OKLAHOMA *Brides*

DREAMS COME FULL CIRCLE IN
THREE PRAIRIE ROMANCES

Vickie McDonough

BARBOUR
PUBLISHING

Sooner or Later © 2005 by Vickie McDonough
The Bounty Hunter and the Bride © 2007 by Vickie McDonough
A Wealth Beyond Riches © 2007 by Vickie McDonough

ISBN 978-1-60260-110-9

All scripture quotations are taken from the King James Version of the Bible.

This book is a work of fiction. Names, characters, places, and incidents are either products of the author's imagination or used fictitiously. Any similarity to actual people, organizations, and/or events is purely coincidental.

Published by Barbour Publishing, Inc., P.O. Box 719, Uhrichsville, Ohio 44683, www.barbourbooks.com

Our mission is to publish and distribute inspirational products offering exceptional value and biblical encouragement to the masses.

Member of the
Evangelical Christian
Publishers Association

Printed in the United States of America.

Dear Reader,

    I was born and raised in Oklahoma, but it wasn't until I started writing that I became fascinated with Oklahoma's unique history. Just a little over 100 years ago, the area I live in was Indian Territory. Indian culture still survives in some parts of Oklahoma, and families still live on land that their ancestors won in the land rush. *Oklahoma Brides* is a collection of three novels set in the Twin Territories about people running from their pasts who find a new life in a new land.

    In *Sooner or Later*, Rebekah runs away from a forced marriage. Mason's wife and sister died in an accident, and he is traveling to the Oklahoma Territory so he can return his young niece and nephew, Katie and Jimmy, to their vagabond father. Then Mason intends on heading west—but God has other plans.

    In *The Bounty Hunter and the Bride*, sheriff-turned-bounty hunter, Dusty McIntyre, has been hunting for the outlaw who killed his wife for over a year. When his attempt to capture the culprit results in the injury of a young pregnant widow and the destruction of her home, Dusty feels obligated to help her. But Katie, the spitfire widow, wants nothing to do with the man who she says is the source of all her problems. Can the two come to an amicable truce long enough for Dusty to get the widow to her family?

    In *A Wealth Beyond Riches*, After her mother abandons her, Sasha flees the New York theater world after learning she has family in Indian Territory. Jimmy is certain the pretty easterner is a carpetbagger after his boss's recently inherited money. He's determined to keep his eye on Sasha. When oilmen pressure her uncle to drill on his land, Sasha and Jim join together to help him. Can Jim protect his boss without losing his heart to the man's niece?

    It is my hope that *Oklahoma Brides* will give readers a taste of life in the Twin Territories. Just as we do today, settlers had physical, emotional, and spiritual challenges, too. Life was hard for early pioneers who settled on the hot, dry prairies, but their faith in God pulled them through. I hope you can set aside your worries for a time and be entertained and inspired in your spiritual walk. Please visit my Web site: www.vickiemcdonough.com and sign my guestbook. I'd love to know what you think about *Oklahoma Brides*.

God is good,
Vickie McDonough

SOONER
OR
LATER

Prologue

Never in her whole life had Rebekah Bailey done anything so daring, but then, she'd never been this desperate. She peered over her shoulder as she tiptoed toward the barn. In silent support, her shadow marched eerily beside her. The full moon illuminated the rickety A-frame house that had always been her home. The breath she'd been holding came out in a ragged sigh. At least she'd managed to get out of the house without Pa hearing her. But she was far from safe.

Her heartbeat resounded in her ears, and she was certain her neighbors miles away could hear it. Hugging her ancient carpetbag against her chest, she hurried faster.

Sucking in a deep, chilling breath, Rebekah managed to squeeze through the narrow barn door opening without it squeaking. Hopefully she'd saddle Prince just as quietly, then slip away without waking the man in the house. If not, her world would end—and all her dreams along with it.

The old horse raised his head to peer at her, snorted softly, then ducked back down as if he knew it wasn't time to be awakened. Rebekah set aside her small bundle of possessions. The bulky saddle was always a struggle to lift; but tonight, under stress and fear, she thought it felt extraordinarily heavy. With a grunt, she labored to hoist it onto Prince's back, stealing glances at the barn door lest Pa sneak up on her. Once she had the saddle in place and cinched, she used the leather strings behind the cantle to secure the handles of the old carpetbag that held everything she owned.

"Come on, Prince. You're my champion—my only means of escape," Rebekah whispered to the old gelding as she led him from the stall. His brown ears flicked back and forth as if he were listening intently. "Ride the wind tonight, my prince."

She looped her canteen over the saddle horn, twisted the stirrup around, and inserted her foot. With a quick hop and a soft grunt, she pulled herself onto the horse, ducking her head to avoid smacking it into the hayloft. Rebekah tapped her heels to Prince's side. He raised his head and snorted but didn't move.

"Oh, no. C'mon, boy. Please go." She nudged him again. Prince blew out a soft nicker and mild snort of resignation, then plodded forward.

Rebekah pushed against the barn door with her foot. It swung open on a groan and high-pitched squeal. Body tensing and every nerve fraying, she darted her gaze toward the house. "Oh, please, Lord, don't let Pa hear. Please, God, help me," she pleaded to the moonlit sky.

No shadows moved in the night, and nobody rushed out of the house to stop her. Rebekah clicked twice out the side of her mouth and nudged the horse with her heels. Prince trotted out of the yard and down the road. The *thunk* of his hooves pounding against the hard ground sounded to Rebekah like the mighty roar of a herd of cattle rumbling by.

She blew out a "Shhh," knowing it did no good. Rebekah took another glance at the only home she'd ever known, wishing desperately that things were different. To the north, the shadowy outline of the mighty oak tree standing guard over the graves where her mother and little brother were buried.

Rebekah slowed Prince to a walk and allowed herself a wisp of a moment to bid them good-bye. "I'm sorry, Mama. I can't do what he demands of me," she whispered to the headstones enclosed behind the weathered picket fence. Her stomach churned with the regret of what could have been, and her eyes burned with unshed tears.

If only I could turn back time. Back to when Mama and Davy were alive. Back to when we were a relatively happy family. Back before Pa hated me. If only...

A sharp creak in the direction of the house jerked Rebekah from her reverie. With a quick tug on the reins and a nudge of her foot to his flank, she turned Prince west. West toward the open plains and Indian Territory. West toward Denver—and freedom. She prayed it was the last place Pa would think to look for her.

The chanting of tree frogs lent music to her ride, and an owl hooted somewhere in a nearby tree. She used to love the sounds of the night, but now they only reminded her of her pain and loneliness. Hoping to ward off the chill, she tugged her worn cloak around her. The world seemed normal, asleep, as it should in the middle of the night. Rebekah felt anything but normal. Her world had fallen apart this evening with Pa's declaration. Nothing would ever be the same for her. She shivered at the memory.

"I've made a deal with Giles Wilbur," he'd said, grinning with pride. "Swapped you for a side of beef and some moonshine. In the morning, you'll be moving in with him to be his woman." Thoughts of the drunken sloth of a man more than twice her age made her blood run cold. How could Pa expect her to live with Mr. Wilbur without even the sanctity of a wedding? How could he simply swap her like she was something to be bartered? Bile churned in her stomach and burned a path to her throat. Tears blurred her vision and streamed down her cheeks.

She'd never felt so alone. Completely alone—as though not a single person in the world cared for her—but the gentle touch of the wind to her cheek reminded her of the One who never failed. Rebekah turned to her heavenly Father as Prince trotted down the dark road.

"Protect me, Lord—and show me the way. And, Father...oh, Father, give me courage for the ride ahead, and strengthen Prince's old bones—"

The faint sound of approaching hoofbeats intruded on Rebekah's prayer.

Oh, no! Pa!

She was certain her heart would jump clear out of her chest. The reins nearly slipped from her trembling hands. Fear of what was behind her overpowered the fear of what was ahead.

Taking a deep, determined breath and a firm grip on the reins, Rebekah dug her heels into Prince's side.

"He-yah," she cried softly.

Prince vaulted into a gallop and raced down the road.

Chapter 1

I gots to go, Unca Mathon."

Mason Danfield pushed the black Stetson up on his forehead and turned in his seat to look at his three-year-old niece. "Aw, Katie, not again." She twirled a lock of golden hair around her pudgy finger and stuck out her bottom lip in a little pout. "You're serious? Not just wantin' out of the wagon?"

"I gots to go weal bad." Katie bounced up and down on her quilt in the back of the covered wagon.

Mason glanced past her to where his seven-year-old nephew sat pretending to shoot Indians with his stick rifle. Jimmy rolled his eyes and shook his head. "Don't forget the last time you didn't stop when she said she had to go." He lifted the edge of the patchwork quilt that hung out the back of the wagon, drying in the warm afternoon sun. Jimmy crossed his arms and sighed. "It's not fair. Why couldn't she go on her own quilt?"

Mason pressed his lips together, holding back the chuckle threatening to escape. "Don't worry about it, pardner. There's bound to be some water up ahead. We'll get your quilt washed out soon as we can." Mason pulled back on the long leather reins. "Whoa, Belle, Duke. Hold up there."

The big Conestoga wagon groaned to a stop, and Mason set the brake. Harnesses jingled as the four draft horses stomped and snorted as though they knew it wasn't time to stop yet. Mason jumped down from the tall wagon seat, sending a cloud of dust flying around his boots when he landed. He stretched and twisted to work the kinks out of his back, then scanned the area as he walked around behind the wagon. The tall prairie grass and gently rolling hills of Indian Territory were a welcome relief after the steep, green hills of the Ozarks they'd recently crossed.

"Come on, Katie. Make it fast." He waved for her to come to him. "We've got a long ways to travel today. You, too, pard. You know the rule."

"Yep; when we stop, everyone goes." Jimmy scrambled over the back of the wagon and headed for a group of small trees before Mason had a chance to lift Katie out.

The little cherub stood with her arms reaching toward him. He looked into her angelic face, and his heart clenched the way it always did whenever he thought of Katie's mother. Taking a deep breath, he pushed the memory of his loving sister back into the hidden recesses of his mind. In the future, he would avoid looking directly into the little girl's face. It only made what he was preparing to do all that much harder.

Mason released a heavy breath and lifted his niece over the wagon's tailgate. "Come on, Katie girl, let's go take care of business."

"You sad, Unca Mathon?" Katie's soft hand stroked his cheek, and against his wishes, Mason leaned into the caress.

"Yeah, sugar, I'm a little sad."

"I sad, too. I miss Mama. When's Mama coming back?" Katie's brow crinkled as her thumb eased toward her pink lips.

Mason sighed. "Katie, how many times do I have to explain this? You know your mama and Aunt Annie are in heaven now. They aren't coming back." Mason shifted the little girl to his other arm and chastised himself for being so gruff with her. He sorely missed his wife and sister. How could he not expect a three-year-old to miss her mother just as much? Life was so unfair.

Mason lowered Katie to the ground, and she ran behind an old stump. He looked heavenward and uttered the silent prayer again.

God, how could You let Annie and Danielle die? Why didn't You protect them?

His throat tightened, and his eyes closed against the burning sensation. He was a grown man pushing thirty, yet every time he thought about the death of his wife, Annie, and their unborn child, and his sister, Danielle, he felt like crying. Sobbing, just like Katie did the time she'd lost her favorite doll.

The accident was his fault. *If only I'd—*

"Got somethin' in your eyes, Uncle Mason?" Jimmy asked, skidding to a stop beside him.

Mason rubbed his eyes. It wouldn't help the kids to know he was upset. "Probably just some dust. Looks like it hasn't rained around these parts for quite a while."

Mason knew they were getting low on water, but he didn't want to worry the boy. He hoped they'd come across fresh water soon. They needed it, their stock needed it, and they could all use a bath.

Katie skipped back a moment later and yanked on his trousers to get his attention. "All done," she said, a darling smile creasing the dimples on her cheeks.

"Well then, back in you go." Mason lifted Katie over the wagon's tailgate and set her on her quilt. Her thumb went straight into her mouth. "Grab your dolly and lie down. It's time you took your nap. By the time you wake up, we should be getting close to where we'll make camp for the evening." Katie nodded and curled up with her doll.

Mason helped Jimmy onto the wagon seat then climbed up beside him.

"How much longer until we get to Dad's place?"

"Don't exactly know, Jim. Maybe another week or so."

"That long?" Jimmy whined. His forceful sigh fluttered his long, straight bangs; and he leaned forward on the seat, resting his elbows on his knees.

Mason shook the reins and clucked to the horses. Snorting and pawing, the large animals lurched forward. He glanced out of the corner of his eye and studied his nephew. His features looked so much like his father, Jake's. But the boy had Danielle's dark coloring, just as Mason did. Except for their lightly tanned complexion, with their dark hair and black eyes, they could have been mistaken for having Mexican or Indian heritage instead of French. In fact, Mason had been ridiculed many times for being a half-breed, even though his mother was French and his father, a Southern gentleman.

Jake. How would he deal with Danielle's death? Would he even care? His scoundrel of a brother-in-law had chased one dream after another ever since marrying Mason's sister. After moving five different times, Danielle had dug in her heels and refused to leave their home on the outskirts of St. Louis to follow Jake into Indian Territory. Mason exhaled a bitter laugh. The ironic thing was, she might still be alive if only she and the children *had* joined Jake. Then Mason would be missing her for a whole different reason. As it now stood, he missed his sister almost as much as his wife.

For the hundredth time, he wondered if he was doing the right thing. Maybe he should just turn the wagon around and take the kids back to St. Louis, or better still, back to Charleston where his parents still lived on the family's large plantation. But Mason knew he couldn't do that either. There were too many bad memories. He needed to rid himself of all responsibilities. As much as he hated to admit it, that included the children. He couldn't keep them; he needed to cut all ties to his past. Then he'd be free to ride west and forget the wonderful life he once had.

Jimmy tugged on Mason's sleeve, pulling him from his thoughts. He looked down at his nephew. The boy pointed to the trail ahead of them. "Look, there's a rider up ahead. What's the matter with 'im?"

Squinting against the bright glare of the afternoon sun, Mason pulled down the brim of his hat to shade his eyes and scanned the road up ahead. He reached down, picked up his rifle, and laid it across his lap. Mason studied the stranger as they pulled even with him, then scanned the tall prairie grass, hoping the rider wasn't simply a decoy for an ambush. A man could easily hide in the thigh-high grass, but he couldn't conceal a horse. His rigid back relaxed, and his heart slowed its quick pace as he realized the stranger was alone. The small man, hunched over and clinging to his saddle horn, didn't even look up as they approached. Jimmy was right. Something was definitely wrong with the rider.

"Ain't you gonna stop?"

"Nope. I'm not picking up someone who may be sick. Since we're traveling alone, I don't want to chance us catching anything out here on the trail. Besides, the man looks more drunk than sick." Mason wondered what could cause someone to be inebriated in the middle of the afternoon. On second thought, he knew exactly the kind of pain that could drive a man to drink.

He studied the stranger as they rode past him. It surprised him to discover the pale-faced rider was just a skinny boy, probably in his early teens. Surely he wasn't drunk. If not, then he *must* be sick—sick enough he didn't even look up or acknowledge there were others on the trail. They passed the rider, who bounced and reeled with each uneven step his old horse took. In truth, the horse looked to be worse off than the rider.

Wrestling with his conscience, Mason continued down the trail. His hands were full enough with two small children. He didn't need a sick teenager to care for on top of everything else.

Then why do I feel so guilty?

A movement flashed in the corner of his eye, snagging his attention, and he turned to look. Jimmy sat on his knees, backward on the seat, and hung halfway around the side of the wagon so that Mason couldn't even see his head. He reached over, grabbing the tail of Jimmy's faded shirt. "You lean any farther off the wagon seat, boy, and you're gonna fall flat on your noggin. What's so interesting back there?"

"I'm waiting to see if'n that stranger gets up. He fell plumb off his horse."

Turning in his seat, Mason ducked his head, peering through the covered wagon's opening and out the back end. Jimmy was right. The stranger lay flat on his back in the middle of the road. His horse grazed nearby. Mason glanced down at Katie. She slept with her thumb smashed against her bottom lip, blissfully unaware of the dilemma her uncle now faced.

"Whoa, Belle, Duke. Here, pardner, hang on to these while I go back and check on that fellow." Mason handed Jimmy the reins and set the brake. He jumped down, grabbed his rifle, and reached into the back of the wagon, searching the supplies until he found the canteen. As he walked toward the boy, Mason looked heavenward. "Don't I already have enough responsibilities without You dumping another kid on me?" He shook his head. "Folks'll be thinking this is one of those orphan trains."

Balancing against his rifle, Mason knelt beside the boy and studied his face. He had a delicate look about him—city boy, maybe—except his well-worn clothes more resembled something from a farmer's scrap bag. Mason pushed aside the boy's hat and laid his hand against the kid's forehead. At least he didn't have a fever. Maybe he wasn't so sick after all. The boy stirred at Mason's touch.

He set his rifle down on the ground. With a twist of his thumb and forefinger, Mason uncorked the canteen and reached behind the boy to lift him up. His eyes widened and he yanked his hand back as though he'd been stung. The boy lay on top of something that felt like a fat snake—with fur. Cautiously, he lifted the boy's shoulder and rolled him over onto his side. *What in the world?*

Mason jumped to his feet and stepped away. He pushed his hat up his forehead and stood with his hands on his hips, staring at the back of his wagon as he fought to get his ragged breathing under control. How was he going to deal with this? He almost wondered if God were laughing at him. Just when he thought things couldn't get worse, God dropped something like this in his lap.

Mason heard a scuffling noise behind him and spun around. The boy—no, the girl—had managed to sit up. Her well-worn Western hat was back on, and her long braid had disappeared.

Why would a girl be out in the middle of nowhere by herself and dressed in boys' clothing? It didn't make any sense. She must be a runaway.

"Please, c–can I have a drink?"

Her soft, timid voice touched something deep within him, and his anger fell away as if someone had doused him with a bucket of cool creek water. In three steps, he was beside her again. Mason knelt next to the girl. Picking up the canteen, he chastened himself for dropping it earlier and allowing some of the precious liquid to seep out.

The girl's small, trembling hands reached for the canteen. She barely had enough energy to hold it, but she managed to get it to her lips. She guzzled the water and choked from the effort. Liquid droplets trickled over her full lips and down her sun-kissed chin.

Mason wanted to tell her to stop wasting the water, but instead he looked toward the horizon, his jaw clenched. He lifted his hat and swiped at the line of sweat on his forehead, then sucked in a deep breath and let it out through his nose.

How could I have mistaken her for a boy?

❧

Rebekah was amazed she'd made it so far. Right now she was so exhausted and famished, she could barely hold her head up. Thank the Lord, the tall cowboy had materialized just when she thought she could go no farther. She closed her eyes and licked the water from her dry, leathery lips, savoring the life-sustaining moisture. Almost two days without water and food had nearly done her in.

Has water ever tasted so good?

Licking her lips, Rebekah looked around the unfamiliar countryside. Where was she now? Still in Arkansas? Missouri, maybe? The dirt had a strange orange tint to it, and the gently rolling hills reminded her of a pan of yeast rolls rising on the stove. Clusters of trees stood here and there, as if afraid to face the ever-changing weather of the plains alone. Knee-high prairie grass danced and swished on the soft spring breeze. This place was so different from the forested woods of her home.

Home.

She longed for it, dreamed about it, but she no longer had a home. Her pa had seen to that. But then, he wasn't really her pa either. Rebekah shook her head and blinked back the burning sensation in her eyes. *How could I have been so naive all those years?*

She tilted her head to look up at the tall cowboy, ignoring the pain it caused. He kicked a tuft of grass and sent it sailing through the air. The man glanced at her and then looked at a covered wagon stopped on the road. His hands rested in his back pockets, and he heaved a loud sigh. He didn't seem happy to be helping her.

Well, she only needed his help a little. It had been foolish of her to leave home with so few provisions, but then, she'd left in a hurry. If only this man could spare some food and water, she'd be on her way.

Suddenly he turned back toward her. His face disappeared in the glare of the noonday sun. "Where you headed, kid?"

"Um. . .Denver." Her scratchy voice sounded foreign to her.

"Denver! On that old thing?" He raised his arm and pointed at Prince. "You'd never make it. And where's your supplies? You don't even have any saddlebags."

Rebekah leaned back, cringing at the disapproval in his voice. What did it matter to him if she rode a horse older than herself and she was ill-prepared for a long journey? Okay, so it mattered if she had to beg food and water from him, but he had no idea how desperate she'd been to get away.

Biting back a retort, Rebekah took another drink from the canteen, then set it down on the dusty road. Her vision had cleared, though her head still throbbed. Probably from too much sun and not enough food, she told herself. She didn't know if her legs would hold her, but she couldn't sit in the middle of the trail all day. Forget the food. If she could just get back on her horse, she could get away from the man's glaring gaze. Easing onto her knees, with her hands firmly anchored in the dirt, she pushed her hind end in the air and straightened her legs. Very unladylike. But then, he didn't know she was a woman.

Her whole body wobbled. Her arms trembled as she tried to push to a stand. She was stuck—not enough strength to get up and too much stubbornness to sit back down. Rebekah imagined she must look like a newborn foal trying out its legs for the first time.

"Here, let me help." A deep voice rumbled in her ear the same moment she felt two warm hands on her waist.

Rebekah stiffened. She turned her head back to see the man's face. She blinked. A pair of the blackest eyes she'd ever seen glared at her.

Why was he so upset with her? Could simply helping a stranger in need cause him to lose his temper? Or maybe he always scowled. Well, she hadn't ridden all this way and left her home just to fall prey to another man like Pa—or Giles Wilbur. She tried to shrug away from the man's hands; instead she felt her body being pulled upright.

The cowboy lifted her up like she was nothing but a five-pound sack of flour and set her on her feet. Immediately her legs buckled. How dare they betray her in her moment of need! Against her wishes, Rebekah clung to the man's waist, her face pressed against his solid chest. She summoned every ounce of energy within her exhausted frame and forced her body upward.

A group of crows floating lazily in the sky cawed as if mocking her. She thought she heard the man gasp—or was he laughing at her? The sky darkened suddenly when a thick cloud floated in front of the sun. Was it raining? She groaned. The last thing she needed was rain. It took her a moment to comprehend that the moisture on her cheeks wasn't from an afternoon shower; it was tears.

No! she chided herself. She couldn't be crying. She just couldn't. She wouldn't cry now—not after all she'd been through.

Rebekah's head sagged heavily, and her tears seemed to have a mind of their own. Blinking, she struggled to dam the tears and focus on her surroundings. She was determined not to show weakness, but her body had other ideas. Her legs shook, her arms trembled, and her head throbbed as if a whole flock of crows were nesting there. Unwillingly, she sagged against the man.

Why is the sky so dark? She tried to ask him that very question, but the words wouldn't form on her thick tongue. Any second now, her head was sure to explode like a stick of dynamite with a short, burning fuse. Rebekah forced herself to lean back so she could look at the man's face, but it swirled into a dark mass and merged into the growing blackness.

"Hey! Hold on now," she thought she heard him say. Then the deep voice faded away into the shadowy abyss.

Chapter 2

Mason hoisted the young woman into his arms and started toward the wagon. "All right. I can take a hint!" he shouted to the sky.

Jimmy peered, wide-eyed, out the wagon opening. "Wha'cha gonna do, Uncle Mason?"

That was a good question. What *was* he going to do? Taking on a sick girl certainly wasn't in his plans. Mason shook his head. "Never mind. Just climb down and get that horse. Tie him to the back of the wagon—and fetch the canteen and my rifle."

Jimmy scampered over the wagon's tailgate and dropped to the ground. "Are we gonna keep that boy? What's wrong with him?"

"Shhh! You're going to wake Katie with all your chatter," Mason hissed. "And I don't know what's wrong yet." He looked into the pale, dirt-smudged, feminine face and studied the woman's soft features. She wasn't beautiful, but she wasn't exactly hard on the eyes either.

He'd nearly come undone when those vulnerable blue eyes, filled with tears, stared up at him. What was it about a female's tears that moved him so? Maybe it was a result of having so many strong women in his life. He'd known the few times he'd seen them crying that things were bad—real bad. He hadn't missed the sudden flash of stubbornness in the girl's countenance when she tried to stand without his help. But despite her determination, she was obviously too weak.

What had happened to her? Why was she out here alone? Against his will, Mason felt a sudden surge of protectiveness. No harm would come to her while she was in his care.

Carefully, he lifted the limp girl over his shoulder, then climbed into the back of the wagon. Thankfully, Katie's little body was curled against the side of the wagon instead of being all sprawled out as usual.

Mason eased down his bundle onto the quilt next to Katie, then knelt beside her. The girl's old felt hat flopped over her face. He picked it up, tossing it aside. Her long braid coiled around her shoulder and rested against her arm. Wisps of soft, brown hair escaped her braid, feathering her cheeks. Now that he knew she was a female, Mason decided she must be older than he'd first thought—late teens, maybe. Still, she had no business traveling alone, unprepared and unprotected.

Katie would enjoy having another female around. Mason shook his head. Having a young woman around wasn't part of his plan. Hopefully, when the girl came to, he could help her get back to her family without deviating from his journey for too long.

Mason pulled his bandanna from his neck and gently wiped at the smudged dirt trails on the woman's pale cheek. He'd need water to get the dirt off, but since he was so low on drinking water, he'd been rationing it, not using any of the precious liquid for cleaning. All he had right now was spit, and he doubted the woman would take kindly to his cleaning her face with that.

"Hey, Uncle Mason," Jimmy said through the back of the wagon in a loud whisper. "Can I ride on this horse instead of in the wagon?"

Mason glanced over the wagon's tailgate and eyed the pitiful beast, wondering how far it had carried its cargo. The bony animal's ribs stuck out, causing Mason to speculate how its saddle had stayed on. The poor creature should have been put out to pasture years ago. He shook his head, and Jimmy's bright smile faded. "Better wait till it's had some water. We don't know how long they've been traveling."

"Oh, okay." With disappointment marring his face, Jimmy slid off the horse and tied it to the back of the wagon. "Here's the canteen and rifle."

Stretching tall, Jimmy barely reached over the top of the tailgate. Mason grabbed both items, noticing how Jimmy's shoulders slumped as he turned and patted the old horse's withers. Mason sighed. He'd planned on getting Jimmy a small horse on his last birthday, but then the accident had happened—and in that instant, everything changed.

Stop it! Move on.

Yeah, move on, he urged himself again. But he couldn't bring himself to do so. He just couldn't. He missed Annie. He wanted her back. He wanted their child. But Annie wouldn't have wanted him to grieve so long, and to this extent. She'd made him promise if anything happened to her that he'd marry again. *What a dumb promise.* As if any woman could ever have a place in his heart after Annie.

"No, Pa—don't." The woman's cry jolted Mason back to the present.

A dull *thud* echoed through the wagon as she kicked a crate with the heel of her worn boot. He glanced at Katie, afraid the young woman's thrashing and crying out would wake her. Katie exhaled a loud breath and turned onto her side but thankfully didn't awaken. With a quick tug, Mason removed the girl's boots and set them near the tailgate.

"Shhh! It's okay." Mason reached out and patted the girl's arm.

She pulled away at his touch. Her forehead gleamed with sweat. Tears running from the corner of her eye formed a tiny river as they cut a trail through the dirt on her sunburned cheeks.

"No, Pa. I—I promise." Anguish contorted her countenance. "I'll be good."

Moved by her tears, Mason went against his own rule and grabbed the canteen. He moistened his bandanna, then ran the damp cloth over the woman's forehead. What had her pa done to her? He shivered at the thought of what the young woman might have endured.

"Please don't," she mumbled.

"Shhh. Hush now, you're all right," he whispered, smoothing her damp hair out of her face. At the sound of his voice, she relaxed and stopped her thrashing. The tears slowed to a single drop, clinging stubbornly to her dark lashes. Mason dabbed at it, then gently wiped her face. Her warm, sun-kissed cheeks were soft in spite of the layer of dust. Almost against his will, he felt his heart going out to her. He turned and looked out the back of the wagon to the bright summer sky.

Well, if I can take care of two kids who aren't mine, I can take care of a third.

❧

Rebekah lay still, trying to make sense of her surroundings. She could hear the soft cadence of nearby voices. A deep baritone, a youthful alto, and a soft soprano wafted on the night like a melody, as a chorus of crickets and cicadas strummed the background music. Lulled by the sounds of peace and contentment, she thought of home and happier times. Of nights on the front porch swing with her mother, listening to a similar string of players. She wanted to drift back to sleep and stay on the porch with her mom forever; then a child's innocent giggle momentarily drowned out the night orchestra and called her back to the present.

Where am I?

In the orange glow of the fading sunlight, she could make out the rounded canopy of a covered wagon. She fingered the quilt beneath her. It felt so good to lie on something soft instead of the cold, hard ground. How long had it been since she left home? Five days?

Her nose twitched. Rebekah caught a whiff of something that smelled like fried chicken, and her stomach grumbled in response. Her last decent meal had been the day she left home. She'd served crispy fried chicken that night—and mashed potatoes with blobs of melted butter, flaky biscuits, and canned green beans. Saliva moistened her tongue. That was almost a week ago. The chicken and biscuits she'd taken with her when she fled her childhood home were gone days ago. A few overripe peaches had been her only source of nourishment since then. No wonder she was so weak.

The murmur of voices floated in again on the warm evening breeze. She listened carefully. The deep, rumbling voice, thick with a smooth Southern drawl, sounded vaguely familiar. The memory of the black-eyed man glaring at her stole the breath right out of her lungs. *Could this be his wagon?* She jerked upright. Pain resonated through her head from the swift movement.

A rustling at the end of the wagon drew her attention. Two small hands grabbed the back edge of the wagon, and a dark head appeared. A pair of black eyes, a smaller version of the one in her memory, stared wide-eyed at her.

"He's awake! Uncle Mason, he's awake." And just that fast, the boy was gone.

Rebekah glanced around for her hat. Quickly she coiled her braid and stuffed it inside, then smashed the hat onto her head. Near the back end of the wagon, she spied her boots. She crawled over to them, staring out the wagon opening as she moved. No one was within her line of sight.

Rebekah glanced down and grabbed a boot. Hearing a scuffling noise, she glanced up. Less than two feet away were the ebony eyes that haunted her memory. She gasped and leaned back. The man's black eyes twinkled momentarily and then dulled.

"Well now, 'bout time you woke up. Thought maybe you'd sleep clean through the night. You hungry, kid?"

Rebekah listened to his voice—a voice smoother than melted butter on warm biscuits. From his accent, she surmised he was from the Deep South—Alabama, maybe. She didn't care; she just liked the sound of it. His eyes didn't seem so threatening now, but he still managed to make her gut contract.

Thank You, Lord, for the boy. At least I'm not alone with this intimidating stranger.

Was the boy his son? It seemed reasonable. They had the same eyes. The same head of dark hair. No, he called him Uncle—Mike or something. Again her stomach complained about its empty state. She pressed her hand to her belly as quickly as she could to muffle the sound.

The man cleared his throat, his lips tilted in an amused smirk. "Sounds like you're hungry to me."

Rebekah realized she'd been staring. Intimidating or not, he was quite handsome, especially with several days' growth of black whiskers that gave him a rugged look. She felt her cheeks warming and looked away.

"Um. . .well, yes. I'm hungry."

"Then get yourself on down here 'fore Jimmy finishes off the roasted rabbit."

Rebekah's heart sank. Rabbit. Not chicken. Oh, well, any food would taste good. She shouldn't complain. Her stomach growled deep and low as if to agree.

She pulled on her boots, stood slowly, then hiked her leg over the back of the wagon. Straddling the tailgate, she set her foot down on a section of wood jutting out the back end. The wagon swirled, fading to darkness then back to light. She paused to catch her balance. The man's hands captured her waist, and warmth radiated up her side. Rebekah froze. *Does he know I'm a woman? Why else would he help me down?*

Straddling the tailgate, she turned, glaring at the man. "I can get down by myself."

"Beggin' your pardon, but you already collapsed in my arms once today. I'm just trying to prevent that from happenin' again. You *are* still weak, you know."

Rebekah felt sure he spat out each individual word on purpose just to emphasize his point. Heat marched up her cheeks. *Collapsed in his arms? What could he be talking about?* Turning away from his penetrating stare, she started to hike her other leg over the side, but the ground below her whirled as if someone had set it in motion. If she didn't know better, she might have believed the solid ground beneath her had turned to water. She clutched the top of the tailgate with a white-knuckled grip. With great resolve she fought the dizziness and weakness. She wouldn't give him the satisfaction of being right.

Regaining her equilibrium, she hoisted her leg over the tailgate and was maneuvering quite well when her pants snagged on the head of a protruding nail. She tugged slightly but couldn't free herself. With a sigh of frustration, she gave her britches a quick yank. The sound of ripping fabric hit her ears the same second her pant leg tore free. The momentum forced her other foot off the wooden ledge, and Rebekah dove over the tailgate—straight into the stranger's arms.

She grabbed hold of the man's shoulders to keep from falling farther. Then she secured her hat just before it slipped off. Rebekah quickly realized she needn't worry about falling. His strong arms held her securely against his solid chest; and his breath, warm on her cheek, still carried the faint hint of roasted rabbit. In spite of her embarrassment and the fact that she'd never been this close to a man before in her whole life, his arms felt entirely too comfortable—too secure.

Rebekah was so mortified she couldn't bring herself to look into his face for fear of seeing a satisfied grin. She'd fallen just like he'd said. Only it wasn't from being weak; it was merely a simple accident that had tripped her up. But she was sure he wouldn't believe her if she tried to explain.

When he stepped back and turned toward the campfire, Rebekah noticed the boy and a younger girl staring at them. The man started toward the campfire, and she realized he wasn't going to set her down. She smacked his rock-hard chest with her open hand. "Put me down," she ordered. "I'm fine."

"Uh-huh. If you're fine, how come I caught you tumbling through the air like a shot goose?"

Of all the nerve. Insufferable man!

Oompf! He hastily deposited her on a rotting tree stump. Then he sat down on the gnarled tree trunk that lay on the ground beside her. Thinking about what creatures might be nesting in such an old, decaying stump caused Rebekah to cringe. There could be spiders, maggots, and all kinds of critters, maybe even snakes. That thought had her on her feet in seconds. Ready to investigate what other creatures might be lurking there, she spun around, and the trunk suddenly blurred. It formed and then faded as if she were looking at it through a fog. Instantly she felt the man by her side, his steadying hand warming her shoulder.

"Sit down before you fall down."

Fine. I'll sit down, but only so I don't end up in your arms again. She pointed to the trunk, and he guided her, offering his silent support until she sat down. With her elbows on her knees, Rebekah rested her throbbing head in her hands.

After a few moments of someone shuffling around, she looked up to see the man standing in front of her with a bowl of roasted rabbit and a biscuit. Her stomach cried, *Hurry!* and she accepted the meal.

"Thank you."

"Don't mention it."

She tore into the meat, ignoring the manners her mother had drilled into her. When the meat was gone, she licked the remaining juice off the bones. Besides, boys didn't have to eat in a ladylike manner; and if she was going to pass herself off as one, she'd have to remember that. The hard biscuit crunched as she chewed it, but she didn't care. It tasted wonderful.

"Uncle Mason don't let me wear my hat when *I* eat," the boy commented, staring at her hat.

She gulped. Seemed there were other things a boy should do. Like be a gentleman, maybe. She just hoped the man wouldn't come yank her hat from her head. She wasn't ready to share her secret.

"Jimmy! That's no way to talk to a guest," the man scolded.

Rebekah sighed with relief and looked at him. Mason. It was a nice name for such an overbearing man. She glanced at Jimmy. His head hung down, and he toed circles in the dirt.

"Sorry," he mumbled without looking up.

So Mason was Jimmy's uncle. Rebekah glanced at the little girl—a darling angel staring at her with wide, dark blue eyes. She held up a ragged cloth doll, whose braided yellow hair hung precariously by several loose threads. "This is Molly," she said.

Rebekah considered how a boy might answer. They'd probably give a disinterested smile, shrug, and say something like, "That's nice"; but she was interested, and she wanted to talk to the child. She'd never had the chance to be around little girls much. "Molly's very pretty. What's your name?"

"Katie. I'm fwee."

Rebekah smiled. "You're three? My, you're a big girl, aren't you?"

Smiling, Katie nodded, and charming dimples dented her chubby cheeks. Rebekah studied the little girl. Her worn dress had seen better days. Her face was covered in what looked like a layer of dirt mixed most likely with grease from the rabbit she'd just eaten. Was she Mason's niece—or maybe his daughter? And why wasn't there a woman around? Jimmy's mom or Mason's wife—if he had one. She glanced around once more, waiting for a woman to appear, but she somehow knew there wasn't one coming.

Savoring the salty dryness of the last of her biscuit, she studied Mason. He squatted next to the fire, stirring the ashes with a stick. The campfire snapped and popped as if complaining about the disturbance. Several days' growth of dark

22

whiskers shadowed Mason's face. What did he look like without a beard? His stature was all man—tall, broad-shouldered, strong. She wondered if he carried Indian or Mexican blood, though his tan complexion didn't carry the reddish tint she figured a man of that heritage would. Those black eyes, probing like a lantern at midnight, had nearly penetrated her fragile disguise. The biscuit churned in her stomach. Jimmy's uncle certainly was an appealing man—too much so for her own good.

Would she be safe if she confessed she was a woman? She'd heard stories about what happened to women who traveled alone. That's why she'd disguised herself in her brother's clothes. She hoped to pass for a teenage boy, hoped to waylay unwanted attention. What would Mason do if he knew the truth? Would he be sympathetic?

Rebekah looked up. Her gaze locked with Mason's. Her heart froze. Flickering shadows from the campfire danced across his face. Flames popped, and a hundred tiny embers sprinkled the air like flittering fireflies on the evening hillside. From under half-lowered lids, he stared at her. His glare burned through her. Disconcerted, she crossed her arms and pointedly looked away.

What have I done to upset him?

Chapter 3

Was he wrong to be cautious? Maybe he should just give the girl some food and water and send her on her way. Mason stood and shoved his hands into his back pockets as he continued to stare into the flickering flames. No. He couldn't do that, even if she wasn't being completely honest with him. He exhaled a heavy breath. Sometimes he hated being chivalrous and caring, but it was his nature.

Mason wondered how much time would pass before the girl trusted him enough to reveal her identity. He always tried hard to give people the benefit of the doubt, but he couldn't stomach a liar or deceiver. A shiver charged up his spine as his thoughts flashed back to his youth, when his father had beaten him whenever he told a lie. Sometime when he was about nine years old, Mason had figured out honesty was a lot less painful than dishonesty. As a boy, he'd entertained ideas of running away from home every time his domineering father took him to the woodshed. Could her father have beaten her? He thought back to her soft cries in the wagon. Was that why she was on the road alone?

He walked away from the heat of the fire. The toe of his boot snagged on a rock, and Mason stumbled, nearly losing his balance. Irritated, he picked up the offending stone with a growl and threw it into the surrounding darkness. He peeked back to see if the woman was watching, but thankfully she was staring into the fire. She looked so scruffy and pitiful.

All his life he'd been rescuing animals and standing up for the smaller kids who were picked on by bullies. Mason wanted to help the woman, but how could he if she wasn't honest with him? He turned back toward the fire.

"What's your name?" Katie asked her.

Something akin to panic dashed across the woman's face. "Re. . .uh. . .RJ."

"That's a funny name." Katie giggled. "How olds are you?"

Mason opened his mouth to scold Katie for her precocious questions, but he decided he'd rather hear RJ's response.

The woman's lips tilted in a melancholy smile. "A lot older than you, sweetie."

Sweetie. At least she was kind to the kids. He'd give her that much. But could RJ be her real initials—or was that a lie? Never in all his life had he heard of a woman who went only by initials. Mason shook his head.

The moon peeked out from behind a cloud, signaling the lateness of the hour. He watched another cloud meander across the sky to cover the moon, and he sighed. Every night Katie gave him trouble at bedtime. He hoped tonight would be different. "Jimmy, Katie, time for y'all to turn in."

"What am I gonna sleep on?" Jimmy asked.

"Ain't you got a bed?" Mason replied.

"Katie wet on my quilt, remember?"

Mason lifted his hat from his head and ran his hands through his hair. He hoped they'd find water soon so they could wash Jimmy's quilt and restock their water barrels. Given the distance they'd traveled without finding fresh water, he'd even considered praying. But his praying days ended when God let Annie and their unborn child die. Why hadn't God prevented it? He could have but He hadn't. As far as Mason was concerned, he had no place in his life for a God who killed women and children.

He looked at Jimmy. "Sorry, pardner, you're gonna have to sleep on your quilt until we can get it washed."

"Oh, great!" Jimmy threw Katie a dirty look and stomped off toward the wagon.

Mason plucked a stem of grass and twirled it between his fingers. He studied Jimmy's back as the boy moved away. Normally all three of them slept together in the wagon, but it wouldn't be proper to make RJ sleep outside, especially in her weakened condition. Mason flicked the grass stem out into the darkening shadows. The girl hadn't been there for a whole day, and she was already forcing changes.

"Jimmy," Mason called. The boy stopped and swirled around. "Throw your quilt under the wagon. We'll sleep out tonight."

The lad's countenance instantly changed. "Woo-hoo!" he yelled. Jimmy punched the air with his fist and burst into a jog toward the wagon. Mason couldn't help smiling. He couldn't begin to count the number of times Jimmy had begged to sleep outside, but he'd always refused the boy since Katie was afraid to sleep alone.

RJ smiled, picked up the canteen, then poured some water into a tin cup. She snapped the cork into the canteen and sipped the water as she stared into the campfire. Mason wanted to talk with her and find out where she'd come from, but first he had to deal with Katie, whose eyes already swam with unshed tears.

"I don't wanna thleep in the wagon by myself. I—I'm scared." The firelight brightened the tears streaming down Katie's cheeks. She hugged Molly tight against her chest.

Mason strode over and knelt beside her. Stroking her silky hair, he pulled her to his chest. "Shhh, sugar. You won't be alone. RJ will be sleeping with you."

Peering past Katie, Mason noticed RJ's head jerk up. He read the probing question in her eyes. He wanted to answer her. *Yes, I know you've been lying. Yes,*

I know you're a woman. But he refrained.

Katie pushed away and sat up, rubbing her sleeve across her nose. "Weally?"

"Really." Mason smiled at her excitement. "And I'll tell you what. How about if you go to sleep under the wagon with Jimmy, and later on I'll put you inside?"

Katie squealed and wrapped her arms around Mason's neck. He loved her little-girl hugs and wet, slobbery kisses.

"Come on, sugar," he said, lifting her into the air. "Let's wash up and I'll tuck you in."

Rebekah watched Mason carry Katie to the wagon. When he tossed her up and caught her, the girl's childish squeals rent the night air. He set Katie down and pulled out a canteen from the back of the wagon, then moistened the edge of his shirt and wiped Katie's face. He replaced the canteen, pulled Katie's dress off, and reached in the back of the wagon, retrieving a small ivory-colored nightgown. Mason slipped it over Katie's head, and she scooted under the wagon. Mason knelt beside her. Rebekah heard the murmur of the children's voices and surmised they must be praying.

Looking toward the night sky, Rebekah marveled again at God's handiwork. Back home, the forest of trees blocked out most of the stars, but here the sky sparkled with hundreds of twinkling diamonds. The soothing glow of the moon rising over the eastern sky, to say nothing of her full stomach, lulled her into a contented state. For the first time in a week, she wasn't in a frantic race away from home, worried about finding something to eat, or fearful for her safety.

She glanced at Mason. Even though the man had barely spoken to her and continually glared at her, she felt safe with him. Just as quickly as the thought came, it was replaced. Irritation seeped in as Rebekah wondered how Mason could allow a total stranger to sleep in the wagon with Katie, especially if he thought she was a boy. It didn't make any sense. Did he discern she wasn't a threat? But how could he know for sure? And why would he take a chance?

The thought angered her so that she couldn't sit still. She bounced to her feet, instantly sorry for her sudden movement. Reaching down, she steadied herself on the tree stump.

"Just what do you think you're doing?" Mason's voice snapped behind her.

The nearness of his voice startled her. Rebekah gasped and whirled around. She pressed her palm to her chest, hoping to steady her racing heart, and flung out her other arm for balance. Strong hands grabbed her shoulders, steadying her. How could a man so big walk so quietly?

"I—I need to tend to my horse and get my blanket." Too exhausted to look into his glaring eyes again, Rebekah stared at a blue button on Mason's plaid shirt. The top edge of his chest pocket flopped over in a frayed triangle where the corner had come unstitched. There was no doubt this motley trio could use a woman's touch. Too bad she would be leaving for Denver after everyone fell asleep.

The pungent scent of smoke and dust permeated Mason's shirt. Rather than finding the odor repulsive, Rebekah had to fight off the desire to lean against his solid torso. For the first time in her life, she found herself attracted to a man.

Why did it have to be this one?

"I already took care of that pitiful beast."

Rebekah sucked in a breath and shoved Mason in the chest. "Prince isn't pitiful. He saved my life. I'd have never made it this far without him."

Mason spewed out a noise that sounded half-laugh and half-snort. "How old is that horse, anyway? Twenty-five years?"

Rebekah narrowed her eyes at Mason's offensive comment. She nibbled at a piece of dried skin on her sun-scorched lips. There was no way she would tell this insufferable man that her horse was probably closer to thirty. In fact, Prince was probably older than Mason. As long as Rebekah could remember, her mother had owned Prince.

"I'm going to turn in," she said, purposely ignoring his question. She tilted her nose toward the stars.

"I think we need to talk." The tone of Mason's voice left no room for objection.

Feeling daring for a change, Rebekah shook her head. "I need to get a good night's sleep so I can be on my way tomorrow."

Mason's eyes blazed, and he looked at her as if she were crazy. He opened his mouth to say something but slammed it shut instead. A muscle flicked angrily in his jaw. Rebekah felt compelled to continue. "I've taken up your time and eaten your food. You've been very kind, and I truly appreciate your hospitality, but I'll be leaving tomorrow."

Mason stalked away then quickly stopped. He pivoted and marched back toward her like a cougar chasing its prey. Rebekah stepped back, the chipped bark of the fallen tree trunk biting into her calves. He leaned into her face. The flickering firelight behind her brought out sparkling flecks of gold in his ebony eyes. His breath warmed her nose, and Rebekah's heart tightened at his intimidating closeness. Mason's steady gaze impaled her. She was suddenly anxious to escape his disturbing presence.

"Kid," he said with cool authority, "you're not goin' anywhere tomorrow."

❧

Rebekah's tears slowed to a mere dribble. Her throat and nose felt thick from her lengthy cry. Though she lay in the back of the wagon next to Katie, she'd never felt so alone. Even her prayers seemed to go no further than the top of the wagon's canvas canopy.

Her emotions bounced from rage to fear and loneliness then back to rage. How could she have been attracted to that beast? How could Mason think he could keep her from leaving? So what if her horse was old? Prince had gotten her this far, and he would get her all the way to Denver. She hadn't run away from Pa simply to fall prey to another tyrant. No. She had to leave tonight.

All her life, Rebekah's mother had told her stories about her hometown. The snowcapped mountains she spoke of had beckoned Rebekah as a child, and when she fled from Pa, it seemed only natural to head for Denver.

Denver was far enough away that Giles Wilbur or her pa wouldn't find her—she hoped. Rebekah still thought of Curtis Bailey as her pa, even though she now knew the truth. The man had raised her and she carried his name, after all. But knowing the truth answered a lot of her questions. How many times had Rebekah asked her mother why she had blue eyes when her pa, ma, and brother all had brown eyes? Now she knew why Curtis—that's what she'd call him from now on—treated Davy so much better than he'd ever treated her. Davy was his true son, and she was merely the unwanted stepchild.

Tears blurred her vision of the moon again. *Oh, Lord, why did You let Ma and Davy die?* Doc said it was influenza. If only Curtis had been home instead of out hunting. Rebekah wouldn't leave her sick mother and brother to go for the doctor. What if she had? Would they still be alive?

Once again, the Bible verse from Ecclesiastes flittered through her mind. *"To every thing there is a season, and a time to every purpose under the heaven: a time to be born, and a time to die."* Was this God's way of telling her it was time for Ma and Davy to die? But why? Davy had filled her life with such joy. He'd been only a few years older than Jimmy when he died. Rebekah wanted so much to be angry with God, but she couldn't. She didn't understand, but still, she wouldn't blame God. Things happened. Life was hard. Right now God was the only constant in her life, her only anchor in a terrifying storm.

A flash of Giles Wilbur's dirty, unshaven face flashed across her mind, sending shivers racing down her spine. The food warming her stomach threatened to come back up as she realized how close she'd come to becoming his wife. How could Curtis consider selling her—and to a horrible man like Giles Wilbur? A man older than himself. His drinking buddy, no less.

Rebekah wiped her nose on her sleeve and breathed a prayer of thanks for her escape. The rider she had thought was Curtis thankfully had turned out to be a stranger. Rebekah had turned Prince off the road the night of her escape and hidden in a cluster of trees while the rider approached and rode past. God had been with her that night and in the days that followed. He would be with her tonight as she made another escape.

It would have been nice to travel under the protection of a man and to enjoy the children's company, but she couldn't afford to dawdle. Even in his old age, Prince moved much faster than the heavy wagon with its cumbersome load. Who knew how close Curtis was behind her? She couldn't give him time to catch up to her. She had to keep moving—and fast. No, this wagon would be much too slow. Her only chance was alone on horseback. God would give Prince the strength he needed to get her to Denver.

"Kid, you're not goin' anywhere tomorrow." Mason's words reverberated in Rebekah's mind like the steady drip of rain on a tin roof.

How dare he think he can keep me here against my will! Come morning, we'll just see about that.

Rebekah flipped onto her side, listening to Katie's steady breathing and the occasional sucking noise she made with her tongue against her thumb. A smile creased Rebekah's mouth. She would miss Katie's sweet smile. There was no guile in her, just innocent childishness. What would it be like to be Katie's mother? To feel her chubby arms wrapped lovingly around her neck as Katie had wrapped them around Mason's? For a moment, Rebekah envied him.

"Mama," Katie called in her sleep.

"Shhh, sweetie, it's okay," she whispered. Reaching out in the darkness, she found Katie's arm and patted it gently.

As if she'd been hit by lightning, Rebekah wondered if this young girl and she shared the same loss. A heaviness centered in her chest. Yes, she would miss Katie. Rebekah choked back a sob.

Katie rolled over in her sleep, and the warmth of her body pressed against Rebekah's stomach. The trust she exuded in her sleep made Rebekah's heart ache even more. If only things were different, she'd love to stay and get to know Katie and Jimmy better. She reached out and pulled Katie against her chest, then placed a gentle kiss on the girl's silky hair.

Mason's voice, soft and deep, filtered through her mind. He called Katie "sugar"—except it sounded more like "suguh." A girl could fall in love with his slow Southern drawl. In fact, most of the words he uttered that ended in *er* sounded more like they ended in *ah. Nevah. Ovah.* A smile tugged at the corner of her mouth. But in the next instant, his flashing obsidian eyes and clipped words branded her mind.

"Kid, you're not goin' anywhere."

"And just who does he think he is?" she whispered to the canvas above her. "God?" Rebekah knew full well Mason wasn't God, which cleared her to be angrier with him. No, she couldn't be angry with God, but she certainly could be angry with the man who seemed bent on holding her against her will. She hugged Katie tighter, as if receiving strength from the little girl. The corner of Rebekah's mouth tilted into a smile and her eyes narrowed.

"We'll just see who's not going anywhere tomorrow, Mr. High-and-Mighty."

❧

Mason flipped onto his side, trying to get comfortable on the hard ground. His head rested against RJ's saddle. The scent of leather, a smell he'd always loved, reminded him of his boyhood home and the huge stables filled with saddles and all manner of horse paraphernalia. It was one of only a handful of pleasant memories he had of his childhood.

His father, Colonel Charles Danfield of the Confederate army, had always demanded strict discipline, especially of Mason, his only son. Mason never doubted the colonel loved him, but he had a unique way of showing it.

The soft sobbing above him shredded his heart. He hadn't meant to be so gruff with RJ. The woman had a way of setting him off with her stubborn foolishness. Not to mention her deception. But there was no doubt in his mind that she hadn't been lying when she cried out while unconscious. Mason knew he should have been gentler with her, considering how much she'd been through and how weak she was. He wanted to go find her father and knock some sense into the man. What had the man done to her?

RJ seemed like a wet kitten someone had left out in a cold rain. Mason wanted to take her in his arms and comfort her like he did Katie. But then, RJ didn't know that he knew she was a woman and would most likely resist. Would she resist if she knew he was on to her little secret? Probably. The woman was too stubborn for her own good.

Mason chuckled softly at the blaze that had penetrated her blue eyes when he said she wasn't leaving. He'd almost had to back away from the heat of them. RJ was most certainly one spirited filly.

RJ. What does that stand for? Ruthie Jane? Rita Jo?

Mason yawned as sleep beckoned. *Ramona J. . .*

From a distance, someone called his name. Mason fought the heaviness of sleep and forced his eyes open. The heat of the morning sun warmed his face. He raised his arms above his head, stretching the kinks from his long frame, and rammed his fist straight into the wagon wheel.

Mason winced and rubbed his knuckles as he stared up at Jimmy, who squatted beside him. "Did you hear me, Uncle Mason? I said, he's gone!"

"He? Who?" Mason lifted his hand up to his mouth and licked the thin line of blood off his knuckles.

"RJ."

Chapter 4

Mason vaulted upward. A loud crack sent fingers of fire radiating pain from his forehead to the back of his head and down his neck. He bit back the urge to shout something neither Katie nor Jimmy's tender ears needed to hear. Reaching up, he pressed the injured area with the fingertips of his bruised hand.

"You okay, Uncle Mason? Your head's bleeding," Jimmy said, concern marring his boyish features. Without waiting for an answer, the boy jumped up and raced to the back of the wagon.

Mason swiped the back of his hand across his forehead. Bright red blood, warm and sticky, painted it. "This is *her* fault," he growled under his breath. He edged out from under the wagon and stood as Jimmy returned.

"Here."

Mason looked down at the fairly clean rag his nephew held in his hand.

"Much obliged, pardner. You're kind of handy to have around," he said. He put one hand on the boy's shoulder to steady himself and took the cloth. Jimmy's bright smile warmed Mason's heart. At the same time, a piercing pain gutted his insides. How could he ever say good-bye to these kids? He'd been the man in their young lives for the last several years. Jake hadn't been home in more than two years, not since Katie was a baby. He would be a stranger to her.

No matter. Jake was their father, so Jake should have his children. It all seemed very logical, but Mason's heart had a hard time agreeing. He squashed down the emotional pain and pressed the cloth to his forehead. He'd do what had to be done. The kids belonged with their father. Surely when Jake found out Danielle was dead, he'd settle down and accept the responsibility of raising his own children. At least, Mason hoped he would.

After that, he would be free. Free to do whatever he wanted. Free to go wherever he wanted. Free to be alone. *Alone.* He'd never been truly alone. The thought didn't bring the comforting reassurance it had when the idea first came to him. The closer he got to finding Jake, the more he dreaded being on his own.

Mason shook his head and was instantly sorry. He pulled the cloth away and stared at the bright red stain. At the moment, he had more pressing needs. He had to find a foolish young woman riding a horse with three hooves already in its grave. Mason needed his morning coffee but decided to forgo it so he could get started looking for RJ.

His knee, injured years ago in a farming accident, hinted at a weather change. This part of the country in April was generally beautiful, but looks could be deceiving when a cold northern blast shot through and cut the temperature in half. When that happened, they could wake up with frost on the ground. Crazy woman didn't even have a cloak with her. He doubted she had any warm clothing.

"I checked on Katie. She's still sleepin'. Ya want me to start a fire for breakfast?" Jimmy asked.

"No, pard, we'll eat on the road. We've got a runaway to find."

❧

Rebekah sat in the grass alongside the trail. She wiped her eyes with the back of her hand. Prince was near death, and it was all her fault. Her faithful steed had stumbled several times during the morning ride, but she'd continued to push him. Each time he'd fallen, she'd urged him on and he'd gone. Then without warning, he fell to his knees and lay down, refusing to stand again. His sides heaved unnaturally in his effort to breathe, and Rebekah knew if he didn't get on his feet soon, he never would.

Only her quick thinking had kept her from being trapped beneath the dying horse. She hated to think what might have happened had she been wearing a dress instead of pants and not been able to jump clear. But thinking about what might have happened paled in comparison to what her faithful friend was going through right now, and she could do nothing for him. If only she had some water, maybe that would help, though Rebekah doubted anything really could. Prince had even refused the fresh prairie grass she tried to poke in the sides of his velvety mouth.

Rebekah now realized the foolishness of her hasty predawn escape. If only she'd stayed at camp, then Prince might not be fighting for his life.

Leaning forward with a hand to Prince's neck and her lips to his ear, she whispered an apology. She laid her head against his and silently berated herself for her stupidity.

"Even Mason knew you needed rest," she said softly to the horse.

Mason had slept with his head on her saddle. He must have thought that would keep her there, but it hadn't. Bareback had always been her favorite way to ride, although it was much more difficult with a carpetbag in tow. If only she could have discovered where Mason had hidden her rifle. But searching for it surely would have caused him to awaken. She'd slept deeper and longer than expected, and the birds were already singing their predawn wake-up songs as Prince first limped away from their campsite.

Now here she was, alone somewhere on the border of Arkansas and the Indian Territory, with no horse, no gun, no food, and no water.

Pulling her knees to her chest, she gave in to the tears blurring her vision.

"Why is this happening, Lord? All my life Mama read the Bible to me. Even as a young child, I believed and tried to obey Your Word. What did I do wrong?"

Rebekah hiccupped and wiped her nose on her sleeve. "Aren't You going to help me?"

"Go back."

She looked around, sure she'd heard a voice. Rolling hills covered in thigh-high prairie grass dotted with clusters of trees arrayed in new green leaves were all that met her gaze.

"Go back."

Go back where?

Back home? She wasn't even sure she could find her way back to her home in southeastern Arkansas.

To Mason?

"No! I can't!" she cried out loud. *I won't.* "He doesn't want to be burdened with me."

"Go back."

Rebekah jumped to her feet. "I can't!" she screamed to the sky. "He already has his hands full. He doesn't need another mouth to feed, and I won't beg charity."

She knelt beside Prince and patted his hard jaw, her dripping tears darkening the short hairs on his neck. Huge, watery brown eyes turned her direction, and Prince blew out a weak snort. "Come on, boy. Get up. Please."

Rebekah stood and took the long leather bridle reins in both hands, pulling with all her strength, willing the big horse to rise. Prince's head slowly began to lift from the earth, but she couldn't hold the weight of him, and the reins began to slip from her grasp. Locking her knees and bracing with all her strength, Rebekah fought to hold the reins; but Prince's head fell back to the ground, and she plummeted onto her backside with an aching *thud*.

"Don't do this, Prince," she scolded the horse as she rubbed her aching rear. Rising on her knees, she crawled to her horse. "Oh Prince, please, please. . . What am I going to do without you?"

"Go back."

Rebekah raised her hands to her face in defeat. The smell of leather and horse sweat lingered on her damp palms. She clenched her jaw to kill the sob in her throat, fighting hard against the tears burning her eyes. Enough tears had been shed in the last twenty-four hours to fill a small river.

Looking up to the graying sky, Rebekah determined it to be shortly after noontime. She needed to find something to eat and drink. She didn't want to abandon Prince to suffer alone, but without her rifle, she could do nothing for him. Mason would have to tend to Prince when he came along. Turning her head, she looked to the west. Her determination faltered.

"I can't go back. Mason will be so angry. He won't want me to come back. He doesn't even like me. I'm a burden he doesn't need."

She rose to her feet. With resolve, Rebekah picked up her carpetbag and walked west into the chilly breeze, hoping and praying she'd find water over the next hill.

Several hills later, Rebekah began to wonder why she'd felt such an urge to get away from Mason. Sure, he'd snapped at her and been upset, but wasn't it because of her stubborn insistence to do things herself when she was far too weak? Her steps slowed. The boots, an ancient pair of Curtis's that were several sizes too large for her, rubbed painful blisters on the sides of her feet.

Rebekah limped over to a grove of trees just off the trail. She dropped her carpetbag and leaned against a tall oak, relishing the support it offered her weary body. A sudden blast of cold air from the northwest taunted the tree's juvenile leaves, while streams of dark, ominous clouds drifted across the gray sky. Wrapping her arms around her chest, Rebekah slid down the trunk of the tree, huddling in a ball, her mind transporting her back to happier, warmer days.

As Rebekah nestled in a quilt with Davy on her lap, sitting in front of the fireplace, they'd listened to their mother read God's Word. One of her mother's favorite verses filtered through her cloud of confusion: *"For I know the thoughts that I think toward you, saith the Lord, thoughts of peace, and not of evil, to give you an expected end."*

Rebekah sucked in a shaky breath. Surely this wasn't the end for her. God's expected end? Surely not. Why would He bring her out in the middle of nowhere just to die? When her mother had read the verse back home, it had always instilled hope in Rebekah. Hope for a home of her own with a husband who loved her and children to cuddle and nurture. As Rebekah reached her teen years, her mother had often said, "Sooner or later, some handsome man will come along and sweep you off your feet."

"Sooner or later," Rebekah murmured. Not if this was her expected end.

"Thoughts of peace, and not of evil. . ." That's the key. Peace. Warmth spread through Rebekah's being as she realized the truth. Thoughts of this being her expected end did not bring her peace; thus they must not be from God. Dying on the prairie was not her expected end. She knew it all the way to her tiptoes.

"Go back."

She heard the words in her mind once more. With sudden composure and deliberate resolve, she jumped to her feet. She picked up her bag, raised her chin, and turned back toward the east.

"All right, Mason Whoever-You-Are, here I come."

The abrupt *ping* of a rifle shot halted the words in her mouth. Her head jerked up. She squinted her eyes, staring off into the distance. Another rapid blast rang out, echoing across the hills. Rebekah began to shake. Fearful images of merciless armed men filled her mind. Her newfound peace and confidence quickly evaporated as icy fear twisted around her heart.

"Oh, Lord, I'm sorry. Sorry for my stubbornness. Sorry for my independence. Forgive me for not being grateful when you sent Mason to help me."

The tears she had successfully held at bay the past half hour spilled forth in a torrent. The tight knot within her begged for release as she turned around again and raced behind the huge oak tree. Once again, she slid to the ground. "Please, God, show me a way out of this awful mess."

❧

Mason rubbed his jaw, which was starting to ache from being clenched all morning. He needed a shave. His bristly beard had grown out the past few days since he'd been rationing their remaining water. As soon as it rained or they came upon a creek, he would shave it off. *RJ must think I look like a hillbilly.*

RJ had headed west; he was sure of it. Shortly past their campsite, he'd happened upon a fresh pile of manure. Since he'd seen no other horses, Mason felt certain it belonged to Prince.

As far as he could tell, the crazy woman had taken nothing with her except a small carpetbag. She even had the gumption to ride off bareback since he'd used her saddle for a not-so-soft pillow. Not for the first time, Mason wished he had a faster horse. On a good horse, he could cover in a half hour the ground that it had taken the slower-moving draft horses all morning to cover. They were great for pulling the heavy Conestoga wagon, but he had to have patience, something he was running very low on at the moment. Besides, even if he had a quick horse, he couldn't ride off and leave Katie and Jimmy alone. That was the whole reason he had sold his other horses before making the move west.

"Look!" Jimmy reached for Mason's sleeve and grabbed a piece of his arm along with it. The sharp pain reminded him he should have been keeping his mind on the job at hand.

"Isn't that RJ's horse?"

Mason squinted and pulled his hat down on his forehead to block the early afternoon sun as he followed Jimmy's finger. He grimaced when his hat pressed against the cut on his head. His heart lodged in his throat when he saw RJ's horse lying alongside the trail, a ring of buzzards eagerly awaiting its certain death. He stood and scanned the countryside, clear to the horizon, but he couldn't see RJ anywhere. A band of tension tightened around his chest, threatening to choke his breathing. Why had he been so crotchety with her? Maybe if he'd been more hospitable, she wouldn't have run off.

"Whoa," he crooned to the big horses as he pulled the equine quartet to a stop. Setting the brake, he grabbed his rifle and fired into the air, scattering squawking buzzards in different directions. In one big leap, he lunged over the side of the wagon and approached the horse. It took Mason only a moment to determine Prince had been down too long and wouldn't be able to rise again. He didn't like what he had to do, but the animal needed to be put out of its misery. The whites of the horse's eyes and his flaring nostrils showed his frantic fear of the buzzards.

"Jimmy, get in the back of the wagon with Katie," Mason ordered.

Jimmy opened his mouth to object then seemed to realize what Mason was preparing to do. He gave a quick nod and hopped over the seat.

Mason cocked his rifle and skillfully shot the horse in the head, putting it out of its misery. Slowly he walked around the large body, studying the footprints in the dirt and the places where the prairie grass was smashed down. As best he could tell, RJ hadn't been injured when the horse most likely collapsed.

Why hadn't she listened when he warned her about the danger of riding her horse in its condition? Especially when they didn't have enough water available to give him a decent drink. Mason grimaced. If they didn't happen upon water soon, he'd be shooting his own horses.

West. Even being on foot, the crazy woman walked west instead of coming back to him. Didn't she have any sense at all? What if she'd run into outlaws or Indians? The muscle clenched in his aching jaw. Had he not hidden her rifle in hopes of keeping her from leaving, she'd be armed right now. If anything happened to her, he'd be as much to blame as she.

Mason climbed back in the wagon and released the brake. "He-yah!" he yelled, startling the big horses into a lumbering trot. "Jimmy, get up here and keep a close eye out for RJ," he ordered.

"Unca Mathon, I gots ta go," Katie called from the back of the wagon.

"Not now, Katie. You're gonna have to wait. I have to find RJ." Mason didn't look back. If he saw his niece's pouting lips and big blue eyes, he might waver. He had to find RJ before some wild creature or ruffian did. As they crested the next hill, Mason pulled the horses to a stop and stood, once again scanning the area.

"See anything, pard?"

Jimmy shook his head. "Why ya think he left in the middle of the night?"

Stubbornness and independence, he nearly blurted out loud. But he wouldn't mention those character traits to a child. Mason clicked the horses forward. "Probably just too proud to accept help. Some folks feel the need to do things for themselves."

"Kinda sounds like you."

He gave Jimmy a sideways glance of disbelief. "Am I that bad?"

Jimmy's cheeks turned a shade of rosy pink, almost matching his sunburned nose. "Well," he started, as if unsure of continuing, "you do like to boss everyone around."

"I *am* the boss." He eyed Jimmy, unsure what point he was trying to make.

"Yeah, but…sometimes you boss grown-ups, too. Pa used to say that." Jimmy ducked his head and picked at the edge of his frayed shirt.

Mason's mind raced. Jake said he was bossy? He struggled to think back two years to when Jake had been around. As if he'd been doused with a bucket of frigid water, he shivered as some of Jake's last words rocked his mind. *"Danielle don't need me around when she's got you. A woman's s'posed to look to her husband for things, not her brother. You two's closer than a possum and its young'uns."*

Ducking his head, Mason stared at the dirt on his boots. His father had always told him he was too stubborn for his own good. But being stubborn helped him survive all those harsh whippings his father had given him—even when his mother begged the colonel to stop. Mason grimaced. His father was stubborn, too. Was he becoming the very man he despised?

"Look! What's that over there behind that tree?" Jimmy cried.

Chapter 5

Glancing in the direction Jimmy pointed, Mason's gaze raked the area, searching for some sign of RJ. In the distance, a hint of soft blue against the green tangle of honeysuckle bushes and wind-tossed grasses snagged his attention.

RJ.

Something deep within him wanted to shout out thanks to God, but he stuffed it down. He wasn't on speaking terms with God these days.

Giving the reins a strong flick, he turned his horses toward her, wishing their plodding feet could move faster. Impatience won out. He jerked back the reins, and the big horses lumbered to a walk. Standing to his feet, he was ready to jump out of the wagon the moment it shuddered to a stop. Mason yanked the brake back and threw the reins to Jimmy.

"Stay put," he told the boy. Grabbing his rifle, he jumped down and set off in a dead run toward his target, certain the blue he'd seen was RJ's shirt.

"RJ!" Jimmy yelled. Fear laced the young voice that was nearly drowned out by the cold wind.

RJ lay on the ground, unmoving. Mason lengthened his steps, dodging prairie-dog holes and leaping over a downed tree. Maybe it was urgency he felt, or fear, or guilt for his harsh treatment of the girl; but his legs, usually agile and swift, felt weighted and sluggish.

"RJ," he called, closing the distance to her prone body. He willed her to move, to let him know she'd heard his calls, but her body remained motionless. Mason's heart plummeted, fearing the worse. He kicked his stride up a notch, his boots thudding against the hard ground. Caught by the breeze, his hat flew off, leaving his sweating head exposed to the chilling elements. He ignored it—ignored the plummeting temperatures and the brisk winds fingering his neck and slipping into his shirt. Easing down beside her, he set his rifle aside.

"RJ. It's Mason."

He checked her arms and head, looking for cuts and bruises, but saw no signs of injury. Still worried she might have wounds he couldn't see, he eased her shoulders off the ground, cradling her in his lap. Without the old brown felt hat covering RJ's features, Mason was gifted with his first real look at the girl in the sunlight. He took a moment to catch his breath and gather his senses while he studied her pale face.

Like tiny feathers dancing in the breeze, long strands of saddle brown hair swirled around her chilled cheeks. A smattering of cinnamon-colored freckles dotted her pink, turned-up nose. Long black lashes rested in a half-moon against sunburned cheeks, hiding her sky blue eyes. He wanted to see those blue eyes snapping in defiance again, but RJ didn't seem to realize he was even there.

"RJ." He whispered her name as he caressed her brow. "Come on, sugar, wake up," he said with a little more force. Then he shook her softly and willed her eyes to open. He nearly yelled for joy when she moved.

"Mmm, cold," RJ murmured against his shirt. Her body shivered and Mason lifted her closer, pulling her against his chest. Turning his body so that the brisk wind buffeted his back, he shielded her from nature's assault. Hugging her and rubbing her arms and back to generate heat, he listened to her soft moans and battled his own private storm.

∞

Snuggled in her quilt, safe at home in bed, Rebekah felt warmth filling her being. The soft, comforting voice poured over her like warm honey on fresh-baked bread. She leaned into the voice rumbling against her cheek and relished its calming reassurance.

"Suguh, wake up," it called again.

Rebekah rubbed her eyes, realizing it was already dawn. Her heart skipped a beat. If she didn't get up soon, Pa would climb the ladder to her small loft and take a switch to her. She had to rise, but she didn't want to leave her cocoon of warmth.

"RJ, you've gotta wake up." The voice was firm this time, the gentle crooning gone.

Forcing one abnormally heavy eyelid open, Rebekah peeked out at a blurry shirt pocket with a torn flap. The faint scent of campfire smoke lingered within its threads. Mason's shirt. She blinked twice, her gaze clearing, but it was still there. With her palm, she pushed against Mason's chest. His arms yielded, allowing her to lean back and look into his concerned face.

Instant relief flooded her. *Oh, thank You, Lord!*

Suddenly the reality of her hasty predawn decision hit her.

"I—I killed Prince." She hiccuped a sob.

Mason pulled her back into his arms, tucking her head under his chin. "No, sugar, that horse was ancient. He probably would've died soon even if you hadn't ridden off on him," he said softly, smoothing her hair with his big hand.

She wanted to linger in the warmth of his embrace. Her problems seemed so far away with his strong arms and gentle voice comforting her. But the problems weren't going away—and one of the problems was Mason. With a start, she realized the glare that had been in his eyes ever since they'd met was gone.

She sighed and pushed away from Mason's chest again.

"Can you stand up?" he asked.

Nodding, she pressed against the ground and struggled to her feet, the chilly wind making a valiant effort to knock her down again. Mason hopped up and reached out to steady her. When her legs trembled, threatening to dump her on the ground, Rebekah took hold of Mason's arm.

A movement caught her eye, and she turned her head just as the stiff breeze picked up her hat and sent it sailing away. Rebekah froze. The only part of her body moving was her long braid, flapping against her back.

He knows!

Swallowing back the sudden queasiness rising to her throat, Rebekah took a deep breath and looked up. Amusement flickered in the gaze that met hers. Mason's inviting mouth quirked up at one corner, along with his dark eyebrows.

Rebekah licked her lips with the tip of her dry tongue. "That's why you let me sleep with Katie, isn't it? You knew I was a woman."

Mason gave her a single quick nod. "Didn't figure you'd want to sleep under the wagon with me." His mouth twitched in his obvious effort to hold back a grin.

Rebekah straightened, not particularly enjoying the pleasure he derived from her discomfort. She wanted desperately to remove her hands from his arm, but she didn't trust her legs, weakened again by a day without food. "How long have you known?" She narrowed her eyes at him.

"Ever since I found you sprawled out along the trail. Your hat was off and I saw your braid."

She couldn't resist smacking him in the chest and nearly laughed herself when his amused expression turned to surprise. "Why didn't you say anything?"

He looked down at his boots then caught her gaze. "I figured you had your reasons. That you probably didn't feel safe enough around me to come clean." Mason looked toward the wagon, and Rebekah noticed a flicker in his jaw.

She felt grateful for his honesty. Her cheeks warmed when she realized how secure she'd felt in his arms. When he wasn't growling at her like an old bear, Mason was rather pleasant to be around. Maybe she had misjudged him. Just maybe, traveling with Mason wouldn't be as bad as she'd first thought.

Rebekah didn't want the flare of anger to be rekindled in his eyes, but she had to know. "Are you angry with me?"

His head jerked back in her direction, and she noticed a fresh cut on his forehead. He stood with his hands on his hips, eyes hooded, lips pursed into a solid line.

Uh-oh, he's mad. Praying her legs wouldn't betray her, Rebekah took a step back and crossed her arms over her chest.

"I ought to be. That was a stupid, dangerous thing you did, taking off without food, rifle, and especially water. What were you thinking—no, wait, you weren't thinking, were you? You scared ten years off my life."

Rebekah ventured a peek at Mason's face.

"I ought to be mad, but I'm just so thankful you aren't dead. . . ."

A smile broke its way through her mask of uncertainty. *He's not mad at me.* Her mother's words flittered across her mind. *"Sooner or later, you'll meet a handsome man who will sweep you off your feet."* Rebekah didn't think she'd mind too much if Mason was that man.

"There's just one thing I gotta know."

"What's that?" she asked, squelching the ridiculous notion of her and Mason ever getting together. *He doesn't even like me.*

Mason combed his fingers through his long dark hair. Rebekah wondered if his red ears were a result of the freezing wind or something else. Butterflies danced in her tummy when Mason's mouth turned up in an embarrassed grin.

"What does RJ stand for? I swear I was awake half the night trying to figure that out."

❦

"Uh. . .RJ's your initials, not something you made up, right?"

The sweet smile that had been on RJ's face faded, and a spark ignited in her eyes. "You're not accusing me of lying, are you? Why would I make that up?" She tugged her arms tighter against her chest, whether in frustration or to ward off the cold, Mason wasn't sure.

He cleared his throat. "Well, you *are* the one wearing a disguise." He smiled back, daring her to disagree.

"I never lied to you. My name is Rebekah Jane Bailey, though most people call me Rebekah." She thrust her chin in the air then wobbled in the breeze, as if she hadn't the strength to withstand it.

"Well, Rebekah Jane Bailey. . .uh, Rebekah, I'm Mason Danfield, and we'd best be getting back to the wagon 'fore you freeze your pretty little self to death."

She nodded and stuck her hand out to him. "Pleasure to meet you, Mr. Danfield."

One eyebrow and the corner of his mouth tilted up in mock consternation. "Mr. Danfield," he said with added precise emphasis, "is my daddy, and he's back in Georgia, living on his plantation. I'm Mason." As if to prove he was in no mood to argue, he took the hand she held out and put it on his shoulder. When her eyebrows pinched into a questioning V, he bent down and lifted her up. He pulled her against his chest, smiling at her stunned expression.

Rebekah squirmed, kicking her feet and pushing against him. "I can walk. I don't need you to carry me."

"It's warmer this way." He took a few steps, stooped down, and holding Rebekah up with his knee, picked up her carpetbag. Turning, he shuffled over to a nearby bush. "Grab your hat." He bent down and she reached out, pulling against his shoulder, and grabbed her hat, which clung to a honeysuckle vine. Then she cuddled against his chest.

Mason started for the wagon, his thoughts on the young woman in his arms. Rebekah was shorter and lighter weight than Annie had been. Annie's Swedish heritage had been evident in her white blond hair and tall, sturdy frame. Mason glanced down at Rebekah's thick braid lying over her shoulder and across her chest. He'd always tried to get Annie to grow out her shoulder-length hair, but she'd refused, saying long hair took too much work.

Mason drew in a ragged breath. Why was he comparing the two women? He wasn't looking to replace Annie. She was the love of his life. Mason stopped at the back of the wagon and helped Rebekah crawl inside.

"You're a girl!" Jimmy stood in the middle of the wagon with his hands on his hips, looking at RJ as if he'd been betrayed. Mason understood how the boy felt. RJ—no, Rebekah—had many secrets, but thankfully she hadn't lied to him. His nephew barreled toward the tailgate, slithered over the side, and dropped to the ground. Jimmy gazed up at him accusingly. "Did you know?"

Mason nodded.

"Why didn't you say something? A man shares his secrets with another man that he wouldn't tell no girl."

Tightening his lips, Mason struggled to hold in his chuckle, wondering what *manly* secrets Jimmy might've shared with Rebekah. "I figured she had her reasons for keeping her identity a secret, and she'd tell us when she trusted us."

Jimmy shook his head and stomped off, mumbling.

Katie hopped up, leaning out of the back of the wagon and reaching out to him. "RJ's a girwl! Yippee! I'm glad." Her bright smile ignited a warmth in his chest that swept through his whole body. "Unca Mathon, I still gots ta go."

He chuckled and reached for his niece.

"It's cold!" Katie burrowed into his chest as he lifted her out of the wagon. "Is it gonna snow?"

"No, sugar, it's too late in the spring for snow. It'll just be cold for a bit, and then it'll warm up again."

Mason set Katie down in the grass and ambled over to where his hat rested, pressed against a mammoth oak tree. The tree branches groaned their resistance to the stiff breeze, and the young leaves hung on for dear life, twisting one way and then the other. He smacked his hat against his leg then pressed it on his head as he gazed heavenward, watching the dark gray clouds drifting past with the speed of an agile roadrunner. He glanced back at his four draft horses. A pang of pity shot through him as he stared at their hanging heads. They needed water, and if they didn't get it soon, he'd have to shoot them. With two small children and a willful young woman, it would be a long walk to the middle of Indian Territory where Jake was supposed to be.

He looked heavenward again.

Come on, we need some rain.

The words were the closest thing to a prayer that he'd uttered in the past six months.

Chapter 6

S ometime in the middle of the night the rains came, fast and furious. A sudden blast of thunder and the initial *pitter-patter* of raindrops alerted Mason to the pending downpour. With the earthy scent of parched dirt and fresh rain filling his nostrils, he scooped up Jimmy and their bedding and made a dash for the protection of the wagon.

The hasty movement didn't faze Jimmy from his deep sleep. With his arms full, Mason stood just inside the tailgate, allowing time for his eyes to adjust to the darkness. A bolt of lightning flashed, illuminating the wagon's insides, and Mason eased Jimmy down along the side next to Katie. A smile tilted his lips when he saw Rebekah, sleeping with her arm around his niece.

After adjusting his bedding at the foot of the wagon, Mason eased down. He'd have to sleep sitting up in order to give Rebekah plenty of room so as not to encroach the rules of propriety. He knew he shouldn't even be in the wagon with her asleep, but he couldn't afford to get drenched in this cold and take sick. If he were down, that would leave the other three helplessly on their own.

Under the safety of the canopy, Mason listened to the steady downpour. Relief flooded him. He was thankful he'd left the lids off the two large water barrels attached to the side of the wagon. He had hoped it would rain; now he hoped the rain wouldn't continue too long and turn the trail into a mud-soaked river. Thunder boomed and another flash of lightning brightened the wagon. Rebekah bolted upright, blinking the sleep from her eyes. Even in the dark, he could tell she stared wide-eyed at him.

"W—what are you doing in here?" She pulled her quilt over her chest, not that it mattered since she still wore her clothes.

"In case you didn't notice, it's pouring outside."

"Oh?"

"Looks like we're gonna get a real toad strangler. I didn't want Jimmy and me to get soaked and possibly sick. 'Sides, I have to keep an eye on the canopy when it rains." The sky lit up, and Mason motioned toward the top of the wagon. "If the top puddles, it'll start leaking and drench everything inside. This is an old wagon, and the canvas has some sun rot. I couldn't see the point in investing a lot of money in a new one when we only needed it for about a month. It's not all that far from St. Louis to the Indian Territory."

He knew he was babbling; he just didn't know why. Running off at the mouth wasn't one of his normal characteristics.

"It's okay," Rebekah whispered. "I really hate storms. I'm glad you're here."

Lightning exploded in the night sky so close he could smell the burn. For a moment, it seemed as if someone had lit the lantern hanging from the wagon's ribbings. Rebekah pulled her quilt clear up to her chin as if to protect herself from the storm—or from him. Her wide eyes looked childlike. Long, sleep-tossed, unbraided hair wrapped around her like a cloak, and Mason had a deep urge to bury his hands in her unkempt tendrils.

Roaring thunder shook the wagon, and in the next instant Rebekah dropped her quilt and scrambled to his side, cowering against his arm. Mason reached for the quilt, tucked it around her, then wrapped his arm around her shoulders, pulling her against his chest. Though surprised by Rebekah's reaction to the storm, he relished the warmth her nearness brought. Outside, he and Jimmy had snuggled together under their quilts, but the frosty temperature had chilled him to the bone.

"I—I'm sorry to be such a baby and so much trouble. I promise tomorrow I'll start pulling my own weight," Rebekah whispered against his shirt, the heat of her breath warming a spot on his chest.

"Shhh. Don't worry about it." Wisps of her hair tickled his chin. With a deep sigh, he brushed it down, stroking her long mane. "I don't care much for storms either, though I'm thankful for the rain. I was getting worried."

"What about?"

"We're running short on water. I was concerned I might have to put the horses down."

Rebekah pushed away from his chest. He could feel her staring at him through the dark. "You wouldn't do that, would you?"

"I shot Prince."

Rebekah gasped and Mason grimaced. "Rebekah," he whispered, "Prince was dying. He was suffering."

"I know and it's all my fault."

Mason heard her suck back a sob. He straightened and leaned forward. In the dark, he reached for Rebekah's face. Lightning flashed. In that brief moment, he smoothed her hair from her face and laid his palms against her cheeks. He wished he could see her eyes, but it was dark again. "Listen to me, Rebekah. Prince was an old horse. It was simply his time. I don't want to hear any more about your killing him. Do you understand?"

He felt her nod. Once again, thunder jolted the wagon. A horse whinnied somewhere outside. Mason pulled Rebekah against his side and wrapped his arm around her shivering shoulders. It was warmer for both of them that way, he told himself.

She wrapped one arm around his back and rested her head against his shoulder. Her warm breath tickled his chin, and her long hair covered his left arm. She smelled of campfire smoke and flowers. She weighed next to nothing—it was almost like holding Katie. No, Rebekah was much different from Katie.

He could tell Rebekah liked to be held and cuddled. Annie hadn't cared for either. She'd been affectionate, but she always said she couldn't go to sleep if he held her, so after a brief hug and kiss good night, she'd skedaddled over to her side of the bed.

Mason enjoyed holding Rebekah. As a boy, he'd hugged his mother a lot. Of course, hugging Rebekah was much different than hugging his mother. After his mother's death, the only hugs he'd received had been his sister Danielle's, at least until Annie had come along. His father's stoic personality had kept the man from showing any sort of affection. Mason was thankful he took after his mother in that respect. If he ever married again, he'd make sure to choose an affectionate woman.

"Mason, can I ask you a question?" Rebekah whispered against his cheek.

"Sure."

"How old are you?"

Mason pushed against a supply crate with his foot and shifted to a better position. "I'm twenty-six. How about you?"

"Twenty-one."

Twenty-one? Mason blinked against the darkness. He'd thought for sure she wasn't a day over seventeen.

"Have you—I mean—you're not—married, are you?" Rebekah stiffened in his arms.

Mason's stomach clenched. He hadn't spoken to anyone about Annie or her death since the funeral. Neighbors had brought food for the three of them, but he'd refused to talk about the sudden deaths. He couldn't then. Could he now? Now that six months had passed?

Rebekah pushed against his chest with her palm, tying to ease out of his embrace. Thunder boomed, and she stiffened but didn't cower in fear this time. "Um. . .never mind. I don't mean to be prying. I just thought since we can't sleep and we'll be traveling together, it would be nice to know each other better." She squirmed again. "And, Mason, let me go."

Mason tightened his arms, not allowing her to escape. He knew he shouldn't, but he wanted to hold her—needed to hold her—if he was going to tell her about Annie. "Shhh. Just relax. The storm's not over yet." He pulled her head to his shoulder, gently pinning it there with his palm, thankful she didn't resist. As if they had a mind of their own, his fingers buried themselves in her wealth of hair.

⚭

Rebekah felt Mason tremble—or was it her? She'd never been in a man's arms before. As far back as she could remember, Curtis had never hugged her. Mason's solid torso felt so different than being hugged by her mother's soft body. As much as Rebekah enjoyed the security of being in his arms, she felt she should move away, but now she couldn't. Her head was anchored against Mason's shoulder by his strong hand; his short beard tickled her forehead. He took a deep, shuddering breath, and Rebekah couldn't resist laying her free arm across his chest.

"I was married. . .for nearly two years." He paused, and Rebekah wondered if she should ask what happened.

"Annie died." Mason exhaled a deep sigh as if it required a huge effort to broach the subject. "She was carrying our first child. My sister, Danielle, Jimmy and Katie's mother, was with her. They both died when the wagon they were riding in overturned as they were crossing a river in a sudden storm. The water in the river was usually only a few inches deep, but not that afternoon. They got caught in a flash flood."

Ah. That explained his desire to hold her. Maybe the storm disturbed him as much as it did her. She wrapped her arm farther around his chest, and he laid his head against hers. Maybe her holding him would help comfort him. *How awful to lose so much in one day.*

"I'm so sorry, Mason."

Here in the dark, in Mason's arms, he didn't seem so intimidating. He was warm, secure, needy. She felt safe in a man's arms for the first time in her life. He, too, had suffered and endured the horrible ache of losing someone he loved.

"I don't know if the pain of that day will ever go away," he whispered against her hair.

"Time has a way of lessening the pain. And God can help the most."

Mason suddenly stiffened. "God doesn't care about our suffering. And what do you know of such pain? Surely at just twenty-one, you haven't been married before." His voice carried a harshness that hadn't been there before.

Releasing her hold on Mason, she pulled her arm down against her chest. *He's mad at God.* Of that much she was certain.

"I know the pain of losing someone you love more than life."

"Who, Rebekah? Who did you lose?" His voice softened to that slow Southern drawl she loved to listen to.

"M—my mother and my little brother, Davy. They died last year from influenza. I tried so hard to save them." She choked back a sob. "Pa. . .uh, Curtis, was out on a hunting trip, and I was afraid to leave them to go for the doctor. He was so angry with me when he got back home. Said it was my fault." Tears wet her cheeks, and she turned her face into the warmth of Mason's shirt. His arms tightened around her.

"He hurried for the doctor, but Davy was already gone by the time he got back, and Ma was close to death. If I'd left them alone and gone for the doctor, they might still be alive." The familiar pain tore at her breast. How many times had she played the "what-if" game? Her fingers tightened on Mason's shirt.

"Shhh, sugar, don't cry. We'll get through this together." Mason said the words against her forehead. He called her "suguh" with that smooth voice of his. Chills, from something other than the cold damp air, raced down her spine. He gently kissed her temple, loosing a storm within her unlike any she'd ever known. She wanted to feel his kiss upon her lips. Just once.

She sniffed back her tears and tilted her head. His gentle kisses angled past her ear and down her jawline. Rebekah's heart pounded louder than the thunder booming in the distance. Their lips connected like a whisper. The warm touch of his mouth deepened on hers, sending a shock wave through her entire body. It was a kiss her tired soul could melt into—her first kiss.

Suddenly Mason stiffened and pulled away. "Rebekah? Uh. . .that was a mistake."

Rebekah's emotions whirled like a leaf in an eddy of wind and then skidded to a halt. She jerked from his embrace, her lips still warm and moist from his kiss. Instantly the chill in the wagon battered her as hard as his words. Grabbing her quilt, she crawled back to her sleeping spot and lay down.

The kiss left her weak and confused. She was stunned at her own eager response to Mason's kiss, but she was more shocked by his words. *That was a mistake."*

No, Mason, it was the best thing I've ever experienced.

"Rebekah? I don't know what came over me." She heard his voice edging closer.

"Just leave me alone." She spat out the words.

"Fine! That's just fine with me."

She heard Mason's shuffling as he exited the wagon, and she shuddered at the cold breeze that followed. The worst of the storm had blown past them. Rebekah listened to the gentle patter of the raindrops against the wagon's covering. Jimmy's and Katie's steady breathing filled the air. Peace reigned everywhere except within her.

Lord, was it a mistake to enjoy Mason's kiss? You know he's the only man I've ever kissed. Does kissing a man always feel like that? Like an explosion? As if a fire were being lit in my belly? How could something that felt so good be a mistake? I don't understand.

Warm tears trailed down her cheeks. *I was a fool to think Mason had a speck of niceness in him. He probably hugged me just so he could get warm.*

"But he called me 'suguh,'" she whispered out loud. Rebekah turned on her side as the tears continued to fall. She didn't want to lose her heart to this bear of a man who despised her, but she feared he'd already staked a claim on a quarter section. She took a deep, trembling breath and resolved he wouldn't claim any more. Until she could find a way to get to Denver, Rebekah determined to keep her distance and make sure she did her fair share of the work. She wouldn't give him cause to lower his opinion of her any further.

Her tears slowed as her determination deepened. Finally, sleepiness claimed her body with its soothing, relaxing heaviness. Rebekah felt herself drifting toward that land without thoughts and pain. A place without those black eyes burning their way into her heart.

A sudden icy coldness splattering against her cheek pulled her back from her haven of rest. With her sleeve, she wiped it away. Instantly the frigid moistness returned, bringing a friend with it. *Drip! Plop!*

"Nooo." *The roof!*

Chapter 7

For the past two days, Mason's level of conversation with Rebekah had been reduced to a series of grunts and nods. He was so angry with himself for kissing her. One minute he was spilling his grief about Annie, and the next he was kissing Rebekah.

Mason shook the sweet memory from his mind. How could Rebekah stir up such feelings within him when they'd just met? He didn't like it. It felt like a betrayal of Annie's memory. He wouldn't let it happen again.

Jerking his hat from his head, he smacked it against his pant leg, sending dust flying. Rebekah looked up from the campfire where she was stirring a pot of rabbit stew. The tantalizing odor caused his stomach to rumble nearly as loudly as the thunderstorm had roared the other night. At least one good thing had happened. Once Jimmy discovered how good a cook Rebecca was, his anger at her being a female shriveled up like a piece of bacon in a hot skillet.

Two days ago they'd huddled together to get warm. Now spring had returned, bringing a taste of summer with it. How could the weather change so fast here? Mason ran his fingers through his sweaty hair. Weather in the heart of the nation was unpredictable—challenging.

"We're done." Jimmy smiled up at him.

"Both barrels are full?" Mason asked, setting his sweat-stained hat on a rock to dry.

Jimmy glanced sideways at Katie and scowled. "Yeah, but it weren't easy. Katie got more water on her than in the barrels."

"Nuh-uh," Katie said. "I helped lots. Jimmy spwashed me."

Mason smiled at Katie. The braids Rebekah had so meticulously woven together that morning were frayed and dripping. Water dribbled from Katie's undergarments, which were stained dark by her numerous encounters with the mud along the creek bank. Rebekah showed good sense in removing Katie's dress before allowing her to help Jimmy.

"Guess she'll be needing a bath after lunch," Rebekah commented.

"Nuh-uh, I gived me one." Katie smiled and smoothed her filthy chemise.

Mason laughed out loud, and with joyous moments in short supply, it felt good. "Oh, sugar." He scooped her up in his arms and smacked a kiss on her moist cheek. "I think it'd do us all good to take a bath. It's been way too long."

"Not me. I ain't takin' no bath." Jimmy crossed his arms and jutted his chin in the air.

Setting Katie on the ground, Mason straightened and turned a stern but playful gaze toward Jimmy. "Oh, yeah?"

"Yeah." Jimmy glanced from Mason to Rebekah and back, as if searching for an ally.

"I don't know, Rebekah." Mason turned to look at her. "What do you think?" She set the wooden spoon on a rock and rested her hands on her hips. "Think this boy needs a bath?"

Rebekah blinked as if surprised by his teasing; then she gave him a conspiratorial grin followed by a playful wink. Mason's heart did a little flip. "Oh, I don't know," she said. "I think the question is more *when* he needs a bath than *if* he needs one."

It was the most she'd spoken to him in days. Pleased that she sided with him so readily in spite of the chasm of unspoken words separating them, Mason smiled.

Jimmy scowled at her.

"You know, I think you're right." Mason took a step toward the boy. "In fact, I think we'd all enjoy lunch a bit more if he bathed beforehand."

Jimmy's dark eyes widened. "What's that supposed to mean?"

"Rebekah, you think Jimmy's got time for a bath before lunch?" He wiggled his eyebrows up and down, hoping she'd continue the playful banter.

She picked up a cast-iron lid from a nearby rock and set it on top of the kettle of stew. Her lips curved into an amused grin. "I don't think it would hurt this stew to cook a bit longer."

"Well, then, I guess now's as good a time as any." Mason turned toward Jimmy.

"You mean, right now?" Jimmy asked, his voice laced with disbelief and his eyes almost ready to pop out of their sockets. "But I don't want no bath, Uncle Mason."

From behind him, Mason heard Katie's excited giggle. "I wanna help. I wants ta spwash him."

Mason edged toward Jimmy. "Aw, come on, pardner, it's not that bad. Just think, you'll get to cool off and clean up all at once."

"I'll get him some clean clothes to put on," Rebekah offered as she moved behind Jimmy and toward the wagon.

"I don't want no stinkin' bath!" Jimmy yelled. He backed away from Mason, casting cautious glances toward the water.

Mason chuckled from deep within. "You're the one who's stinkin', son."

Jimmy tilted his chin down and sniffed his shirt. "I don't smell no worse than you."

An unladylike snort erupted from Rebekah as her shoulders curled and she bent forward. Her eyes danced with amusement as she struggled to hold back her tight-lipped smile. She sucked in her lips and raised her eyebrows as if daring him to object to Jimmy's observation.

With one eyebrow raised, Mason looked at her in mock indignation. He rather enjoyed this playful side of Rebekah.

"Well, Jimmy does have a point," she finally said, still struggling for some semblance of control. "I—" She seemed to struggle to speak. "I'm just glad I'm upwind of the two of you."

Mason stopped in midstep. "I'm not taking a bath in the middle of the day."

One of Rebekah's eyebrows and one side of her mouth tilted upward. "Hypocrite."

"This isn't about me. It's about Jimmy." Mason straightened. "C'mon, Jimmy, grab the soap and let's get you washed up."

"Me, too. I wants ta be washed up." Katie ran over and grabbed Rebekah by the leg. "I want Webekah to wash me up."

A roguish grin tilted Mason's lips. "You know, Katie, now that you mention it, Rebekah doesn't exactly smell too good herself."

All amusement faded from Rebekah's face, and Mason had to hold back his own chuckle. A rosy tinge painted her cheeks. Somehow he didn't think it was from working over a hot fire on such a warm, humid day. With her palm, she gently fingered Katie's hair. It suddenly dawned on him how much Katie had taken to Rebekah. His stomach clenched and he felt his smile fade. He didn't want Katie to have to suffer another loss when Rebekah left.

"I—I don't have any clean clothes to wear," Rebekah said. She stood rigidly and thrust her chin in the air.

Mason read the unspoken words he knew must be on the tip of her tongue. *I'm not about to wash when you're anywhere nearby.*

An idea popped into his mind. "I know just what you need." He turned and hurried toward the wagon and climbed in. After rummaging through a trunk of clothing, he found his objective.

Hopping down off the tailgate and sending dust flying, he turned and marched toward Rebekah, smiling inwardly, knowing he'd won this round. He relished her questioning stare.

"Close your eyes."

Rebekah's curious gaze caught his. Excitement filled him, knowing she'd be pleased with his gift.

"Go on, Rebekah, close your eyes," he encouraged. *C'mon, trust me.*

"What you got, Unca Mathon?" Katie giggled. "You gots a th'pwise for Webekah?"

Mason nodded at Katie then looked back at Rebekah. A tiny smile graced her lips, sending his stomach bucking like a back-busting bronc. Rebekah's eyelids eased shut.

From behind his back, Mason pulled out a dark green cotton dress and gave it a gentle shake. Holding it under his chin, he smoothed the wrinkles and then held it up by the shoulders.

"Ohhh," Katie exclaimed. "That's Mommy's."

Obviously overcome by curiosity, Rebekah peeked out of one eye. She threw him a questioning look; then her eyes twinkled with what looked like delight. Mason felt a surge of pride race through him. Suddenly Rebekah's pleasant expression was replaced by something else as she turned toward Katie.

"That's your mama's dress?"

"Uh-huh." Katie nodded.

Rebekah knelt down and took Katie's hand, turning the little girl toward her. "It must be a special dress if it was your mama's. I understand if you don't want me to wear it. I have a dress in my bag I can wear, but I need to wash it first."

"You can wear it," Katie offered with a hesitant smile.

Rebekah glanced up at Mason. A warmth flooded him at her concern for Katie's feelings. He felt his wall of reserve toward Rebekah crumbling, and he didn't know what to do about it.

"Are you sure, sweetie? You really don't mind?"

Katie nodded and Rebekah looked toward Jimmy.

"What about you, Jimmy? Would you mind if I borrowed your mama's dress? I promise to give it back before I leave for Denver."

Denver. Like a bucket of ice-cold water on a flickering flame, Mason's enjoyment of the day's antics dissipated in a plume of smoke. As if someone had reversed the biblical scene of Jericho, his wall of reserve and self-protection rose again.

"It's okay," Jimmy offered.

Rebekah stood up and looked back toward Mason. Amusement once again flickered in the blue eyes that met his. Her mouth quirked with humor. "It's a very pretty dress, Mason, but don't you think it's a bit small for you?"

Only the sounds of nature could be heard as he processed her comment. Birds flittered and chirped in the overhanging trees. The gentle ripple of water cascading over rocks mingled with the *caw* of a lone crow.

"You gonna wear Mommy's dwess, Unca Mathon? Daddies don't wear dwesses."

Jimmy sucked back a loud snort and then exploded into a ball of laughter.

Rebekah's hand came up to stifle her giggle. Teasing laughter danced in her eyes.

"Yeah, Uncle Mason, you gonna wear that dress?" Jimmy slapped his leg and hee-hawed like the joke had been his idea.

Mason wadded the dress in one hand and tossed it toward Rebekah. He moved so fast in Jimmy's direction that the laughing boy didn't realize he'd been captured. "Let's go, Jim. You're gettin' a bath whether you want it or not."

"Wait." Instantly Jimmy's laughter died. "But I thought Rebekah was gonna take a bath. You gave her the dress. I don't want a bath," he yelled as Mason dragged him toward the creek.

❧

Rebekah watched Mason stomp toward the water. She fingered the pretty dress as she considered the kindness he'd offered. If she knew her teasing would have upset him so much, she'd have kept quiet.

Jimmy and Mason sat down along the creek bank and pulled off their boots. Mason helped Jimmy out of his clothes and then rolled up his own pant legs. Mason stood, never releasing his hold on his nephew. Rebekah smiled at Mason's lily-white legs covered in dark hair, wondering when they'd last seen the light of day. Yanking Jimmy up into his arms, Mason waded out into the knee-high water and gently tossed the boy in.

Jimmy's squeal rent the air until a loud splash drowned it out. When she felt a tug on her pants, Rebekah look down at Katie.

"I wanna baff, too."

A bath sounded delightful. Rebekah looked down at her dirty, sweaty clothes. How nice it'd be to get out of these pants and back into a cool dress. When they'd pulled alongside the creek an hour ago, Mason declared they were taking a day off to rest the animals. The first thing Jimmy had done was drag his quilt to the creek and wash it out.

Rebekah eyed the water again. Even if she didn't take a bath now, she could wash Katie and enjoy the water's coolness on her hot feet. Maybe Mason and Jimmy could keep an eye on Katie during her nap, while she walked farther down the creek and bathed. Rebekah put the green dress in the back of the wagon, then walked back to the fire to stir the stew.

"Webekah, can I wash up, too?"

Rebekah smiled at the youngster. She was becoming very attached to the little girl. Pushing back the pain she'd face when leaving for Denver, Rebekah took Katie's hand and started for the water. "Sure, sweetie, let's give you a bath."

Katie tiptoed into the ankle-deep water and flopped down. Rebekah eased down on the creek bank and removed her boots and socks. Jimmy's squeals split the air as Mason flipped water at him. Rebekah grinned. It looked like Mason was getting wet after all, as Jimmy splashed back at him. Mason took another step in, and the water covered his knees.

Suddenly Rebekah got an urge she couldn't resist. She put her finger to her mouth, silencing Katie, and tiptoed into the creek. She resisted the urge to cry out when she stepped on a sharp rock. The cold water stung the blisters on her feet and sent goose bumps racing up her legs and onto her arms.

Easing up behind Mason, Rebekah held her breath. She caught the excited glint in Jimmy's eyes as she sucked in a deep breath and gave Mason the shove of his life.

"Hey!" he yelled as he landed in the creek, creating a huge splash that washed Jimmy several feet downstream. Katie's laughter warmed Rebekah's heart just as Mason surfaced and turned a dark glare on her. *Uh-oh.* A spark of amusement instantly kindled in his eyes, turning into a blaze. Like a wild stallion tossing his thick mane, Mason shook his shoulder-length black hair, sending sun-glistening droplets of water cascading in every direction.

"Seems I was destined to take a bath today after all." A flash of humor crossed his face, and his mouth twitched with amusement.

Katie clapped her hands. "Unca Mathon got washed up."

Mason smiled at her; then his eyes narrowed. "What do you think, Katie? Think Miss Rebekah needs to get washed up?"

Rebekah's smile melted even as her heart gave a small leap. *He wouldn't dare.*

"Yep." Katie giggled. "Mith Webekah needs to get washed up." Rebekah turned her head to see Katie toss a handful of water at her.

A dark blur entered her side vision, and she turned to see Mason charging toward her. How could such a big man move so fast? Rebekah's eyes widened and she felt frozen to the spot. A scream tore at her throat, and she heard Jimmy's cackling laughter as Mason scooped her up and turned back toward the water.

"No, please, Mason, I'm sorry. Really, I am." Mason's breath warmed her face. His playful but roguish grin told her she'd get no mercy from him. Rebekah clung to Mason's damp shoulders, hands locked behind his neck, determined if he was going to toss her in, he'd go with her. His dark hair curled at his neckline, dripping tiny droplets of water on Rebekah's arm.

She felt her backside chill as Mason eased into the deeper water. When she saw Jimmy following, she looked up at Mason and indicated him with a nod of her head. Mason stopped and turned.

"Jimmy, it's too deep for you here. Move back there and keep an eye on Katie. I have business with Rebekah."

"Oh, shucks!" Jimmy commented.

Rebekah saw the boy turn back and felt relieved. She looked up at Mason, who'd stopped walking. His eyes glinted with mischief. This was a side of Mason Danfield she could easily learn to love. *Love? Where did that thought come from?*

"I predict Miss Rebekah's 'bout to take a plunge." His dark eyebrows bounced up and down in eager playfulness.

Rebekah took a deep breath, hoping to get her tumbling emotions under control. Being in Mason's arms was something she could easily get comfortable with. Did he have any idea the effect he had on her?

"If I go in, I'm taking you with me," she ventured.

Mason's eyebrows arched in skepticism. "Is that a threat?"

Rebekah pushed up, tightening her grip around his neck. "No, it's a promise."

Mason flashed a grin that could light a moonless night sky, and Rebekah's stomach churned at his nearness. He leaned his face closer to hers, and she thought for a moment he was going to kiss her.

"We shall see," he whispered.

The next moment, Mason gave her a hefty toss in the air and yanked his head from her frantic embrace. Rebekah landed with a splash about three feet away. Coldness gushed over her body, taking her breath away. Her feet slipped on the muddy bottom, and she sank down, hearing Mason's laughter booming through the air.

Rebekah managed to get her head above water and cried, "Mason," before she was sucked down again. Once again she broke the surface, searching, clawing for Mason. "Can't swim!" she yelled as once again she sank down.

Strong hands lifted her out of the water, and Mason pulled her against his chest. "I'm sorry, sugar, I didn't know you couldn't swim."

Rebekah took a deep, shuddering breath. As Mason took a step back toward the bank, Rebekah snagged her foot around his leg, causing him to lose his balance. In the next instant, Katie screamed as Mason and Rebekah hit the water together, a tangled mass of arms and legs.

Breaking the surface first, Rebekah shoved Mason back down. He grabbed her waist and carried her out of the water. Rebekah threw her head back and laughed. It had been so long since she'd felt this free and full of joy.

"Rebekah!" Mason's harsh voice cut into her joy like a dull knife. "That wasn't funny. Never joke about something as serious as drowning."

Setting her down in the shallow water, he grabbed her by the arm and roughly pulled her to the shore. "C'mon, Jimmy, you're clean enough. There's work to be done."

Rebekah watched Mason jerk his socks on, stuff his feet into his boots, and stomp off. *Why would a little horseplay affect him so?*

Jimmy splashed toward the bank. He paused beside her, wiping the dripping water from his face. "Don't be mad at Uncle Mason. He's just upset. Mama and Aunt Annie drowned when a flash flood raced through the creek they were crossing."

Rebekah stared at the little boy as he trudged to the bank, grabbed a towel, and dried himself. She glanced down at Katie's stricken, tearstained face.

"Oh, sweetie, I'm sorry. Did I scare you?"

Katie nodded, wiping at her cheeks with a pudgy hand, smearing dirt and tears. Rebekah pulled the little girl into her arms.

Remorse stormed through her being. Just the other night Mason explained how his wife and sister had died. How could she have forgotten so quickly?

Oh, Lord, she prayed, *what have I done?*

Chapter 8

Mason sat on the ground, rubbing the oil into the leather harness with more force than necessary. His heart had finally returned to a normal beat after Rebekah's stupid stunt. Through narrowed eyes, he glanced up to watch Jimmy moving the horses, one at a time, to a new grazing area. He sighed a deep breath of relief that they'd finally found water.

Peeking out from under his hat, he glanced over to where Rebekah sat under a tree. Katie lay next to her on her quilt, sleeping. Mason stifled a grin at the sight of Jimmy's freshly washed quilt lying over a bush, drying in the sun.

Mason's gaze drifted back to Rebekah, his emotions swirling faster than a cyclone. Rebekah had gone downstream and bathed after putting Katie down for a nap. Now she sat there, wearing Danielle's dress and drying her waist-long hair in the sun as she used yellow thread to sew the hair back on Katie's dolly.

She was kind that way, doing little things that were important—things he'd never think to do. He couldn't help smiling when he thought how pleased Katie would be to see that her doll had sewn-on hair and blue-button eyes again. In her grief over her mother's death, the young girl had chewed the original buttons off.

Glancing down at his shirt pocket, Mason raised his hand to finger it but decided he didn't want to get oil on it. Last night Rebekah had asked him for his shirt—the one with the torn pocket. She'd washed it and laid it over a bush to dry overnight. This morning she took out her little tin box and stitched up the corner where it had flopped over for as long as he could remember. She even replaced the missing button. Afterward she made him change into it so she could wash his other shirt.

Rebekah laid Katie's doll aside to run the brush through her long tresses. Mason wanted more than anything to go over and take the brush from her hand and run it through her hair. Evidently it was dry, because Rebekah set the brush down and began braiding. It amazed Mason that she could plait it behind her back. He still couldn't braid Katie's right even after lots of practice, but there sat Rebekah deftly plaiting her hair without even seeing what she was doing. After getting it started at the base of her neck, Rebekah pulled the thick, trifold cord over her shoulder and continued until she ran out of hair. Pulling a dark green ribbon from her pocket, she tied it off and flipped it back around behind her. He liked this version of Rebekah. Her hair wasn't hidden behind some dirty hat, and she looked quite feminine wearing a pretty dress instead of those old farmer's clothes.

When she wasn't being stubborn or foolish, Rebekah was an amazing woman. Her cooking, though not as delicious as Annie's, tasted good and warmed his belly. She had more patience with the kids than Annie. Mason shook his head. *Why am I comparing them?*

A warm breeze tugged at his hat, and Mason had to reach up quickly to keep it from sailing away. The children's clean clothing, drying on the nearby bushes, floated to the ground and lay in the dirt. Rebekah squealed and jumped up, chasing after them as the wind lifted them again and blew them out of reach. Mason grinned as she zigzagged from a shirt to a tumbling sock, then chased down a towel.

Danielle's green dress fluttered in the wind, grabbing at Rebekah's ankles. She looked good in green, even though the dress hung more loosely on her than it had on his sister.

"I don't suppose you could help," Rebekah said, shaking the dirt from the shirt in her hand. "All my clean laundry is getting dirty. Where did this wind come from?"

Mason grinned and held up an oily palm. "Got dirty hands. Didn't figure you'd want oil on your clean clothes." He set aside the harness and grabbed a rag, wiping his hands as he stood. Another stiff breeze snatched up his hat, then dropped it next to one of the wagon's wheels. Mason glanced upward. He'd been so focused on studying Rebekah, he hadn't noticed the dark, grayish green clouds streaming across the sky.

"Look's like a storm is brewing."

"We've got to get these clothes inside," she said, snatching up a pair of Katie's undergarments. "How can the weather change so quickly?"

"It does that here in the heart of the country. You'll be swimming in the creek one day and wake up to snow on the ground the next." Mason tapped down his hat and grabbed a pair of his pants as the wind whipped them against his leg. He gave them a sharp shake, and dust flew past on the stiff breeze.

Together they dumped the pile of clothing in the back of the wagon. "I need to make sure the horses are secured." Mason pointed toward the campfire. "You gather up all the loose things and get them in the wagon. I don't like the look of those clouds."

Rebekah looked skyward and her brow creased. She turned her gaze back toward him, and he saw the unspoken concern etched in her face.

"Uncle Mason!" Both their heads jerked toward Jimmy's frantic voice as he raced toward them. "Look!"

Mason and Rebekah hurried around the wagon to look in the direction Jimmy was pointing. Mason's stomach knotted as he took in the swirling, churning black mass of clouds ripping the earth apart as it cut a crooked path across the countryside. Rebekah's fingers clutched his arm, sending shafts of pain racing toward his shoulder.

He loosened her frantic grip and turned her to face him. The breeze whipped the shorter tendrils of her hair loose from her braid. A small, wind-tossed stick slammed against her cheek, and Rebekah jerked her head and grimaced. Her eyes, squinting against the flying dust, gazed up at him with near panic.

The cyclone roared closer. Its screams reminded Mason of a train barreling down the track. He leaned close to Rebekah's ear. "It'll be okay. Get Katie."

Rebekah's heart raced faster than a wild mustang. She'd never been so afraid in all her life. Even marriage to Giles Wilbur didn't seem so awful at the moment. The closer the twisting black monster came, the more she shook. Her cheek stung from the debris flying around, slapping her face.

Mason's fingers cut into her arms. She turned to face him again. A depth of concern she'd never before seen enveloped his features. "Did you hear me?" he yelled. "Get Katie!"

Katie.

Instantly spurred into action, Rebekah raced toward the sobbing child. She scooped her up and turned around. Mason had Jimmy in his arms, racing toward her.

"The creek," he yelled, his black hair flying in all directions, making him look like some majestic warrior. Jimmy clung to him, his face buried against Mason's chest.

Mason's hand grasped her upper arm, pulling her toward the creek. Rebekah fought against her skirt, whipping in the wind, entangling her legs. She stumbled. Mason lifted her, dragging her forward. Rebekah clutched Katie with a death grip, lest the girl be ripped from her arms. The cyclone roared behind her, a heinous, black creature seeking to devour them. Cracking tree limbs splintered nearby. Rebekah ducked and ran faster.

A horse's terrified whinny stabbed at her heart as the earth rumbled when the large animal galloped past. Katie clung to Rebekah's neck with trembling arms. She held on so tightly, Rebekah felt her skin tingling with numbness, but with the cyclone bearing down on them, she couldn't take the time to loosen the child's grasp. Besides, the girl was terrified. Rebekah could hear her wailing cries over the howls of the wind. She could feel Katie's tears warm and wet on her shoulder.

Reaching the creek bank, Mason turned them south. He hurried along the water's edge, steadily urging Rebekah forward. When she stumbled again, nearly dropping Katie, his strong grasp hoisted her up and urged her to run. She ran on coltish legs, her fear spurring her on. Finally, when it seemed like the cyclone might overtake them, they rounded a bend. Here, past floodwaters had dug out a four-foot-high section of the bank, making a natural shelter, and Mason pulled them to the ground on dry dirt.

Rebekah peeked around Mason's arm. She couldn't see the monster, but its presence was evident. The shallow water whipped about as if struggling to escape its banks. Tree limbs, Jimmy's quilt, and their wooden bucket flew by. Thanks to their earthen shelter, the worst of the wind skittered around them. Grateful for his masculine strength, Rebekah turned her cheek into Mason's shoulder, shutting out nature's fury.

He set Jimmy down next to Rebekah, with a reassuring ruffle to the boy's head. Leaning over, Mason gave Katie a kiss on top of her head. His black eyes held Rebekah captive, urging her to be brave. Suddenly Mason jumped to his feet then leaned down toward Rebekah. His lips, warm against her ear, sent chills tunneling down her spine. "Need to check horses. Stay here. But get out—no matter what—if the water starts to rise."

Rebekah practically tossed Katie into Jimmy's arms. Turning, she grabbed at Mason's ankle. "No! Don't go!" His boot slipped out of her grasp. Rebekah squinted into the gray darkness, but Mason was already gone.

She turned back to the sobbing children and sheltered them with her body. A cold, stinging rain pelted her back, seeping into her dress.

Oh, Lord, watch over Mason. Keep him safe. Please.

After what seemed like an eternity, though Rebekah knew it was only minutes, she dared to raise her head. The sky had brightened, and the wind diminished. As quickly as the storm had come, it was gone, the rains reduced to a mist. Pushing her hair out of her face, she checked the children. They were wet and visibly shaken, but they were alive and unharmed. *Thank You, Lord.*

Katie jumped into her arms, burying her face against Rebekah's chest. "Shhh, it's okay, sweetie. The storm's passed us. God kept us safe."

Jimmy started to shinny up the bank, but Rebekah snagged his pant leg and pulled him back. She smoothed Katie's damp hair from her face. "Katie, sweetie, go to Jimmy for a few minutes. I need to check things before you two come out."

"Aw, Rebekah, let *me* go," Jimmy pleaded. "I can check things."

Katie clutched Rebekah tighter, choking off her breath. She loosened Katie's arms. "Sweetie, come on, I need to have a look around and make sure the storm's over. Jimmy will hold you for a few minutes; then I'll be right back for you."

"But where's Unca Mathon? Did he get blowed away?" Her bottom lip trembled as she put words to Rebekah's own fears. Tears cascaded down Katie's cheeks, mingling with the rain and mud already streaking her face.

If Mason were okay, surely he would have returned for them by now. But he wasn't back, and she didn't hear him calling. What if he was hurt? Rebekah's concern for him grew by the second.

"Don't go, Webekah." Katie's sobs wrenched her heart even as her little arms strangled Rebekah's neck again.

"I'll be right back. I promise."

"Mama didn't come back."

Rebekah looked at Jimmy's wide-eyed stare. His black eyes looked so much like Mason's.

"C'mon, Katie," he finally squeaked out. "I'll hold you till Rebekah comes back."

Giving Jimmy a smile of gratitude, Rebekah disentangled herself from Katie's death grip. She rose to her feet, futilely brushing the dust and wrinkles from Danielle's dress. Standing on her tiptoes, she gazed over the top of their sanctuary, stunned at the destruction and disarray of their camp. She looked down at the children and smiled then turned and walked back alongside the peaceful stream. The calm water rippled along, belying the mayhem of the storm. In the far distance, Rebekah watched the cyclone continue its black path of destruction, the ever-hungry monster seeking other innocent, unwary victims to devour.

The canopy over the wagon, split in three pieces, rippled in the light breeze like an embattled flag. Thankfully, the wagon still stood, a brave survivor of the destruction. Ironically, Rebekah's pot of stew still sat over the campfire. She stared, amazed that the small fire had withstood the sudden, vicious downpour. Her clean clothes dotted the ground along the cyclone's path. The one thing she longed to see eluded her scope of vision.

Where is Mason?

Most of the trees in the area lay eerily on their sides. Those still standing resembled besieged soldiers with broken arms. In the field across the trail, Rebekah could see two of their horses grazing on the knee-high prairie grass as if nothing had happened.

Mason must be looking for the other horses.

Rebekah decided the most important thing she could do was secure the horses, but first she had to tend the children.

"Jimmy," she called from the ledge up above them, "bring Katie on up here."

Immediately she heard the children running along the creek bank, and then they scrambled over to her. Wide-eyed, they stared in amazement at the destruction. Katie wrapped her arm around Rebekah's leg, her dolly tucked in her other arm and her thumb in her mouth. Jimmy scanned the area, running his fingers through his hair just like Mason did whenever he was nervous or deep in thought.

"Where's Uncle Mason?" He turned to her with panic written all over his face. "Is he gone?"

Rebekah had hoped to see him returning by now and nearly voiced her worry, but she had to be strong for the children. She couldn't let them see that she was wondering the same thing.

"I figure he went looking for the other two horses. We need to get busy and clean up as much as we can before he gets back. He'll be so proud of us."

Jimmy straightened, as if in agreement.

"I want you two to stay together. Jimmy, you watch out for Katie. There may be sharp things around like broken tree limbs. You two start by gathering up all the clothes and putting them in the back of the wagon. Then stock up a pile of wood and set it near the campfire. I'm going to run over there"—she pointed to the field behind the wagon—"and bring back the two horses. Okay?"

Katie tightened her grip on Rebekah's leg. "I wanna go wif you."

Stooping down, she gave Katie a hug, then pulled a leaf from her hair. "Sweetie, I'll need both hands to bring back those two big horses. I need you to help Jimmy. It's very important that we find all of our clothes and other belongings before dark. It will be like a treasure hunt. Can you do that for me?"

Katie's eyes sparkled. "I can find tweasure. And Molly can help, since she gots eyes now." Touching a chubby finger to each eye, Katie turned Molly away from her. "See, Molly, there's Unca Mathon's shirt." Running over to the blue plaid shirt, she snatched it up and turned a victorious smile toward Rebekah.

"Good job, Molly, Katie. Go on, Jimmy, get busy and help Katie and Molly." Jimmy rolled his eyes as if he were too mature to partake in Katie's game.

"Watch her carefully," Rebekah whispered for his ears only. "I'll be back as soon as possible."

He nodded and turned, taking Katie by the hand.

Rebekah hurried toward the horses, slowing as she got closer so as not to spook them. She recognized the closest horse as Mason's lead gelding, Duke. Rather than wrestling with two of the huge animals, she grabbed the rope attached to Duke's halter and tugged him back toward the wagon. He came willingly with a soft whinny. Rebekah wondered if he was thankful for the human companionship. She tied Duke to one of the few trees still standing and turned back to get the other horse.

Scanning the countryside, she again wondered where Mason and the other horses were. As she neared the second horse, Rebekah spied a patch of red against the raw browns and dusty hues the tornado had left behind. A sudden sense of foreboding assaulted her so strongly she could almost smell it. Inching forward, she felt the blood drain from her face, causing it to go nearly numb. Raising a trembling hand to her mouth, she fought back the scream that sought so viciously to escape.

No! Mason!

Chapter 9

Rebekah slumped to the ground, ignoring the wetness saturating her dress. Mason's shoulder bulged upward in an unnatural manner. She doubted it was broken—maybe dislocated—but panic swarmed her mind at the sight of it. How could she fix a dislocated shoulder?

With trembling hands, she reached under her skirt and tore off a strip of her petticoat. She dabbed the blood on Mason's forehead, thankful when she realized the injury was only a small gash.

"Mason," she called, gently jostling his good shoulder. *Oh, Lord God, please help us.*

A moan erupted from somewhere deep inside Mason, softly reverberating through his body. Pain etched his face as he struggled to open his eyes. His eyelids fluttered then closed again as if the effort were too difficult. He lifted his good arm and squeezed his forehead, then reached for his wounded shoulder. "Ahh!"

Rebekah saw a muscle twitch in the side of his jaw as he gritted his teeth, and she clenched her jaw in sympathy.

"Shhh. I'm here, Mason. Try to relax and tell me how I can help you." Rebekah brushed his dark hair off his forehead, then ran her hand down his cheek.

"My arm—knocked—out of joint."

Rebekah dabbed at the sheen of sweat covering Mason's forehead.

"Gotta pop it back—happened before." Mason's chest rose in staccato rhythm as he sucked in short gasps of breath.

Rebekah felt a woozy darkness threatening to overpower her. This couldn't be happening again. A picture of her pale mother and little brother lying on their deathbeds, burning up with fever, haunted her. If only there'd been a doctor nearby. And here she was again, out in the middle of nowhere with Mason injured and maybe dying. Rebekah looked all around her. She didn't even know in which direction the nearest town was. She raised her hands to her face as unshed tears burned her eyes and tightened her throat.

No, God, please don't do this to me again.

"Bekah—I'm okay." She felt Mason's warm, calloused hand gripping her wrist. "It happened before. Help me—pop it back."

Rebekah spread her fingers apart and peeked at Mason. He didn't sound like he was dying. She took a deep, shuddering breath. "I don't know what to do."

"Put your foot—in my underarm. Grab my arm and jerk it—back in place."

"No, I can't do that. It'll hurt you." She laced her fingers together and pressed her hands to her mouth. The thought of bringing Mason more pain made her want to jump up and run away, just like she'd done when Curtis said she had to marry Giles Wilbur.

"And who knoweth whether thou art come to the kingdom for such a time as this?" The words she had read that morning from the book of Esther burst into her mind. Rebekah dropped her hands to her lap and sat up straight. Could everything that had happened to her have been God's plan to bring her to this exact place? What would Mason have done if he'd gotten hurt like this when he was alone with the children? Maybe she could redeem herself by helping them. The thought gave her courage. Even though she was on her way to Denver, it blessed her that God could use her along the way to help this man and the children. Swallowing back her remaining fear and doubt, she glanced up and met Mason's pain-filled gaze.

He lifted his head off the ground as if he needed to get closer to her. "I need your help, Bekah."

Bekah. That was the second time he'd called her Bekah, and he'd never called her that before. It seemed almost as if saying her full name took too much effort. How could she not help him?

"Tell me what to do." She heaved the words with a heavy sigh. A smile tilted Mason's lips, bolstering her courage.

She slipped around to his wounded side, then sat down and removed her boot. Gently she eased her toes into Mason's warm underarm, the heel of her stocking instantly absorbing the moisture of the damp grass underneath. He grimaced, whether in real pain or anticipation, Rebekah wasn't sure. Wrapping her hands around the wrist of his useless limb, she gazed into his eyes. "I'm afraid I'll hurt you," she whispered.

"You can't hurt me any more than it hurts now." His eyes begged her for understanding. "Yank hard or you might have to do it again—and we don't want that, do we?" He gave her a weak smile and laid his head back down on the wet ground.

"How hard?" Rebekah didn't like the way her voice trembled. She needed to be brave for Mason's sake.

"Hard." The gritty tone in his voice left her no doubt.

"Wait," she cried. Reaching under her skirt, she tore another strip off her petticoat, then folded it into a square. "Bite down on this. Maybe it will help."

"Thanks." Mason's sweet grin sent her stomach turning flip-flops—or maybe it was just the sight of his abnormal-looking shoulder. Mason opened his mouth, and she laid the pad of cloth between his teeth.

"You ready?"

Mason stared deeply into her eyes, as if fortifying her for the task ahead. After a moment, he gave a brief nod.

God, help me do this right the first time—for Mason's sake.

Anchoring her foot into Mason's armpit, she gave him a final glance. His eyes were shut, dark eyebrows drawn down, and teeth clenched tightly on the fabric. Rebekah tightened her grip around Mason's forearm. She closed her eyes, heaved another quick prayer, and yanked with all her strength.

"Ahhh!" he cried out. His head dropped to the ground.

"I killed him!" Rebekah dropped Mason's arm and rose to her knees. Leaning over his still form, she cradled his face in her hands. "Please don't die," she whispered, patting his clean-shaven cheeks. Tears from her eyes dripped down onto his face and the backs of her hands.

In that moment, Rebekah suddenly realized how deep her feelings for Mason ran. She blinked in surprise. Though he irritated her with his stubbornness, she knew she'd never felt this way for a man before. Did she love him? How could she tell? She'd never known the love of a man—only Davy. But he wasn't a man, just a boy. And even though she cared for Mason, she knew he didn't love her. He still grieved for Annie.

She told herself to remember that God had put her here to help Mason and the kids through this rough time, not to fall in love. The thought brought more tears gushing forth. Tears of gratitude that she could be here to help. Tears of sorrow that Mason could never feel for her what she felt for him.

He uttered a soft moan, and his breathing returned to normal. With her thumbs, Rebekah wiped her tears off his face. She brushed back a lock of his damp hair and ran her fingers over his scalp, checking for other injuries. Mason heaved a deep sigh.

"Mmm. Do that again." Rebekah's hands halted. He was alive—and conscious? "Don't stop, Bekah. That feels great."

Staring at him in confusion, she leaned back, sitting on her heels, and wiped the tears from her face. The deeply etched pain no longer contorted Mason's handsome face. Instead, he seemed almost at peace. She glanced at his shoulder, relieved it no longer held that unnatural shape. She'd done it. A smile of pride tickled her lips and swelled her chest. In spite of her fear and insecurities, she'd held her ground, she hadn't run away, and Mason seemed better.

"Where are the kids?" He peeked out one eye for a moment then shut it again.

"They're picking up." She glanced back toward camp then realized she couldn't see the campsite because of the wagon. At least the wagon had served to keep the children from seeing Mason on the ground.

"You're not hurt?"

"No, I'm fine." Rebekah glanced over her shoulder and saw that the horse still grazed nearby. "Do you think you could get on the horse so I could get you back to camp?"

He shook his head. "No, I'd be better off walking. You can help me if I need it."

"All right." Rebekah put her boot back on, trying to ignore her soaked stocking, and rose to her feet, taking a moment to brush off her dress while she willed her legs to stop trembling. Grimacing, Mason used his good arm to push himself into a sitting position. Rebekah noticed his gaze drift down to his wounded arm, which hung useless at his side. He'd need a sling or something to support his shoulder until it could heal. For now, she could stick his arm inside his shirt.

Kneeling back down, she undid the button she'd just sewn on his shirt—had it been only this morning? It seemed so long ago. Mason's eyebrows lifted in surprise, and a cocky grin tilted his lips.

"I've still got one good arm. I think I can tend to my own dressing."

Rebekah felt her cheeks flame. Lowering her eyebrows in a challenging glare, she picked up his wounded arm and stuffed his hand inside his shirt.

"Ow! You're brutal, Doc." Though Mason's words sounded gruff, she could see the teasing glint in his eyes. Eyes that reminded her of black onyx.

"Sorry," she murmured.

"Oh, yeah, I can tell you're real sorry." Mason nodded his head and rubbed his shoulder.

Rebekah nibbled on her bottom lip. She really didn't mean to hurt Mason, but sometimes his teasing irritated her as much as his stubbornness. He had no idea how much his being hurt had rattled her and brought back memories of her failure to keep her mother and Davy alive.

"Hey, I'm okay." Mason reached out, touching her cheek. "You did good, see? My shoulder still hurts, but I'm better."

She gave him a weak smile and shrugged her shoulders. "I. . .uh, need to wrap your head. Your cut's still bleeding." She took the two pieces of frayed cloth that she'd ripped from her petticoat and quickly formed a head bandage.

"Where're the other horses?"

"Duke's at camp. I don't know about the other two." She glanced down to see Mason staring off in the distance, his mouth cocked in frustration. "Can we pull the wagon with two horses?"

"No."

His curt answer didn't allow for exceptions. Without the other two horses, they were either stranded or would be forced to abandon the wagon and most of their supplies. Rebekah exhaled a deep sigh. This would be a long day. As soon as she got Mason settled in camp, she'd have to go looking for the horses while there was still daylight. At least dinner still simmered on the campfire.

Rebekah helped Mason to his feet. He wobbled a bit then slung his good arm around her shoulders. "You okay?" she asked.

"Just a bit dizzy—and my shoulder aches, but that's normal."

"How many times have you dislocated it before?"

"Twice. One as a kid and once. . .uh, never mind." He tightened his grip on her shoulder. Rebekah's frame sagged from the weight of Mason's big body. With one arm around his waist, she used her other hand to help hold his injured arm against his chest. The going was slow as they stepped over and around all kinds of debris, from tree branches to a dead duck to a derby hat, uncrushed and in perfect condition.

Mason gave a chuckle. "Where do you suppose that came from? I think we're days from the nearest town."

"I don't know. The storm was so strange." Rebekah reached up and tucked a loose strand of hair behind her ear. "Things are torn up all over the place, and yet my stew still sits over the burning fire, untouched."

"Twisters do weird things." Mason stopped and looked down at her. "We were lucky, Bekah." His gaze roved over her face and rested on her cheek. Conscious of his gaze, she reached up to touch her face. Mason gently nudged her hand away and ran his finger across her cheek. "You have a scrape."

"It's nothing—not like your injuries." Chills raced down her spine as Mason fingered the area near her cut.

"Looks like you'll have a bruise. Uh, listen. . ." He stared off toward their campsite a moment, then turned back to her. "I'm really glad you were here. I don't know what would have happened to me and the children without your help." He slid his fingers down her cheek and around to her nape.

Rebekah's breath caught in her throat. She closed her eyes, enjoying the warmth of his hands on her skin. Her heart danced and her breathing hurried to keep pace. He had no idea what his touch did to her.

"Sugar?"

Her eyes flew open, expecting to see Katie nearby, but instead Mason was peering down at her with an endearing smile tilting his fine lips. His warm breath tickled her face as he leaned closer. His eyes nearly begged her for a kiss. Rebekah couldn't breathe. She studied his gaze, expecting to see a teasing glint. He leaned closer. Rebekah leaned forward to meet him.

"Hellooo in the camp," came the distant intruding call.

Chapter 10

Reluctantly, Rebekah forced her gaze away from Mason's mouth and turned to see two men coming down the trail. Her heart skidded to a halt. Curtis and Giles Wilbur! Like a frightened deer, her gaze darted for a place to hide. She couldn't have come this far only to be caught and taken back and forced to marry against her will.

"Ow, easy there." Mason flicked the wrist of his injured arm, forcing her to loosen her death hold on his arm. Rebekah realized just how hard she'd been gripping it. He looked down at her, and his expression darkened. "What's wrong?"

She looked back to the men. Both were riding horses she didn't recognize, and behind them they led Mason's other two horses. A small measure of relief filled her knowing Mason and the kids wouldn't be stranded. She looked toward the creek. If she took off running now, she might be able to get away.

Oh, God, why now? Mason needs my help. The children need me. What do I do?

Mason loosened his grip on her shoulders and turned to look her in the face. "Tell me what's wrong, Bekah."

Avoiding his probing gaze, she looked back toward the two men. They were closer now. Suddenly she realized the men truly were strangers—not Curtis and Giles. Knee-sagging relief flooded her. *Thank You, God.*

"You know 'em?"

Rebekah shook her head. "For a moment I thought I did. But, no, they're strangers."

"C'mon." Mason wrapped his arm around her shoulders again. "Get me to the wagon. I need my rifle."

The men drew closer, moseying along, not seeming to be in any big hurry. Rebekah was grateful for that small fact. As she and Mason approached the wagon, Katie and Jimmy came into view.

"Nuh-uh," Jimmy said. "I don't care if I am dirty again, no one's making me take two baths in one day."

"Uh-huh. Webekah will. You's all dirty again." Katie stood with her hands on her waist, looking like a little mama. Suddenly she caught sight of them. "Unca Mathon. You's hurt." Worry tilted her slim blond eyebrows, and she raised Molly to her chest in a fierce hug.

"I'm okay, sugar. Don't worry."

Katie studied him a bit to see if he was telling the truth; then she looked to

Rebekah. She flashed the little girl a reassuring smile, and Katie gifted them with a dimpled grin. She gave Molly a kiss and a hug. "See, Molly, Unca Mathon's only hurt a wittle bit."

"Popped out your shoulder again, huh?" Jimmy sounded like a knowledge-able old man as he tossed his wet and dirty quilt onto the wagon's tailgate. Rebekah bit back a laugh, not wanting to embarrass him. She helped Mason to where he could lean against the wagon; then she climbed inside and found the rifle. As she exited the back of the wagon and jumped to the ground, the two strangers ambled into camp.

Mason reached toward the rifle, but Rebekah pulled it away, shaking her head. He couldn't shoot one-handed. He gave her a questioning glare, but she cocked the weapon and aimed it at the men. Mason's glare turned into an expression of surprise. She thought she caught a hint of wonder in his dark eyes before he turned back to face the two men.

For once, she felt thankful for all the hunting Curtis had forced her to do. It had paid off—she now had a dead aim. She stepped in front of Mason where she could get a clear view of the strangers. Mason grunted a little moan of frustration, and Rebekah felt herself being pulled back beside him. He gave her another intense look, clearly letting her know she wasn't in charge, even if he was banged up.

"Jimmy, Katie, over here," Mason ordered. The children must have caught the warning in his voice, because they both hustled forward. "In the wagon." Mason nodded his head toward the Conestoga. Jimmy lifted Katie with a little help from Mason; then the boy scrambled in behind her. Both children ducked down and peered over the back of the wagon.

In spite of her nervousness, Rebekah pursed her lips together to hide her smile. She'd never seen either child obey so quickly or quietly. She wondered if it had more to do with Mason being hurt or the strangers.

"Howdy," said the older of the two men, who looked to be in his late sixties. "Looks like y'all got a nasty taste of that cyclone what passed through. You folks all right?"

Mason nodded. "Been better off before, but then again, we've been worse off, too."

The old codger chuckled. "I hear ya." He nodded his head back toward the two horses he was leading. "These wouldn't be yours, would they?"

"Matter of fact, they are. I'm much obliged for your returnin' 'em."

"We saw them hightailing it away from the cyclone and figured somebody down this way'd be lookin' fer 'em." The old man turned to the younger man, who looked to be in his mid-forties. "This here's Beau, my son, and I'm Sam Tucker. Y'all mind if'n we share your camp for the night?"

Mason looked down at Rebekah. She saw the wariness in his gaze. "I reckon that would be the neighborly thing to do, seein's as you brought my horses back.

Come on down and sit a spell. I could use a good sit-down myself." Mason turned and looked in the wagon. "Jimmy, hop down and tend to the horses. Then get out to that field and fetch Hector back 'fore he wanders off."

Rebekah felt Mason's arm go around her shoulders, and she looked up at him. Lines of pain and fatigue etched his face. "Help me over to that tree. Think I'll sit and rest up a bit; then I'll help get the camp back in order."

She uncocked the rifle and slipped one arm around Mason's waist. She tried hard not to think of how nice it felt to be able to cling to Mason's solid body, not to mention how having his arm wrapped around her felt better than being tucked into a toasty bed on a freezing cold night. She shook her head. She couldn't afford to think thoughts like that. Denver was her future, not Mason. A sigh of longing slipped through her lips, and Mason tightened his grip on her.

He leaned his head down next to her ear. "You all right?"

How could she be all right with his warm breath tickling her cheek? She nodded, not daring to look up and be face-to-face with the man filling her thoughts. "I'm sorry about all this," he whispered. "I know my getting hurt will mean extra work for you. And having these two men around might make things tense."

Mason's concern sent a sudden warmth racing through Rebekah's body. She ventured an upward glance. She never knew what she'd see in Mason's black eyes. Sometimes he glared back, making her wish she were a turtle and could just crawl into her shell. Then other times, the looks he gave her sent her blood churning. The feeling rumbling through her body now fell into the latter category.

"I don't mind the work," she said on a shaky breath.

"You wouldn't," he said with a smile. "But you already do so much; I don't know what I'll do when you leave us."

Rebekah's smile faltered. All he was worried about was how he'd get along after she left? What about her? How would she ever get Mason Danfield out of her mind? She'd best start right now. She helped Mason ease down to the ground and lean back against the tree's rough trunk.

"Thanks," he mumbled.

Sam and Beau Tucker had dismounted and were leading their horses toward the creek. She started to walk away, then felt a tug on the rifle. Glancing down, she caught Mason's gaze.

"I'd best hang on to that till we know for certain what these fellows are about."

"You couldn't even use it if you had to," she countered.

"If I have to, I'll manage. You can't lug it all over camp with you."

Rebekah relinquished the weapon and turned to check her stew. A deep emotional exhaustion seemed to make each step harder to take than the next. She'd allowed herself to think Mason felt something for her, but now she knew the truth. No man had ever loved her, and no man ever would.

She stopped in front of the campfire, trying to find the strength to stir the stew. Between the storm, Mason's getting hurt, and her realizing the truth about her relationship with him, she just wanted to curl up and go to sleep, but she had too much work to do. Rebekah looked around the camp area. Her wooden spoon was missing.

"Can I get down now?" Katie yelled from the back of the wagon.

Rebekah forced her feet to move. A hug from Katie just might be what she needed to suck her out of her depression.

⋙

Mason laid the rifle in his lap. Until he got to know these strangers better, he'd rather play things safe. He drew the rag from his pocket that he'd used to wipe the oil from his hands earlier. It would serve well to polish the rifle's wooden stock and maybe distract his company from the real reason it rested in his lap.

He watched Rebekah amble toward the fire. She looked tired. He couldn't imagine what he would have done if she hadn't been here. He admired her brave spirit. With just a bit of encouragement, she'd pushed back her fear and popped his arm back into place. With a little shrug, he tested his shoulder, instantly sorry when a sharp pain jolted his torso.

Sam and Beau Tucker had watered their horses and filled their canteens and were making their way back toward him. Both men strolled under the tree's shade and flopped down on the ground.

"Whewee! That cyclone was a big un," Sam said.

"Yep." Beau plucked a stem of dried grass and stuck it in his mouth.

"The worst of it missed us," Mason said. "I got Bekah and the kids tucked in a shelter next to the creek and went to secure the horses. Next thing I knew, somethin' knocked me in the head. I'd just raised my arm to check my forehead when a branch or something hit me from behind." Mason left the rag lying on the rifle as he rubbed his aching shoulder. "Ain't too bad, though." Until he knew what these men were about, he thought it best not to let them know just how badly he was injured.

Katie skipped over with a tin cup, water sloshing everywhere. "Webekah says I'm s'posed to give you this."

Mason smiled and peered into the blue tin mug. Only about a half inch of water remained. He bit back a grin and swallowed it in one gulp. "Mmm, delicious. You reckon you could fetch me some more?"

Katie giggled. "I can't, but Molly will."

Mason smiled. "That would be fine. Tell Molly thanks."

"That's a cute kid you got there." Sam watched Katie skip off toward the water.

"Actually, she's my niece. Her name's Katie. The boy is Jimmy, my nephew." Mason resumed polishing his rifle.

71

"So is Molly your wife then?"

"What?" Mason looked up in surprise. "Oh, no." He grinned. "Molly is Katie's doll."

The three men shared a laugh as Katie, carrying Molly, tiptoed back with another cup of water.

"That's a mighty fine-lookin' wife you've got. Lost my wife a couple years back." Mason's gaze darted toward Sam, and he studied the old man's face, not sure how to respond to that. Probably just as well that they thought he and Rebekah were married. Mason's gaze drifted back to Rebekah. A smile tilted his lips. Life definitely would be interesting married to her. Too bad she was so dead set on traveling to Denver.

"Yup, I lost my Hazel, and Beau lost his ma."

"Yep," Beau echoed.

Mason looked at Beau. The man dressed in faded overalls had to be near forty. So far all he'd said was "Yep." Somehow Mason wondered if Beau wasn't a few turnips short of a bushel.

"Where y'all headed?" Sam asked as he rifled through his saddlebags.

"Up Tulsa way," Mason said. "We're looking for the kids' dad. The last letter I got from him was posted in Tulsa."

"Ya heard what's goin' on in the Unassigned Lands in the Oklahoma Territory?" Sam pulled a wad of beef jerky out of his bags and bit off a hunk, then handed it to Beau. He bit off a chunk and offered it to Mason.

Shaking his head, Mason tried not to grimace at the thought of eating after these two less-than-clean men. They looked like trappers who had been up in the mountains for years. "Hillbillies" is what folks in this part of the country called them.

Unassigned Lands. He'd heard about the lands originally plotted out for Indian reservations but never assigned to a specific tribe. Mason racked his brain, trying to think if he'd heard something about them lately. Finally he shook his head. "What's happening there?"

"Ain't you seen a newspaper lately?"

Mason shook his head, more than a little surprised that Sam could read. "Nope. Been travelin' awhile."

"Well, that new president of ours, Benjamin Harrison, signed a bill opening up the Unassigned Lands in Indian Territory for settlers. There's gonna be a big race—a land run. They's callin' it Harrison's Hoss Race."

"How's it work?" Mason asked, setting his rifle aside.

"The Land Run starts at noon on April 22. Folks can race for a lot in town or a 160-acre plot in the country. The paper says ya gotta register in either Guthrie or Kingfisher in the Oklahoma Territory if you git lucky 'nough to stake a claim. Costs fourteen dollars. That's an awful lot, if'n you ask me."

Mason knew Jake would want in on the run. It was just the kind of opportunity he'd jump at. Jake probably wasn't even in Tulsa anymore—not if he knew about the Land Run. The problem was, he'd told Rebekah he'd drop her off in the first big town they came to. Of course, if they didn't stop in Tulsa, she'd have to continue traveling with them.

He looked across the campfire and watched Rebekah redo Katie's hair. She nibbled her lip and looked deep in thought. He glanced around to check on Jimmy. The boy, wearing the derby hat, was leading Hector back from the field where Bekah had found Mason.

Would that be fair to Bekah—to make her travel to the Oklahoma Territory? It *would* get her closer to her destination.

The truth was, he wanted to spend more time with her. He wasn't ready for her to leave. Of course, he needed her more than anything now that he'd been injured. Hadn't he heard that the train cut across the Territories from Kansas all the way down to Texas now? If they headed far enough west, they'd have to come across it sooner or later. Then she could catch the train up to Dodge City and on to Denver. Until then, he'd have time to heal and get himself ready to say good-bye.

Mason turned back to Sam. "You know if there's a train that crosses the Territories?"

"Yup. Yup. The Atchison, Topeka, and Sante Fe Railroad runs through there."

Stretched out on the ground beside Sam, Beau began snoring. The irritating noise reminded Mason of a badger's snarling growl.

Mason looked back at Rebekah, and a small grin tilted his lips. She and Katie had filled their arms with the tornado-tossed clothing they'd washed that morning. The two females were headed back to the creek, evidently to wash the clothes for the second time in one day.

"Yup, that's a mighty fine-lookin' woman you got there." Sam laid back, his head on his crossed arms, and closed his eyes.

Mason felt his ears warm, knowing the old man had caught him staring at Bekah. He forced away pleasant thoughts of having her for a wife. "How long you reckon it would take to get from here to the Territories?"

"You're already in Indian Territory, but I imagine it'd take less than a week on horseback from here to cross into the Oklahoma Territory. Course, pullin' a wagon the size of your'n, more likely two weeks."

"Got any idea what the date is?" Mason asked.

"Yup. Early April—somewheres around the fourth or fifth." Sam yawned and turned onto his side.

One-handedly, Mason calculated the days. That gave him barely two and a half weeks to get to Oklahoma before the Land Run—if they didn't stop in Tulsa. It wasn't like he'd promised Bekah they'd stop there, and sure as shootin',

Jake would be off somewhere else once the Land Run was over. Mason couldn't afford to miss him.

Almost against his will, his gaze drifted back to Rebekah again. She wrung the water out of one of Jimmy's shirts then flipped a handful at Katie. His young niece giggled and whipped a dripping sock in the air, getting more water on herself than on Bekah. Rebekah unrolled Jimmy's shirt and gave it a ferocious shake. Katie squealed and ran back toward the creek bank. Mason chuckled.

He loved Bekah's playfulness. *Whoa! Loved? Where did that come from?* Mason ran his hand through his hair, suddenly wondering where his hat had ended up. Loved. It was simply a figure of speech, wasn't it?

Yeah, then why did you kiss her, Danfield?

Mason laid his head back against the tree trunk. He didn't want to have feelings for Rebekah. He had plans. Take Jimmy and Katie to Jake, then head west—alone. Suddenly, being alone didn't sound so great.

The sound of water splashing and Katie giggling tickled his ears. Songbirds had returned to the wind-tossed trees and trying to outdo each other in their cheerful choruses. A gentle breeze tugged his hair. Maybe it would be best to take Rebekah to Tulsa after all.

But how could he manage without her now that he was wounded? He opened his eyes and studied the ground nearby. He reached out and snatched up a small stone. With a deep sigh, he heaved the rock to the far side of the camp, instantly regretting his sudden movement when pain riveted across his chest. The rock landed in the dirt near Duke. The big horse snorted and jumped, his brown hide quivering.

"Don't splash me, Katie. I'm warnin' you." Jimmy's stern tone drew Mason's gaze back to the creek. "I told you I've had all the water I want for one day."

"But you's dirty again," Katie reasoned.

"It's okay for men to be dirty."

"Nuh-uh. It ain't okay for anybody to be dirty." Katie stood ankle-deep in the creek with her dripping fists on her waist. "'Sides, you ain't a man. You's just a boy."

"Well. . ." For once, Jimmy didn't seem to have the words to argue with his sister. "Well, I'm not gettin' wet—and that's final." He plastered his fists on his hips, daring Katie to argue more. Suddenly Hector lifted his dripping muzzle from the creek where he'd been drinking. The horse stepped toward Jimmy and nudged him in the back with his big head, sending the boy flying into the creek. Jimmy rose from the water, sputtering and fuming. Like an Indian on the warpath, he danced in the creek and glared at the horse. Good thing for Hector, Jimmy didn't have a tomahawk handy.

Mason's lips split into a grin, and he couldn't hold back his chuckle. Katie and Bekah howled with laughter. Jimmy whirled around, glowering at them both. Hector whinnied as if joining in the fun.

"You's did get two baffs in one day." Katie covered her mouth as she giggled.

Jimmy grabbed Hector's lead rope and led him out of the creek. "Some friend you are," Mason barely heard him mutter as the boy stomped away, dripping water everywhere.

Smiling, Bekah followed Jimmy out of the water. She shook open the boy's shirt and laid it across a bush. Cupping her palm over her eyebrows, she looked in Mason's direction. A warmth saturated his being. She was checking on him. He raised a hand in a little wave. A pale rose color stained Bekah's cheeks as she waved back. Bending down, she picked up one of his shirts and turned back toward the creek.

Mason laid his head back against the tree trunk. His eyelids drifted shut. Who was he kidding? He wanted Bekah around as long as he could manage. Just maybe, getting laid up was the best thing to happen to him in a long while.

Chapter 11

No, I'll do it. You just sit down and rest." Rebekah glared up at Mason, daring him to argue with her again. For the past two days, he'd been cranky, fussing to get back to work. The foolish man wouldn't lay still and allow his arm to heal. And, as if that wasn't enough, he'd been bossing everyone around as if they didn't know enough to do their chores without his oversight.

Mason's eyes narrowed. He seemed to be contemplating his response. "Look," he finally said, "I hurt my shoulder. I'm not dead or dying, Bekah. I don't need to be babied like an infant still in the cradle."

"Well, you don't need to be messing with the horses just yet either. It's only been two days since your shoulder was dislocated." She moved closer and tilted her head back farther to see clearly into his dark eyes. " 'Sides, I haven't been babying you."

Mason stepped forward, the toes of his boot knocking into her shoe as Rebekah tried to gulp down the knot in her throat. Knowing full well she had been doing everything she could to make his recovery easier, she now avoided his gaze and stared at the stubble on his chin. The very chin she had shaved just yesterday. Her heart had barely slowed its erratic throbbing from being so close to him and from rubbing her hands across his rough cheeks. She was so thankful he hadn't perished in the storm that she'd been willing to do almost anything to help him.

"I—I don't want you to hurt your shoulder," she whispered as she read the words *Blue Creek Mills* on the sling she'd made for Mason out of an old flour sack. He reached behind him and adjusted the knot against his neck.

"I told you this has happened before. I know my limits. You're gonna have to trust me on that."

"But the horses—" Mason's warm finger on her lips halted her next words. She swallowed, willing her heart to slow down. Being close to Mason like this was making Denver look less and less appealing.

"You and Jimmy can help me with the horses. I'm trying to be careful and not do too much, but you're gonna have to trust me." His eyebrows arched as if waiting for her to disagree.

Oh, but I do trust you. If you only knew how much.

"Hee-hee." Sam shuffled past them, chuckling and tugging on his faded suspenders. "You two's not gonna have a very happy married life if'n y'all argue all the time like that. Best y'all should just kiss and make up."

Rebekah felt as if her cheeks had caught fire. "They've been here two days, and you never told him we aren't married," she hissed at Mason.

Mason grinned at Sam, but his smile faded when he caught her glare. He looked like a schoolboy with his hand caught in the pickle barrel. He opened his mouth to say something then clamped it shut.

Straightening, Rebekah leaned toward Mason. "Well, if you won't tell him, I will." She swung around, mouth open, ready to inform Sam of her unmarried status. "Sa—"

Mason's warm, calloused hand settled over her mouth, halting her words. He pulled her against his chest, holding her tight. Frustrated, Rebekah wanted to fight against him but was afraid she'd hurt his shoulder, so she allowed herself the luxury of leaning back against Mason's solid body.

Sam had stooped down to load his saddlebags and had his back to them. Beau was on the other side of the wagon, taking his horses to the creek, with Jimmy and Katie tagging along. Rebekah felt Mason's cheek against her head as he leaned down close to her ear. His nearness shot spikes of attraction up her spine. "At first, I didn't want them to know. I thought it was safer for you that way." Mason's warm breath tickled her ear. "Then I decided not to tell them. I didn't want them getting any wrong ideas about us."

Rebekah snorted an unladylike laugh against his warm, salty hand, which remained lightly against her lips. What about the wrong idea that they were married?

Sam stood and turned. Mason released her mouth and ran his hand along her cheek; then he let it rest against her neck. She couldn't move. Could he feel her ferociously pounding pulse?

Sam chuckled. "Yup, making up's the best part. Give the little woman a kiss for me, Mason." He grinned his gap-toothed smile and ambled toward the creek.

Mason tightened his grasp and leaned down, kissing Rebekah firmly on the cheek. She stiffened at his unexpected display of affection, then shoved her elbow in his belly. He *oompfed* a gasp of air then chuckled. "I'm just obeying my elders, sugar."

Rebekah grabbed his arm and yanked it away, then stomped off to finish packing the wagon. "Of all the nerve." She swatted at her cheek where it still burned from Mason's kiss. Tears stung her eyes. Why couldn't he kiss her for real, instead of making it a big joke? If only Prince hadn't given out on her, she'd be in Denver by now and Mason Danfield would be a distant memory. So why didn't that thought make her feel any better?

❧

Rebekah hadn't talked to Mason all day. She sat stiffly beside him on the wagon seat as if he weren't there. Mason lifted his hat, thankful he'd found it under a

bush near their camp, and scratched his head. He couldn't for the life of him figure out what he'd done—unless it was the kiss. But he was just funnin', humoring
Sam really. Surely she didn't take offense at something so harmless.

Sam and Beau had said their good-byes and trotted their horses down the
trail toward the Unassigned Lands. Actually, Sam had said good-bye and Beau
had just said, "Yep." Mason racked his brain, trying to remember if Beau had said
anything else the whole two days they'd spent together. The son was as quiet as
his father was chatty—a strange but friendly pair.

Mason peeked out the corner of his eye at Bekah. She'd loosened her braid,
allowing her long brown tresses to spread out over her shoulders like a soft cloak.
Her hair reached all the way to the wagon seat. He wondered how she ever managed to stuff it all up under that silly felt hat she often wore. His fingers itched to
reach out and touch her hair. Instead he tightened his grip on the reins.

If only she weren't so dead set on going to Denver. . .

Mason heaved a sigh as he realized his thoughts had ambushed him again.
When had he started developing feelings for Bekah? Adjusting his hat, he sneaked
another glance. She combed her fingers through her hair, then began rebraiding
it. He turned his face forward, concentrating on the fly buzzing around Duke's
head. It was either that or stare at Bekah like an enamored young pup.

The wagon jostled and squeaked down the dirt trail. The horses' hooves *clip-
clopped* slowly in the soft dirt and prairie grass. Katie and Jimmy giggled from the
back of the wagon as they used stick rifles and pretended to shoot the flock of
crows that seemed intent on following them. Mason's right arm, still supported
by Bekah's sling, felt hot against his chest as the warm afternoon sun beat down
on them. He yawned. At least they were no longer fighting that blast of cold that
had run in and pelted them with sleet and rain, then hurried back to the north
like an ornery kid playing tag.

Mason slouched forward, resting his good arm on his knee, and closed his
eyes. If things went right, in less than a week he'd find Jake, return the kids to
him, and put Bekah on a train to Denver. He squeezed his eyes tighter, trying to
determine which action would hurt the most. How had Bekah managed to wind
her way into his life so soundly? Into his heart? Maybe it was just because they
were thrown together with no real choice in the matter. He couldn't exactly have
left her alone on the prairie. Then when he got hurt, he needed her even more.
He needed her. . . .

Mason clenched his jaw. He didn't need Rebekah. He was going west—alone. If
he came to love Bekah, it would be just a matter of time before something took her
away from him. And he couldn't endure losing the woman he loved a second time.

"Mason, are you in pain?" Bekah's hand warmed his shoulder where she
touched him.

Pain. Yeah, but not the kind she meant. How could he say good-bye to Katie and Jimmy? To Bekah? Why couldn't something go right in his life—just for once? How far west would he have to go to outrun his pain?

"Mason? Are you all right?"

"Yeah. Fine," he grunted without looking at her.

"I just hope you aren't overdoing it."

Mason turned a glare on Bekah. "Don't mollycoddle me."

"I . . ." Bekah turned her head away, but not before he caught a shimmer of tears glazing her eyes.

Mason snapped the reins, sorry for losing his temper. The four horses had nearly slowed to a crawl as they pulled the heavy wagon up another round-topped hill. "He-yah! C'mon, Duke. Get a move on."

"I didn't realize I was babying you. I'm sorry." Bekah's soft whisper sent daggers of condemnation spearing into him.

Mason pressed two fingers against the bridge of his nose, chastising himself for taking his frustrations out on her. She was only watching out for his welfare. He turned in the seat to face her. "No, I'm sorry. I shouldn't take offense to your watching out for me."

She flashed him a brief, tight-lipped smile. "It's all right." Rebekah fiddled with her dress, folding a section in her lap and unfolding it. "How much longer do you think it will be 'fore we get to Tulsa?" She looked up at him, hopeful expectation glistening in her blue eyes. Mason's gut twisted when he saw her damp eyelashes clinging together in tiny spikes—or maybe it was because of what he had to tell her.

"Uh. . .we already passed Tulsa."

"When? I never saw it." Bekah's eyebrows scrunched together as if she were struggling to remember.

"We skirted around it yesterday. Sam told me it was quicker to get to the Oklahoma Territory going as the crow flies rather than turning off the trail to Tulsa."

Bekah nibbled on her bottom lip. "Those train tracks we crossed yesterday went to Tulsa?"

"Yeah."

"I could be heading for Denver right now."

Mason winced. Denver again. The woman obviously had a one-track mind. Why did he ever think she'd be interested in a life with him? "My mistake." There could be no confusing the tone of his voice. "I figured you'd want to stay on with us awhile longer—with me being laid up some."

Rebekah turned a hurt gaze toward him. "You could've at least asked me before deciding on your own. It was my choice to make."

She was right, but in the mood he was in, he didn't feel like giving her the satisfaction of admitting as much. Instead, he picked up her long braid and flicked it like a whip, then nudged her shoulder with his. "You know what your decision would have been anyway, right?"

She gave him an indistinguishable stare. Kind of like a hunter staring down a cougar.

"I'm helpless, remember?" He wiggled his eyebrows and the arm in the sling, ignoring the twinge of pain bolting through his shoulder.

Her pretty mouth twisted into a wry grimace.

Mason decided to pull one of Katie's stunts. "Don't be mad at me, sugar." He pressed his lips into a pout.

Bekah maintained her stoic expression only a few seconds before she tucked in her lips in her effort not to crack a smile, but the sparkle in her eyes gave her away.

"We could always kiss and make up, like Sam suggested." Mason gave her an ornery grin then struggled to return his lips to a pout again.

Bekah crossed her arms over her chest and glared at him.

Mason heard a scuffling sound; then Katie popped her head out from the back of the wagon. "What's the matter? You sad, Unca Mathon?"

Bekah gave a little laugh that sounded like it came out of her nose.

"No, sugar, I'm not sad." He reached back and ruffled her already-messed-up hair. "Just playin' with Bekah."

"I gots ta go again." Katie stared up at him expectantly. He narrowed his eyes, trying to determine if she was telling the truth or just looking for a way out of the wagon. Katie looked at him with wide blue eyes; then her pink little lip pushed out into a darling pout.

Mason glanced up at Rebekah. Their gazes locked. Bekah's eyes twinkled with mischief, and she stuck out her lip at him. He couldn't hold back his howl of laughter. Bekah's shoulders bounced with her own mirth. Katie looked at them like they'd both gone crazy.

"Don't waff at me." Katie shook her head like an offended matron. "I gots ta go weal bad. Weally, Unca Mathon."

Mason and Bekah's laughter only increased. Tears blurred Mason's vision as he reached back and lifted Katie onto the wagon seat, ignoring the sting in his wounded shoulder.

Katie sat stiffly on the seat with her pudgy little arms crossed over her chest. "It's not funny," she huffed.

"What's not funny?" Jimmy poked his head up then grabbed Mason's arm. "Look there." He pointed over the horses' heads. Mason choked back his laughter at the sudden urgent tone in Jimmy's voice. Up ahead, a buckboard listed unnaturally to the left. A man squatted beside the broken wheel as if trying to decide what to do. They pulled up closer to the busted wagon.

Suddenly a woman stepped from behind a tree, her rifle pointed straight at them.

Chapter 12

Rebekah's heart pumped with anxiety. Were they about to be robbed? Would they lose their wagon—or worse? Mason couldn't defend them with an injured shoulder. She breathed a quick prayer as she leaned forward and reached toward the rifle resting on the floor near her feet.

Mason firmly but gently grabbed her shoulder, giving her a quick shake of his head as he turned his gaze toward the strangers. "We don't mean you folks any harm. We'd like to help if we can."

The woman studied them for a long moment; then Rebekah sighed with relief as the older woman lowered the barrel of the rifle till it pointed at the ground.

"I don't reckon you'll do us harm if you got your wife and kids with you."

Rebekah groaned. *Not the wife thing again.* She sat up on the hard seat. First chance she got, she was going to set the woman straight.

"Come sit a spell. Maybe we could share dinner tonight," the woman offered. Suddenly the thought of talking with another adult woman tickled Rebekah's insides. She hadn't had a conversation with a woman since her mother died.

Mason clicked the horses forward then guided the wagon to the side of the trail. One-handedly, he helped Rebekah and Katie descend from the wagon. Jimmy hopped out the back and hustled around to the front. He started to unhitch the horses but stopped and looked at Mason for permission. Rebekah saw Mason give the boy a swift nod; then with the grace of a three-legged bear, Mason climbed down from the wagon. His jerky motions made her wonder how much his shoulder still hurt him. And she didn't miss the fact that he left the rifle on the wagon floorboard. Knowing he felt that comfortable already with these strangers eased some of the tension tightening her neck and shoulders.

Feeling a tug on her skirt, she looked down to see Katie's forlorn face. Rebekah bit back a smile at Katie's cross-legged dance. She grabbed the girl's hand and rushed her behind the wagon, grinning as Mason's soft chuckle followed on the warm afternoon breeze.

By the time they returned, the horses were grazing in the nearby field and Mason had squatted beside the man, looking over the broken wheel. Rebekah headed toward the woman, her arm jerking as Katie held her hand and skipped along beside her. The woman looked to be in her late fifties or so. Her plump figure amply filled out the faded blue calico. Graying brown hair was bunched in a loose bun at her nape, and a bonnet hung down her back with the tie forming a strange bow under the woman's two chins.

"Howdy! I'm right pleasured to meet you'ns. I'm Ella Robinson, and that's my Luther fixing the wagon wheel."

Rebekah smiled. The woman had kind blue gray eyes and a friendly grin. "This is Katie, and I'm Rebekah Bailey." Katie blessed the woman with a dimpled smile and a brief wave; then she tugged her hand free from Rebekah's and skipped off toward Jimmy, who had squatted next to Mason.

"Your Mr. Bailey was kind to offer us help. We's anxious to get back on the road to Oklahoma. Gonna get us some land in that big race they's gonna have there."

Rebekah watched Ella Robinson rustling around in the back of her wagon. She pulled out what looked to be biscuit fixings. Suddenly it dawned on Rebekah what the woman had called Mason. Mr. Bailey. She didn't know whether to laugh or scream, but she knew she had to set the woman straight. "We're heading there, too." Rebekah turned and pointed to Mason. "His name's Mason Danfield, and the boy is Jimmy. The children are Mason's niece and nephew." Rebekah cleared her throat. "And we aren't married."

Mrs. Robinson stopped almost in midstride. She looked at Mason and back to Rebekah. Her gaze darkened, and her thick lips thinned into a straight white line. "Oh, my. That's not at all proper." Her withered hand rose to her mouth.

Rebekah stepped forward and laid her hand on the woman's arm. "Please, it's not what you're thinking."

The woman's gaze looked skeptical. Rebekah's words rushed forth as she told the story of how Mason had rescued her, but she left out the part about how she'd run away from home—away from an unwanted marriage. Mrs. Robinson seemed to ponder her words for a moment, then shook her head. Before Rebekah could blink twice, the woman set her bowl of supplies on the tailgate and tugged Rebekah into her plump arms. "You poor thing. You must have been so frightened. Well, you're safe now. Luther and I'll take care of you. Since we're both goin' in the same direction, you can travel with us."

Rebekah was flabbergasted. Not travel with Mason? But he needed her, didn't he? She felt a sudden warmth at her shoulder and knew instantly that it was Mason.

"Uh. . .that's mighty kind of you, ma'am, but you can see I'm laid up some and sure need Bekah's help, especially with the kids and the cookin'."

Mrs. Robinson gave Mason a thorough dressing-down with her eyes. Rebekah didn't think she'd like being on the wrong side of the older woman's temper, but she had to give Mason credit for not squirming. "I promise, I've been a perfect gentleman the whole time Bekah's been with us. Right, Rebekah?"

She was tempted to toy with his emotions a bit, but the look in his eyes told her that his reputation was too important to tease about. "Yes," she said, pushing away the thought of Mason's kisses. "He's been nothing but kind to me—probably even saved my life."

"Well, I supposed ya did what ya had to, given the circumstances." Mrs. Robinson's gaze softened a fraction toward Mason. "But since we're headed the same direction, Luther and I can be chaperones. That way, Rebekah can help you and sleep with us, and things will be all proper-like." Mrs. Robinson turned around and scooped up her biscuit fixings again, then pivoted back to face them. "Oh, and another thing, we're just plain ol' Luther and Ella."

Rebekah turned to study Mason's expression. Here was another situation he couldn't control. She wondered if he was fuming inside or if he was glad to be relieved of her. The muscle in his jaw twitched just before he spun away and stalked back to his wagon.

She didn't particularly like the change herself. Things had been going along just fine without the Robinsons chaperoning. Suddenly Rebekah's mind flashed back to the nighttime rainstorm when Mason and Jimmy had climbed in the back of the wagon to stay dry. She felt her cheeks flame. What would Ella say if she knew Mason had taken her in his arms and kissed her?

It probably was a good idea to put some distance between her and Mason—before her heart became any more entwined with him and the children. Each day of their journey brought them closer to their destination—and a train or stage that would take her to Denver and away from Mason forever.

Suddenly Denver didn't sound as appealing as it once had. Pushing those unwanted thoughts from her mind, Rebekah tucked a wisp of hair behind her ear and turned to Ella. "What can I do to help?"

≫~

One week later, the roads near the border of the Unassigned Lands were thicker with people than a wheat field covered in a swarm of grasshoppers. Mason had never seen so many humans in one spot, not even back in Atlanta. Wagons of every kind and size parked along the sides of the road and across the fields. The air was thick with the odor of campfires, horses, and unwashed bodies.

Water was sure to be a problem with so many people congregating in such a small area. He felt thankful he'd had the sense to fill both of his barrels at the last creek they'd crossed.

"Have you ever seen so many tents and people?" Rebekah said, her voice filled with awe. "I never dreamed there'd be so many here."

"It's downright shocking, ain't it?"

Rebekah nodded. "I don't think I've ever heard so much noise before. I grew up in the woods. The only noise there is the sound of insects and the wind whipping through the tall pine trees."

A man clad in worn overalls whistled at a boy about Jimmy's age who ran across the path in front of the slow-moving wagon. Duke snorted and tossed his head then continued down the road. Tired-looking women seemed to be making camp the best they could under the circumstances. Mason felt a twinge of regret that Bekah would be subjected to living in these awful circumstances. Then again, she might be on the train to Denver by nightfall.

With Ella's close chaperoning, they'd hardly talked the past week. The only time they'd had together without the Robinsons was when Bekah rode with him on the wagon, and then the children were constantly vying for their attention. Mason didn't know how Katie would handle Bekah's leaving. He wasn't sure how he would handle it.

Maybe he should just ask her to stay. . .and do what? Travel west with him? Mason shook his head. He wasn't going to come between Bekah and her dream. And he wasn't going to let her come between him and his plans. It was better this way. He'd lost everyone he'd ever loved except Katie and Jimmy—and they'd soon be gone, too. If he gave Bekah his heart, it would only be a matter of time before something took her away. Better she should go now while she claimed only a portion of his heart rather than the whole thing.

"Where will we camp?" Rebekah's words jarred his thoughts.

"Let's see where Luther and Ella go." He pulled off his hat and ran his fingers through his sweaty hair. "I'd like to camp with someone we know so they can help with the kids." *After you leave.* He couldn't voice the final words out loud.

"Maybe it won't be so crowded on the other side of town."

"Maybe."

The long screech of a train whistle screamed over the din of the crowd. Mason saw Bekah jump; then she turned to face him. Their gazes locked. The noise surrounding them faded as Mason sat captivated by Bekah's melancholy gaze. The reality of her leaving hit him in the gut. It almost seemed as if she didn't want to go. But probably she was just dreading saying good-bye to the kids. He could tell she loved them.

"Unca Mathon, what was that noise?" Katie's blond head popped up from the back of the wagon.

"I told her it was a locomotive, but she don't believe me," Jimmy said.

Mason chuckled. He doubted Katie even knew what a locomotive was.

"It sounded like a monk-ster," Katie said, her gaze darting in every direction.

Bekah reached back and patted the little girl's head. "Don't be afraid, sweetie. It's just a train. It won't hurt you."

"Why is there so many peoples here?" Katie asked.

"This is where they're having that Land Run Sam told us about. Right, Uncle Mason?" Jimmy sounded like a little man, trying to impress the ladies. Mason suppressed a smile.

"Nuh-uh. Land can't run, can it, Webekah?" Katie crossed her arms, looking to Rebekah for support. "It ain't gots no legs."

Mason's heart somersaulted at the way Bekah's eyes twinkled while she fought to keep from laughing. The wagon croaked and groaned down the trail as he watched her struggle to answer. After a moment, she seemed to have regained control.

"You're both right, Katie. The land doesn't have legs, so it can't run. But the race Jimmy mentioned is called a Land Run because people run to get free land."

"Water doesn't have legs, but it runs," Jimmy mumbled.

"Nuh-uh," Katie said.

"That's enough," Mason said, using his no-tolerance voice. "You two go watch out the back for a while. We'll be camping soon."

"Yes, sir," Katie and Jimmy said in unison; then they disappeared into the wagon.

Mason turned his back to Bekah. "Untie this thing, will ya?" His arm had been immobilized in the sling for nearly a week and a half.

"Are you sure you're ready to be using your arm?" Rebekah asked over his shoulder. Her warm breath tickled his cheek, doing strange things to his insides.

He pushed the feeling away. "There may be lots of rough people around here, and I don't want to seem an easy mark. I'll be careful. 'Sides, it hasn't hurt much the past few days. I've been moving it around some when you weren't watchin'."

Rebekah smacked him on his good shoulder; then her fingers fiddled with the knot, tickling the hair along his nape and sending shafts of excitement coursing down his spine. After a few moments, the sling fell loose around his chest, and his arm was free again. He carefully moved the stiff limb back and forth, testing his range of motion.

"See, good as new." He flashed Bekah a smile, hoping to prove his point.

She seemed to be observing him for signs of pain. Beyond her shoulder, a familiar figure darted by and disappeared behind a tent, loosing a cyclone in his belly.

Jake!

Chapter 13

Mason jumped to his feet, throwing the reins at Rebekah. He had to catch up with Jake before he disappeared again, or he might never find him again in this massive crowd. Mason stepped in front of Bekah, but she grabbed his sleeve, forcing him to stop.

Standing, she looked over her shoulder in the direction he stared. Mason offered a supporting hand against her back as the wagon jostled them down the road, moving in and out of dried ruts made by previous travelers. The wagon tilted to the side in a deep furrow. Mason grabbed Bekah's arm to keep her from tumbling over the side, all the while continuing to scan the crowded tent city, hoping to see Jake again.

"What is it?" Rebekah asked. Her voice sounded shakier than normal.

"I saw Jake. I've gotta catch up with him before he gets away."

She turned to face him, placing her hands against his chest for balance. "Think, Mason. You can't go chasing after Jake until we've set up camp; otherwise, you'll never find us in all the mess."

Mason clenched his teeth together, fighting his fierce desire to run after Jake and knowing her reasoning made sense. She and the children were his first priority. He focused his gaze on the Robinsons' wagon in front of him as it veered off the trail toward a small cluster of trees standing in a less crowded area of the tent city. Ella glared back at them, obviously wondering why they were standing while the wagon was still moving. For some reason Mason couldn't explain, he still didn't think Ella trusted him. Maybe it was because she'd become a mother hen to Bekah. He'd enjoyed Luther's company in the evenings, but at the same time, it meant less time with Bekah—although that was probably for the best since she'd be leaving soon.

He flopped down on the seat, biting back a grimace when his shoulder twinged with a brief spear of pain.

Think about finding Jake—not about saying good-bye to Bekah.

❧

Rebekah sat down on the hard wagon seat next to Mason. She handed the reins to him, hoping he didn't notice her trembling. His sudden outburst had shaken her. In the weeks they'd traveled together, she hadn't seen him so intense and uneasy except maybe when she'd first met him. She couldn't understand why Mason was so intent on returning Jimmy and Katie to their father. After all, the man had abandoned them like Curtis had said her own father had left her. From what Mason had told her, Jake would be a complete stranger to Katie.

A pang of unexpected sympathy knotted her stomach. She leaned forward, elbows on her knees, and put her face in her hands. They smelled of leather and dust. How could she make Mason see that the children needed him to hang around, at least until they got used to Jake again?

Rebekah slid her hands over her ears. How would she ever sleep with the awful din of thousands of people roaring in her ears? Having grown up almost alone in the woods of Arkansas, rarely seeing anyone except her family, she felt the noise crowding in on her. She moved closer to Mason, but he didn't seem to notice.

He pulled the wagon to a stop beside the Robinsons' buckboard. "This looks like as good a place as any to camp," Luther hollered.

Rebekah's gaze traveled around the area, coming to rest on two tiny wooden structures, both with a long line of ragtag people winding away from them. The buildings were only about fifty feet from where the two wagons had stopped. This certainly wouldn't do.

She glanced past Mason to see Ella in an animated discussion with Luther. Ella's plump hands moved faster than a nervous cat trying to escape a room full of active children. Rebekah could just imagine the tongue-lashing Ella was giving him for suggesting camping so near the busy, aromatic outhouses.

Luther turned a frustrated gaze toward them. "Guess we'll be moseying on down the road a bit farther." He clicked his tired horses forward as Rebekah tightened her lips to hold back a grin.

"Don't know what's wrong with this campin' spot," Mason mumbled. "That Ella's just too picky."

Rebekah tried hard not to giggle, but a loud, unladylike snort broke loose. She couldn't hold back any longer. A loud laugh blasted past her lips. She leaned forward, forgetting her fear of the crowd, and enjoyed the feeling of amusement.

Mason peered down at her. "What's so funny?"

She shook her head as her whole body jiggled with laughter.

"*What?*" he asked with added emphasis.

Regaining control, Rebekah wiped the tears from her eyes. "I just imagined a glimpse of your face at dinner, trying to eat while sitting fifty feet downwind from the outhouses."

Mason's dark eyebrows crinkled in confusion. He pushed his hat up, revealing his pale forehead—an odd contrast to the rest of his tanned face. He looked back at the two little buildings, then turned to face her. His dark eyes glistened like the blue black of a crow's wing in the bright sunshine. "Oh," he said.

Rebekah turned her face away to keep from laughing at him. Men had such a different perspective on things. And Mason was all man; she couldn't deny that.

Nor could she deny the way his nearness made her get all antsy inside. Their shoulders knocked together as they continued down the rutted road, giving her a sense of security and happiness like she'd never felt around any other man. Thoughts of her stepfather doused the joy in her spirit, sending her mirth fleeing as a pang of regret flooded through her. Her smile vanished, and once again she thought about leaving.

She scanned the crowd of people. Would she be safe from Curtis here? Was he even following her? And if he was, could he find her in this crowd? Children raced about, playing tag and squealing to one another. Jimmy shouted out the rear of the wagon at some boys as they galloped past, whooping like Indians. Tired women hung up faded clothing that looked even more worn out than their owners.

Rebekah shook her head; she didn't understand it. What could make so many people leave their homes, come to this horrid place, and live in such squalor, just for a chance at a small farm? She had a feeling most of them would leave empty-handed and disappointed. There couldn't possibly be enough land for all of them.

A nearby train whistle startled the horses. They snorted and whinnied and pranced sideways in their harnesses. Mason had to grip the reins to keep them from bolting. His arm, muscles tight, pressed against hers. He muttered soothing words to his team. She glanced down, realizing just how close she sat to him. She had to start distancing herself from Mason and the children, or she'd be suffering the pain of separation for a long time.

Rebekah slid over to the far side of the wagon seat, wondering how much a train ticket to Wichita, Kansas, would cost. She'd counted her little pile of coins a few days ago. The money she'd made back home from selling eggs and the fowl she'd hunted was pitifully meager. She calculated the amount again. Would it be enough? She could only pray it would.

Luther eased off the trail to an area that looked large enough for both wagons. He set the brake and hopped down before Ella could comment on the spot he'd selected. Mason pulled alongside, leaving about ten feet between the wagons. They could set up their campfire in the middle, giving their little group a bit of privacy.

Rebekah stretched, wishing she could take a nap like Katie had earlier. With her thoughts on leaving and never seeing Mason again, sleep had been hard to come by lately. She hoped Mason could find Jake quickly so she'd be free to leave. No sense in postponing the inevitable.

She shook her head. It was best not to think on those things. Wasn't there a verse in the Bible that said to think on good things? Tonight, after dinner, she'd try to find it.

Good things. Denver. Jimmy and Katie seeing their dad again. At least she hoped that was good. Mason's smile—no, that didn't count. A home of her own. Children someday. A vision of Jimmy and Katie chasing butterflies in a field with her watching from the porch swing of her own little home and Mason sitting next to her flittered across Rebekah's mind. Ohhh! Thinking good thoughts was harder than she had imagined.

She didn't even notice Mason had climbed off the wagon until he reached up to help her down, pulling her from her mental battle. *Don't think so far ahead—maybe that's the key.* Dinner. Setting up camp. She reached out, holding on to Mason's broad shoulders as he lifted her down. She noticed his lips were pursed into a tight line.

"What's the matter?"

"Nothin'. Lots of things." He released her and reached up to adjust his hat. "I've gotta find Jake, but I need to get you all settled first."

"We can set up camp if you want to start searching," she offered.

A spark flickered in his eyes then quickly faded. He looked up at the sky and shook his head. "It'll be dark before too long. We need to get supper and get the kids bedded down."

"All right. I'll get the food started." She looked around. "I guess it's a good thing we gathered up some firewood this morning. I don't know what we'll do when we run out, what with all these folks around here needing wood, too." Mason's gaze drifted away from her face and focused somewhere behind her.

"Howdy, neighbors."

Rebekah turned to see a tall, thin man walking toward them. His worn overalls were covered in multicolored patches, and some of the patches had patches. She looked down to his bare feet, filthy dirty from who-knew-how-many days of walking.

"My name's Homer Banning. You reckon you and your missus could spare some water?"

"I—" Rebekah slammed her mouth shut when Mason squeezed her shoulder. She wanted to set this man straight right off. He needed to know she wasn't Mason's wife, but with Mason's arm hanging lightly around her shoulders, she couldn't think straight.

"I see that you folks just rode in, so's I figured you must have some fresh water," Mr. Banning said.

"Sure—" Mason's grip tightened on her shoulder, cutting off her words again. He pulled her close to his side, sabotaging her brain. "I'd like to be hospitable, but we don't have any water to spare. Sorry."

"I'm willing to pay—a nickel a cup." Mr. Banning reached in his pocket and pulled out a handful of coins. "Some folks is charging up ta fifteen cents a cup, but I cain't pay that much. Ten's more reasonable."

Horrified, Rebekah gaped at the sea of humanity. People were actually buying water? She'd never heard of such a thing. Surely they could spare a bit of water. Mr. Banning didn't look like he had a nickel to spare. She turned to face

Mason and leaned in close. "Surely we can spare a little water," she whispered.

Mason glared at her with that look he'd used when she'd first tried to leave his camp. "No."

"But—"

"I said no, Bekah." Mason looked past her and scowled. "See why." He gently turned her around. A group of six or seven people headed toward them. Rebekah took a step back until she could feel her back touching Mason's chest. Surely all these folks didn't need water.

"I'm real sorry, Mr. Banning, but we've got two kids to care for and four horses. We need all the water we've got." Mason's voice tickled her ear. She loved his smooth Southern accent. When he said "I'm," it sounded more like "ah'm."

"Now see here, you've got two barrels. All I want is a canteen full." Homer Banning moved forward just as Jimmy popped his head out of the front of the wagon.

"Got my boots on. Can I get down?" he asked.

"Back inside, now!" Mason snarled. Rebekah glanced up in time to see Jimmy's shocked expression, but the boy didn't argue. He simply disappeared inside. She heard Katie's little voice talking to Jimmy. He shushed her quiet, obviously hoping to hear what was going on outside.

Mason moved around, then stepped in front of her, rifle in hand. "I don't want any trouble," he said. "I'm just looking out for my own." She peeked around him so she could see Mr. Banning. "There's a whole river full of water half a mile away."

Mr. Banning looked at the rifle and scowled. She wondered if the thought of going the half-mile to the river was so much of an effort for him that he'd risk getting shot. He glared at Mason again then turned and stomped off. The small crowd of people gathered around Mr. Banning. "He's not sharin'," she heard him mutter.

In unison, the group of people glanced at Mason. He straightened, raising his chin in the air as if daring them to approach him. After a moment, they turned away, looking tired and discouraged, and dispersed in different directions. Rebekah blew out the breath she'd been holding.

"I want Webekah," Katie cried through the canvas wagon top.

Mason pivoted around, nearly smacking Rebekah in the head with the rifle because she was so near. "I want you and the kids to stay real close to the wagon and the Robinsons until we know which way the wind's blowin' around here. Could be they were just testin' us to see how soft we are." He glanced over his shoulder, and seeming to feel the danger was past, he leaned over her and set the rifle on the wagon seat.

Rebekah closed her eyes, savoring his closeness as his chest brushed against her forehead. She suddenly saw Mason's wisdom in removing his sling. Would those people have forced the issue if he had faced them one-armed? She didn't even seem to mind that he was bossing her around again.

"Thanks for backing me up, Luther." Mason looked past her, and Rebekah peeked over her shoulder to see Luther walking around the front of the horses, back toward his wagon. She hadn't realized he'd been there to support them. Warmth flooded her. It felt good to have friends watching out for her. That was something she'd never had before.

"Bekah." Mason grasped her chin and turned her face toward him. "I'm serious. Stay close tomorrow while I'm gone."

She tilted her head back and glanced up at him. By the tone of his voice, she could almost convince herself that he cared for her. "You're not going looking for Jake tonight?"

He removed his hat, ran his hands through his hair, then blew out a breath that warmed her cheek. "No. I don't think I can risk leaving you and the kids after what just happened." He rolled the edges of his hat then slapped it back on.

Rebekah's spine tingled with excitement as she stared up at his stubbly chin. He wanted to protect her *and* the children. Maybe he really did care—at least a little.

"I don't want to lose the water. Did you see that water in the river? It was almost yellow."

The water. Her excitement plummeted and mixed with the dust at her feet. She should have known he was concerned for the water, not her.

"Tomorrow I'll start looking for Jake. That is, as long as we don't have any more trouble." Mason walked to the back of the wagon. "C'mon out, kiddos."

Tomorrow. Tomorrow she'd find out how much train fare to Denver was.

Chapter 14

Rebekah yawned and stretched, not quite ready for dawn. Half the night she'd tossed and turned, trying to erase the pain of Mason being more concerned about the water than about her. She didn't know why she expected more when no man had *ever* cared for her. Her real father died. Her stepfather was willing to trade her to his old drinking buddy for a few bottles of moonshine and half a side of beef.

Was there something wrong with her? Rebekah shook her head. No, she wouldn't believe that. Her mother had told her that God loves everyone and that each person is special in their own way. There must be some way that she was special.

Sitting up, she rubbed the sleep from her eyes then peeked at Katie. The toddler lay on her side with her thumb halfway in her mouth. Tears blurred Rebekah's eyes at the thought of never seeing her sweet smile again. At least Ella had softened her stance on what was respectable and allowed her to sleep in the wagon with Katie.

It would be good for the children to have a real home again. Maybe Jake would get a piece of land in the Run and settle down with the kids. Then she could write to them—if Jake would allow it.

Ignoring the chill in the air, she quickly dressed in the early morning light. Crawling out the back of the wagon, she looked for Mason. She'd heard him walking around outside the wagon until she finally drifted off to sleep. Must have been protecting his precious water.

Rebekah wanted to slap herself for her bad attitude. Come the heat of the day, she'd be thankful for that water. She couldn't help feeling sorry for all the other people who were running low, but Mason was right: If they started handing out water, it would be gone in no time.

Mason must have been up half the night, because he was still curled up beside Jimmy next to the cold campfire. He rarely slept past dawn. Against her will, Rebekah studied him. She seldom had the luxury of staring at his hair, since it was usually hidden under his big Western hat. Now the ebony locks fell across his forehead, giving him a youthful look. Dark stubble shadowed his firm jaw. Deep breaths of sleep blew across lips that were wonderful to kiss.

She blinked back her tears, knowing she'd never kiss them again. Rebekah turned abruptly. She had to find something to occupy her thoughts, or she'd stumble into the quagmire of self-pity and be stuck for good.

"You ever gonna tell him how you feel?"

Rebekah jumped. She looked up, surprised to see Ella sitting on the tailgate of her buckboard. "I. . .uh, what do you mean?" She rubbed her eyes, hoping Ella would think she was clearing the sleep from them rather than tears.

"You're crazy in love with Mason. It's written all over your face." Ella pulled her foot up onto her knee and began lacing her shoes.

Rebekah's hands flew up to touch her cheeks. Did she love Mason? Was that what she was feeling? And was it obvious to everyone else? She glanced around to see if any of their close neighbors were listening. Thankfully, nobody nearby was stirring yet.

"Now don't go fretting on me. I doubt he knows. Men are slow on the uptake 'bout things of the heart."

She moved over closer to Ella. If the older woman kept talking so loudly, everyone in the camp, including Mason, would know how she felt. She was thankful Luther was nowhere in sight. He wasn't the type to keep information to himself.

"You gotta plain tell a man. Don't 'spect him to figure it out on his own."

"It doesn't matter anyway." Rebekah peeked at Ella then glanced back down at her laced fingers. "Mason doesn't love me; he still loves his dead wife."

Ella slipped off the wagon and came to stand in front of her. The older woman took Rebekah's hands in hers. "I don't know as I believe that. I've seen how he looks at you. That man's just full of hurt and anger at God. Till he gets that out of his system, he don't have room to love someone else."

Rebekah absorbed Ella's words. There was wisdom in what she said. The only problem was that by the time Mason got over his hurt, he'd be out West and she'd be in Denver. At least she could pray for Mason to find peace with God. Knowing he did would make her happy.

"Thank you, Ella." Rebekah pulled Ella into her arms. She appreciated having a woman to talk to and share things with. "Will you write to me in Denver?"

Ella pushed away. "Denver. Hmpff!" She turned back to her wagon and began pulling out cooking supplies. "Best get that notion out of that pretty little head of yours," she mumbled.

Rebekah smiled. It felt good to know someone would miss her after she was gone. She turned back to her own wagon—Mason's wagon—and began hunting for something to cook for breakfast.

❧

Mason wandered from tent to tent looking for Jake. He'd started in the area where he'd seen the man the day before and was now working his way back toward the Conestoga. The sound of hammers echoed behind him. Today he'd witnessed the birth of a town as people began erecting buildings that would make this more than just a tent city. Bekah's delicious pancakes warmed his belly while thoughts of her warmed his heart. Just as quickly those thoughts grew cold.

Things had been so much easier before she came. No, that wasn't true. Not easier—less complicated. Bekah's help had been invaluable. Now he wondered how he'd managed to cook and care for the kids and handle everything else without her help.

But he'd been focused then. Give the kids back to Jake and head west. Simple. He yanked off his hat and rubbed his forehead with his palm. Why did women always have to mess up a perfectly good plan? He didn't like his mind being all frazzled, useless like an old frayed rope. A man needed a plan. He needed to think clearly—and women had a way of fogging up a man's mind.

"Well, well, if it ain't that no-good brother-in-law of mine."

Mason slapped his hat back on as he spun around at the sound of the familiar voice. Jake stood there, dressed in nearly new black pants and a fancy pale blue shirt with frills on the front. He looked like a dandy—a gambler. Mason narrowed his eyes. He could handle his brother-in-law's restlessness and inability to settle down, but to find out he was a low-down gambler sparked Mason's short fuse. He clenched his teeth together to keep from saying something he'd regret.

"Whoa, now." Jake raised his hands in defense. "That's not a very friendly welcome for a relative."

Mason fought the urge to plow his fist through that big, toothy grin of Jake's. "We're no longer relatives—or did you not get my telegram?" The man finally had the decency to look chagrined, and his smile faded.

"Yeah, I got it."

"And you couldn't see your way clear to come home and visit your wife's grave?"

Jake pulled off his bowler hat and fiddled with the short brim. "I didn't get the message until about a month afterwards. By then it was too late to do anything about it."

Mason ground his teeth together. "And what about your kids? Did you think even once about them and what they were going through losing their mother after they'd already lost their father?"

"They didn't lose their father," Jake ground out defensively. "I've been working—trying to make some money for 'em."

Mason noticed people staring as they walked by, giving a wide berth around them. He turned his gaze back on Jake and lowered his voice. "And just what do you think would have happened to Jimmy and Katie if I hadn't been around to care for them?"

Jake shrugged. "I knew you would, so I didn't worry."

"Do you have any idea how hard it is to run two farms and care for two young children? They aren't my responsibility—they're yours." As soon as he said the words, a sharp pain gutted him. It sounded almost like he didn't care for his niece and nephew.

"So did you sell my farm?"

Mason balled up his fist in his effort not to slug Jake. Was money all he cared about? "Yep, I sold it. Mine, too. How else could I get the money to bring the kids out here?"

"Jimmy and Katie are here?" Jake looked around. "Where?"

"Back at camp," Mason grumbled.

"Well, let's go see 'em. They'll be happy to see their ol' man." Jake set his hat back on his slicked-down hair; then he grinned.

"What are you grinnin' about?"

"Just trying to imagine you changing Katie's diapers."

Mason straightened. "Katie doesn't wear diapers anymore—hasn't for a long time."

Confusion flickered in Jake's eyes. "Guess they've grown some, huh?"

"Kids grow a lot in two years." Mason started for camp. The last thing he wanted to do was take Jake to see the kids, but this was the whole reason he'd made the trip, wasn't it? Jake walked along beside him with a slight limp Mason didn't remember. His brother-in-law was thinner and looked older than his thirty years.

Moving around a group of children playing ring-around-the-rosy, Mason watched Jake from the corner of his eye as they walked toward camp. "So you been gamblin'?" Jake wore a poker face if Mason ever saw one.

"Uhh. . .yeah. I've made a nice little nest egg. I'm planning on racing in the Run and getting me some land. I've already scoped out a nice little quarter section." Jake smiled his first natural smile. "You should see it, Mase. Prettiest section of rolling green hills with a creek flowing through it."

Mason stopped and turned to face Jake. "You're one of those Sooners—those folks who've snuck in and tried to stake a claim before the Run?" He couldn't believe it—on second thought, it sounded just like Jake.

"Pretty smart, huh?" Jake straightened his lapels then tucked in his fancy shirt.

"Pretty dumb. The army's shootin' Sooners."

"Well, they are now, but they weren't last month." Jake tipped his hat at two teenage girls who giggled and snickered as they walked by. "Nice." He whistled through his teeth.

Mason wanted to be sick. Jake was making eyes at schoolgirls. What had Danielle ever seen in him? Jake had never been any good, as far as he was concerned. Suddenly Mason stopped dead in his tracks. How could he honestly turn Jimmy and Katie over to a no-good like Jake Conners?

"What is it?" Jake stopped, too, and looked at the people passing around them.

The cadence of voices buzzed in Mason's ears. The reality of his plan slapped him full in the face for the first time. There was no way he could give the children to Jake. The man would never take care of them or protect them.

"C'mon, Mase. I wanna see my kids."

Mason's first thought was to turn around and lose Jake in the throng of the crowd. It wouldn't take much effort. Then he could pack up Rebekah and the kids and head out. But to where? He had enough money to buy a little farm somewhere, but his plan had been to head west, and he didn't have enough money to get four people halfway across the country and still have enough to start over.

Who was he kidding anyway? The children didn't belong to him. Rebekah didn't belong to him. In fact, almost half the money he had hidden in the bottom of his wagon belonged to Jake and the kids.

"What is wrong with you?"

Mason stared at Jake. How could he explain his feelings to this man when he didn't understand them himself?

"Uncle Mason!" Jimmy's call broke into his thoughts. He hadn't realized they were at camp already. "Where ya been all day?"

"I. . .uh. . ."

"Jimmy, boy, have you ever grown!" Jake looked at his son like any proud papa would.

"Do I know you?" Jimmy's gaze focused on Jake's face; then his boyish features registered alarm, and he glanced at Mason. Suddenly he took a step back, almost knocking down Katie. "Pa?"

Jake slapped his thigh and cackled. "That's right, son. I'm your pa."

Worry crinkled Jimmy's forehead. Katie's features resembled her brother's. She stepped around him and surveyed Jake, looking him up and down. Katie crossed her pudgy arms across her chest and tapped her toe.

"Nuh-uh, you ain't our pa. Unca Mathon is."

Chapter 15

Jake whirled around, and his usual congenial countenance sparked into something almost vicious. "You told Katie you were her pa?"

Mason stood speechless. He'd never so much as insinuated such a thing. He shook his head, noticing a blur of skirt and blond hair as Katie rushed over and grabbed him around the leg.

"He's not my pa. You're my pa!" Katie screamed into his thigh.

Jake reached out and tugged on her arm. "Katie, I'm your pa. Don't you recognize me?"

She turned her head away and tightened her grip on Mason's leg. "Nooo! You's not my pa."

Mason reached down and patted her head, pressing it against his leg. "Shhh, sugar, it'll be okay."

Jake tugged on Katie's arm again. The little girl let out a bloodcurdling scream.

Holding up her skirt, Rebekah raced around the side of the wagon, her blue eyes wide with concern. "Katie—"

She halted so fast, her long braid flopped over her shoulder and slapped her across the chest. She looked from Katie to Mason to Jake. "Is everything okay? What's going on?"

"Webekahhh!" Katie cried as she suddenly released Mason and ran to Rebekah. Bekah stooped down, opening her arms, and Katie hurried into her embrace. "Tell him Unca Mathon is my pa."

"Oh, sweetie, it's okay." Rebekah stood and hugged Katie, her questioning gaze locked with Mason's.

After a moment of drawing strength from Rebekah's stare, Mason broke his gaze free. He realized they were drawing a crowd. Jake paced back and forth, looking like a polecat that had eaten some rank meat. Jimmy watched his dad with wide eyes. Luther, armed with his old shotgun, stood next to Ella.

"Show's over, folks. You'd best just tend to your own business," Mason said to the crowd. He placed his hands on his hips and glared until people slowly began to disperse and the buzz of speculation faded.

"You're the last person I'd expect to shoot me in the back like this, Mase." Jake stood in a stance similar to Mason's, glaring through his pale blue eyes. The words gutted Mason worse than the point of a brand-new bowie knife.

"Let's take this to the privacy of our camp." With a wave of his hand, Mason motioned the direction to Jake. Jimmy raced off ahead of them, while Rebekah carried Katie. His neice wrapped her arms around Bekah's neck and her legs around Bekah's waist.

In silence, they walked together to the campsite. Blocked by the wagons on two sides and grazing horses on the third, they had a fair amount of privacy. They gathered in a rough circle, and Mason opened his mouth to speak. In that instant, he heard the *click* of a rifle being cocked.

Jimmy stood on the wagon seat, looking like a fierce soldier, the rifle pointed straight at Jake. "You ain't takin' my sister," he glowered.

Mason heard Rebekah's gasp as he moved toward Jimmy. "Now just hold on there, pardner. No call to get all fired up." Jimmy eyed him with a mixture of defiance and uncertainty. "Give me the rifle and hop down. We'll get this all worked out, okay?"

Rubbing the back of his neck, Mason watched the different expressions cross Jimmy's face as the boy decided what to do. Mason felt certain Jimmy wouldn't shoot his own father. The boy could barely shoot a duck for dinner.

For the first time, Mason considered how his leaving might affect the children. In his mind, he'd been planning this ever since Danielle's death; but to the kids, finding their father had been an adventure until the reality of their separation with him set in. He'd never once thought how hard that might be on them. His leaving would be another loss they'd have to suffer.

"Jimmy," Rebekah's firm but gentle voice called softly beside Mason. The boy looked from his father to her. "Please, Jimmy, give Mason the rifle. I know you don't want to hurt your father." Defiance flickered in his nephew's dark gaze. "What if you missed and hit me—or Katie?" Instantly Jimmy wilted and lowered the rifle. Mason blew out a deep breath he just realized he'd been holding, then snagged the weapon out of Jimmy's hands, tossing it into the back of the wagon. He pulled Jimmy off the wagon seat and wrapped his arms around the boy.

Like two parents ready to do battle for their children, Mason and Rebekah stood side by side, each holding a child. Jake whirled to face Bekah, fury blazing across his lean features. "Just who are you to be telling my boy what to do?"

"Don't yell at Webekah," Katie cried.

Mason cast a glance at Ella, beseeching her with his eyes for help. The older woman immediately picked up his signal. "Luther and me had a hankering to take a walk about town and see them new buildings they're tossing up. Jimmy, you and Katie come on along with us and give the grown-ups here a chance to yammer some."

"You won't leave?" Jimmy asked Mason. His eyes reminded Mason of a skittish mustang.

"No, pard, I'm not going anywhere." He gave his nephew a hug then set him on the ground. For the first time in months, Mason had a feeling he might not be heading west after all.

Katie took a little longer to be convinced to leave Bekah's arms, but finally the Robinsons and the children walked out of camp.

"Why don't we all sit down and have some coffee?" Rebekah gave a little half smile then turned without waiting for a response.

Mason could sense her apprehension. He shook his head. Never once had he considered the children wouldn't want to go with their father. Mason and Jake sat down on a couple of large rocks and waited for Bekah's return.

"You wanna tell me what's goin' on and who this woman is, Mase?" Jake's tone had softened somewhat. Evidently, having his own son point a rifle at him had shaken him up, too.

"Her name is Rebekah," Mason said. Bekah disappeared in the wagon, looking for tin cups, he guessed.

"Yeah, but who is she? You and her ain't married, are you?"

"No." Mason shook his head, knowing a part of him deep inside wished he could answer yes.

Jake's eyes flashed and his nostrils flared. "She's not a—you know, a loose woman, is she?"

Mason jumped to his feet, ready to pommel Jake's face into mashed potatoes. How could he think that about her? *God, I could use some help here.* Unclenching his fist, Mason realized he'd just uttered his first proper prayer in half a year. He heard the clinking of metal behind him then felt Bekah's soft touch in the small of his back.

"Let it go," she whispered. "It's not important." She stepped around him, trailing her arm along his waistline, sending tingling sparks shooting up his spine. The fingers of her other hand were looped through the handles of three blue tin mugs, making her fist look like some kind of strange club. She held her right hand out to Jake and smiled. "I'm Rebekah Bailey, and your brother-in-law saved my life."

Jake's mouth fell open, and he halfheartedly shook Bekah's hand. Mason's chest swelled. She'd been more concerned with his pride than her own.

For the next half hour, they sat talking and drinking their coffee. Rebekah shared how they'd met. Mason told Jake how much help she'd been caring for him and the kids, especially after he'd been injured. Bekah blushed and all but hid behind her coffee cup. He told Jake of his quest to locate him so he could return the kids and then go west. Bekah's gaze darkened and she took on a faraway look.

All too soon, the children returned with the Robinsons. Jimmy and Katie squeezed in between Mason and Bekah. Neither seemed excited at all to see their father; in fact, they were just the opposite.

"I can't believe how much you two have grown," Jake said. "Jimmy, you'd just turned five last time I was home, and you, Katie, were still a baby."

"I'm not a baby," Katie said, a little louder than necessary. "I'm fwee."

"Well, three's still little." Jake gave her a wry smile.

"Nuh-uh. I'm a big girwl."

Mason knew he should scold Katie for talking to Jake so, but he didn't have the heart.

"Katie," Bekah said, "it isn't nice to talk to your father like that."

Great! Bekah's braver than me. But then he already knew that. Hadn't she boldly faced him every time he'd tried to get her to do something she didn't want to? She wasn't one to back down—though she did have a problem with running away at times.

Mason tore his gaze away from Bekah and realized Katie was crying.

"C'mon, sweetie," Bekah said. "I think you're ready for your nap."

Bekah picked up Katie and took her inside the wagon. The Robinsons were nowhere to be found. Jimmy had finally warmed a bit and was talking with Jake. Watching them, Mason knew his life was fixing to change in a big way, but he didn't know if he was ready to handle that change. He suddenly realized that it had been days since he'd thought of Annie—maybe even a week. It was one thing to lose a woman to death, but totally another thing to lose one because she wanted something more than she wanted him. Mason looked heavenward. *God, I think I may need Your help with this.*

❧

Now that Katie had fallen asleep and the men were still talking, Rebekah finally had a chance to slip away and check on the price of her train ticket. She'd counted her money last night and hoped her measly amount would be enough.

Please, God, make it be.

She slipped out of the back of the wagon and headed for the depot. Soon she spotted the brand-new pine building that housed the ticket booth and waiting area. As she approached the building, the smell of freshly cut pine mixed with the pungent aroma of coal. The new platform was already darkened from coal dust and the shoes of travelers hoping for a new start. A few hundred feet from the depot, the train tracks ended.

Rebekah hopped up the three steps to the platform just as the train chugged and spewed backward out of the depot. She raised her hand to her mouth to keep from inhaling the black smoke and coal dust. Her insides quivered. What would it be like to journey in the belly of such a beast and to travel so fast? Shaking off her apprehension, she looked around the depot. Some of the people who'd recently arrived still wandered about with the same dazed expression she knew must have been on her face the first time she saw the enormous tent city and the myriad of people, all vying for the same land.

The arrival times posted next to the ticket cage indicated three trains per day arriving every day except Sunday. With the Land Run only fours days away, the population in the area could easily double if each of the trains was full. Where would all these people live and find water?

Rebekah stepped up to the counter and waited until the clerk turned around and noticed her. He wore what she figured was the typical train clerk garb—black pants and white shirt, with a flat black cap and string tie.

"Howdy, ma'am. What can I do for you?" He laced his slender fingers and gave her a businesslike smile, reminding her of a fox she once nursed after it had gotten caught in one of Curtis's traps.

"Can I get a ticket to Denver?"

"You betcha." He rubbed his pale hand over his jaw. "Course, you'll have to switch trains a couple of times. Be best to go to Wichita first and overnight there."

"Okay, then, I'll take a ticket to Wichita." Rebekah fingered the coins in her pocket, praying they'd be enough. She'd worry about what she'd do next when she got to Wichita.

"You'll pert near have the whole train to yourself, I reckon. Folks these days are wantin' to come *into* the Territories, not leave." He cackled like he'd told the funniest joke in the world. When she didn't laugh, he sniffed then looked down into a book filled with prices.

He quoted the price. *Two dollars and twenty-five cents!* That was almost twice the money she had. Rebekah thanked the man and headed back to camp. How could she earn the money she needed in such a short time? The last thing she wanted was to be stranded here or live with the Robinsons, as Ella had suggested. With the kids back with Jake soon, she knew she couldn't travel with Mason any longer.

Rebekah fought against the tears blurring her vision. She wouldn't cry—not here where so many people could see. Holding her head up, she ignored the stares and whistles of the men she passed.

Please, God. Show me a way to make the money I need. You helped me get away from Curtis and sent Mason to help me and protect me. Now I'm asking You to show me a way to make some money.

Walking back to camp, she decided to make a stop at the ever-busy outhouse. The bright afternoon sun had nipped the chill out of the spring day, making her crave a drink of Mason's water. As she waited her turn in the long line of women, she studied the men in the nearby line to their outhouse. They ranged from young boys to old, bent seniors; some dressed in fancy city clothes while others sported faded overalls.

After about ten minutes of waiting, her ears honed in on a particular voice. "Lookie here," said a middle-aged man dressed in a flannel shirt and black pants.

"I only got one button left on this here shirt. There ain't no general store here so's I can buy some new ones, and even if I did, I don't know nuthin'bout how to fasten them on." He heaved a sigh.

"Just look at all those women." The tall, thin man standing next to him waved his hand in the air, pointing at the line of ladies. "Can't you get one of them to hook them buttons onto your shirt?"

The other man looked up and down the line then shrugged. "You know I don't know any of them womenfolk. Their menfolk might not take kindly to me askin' one of 'em to take up clothes fixin' fer me."

"You could pay her."

A lady with a young girl exited the privy. Rebekah stepped forward with the other women, her mind buzzing with ideas, and formulated a plan. Suddenly she swirled around to the woman standing behind her. "Would you hold my place in line for a moment, please?" The woman nodded, eyeing her skeptically.

Rebekah took a deep breath, hoping to steady her wobbly knees, and started forward. "Uh. . .excuse me, sir, I don't mean to be eavesdropping, but I just happened to hear your conversation." The two men glanced at one another, then broke into grins like children at Christmas. Rebekah wondered if it was because a female had had the nerve to approach them. "I can sew buttons on your shirt. Uh. . .I mean for ten cents each—and I'll supply the buttons. Course, they might not all match."

The men exchanged glances again; then the buttonless man looked down and counted the buttonholes on his shirt. "That'd be forty cents. Why, I can pert near buy a whole shirt for that."

"Not in this town, you can't." Rebekah held her ground, knowing she'd just come upon an idea that could easily earn her the money she needed.

"Twenty-five cents," he countered.

Rebekah straightened. Thrusting her chin in the air, she turned her back to the man and started to walk away. "Oh, all right, how about thirty cents for this shirt, and I'll pay you to fix my other shirt, too?"

She knew she must be grinning like a possum as she spun back around. Maybe watching Curtis barter so many times had taught her a thing or two. "Done!"

"My name's Ben Hopper, and this here's my sister's boy, Carl." Ben undid the single button on his shirt and started to shed it right there.

Rebekah glanced around, noticing for the first time all the people watching them and how the buzz of voices near them had quieted. Most of the faces were filled with curiosity and a few with disapproval. "Uh. . .wait, Ben." She raised her hand to halt his undressing. "I'm gonna have to go back to my wagon and fetch my box of buttons and sewing supplies. Why don't we meet under that big tree in about half an hour?" She pointed across the field to one of the few trees offering shade to the weary bunch of travelers.

"All righty. I'll do it, and I thank ya kindly." Ben stuck out a not-too-clean-looking hand. Hesitantly, Rebekah reached forward with her fingertips and gave it a little shake. She had just started her own little business. She raised her head, proud of her accomplishment. "Oh, by the way, my name is Rebekah. And please tell your friends I'd be happy to sew buttons or do repairs on their shirts, too."

The men tipped their worn hats and mumbled, "Pleased to meet'cha," in unison. Rebekah smiled then returned to her place in line, thanking God for answering her prayer so quickly.

From behind her she heard someone mumble, "Ain't proper-like for a young woman to be mending clothes for total strangers."

Rebekah cringed at the rude comment but refused to turn around to look at her accuser. That person had no idea how desperate she was. If she didn't find a way to earn some money, she could soon find herself living alone without home or friends. Maybe it wasn't exactly proper, but if she stayed in plain view of everyone, surely she and her reputation would be safe.

She felt certain God had arranged this opportunity for her. If only she could be sure Mason would feel the same way. If he opposed the idea, he would try to stop her. Maybe she wouldn't tell him. He wasn't her boss. After all, he cared more for a barrel of water than he did for her.

Rebekah began calculating how many buttons she'd have to sew on in order to have enough money to buy her ticket. If she were lucky, she might make enough to get her all the way to Denver without having to stay and find work in Wichita. It felt good to focus on her goal. She wouldn't think about how much leaving Mason and the kids would hurt. But she was happy to have met them and to have had a glimpse at what it felt like to be part of a loving family. Mason didn't think of himself as father material, but she had a feeling he was a much better father to Jimmy and Katie than Jake would ever be. If only there were a way Mason could keep the children. . .and her. But then, he didn't even want her.

Back at their camp, Rebekah climbed into the rear of the wagon. She peeked at Katie, thankful the little girl was still asleep. She folded a pile of clothing and picked up the toys Katie had played with earlier, then located her carpetbag. Inside was a small tin can filled with her mother's button collection, several spools of thread, and a couple of needles. When she ran away from Curtis, she'd wondered why she'd felt such a strong inclination to take her mother's button box; now she knew it had been God's prompting. God's provision.

Holding the tin steady so it wouldn't rattle, she climbed out of the wagon. Mason, Jake, and Jimmy still sat around the campfire, talking and reminiscing. As she approached they stood, though Jake rose a bit more slowly than Mason and Jimmy, almost as if it were an afterthought. Mason greeted her with a reserved smile.

"I don't mean to disturb you all," she said, glancing from Mason to Jake and

Jimmy, "but if you're going to be here talking for a while, I thought I'd go help some folks for a bit."

"What folks?" Mason said as he approached her.

Rebekah shrugged. "Just some people I met—who need some help."

"I don't think it's a good idea for you to go running around here unescorted." Mason waved his hand in the air. "There's a whole passel of unsavory people here."

"Aw, let her alone, Mase." Jake strode over and stood next to Mason. "'Sides, you don't own her. She's got a right to go wherever she wants."

Mason scowled at Jake then skewered Rebekah with his glare. She lifted her chin and met his gaze evenly, though her heart raced faster than a mustang on the run. Jake was right; Mason wasn't in charge of her. Still, she didn't want to displease him. He'd been good to her, but she had no choice. She had to make the money she needed, even if Mason didn't like her traipsing about on her own.

"There's nothing to worry about," she said. "I've been walking about for more than an hour, and nobody has bothered me. In fact, most folks are friendly."

Mason crossed his arms, stared down at her for a moment, then turned back toward the camp. "Guess you'll be on your own soon enough," he mumbled.

"I've been on my own for a while now," she said as she turned and walked away from camp.

Chapter 16

No, Jake. I'm not riding in the Land Run, and that's final!" Mason wasn't about to be sucked into one of Jake's schemes.

"Now listen to me, Mase." Jake glanced around and moved in closer to him. "I've seen the land," he whispered. "I've been there already."

Mason narrowed his eyes, struggling to grasp Jake's meaning.

"I've found the most beautiful quarter section of land. Rolling green hills. A creek that cuts across the top third of the land. A section of trees just begging for a house to throw shade on."

Mason had seen that faraway look in Jake's eyes before. It was the same look he got every time he birthed another one of his harebrained ideas that took him from his family. He shook his head, unsure of what land Jake was referring to.

Jake's eye sparked with excitement. "It's perfect, I tell ya, and it's gonna be mine."

"What's going to be yours?"

"Aren't you listening? I told you I've been in the Unassigned Lands."

Mason blinked, remembering what Jake had said the day they'd found him. "I still find it hard to believe you're one of those Sooners."

"Boomer. Sooner. Lots of folks got different names for it, but, yeah, I'm one of them."

"That's just plumb crazy, Jake. The soldiers are arresting and even shooting Sooners." Mason thrust his hands on his hips. "You're just beggin' for trouble, aren't you?"

Jake curled his lip but didn't respond. He squatted by the campfire and poured himself a cup of coffee. The fresh scent tickled Mason's nose. He stooped beside his brother-in-law, helping himself after Jake set the coffeepot back on the fire. He swirled the black liquid around, listening to the sounds of people all around. Children squealed; a baby cried. Dogs barked; horses whinnied. Life went on all around him. A smile crept to his lips when he saw Jimmy lasso one of his friends across the way. Every so often, he'd hear Katie or Bekah's soft chatter in the wagon.

What if he went west and something happened to Jake? What would become of the children then? How could he just get on his horse and ride away? Maybe if Jake married again—but where would he find someone willing to marry a homeless vagabond with two children?

Rebekah's laugh drew his gaze toward the wagon. Hoisting her skirt, she climbed backward out over the tailgate. Katie's chubby arms emerged from behind the yellowing canvas, and Bekah lifted her out of the wagon. "My, but you're getting big," she said. Katie giggled, giving Rebekah a tight hug around the neck before being set on the ground.

Rebekah turned her head, smiling when her gaze caught Mason's. Somewhere in his belly, he felt a zing of emotion. "Katie and I are going for a little walk." She smiled and gave a wave. She and Katie had been going on lots of little walks in the past few days. Bekah's arms held several articles of clothing he didn't recognize. He wasn't sure, but he had a feeling Bekah was working on her own scheme of some sort. She and Jake would make quite a pair. *Whoa!* Where had that thought come from—and more importantly, how did he feel about it?

Her long braid swung like the pendulum of a mantel clock, ticktocking back and forth. Katie skipped along beside her. Anyone who didn't know them would surely think they were mother and daughter. Mason peeked over at Jake. Bekah needed a home. Jake needed a wife. The kids loved her. It seemed like a perfect solution. He could ride west and no longer have to worry about the children— Bekah would take care of them. But who would take care of her? He sure couldn't count on Jake for that. *Bekah deserves better than Jake,* he thought, pushing away the feelings of unrest and jealousy that surfaced at the thought of Bekah and Jake together. Still. . .it would solve his problem.

"Why you scowlin'? I don't think you heard a word I said." Jake tossed his coffee grounds into the fire. The flame flared and sizzled, filling the air with the pungent scent of burnt coffee.

"I heard you."

"So what do ya think? Will you ride with me and try to get the land next to mine?" Jake pinned him with a hopeful stare.

Okay, so maybe he hadn't been listening all that closely. He didn't want the land next to Jake's. His heart couldn't handle seeing Rebekah with Jake. That would be worse than watching her get on the train and head for Denver. When had he started to care about her so much?

"Mason. Pay attention. This is important." He looked up to see Jake staring at him. "If we both ride, we'll have a double chance of getting the land I want. If something happens to me, you can claim it."

For once, what Jake said made sense, but Mason shook his head. "It's too late. The Run's tomorrow and I haven't registered."

Jake broke out in a smile that would rival a kid's at Christmas. "Not a problem." He strode over to where his saddle lay next to the wagon. For several moments, Jake rustled around in his pack. Then he turned, raising his arm in victory. In his hand, he held two wooden stakes with colored fabric flags nailed to them.

"Are those what I think they are?"

"Yep." Jake beamed with excitement. "I've got two stakes for the race. Now all we've gotta do is get to the land first, hammer in our stakes, file the claim, and the land's ours."

Mason set his coffee cup on a rock near the fire and stood. "How'd you manage to register twice? Isn't that illegal?"

Jake shook his head. "Nope. Not since I signed your name in the registration book for one of them."

"Jake!" Mason hissed. "You got no right signing my name to anything. If Jimmy wasn't so near, I'd be tempted to knock you clear back to Missouri."

"It's no big deal, Mase. All I did was sign your name. Now you can ride with me."

Mason rubbed the back of his neck. "Even if I wanted to ride with you, I don't have a fast horse."

Jake beamed. "Then I guess it's a good thing I've got two."

Mason glanced over to where Jake's two mounts grazed with his four horses. He studied them for a moment. Both looked solid. Long-legged, trim—probably fast. Maybe Jake was finally ready to settle down. If Jake had thought this thing through so well, it might be a sign he had matured—finally.

He sighed, feeling cornered. He could ride for Jimmy and Katie. Getting the land would ensure they would have a home. But they still needed a mother.

"All right. I'll ride." Mason straightened and looked Jake square in the eye. "Under one condition."

Jake's eyes glowed. He smiled the smile that Mason felt sure was the one that had won his sister's heart. "Sure, Mase. Anything. This is the opportunity I've been dreaming about all my life."

Mason closed his eyes, gathering the strength he needed to utter the words that made him sick to his stomach. "I want you to ask Rebekah to marry you and be Jimmy and Katie's mother."

❧

Rebekah stumbled and nearly fell down. She'd forgotten her button box and had come back to fetch it. From the far side of the wagon, she couldn't see the men, but she heard them. "I want you to ask Rebekah to marry you. . . ."

If she'd had any doubts about leaving Mason and going to Denver, they suddenly evaporated. She felt as if he had plunged a knife into her heart. He had no way of knowing she'd fallen in love with him. Now he never would.

Holding on to the side of the wagon, she leaned her head against her arm. How could she have been so wrong? She felt certain Mason had feelings for her.

"I can't marry Rebekah," she heard Jake say on a choked gasp.

"Then I can't ride with you."

"Now be reasonable, Mase. I don't love her—I don't even know her."

Bekah eased back behind the wagon. She wanted to run away, but her feet wouldn't budge. With blurred vision, she looked up, checking to be sure Katie was still playing with the neighbor's puppy.

"But she loves the children—and she needs a home. She'll take good care of them and you, too. She's sweet, pretty—sure, she has a temper and can make you madder than a cornered bear, but she's fun to be with. You'll really like her if you just take the time to get to know her. It just makes sense for you two to get together."

Rebekah blinked back her tears as she listened to the words glide on Mason's smooth Southern accent. If he thought all those things about her, why couldn't *he* love her? Maybe she'd pushed him too far—bucked his authority one too many times. If only she could go back and change things. But she hadn't known him back then. She'd been wrong about him. Mason had a heart bigger than the whole West.

"I just don't know, Mase. It seems. . .well, odd, marrying up with someone you don't know."

"Danielle barely knew you when she married you." Rebekah could hear the unspoken censure in Mason's words. "If she'd known you, she never would have married you. I wouldn't have let her."

"Let me think on it a bit, okay?"

"All right, Jake. You've got till noon tomorrow—that's when the race starts, right?"

She didn't hear Jake's response. Fighting back her tears, she tiptoed away from the wagon, her heart in more pieces than a new quilt ready to be assembled. She spied Jimmy playing with Katie and the puppy and numbly moved in their direction. Jimmy gave her an odd look when she asked him to watch Katie for a while. Could he see that she was upset?

She hurried through the field of humanity, desperately looking for some-place she could be alone. People were everywhere. With the big race being held tomorrow, an epidemic of hope and excitement ran rampant throughout the huge tent city. By evening tomorrow, how many of them would feel like she did now—disillusioned, disappointed, their hopes destroyed? All the time she'd been sewing on buttons and repairing clothes to make money, she had hoped deep inside that Mason would ask her not to go. That he would take her west with him—or even better, that they would stay here and make a home near Jimmy and Katie's.

"Hey, lady," a heavyset man in baggy overalls hollered to her. She turned her head, quickly wiping the gathering tears from her eyes. "Yer that Button Bekah lady that fixes shirts, ain't ya?"

She forced a smile and nodded, though thinking about clothing was the last thing on her mind.

"I gots me two shirts that need fixin', and my other pair of overalls gots a hole right in the—" He reached toward his seat then halted his hand and blushed. "Well, they's got a big hole. . .um, well, you'll see."

She couldn't help but smile at his discomfort.

"I'm figuring on gettin' me some land come tomorrow. I don't reckon I'll be back in town fer a while, so I need to get my duds fixed up 'fore I go. You reckon you could have 'em done before tomorrow? I'll give ya a silver dollar."

A whole dollar. Though she hadn't prayed yet, God was already providing for her again. *Thank You, Lord.* If she had any doubts as to what to do, they just went up in smoke.

She followed the man back to his camp, got his clothing, and arranged to meet him tomorrow, then headed for the train station. Tallying up her funds in her mind, she figured she had close to twelve dollars—thirteen with what she'd make today. That was more money than she'd ever seen in her whole life.

It suddenly dawned on her what the man had called her—Button Bekah. The label brought a soft smile to her face.

In a matter of minutes, Rebekah had purchased her ticket to Wichita. She felt certain she'd have enough money to get to Denver now—maybe even enough to stay in a hotel in Wichita and get her first bath in one of those fancy porcelain bathtubs.

Now all she had to do was figure out how to say good-bye. It would break her heart to leave Jimmy and Katie. For the past few weeks, she'd almost felt like a mother. She'd grown to love them both, but they weren't her children—they didn't belong to her—and wishing wouldn't make it any different.

Then there was Mason. How could she have been so wrong? She'd felt certain Mason was beginning to care for her.

But she must have been mistaken.

Growing up in the wilds of Arkansas had not prepared her for dealing with men. She knew she couldn't tell him good-bye without collapsing, so her only other option was to leave while he was riding in the Run. That's what she'd do. Get Ella to watch over the children and she'd be free to leave and chase her dream.

So why was her heart breaking?

Chapter 17

Mason sat astride the prancing gelding, studying the starting line of the race. As far as he could see in both directions, thousands of people were lined up to the sides and rear, ready to grab a section of free land. Resembling a long, slithering rattlesnake, the line of people, animals, and all manner of vehicles glided back and forth as if it were alive.

Like he and Jake, many folks were mounted on sleek horses bred for speed, while others sat in covered wagons or buckboards filled with all their worldly possessions. A few men dared to venture the untamed land on the back of a contraption they called a bicycle. Mason shook his head, wondering how a man could stay on one of those strange two-wheel ditties.

Give me a horse any day.

The noise was deafening. People yelling, horses neighing, children crying. He wondered how they would ever hear the army bugle indicating the start of the race.

He glanced at his brother-in-law. Jake was more animated than two roosters in a cockfight. He bubbled with excitement over the prospect of winning the land of his dreams. Mason had to admit his excitement was contagious.

He hadn't wanted to ride in the Run, but now he was glad that he'd be a part of history. Win or lose, he would have something to tell his grandkids.

That thought suddenly threw a bucket of cold water on his enthusiasm. Would he ever have grandkids?

Someday. Maybe. But first a man needed a wife.

His thoughts turned to Bekah. Jake had agreed to propose to her if he won his land. All night long, Mason had wrestled with the desire to claim Bekah for his own. If Jake didn't win the land, he'd have no place to call home. Bekah and the kids couldn't live in a tent or hotel room forever. He scouted the land before him. He *had* to get a claim so he could ensure they had a home.

Jake leaned toward him, his eyes twinkling. "Yep, that Rebekah's a fine-looking woman, Mase. She'll be cozy to cuddle up to on a cold winter's night. I'm right glad ya didn't want her for yourself."

Mason's indignation grew. Did Jake have to rub his nose in the fact that he was marrying Bekah? Had Jake actually asked her? And had she said yes?

He closed his eyes and pulled back on the reins to steady his prancing mount. If only he could steady his heart. How could he let Jake marry Bekah?

It was time he faced the facts—he was in love with her. He loved Rebekah.

What a fool I've been to push Bekah into Jake's arms. I can't let him marry her. I won't.

Hope soared like the eagle floating lazily in the sky high above him. If he won a plot of land, he could build a home for the two of them—and Jimmy and Katie, if Jake decided not to stay. He could farm the land. It was good land with rolling greens hills, apple trees promising a good fall harvest, plenty of decent-sized creeks that could support a family—though not this sudden influx of thousands of people. The Indians had well-named Oklahoma the *beautiful land*.

In his mind he heard a bugle, then rifle fire and a huge roar. Yanked from his introspection, Mason realized the race had begun. His horse jerked the bit with his teeth and took off like he'd been shot from a cannon. Mason almost lost his seat because his mind had been on Bekah.

"He-yah!" Mason lashed his horse with the reins. Jake was already topping the hill and disappearing over the other side. The roar of the multitude and thunder of hooves echoing across the land matched the throb of his heart in his ears. He would ride for Rebekah. He would win the land; then he'd return and ask her to marry *him*—not Jake.

❧

Rebekah bit back the tears as she watched the huge crowd of home-seekers disappear into a cloud of dust. Mason was out there somewhere, probably at the front of the pack, racing away from her—seeking land he didn't even want.

It had taken a monumental effort to keep a smile on her face all morning when her heart was breaking. Who ever would have thought following her dream would be so painful? Mason had looked at her strangely a couple of times, and she was afraid if he asked what was wrong that she'd burst into tears and tell him how she felt. But it would be too mortifying to tell him of her love only to have him reject her.

She cringed at the looks Jake had given her this morning, like he was already envisioning them married. They reminded her of the same looks Giles Wilbur had given her. How could Mason think she would agree to marry a man she didn't love? Not even for Jimmy and Katie could she do such a thing.

"Are you sure you want to do this?" Ella asked.

Rebekah looked at her friend and nodded. "I have to do this. Mason wants me to marry Jake, but I can't. As much as I love Jimmy and Katie, I won't marry someone I don't love."

"You should marry Mason. Can't imagine what's goin' through that boy's mind for him to tell Jake to marry you. Anyone can tell he's in love with you hisself."

Rebekah shook her head. "You're wrong, Ella. He doesn't love me."

Her things were packed, her train ticket was burning a hole in her pocket, and all that was left was to say good-bye. She knelt in front of the children, studying their cute faces, memorizing every inch.

"But I don't want you to go, Webekah," Katie said, burying her face in Rebekah's shoulder.

"I know, sweetie, but I have to."

"Why can't you stay and be my mommy?" Katie grabbed her around the neck so hard that Rebekah nearly lost her balance.

"It's complicated. I'm not in love with your father, so I can't marry him."

"You could marry Uncle Mason," Jimmy said, his cheeks turning a bright red. "You love him, don't you?"

Rebekah gasped. Were her feelings obvious to everyone? She glanced at Ella. The older woman crossed her arms over her chest. An I-told-you-so grin tilted her thick lips.

"Even if I did, Jimmy, he doesn't love me. You need to have two people who love each other to have a good marriage." She smiled at him and cupped his cheek. "I do love you and Katie, though. I'll never forget you. When I get settled in Denver, I'll write to the post office here—surely by then they will have one—and you can write back to me. Okay?"

Jimmy didn't look too appeased. Katie still clung to her neck for dear life, her tears dampening Rebekah's dress and her tight grasp making it hard to breathe. Rebekah gave Ella a beseeching gaze. The older woman sighed and moved forward, looking disappointed.

"C'mon, kids. Rebekah has a train to catch."

An hour later, Rebekah waved at Ella and the children as the near-empty train lurched out of the station. She grasped the wooden arm of the seat with one hand while pressing the other hand against her churning stomach.

Her heart finally beat normally again after its frantic pace at nearly missing the train. The unimaginable swarm of people getting off when it first arrived had pressed them back away from the station. There had even been people riding on top of the train, clinging perilously to the ventilators. Rebekah, Ella, and the children had been forced to stand under the shade of an old oak tree while the throng of people hurried by, anxiety and hope written on each face—hope that they could still get free land, anxiety that they were too late. She felt thankful that she didn't have to be the one to tell them they were.

Now Rebekah raced toward her own dream: Denver. She felt grateful for her time in the big tent city. Being around so many people allowed her to prepare for the congestion of city life. She felt the same anxiety and hope of those just arriving. Hope for a new beginning—a new home where no one could force her to marry against her will. She felt anxiety over leaving the children...and Mason. And she felt concern about what the future held.

She watched the landscape speed by. Trees, bushes, and hills blurred into splotches of green and brown as her eyelids sagged. Worry and thoughts of never seeing Mason again had stolen any hopes of sleep last night. She leaned her head against the seat and closed her eyes. The swaying motion and *clackety-clack* of the rails soothed her like a lullaby as she drifted to sleep with thoughts of what could have been on her mind.

"Miss...uh, miss?" She felt a hand shaking her shoulder as she awoke. "Miss, we're coming into Wichita."

"Oh." Rebekah sat up. "Oh, thank you, sir." The thin man smiled and moved on down the aisle. Rebekah picked up her old carpetbag and hugged it to her chest, blinking her eyes to moisten them.

The ticket agent ambled to the front of the coach, rocking back and forth with the sway of the train. "Rock Island Depot, Wichita," he called out, as if she weren't the only person in the whole coach.

Wichita. Why did the name of the town send chills down her back?

Wichita! Curtis's hometown. She straightened in her seat, fighting back a panic that threatened to overpower her. Why hadn't she remembered that?

She turned her gaze toward the city, the first big city she'd ever seen. Rebekah felt her mouth drop as she surveyed the tall buildings and huge houses—some even three stories high. Surely in a town so big, one could go unnoticed. Even if by chance Curtis's family still lived here, they wouldn't know her. She'd never met any of them. And Curtis had no reason to think she'd come here. She drew in a slow, steadying breath. Things would be okay.

Minutes later, the train screeched and groaned as it pulled to a stop at the Rock Island Depot. She covered her face, hoping to block the unpleasant odor of the coal plume streaming from the engine. Her clothes were hopelessly covered with a gritty layer of soot.

Gathering her courage, she stood and followed the ticket agent to the door and down the three steep steps to the wooden platform. For the first time in her life, she was in Kansas. Even the massive tent city she'd just left hadn't prepared her for the enormous town of Wichita. She took a breath and looked around, spotting the ticket booth after a few moments.

Making her way through the waiting crowd, she finally reached her goal. She waited in line, listening to the conversations around her. Over and over, she heard the Land Run mentioned. She sincerely hoped all these people weren't wasting their money on a ticket there.

She'd heard Wichita was a big cow town, and as she looked around, she saw evidence of the Western influence. Cowboys dressed in denim and boots stood next to men in fancy three-piece suits. Occasionally she caught a whiff of the stockyards when the wind gusted.

Half an hour later, Rebekah sat on the bed in her room in the Occidental Hotel, probably the biggest structure she'd seen so far. The whole three-story building was built of brick, and huge, white pillars supported the ten arches along the front. She'd never imagined staying in a place so fancy. The little house in the backwoods of Arkansas paled in comparison to this fine place.

The brocade bedspread, the color of ripe wild raspberries, matched the ceiling-to-floor draperies. An ivory-colored desk with an opulent chair sat between the room's two windows. A small divan and two end tables rested along the wall across from the bed. Never in her life had she seen anything so luxurious.

As amazing as the room was, Rebekah had a hard time enjoying it. Though her body wasn't in Oklahoma anymore, her heart certainly was. Yawning, she eased onto the fancy bed and closed her eyes. Thinking back over the last few weeks, she breathed a prayer of thanks. "Thank You, God, for keeping me safe on the trail and for sending Mason to watch out for me. Thank You for showing me how to make the money I needed. Please show me how to deal with the pain of losing Mason and the children. Keep them safe, Lord."

Like lemonade without enough sugar, the words left a sour taste on her tongue. "What's wrong with me?" She pulled a fluffy pillow out from under the bedspread and tucked it under her head. Tears blurred her vision. Instead of facing Mason and telling him how she felt about him, she'd taken the coward's way out and run away—again.

Mason would be furious with her. But why? Why would it matter if she were gone? He probably didn't care. He'd be happy to be rid of her. Immediately she felt guilty and shook those thoughts from her head. Mason might not love her like she did him, but she knew he cared what happened to her. It was his way. He might be gruff and bossy at times, but in his heart, he was a caring person.

So what now?

The words she'd heard out on the trail reverberated in her mind.

"Go back."

"No, I can't. Don't ask that of me." She wrapped the pillow around her head as if to keep the words at bay.

Why had she ran from Mason this time when she'd stood up to him so many other times? She knew the answer. She couldn't stand to find out he didn't love her. But wasn't it better to know for sure than to wonder the rest of her life? "What do I do, Lord?"

"Go back."

Rebekah sat up and wiped her tears. Resolve was winning the battle over doubt.

"I can do all things through Christ which strengtheneth me." The words from the Bible seeped into her mind, filling her with warmth like a cup of hot coffee. The only way she'd have peace and be able to set up a new home was to know the truth. She had to face Mason, tell him how she felt, and see if he felt the same.

She reached in her pocket, fingering the ticket to Denver. In her mind, she calculated how much money she had left. If she was very careful, she could go back to Oklahoma and still have enough money to make it to Denver. She'd arrive penniless, but she could worry about that when she got there.

That's what she'd do. She'd go back and face Mason—one more time.

❧

Mason rode slowly back into town. Both he and his horse were exhausted after riding all day in search of a plot of land that hadn't already been claimed by those sneaky Sooners. Time and again, he thought he'd found unclaimed land, only to end up with a rifle in his face, urging him to look somewhere else.

He'd tried to keep up with Jake, but after spotting him riding over that first hill, Mason had lost him in the swarm of racers. The directions Jake had given him to the land he wanted weren't as clear in reality as they had been when Jake first drew them in the dirt by their campsite. Mason sincerely hoped Jake had secured his land.

He rubbed the back of his neck as he guided his horse back to camp. Already the town looked much different. The population had shrunk enormously, and now there seemed to be mostly women and children left behind while their men raced for their future. Pieces of broken wagons littered the initial race area. It looked as if some people's dreams had died before they'd gotten out of town.

For a time, he'd allowed himself to get caught up in the excitement of Jake's scheme. If he'd won a claim, he could have asked Rebekah to marry him, and they could have settled there. But what now?

Mason didn't like feeling as if he'd failed. He didn't know how to deal with failure. All his adult life, except for when his wife had died, he'd pretty much been able to control things around him—other than the weather.

The smell of fresh-cooked beans and salt pork tickled his stomach as he rode into camp. He couldn't wait to hug the children—and Rebekah. The thought of her waiting for him wrapped around him like a warm blanket on a chilly night. When had he fallen in love with her? When he'd found her helpless on the trail? When she'd stood in his face, refusing to allow him to tell her what to do? He didn't know when; he just knew it had happened.

His gaze searched the campsite as he dismounted. He wondered where everyone was. His mount's head sagged with exhaustion as Mason removed the saddle and rubbed him down. The horse was a fine animal. Maybe he'd see if Jake would swap him for a couple of his draft horses. A decent saddle horse would suit him better on his trip west than one of the big, slow-moving horses. But was he still going west? No, not unless Rebekah would go with him—he knew that much.

"Uncle Mason!"

He spun around to see Jimmy running toward him, closely followed by Katie. Both children looked upset—red eyed, as if they'd been crying. Mason squatted so he could look them in the face. "What's wrong, pardner?"

"Rebekah's gone. She left on the train."

Chapter 18

Rebekah was gone?

The words crashed into Mason as if the locomotive had physically run him down.

A tearful Katie crawled up into his lap. Standing, he tucked her to his chest as Jimmy wrapped his arms around Mason's waist. He hadn't seen the children this upset since their mother died.

"When?" he whispered, his voice cracking.

"This morning," Jimmy said, wiping his damp face against Mason's stomach.

"Why did she leave?" It hurt him more than he could say to know she'd run away again.

"She—she didn't want to marry Pa." Jimmy looked up at him. "She said two people had to love each other for a good marriage to work—and she doesn't love Pa."

She knew about his crazy suggestion for her to marry Jake? How?

He gritted his teeth. He knew why she'd run away. Rebekah surely felt he was pushing her into an unwanted marriage to Jake just like Curtis had tried to force her to marry that Wilbur guy. A sharp pain gutted his midsection. How could he have done that to her?

"She wuvs us," Katie said as she raised her head off his shoulder, rubbing a fist in one of her damp eyes. Her little face was splotched with red—obviously she'd been crying a lot today. "She wuvs you but not Pa."

Mason blinked. Rebekah loved him? How could Katie know that?

"What makes you think that?"

"Ella said so," Jimmy offered. "She told Rebekah she should stay here and marry you 'cuz she loves you."

A tiny smile tilted Mason's lips in spite of his concern. "What did she say then?" he couldn't help asking.

"Webekah said you don't wuv her. Is that true, Unca Mathon?" Katie looked at him with her big, watery blue eyes. She wiped her nose on her sleeve and stared at him with childish innocence, waiting for his answer.

"Well, do you?" Jimmy asked.

"That's what I'd like to know, too." Mason glanced up to see Ella standing there with her arms crossed over her ample bosom.

"Well, uh...yes, I do love her." He straightened, feeling more confident now that he'd voiced the words out loud.

"Good. That's what I thought. So what you gonna do about it? Just gonna let her run off, or are you going after her?" Ella pinned him with that matronly glare of hers, making him feel like a naughty schoolboy.

"I'm going after her." He glared back then kissed Katie's cheek.

"Weally?" Katie asked, wide-eyed. "You gonna bring Webekah back?"

"Yeah, I am." Determinedly, he set Katie down. "Where'd she go, Ella?"

"Wichita. You're gonna need to eat first." She hurried toward her campfire. "Won't do to have you passin' out from hunger."

An hour later, with his belly filled with beans and corn bread, Mason headed for the train station as he breathed a prayer. "Lord, I need Your help to find Rebekah. Wichita is a big town."

Mason stopped dead in his tracks. He'd actually uttered another prayer—and it felt good. He moved off the road and sat down on a pile of lumber.

He yanked off his hat and rubbed his head. Before he could face Rebekah, Mason had bigger fish to fry.

"Dear God, You know I've been angry with You for a while. Sorry 'bout that. I nearly died when You took Annie and Danielle from me. Okay, sorry, I know You didn't take them. I'm sorry for blamin' You. Please forgive me. Lord, help me to make things right with Rebekah. Don't let me lose her, too. And thanks for being patient with me."

He blew out a cleansing breath and smiled. It felt good to be right with the Lord again. He'd stayed away too long. Mason stood and started jogging toward the train depot.

"Mase!" Jake called. Mason pulled to a halt and turned to see Jake running toward him. "I did it, Mase. Got that purty little quarter section I told you about. What happened with you? Did you get any land?"

Mason shook his head. "No luck, I'm afraid. Everywhere I went some Sooner was already setting up camp."

"I'm real sorry about that. But I did it!" Jake grabbed Mason around the neck and gave him a brotherly hug. He couldn't help but smile. If Jake felt this happy, maybe he'd settle down and be a decent father. "Never had such luck—"

A shot rang out. Mason jumped as Jake slumped against him, his eyes registering complete shock. "Got me, Mase." His words slurred together as his body slid down the length of Mason's. He tried to hold him up, but the dead weight pulled him down with Jake.

Mason jerked around to see where the shot had come from, hoping he wasn't next to get a bullet in the back. A skinny old man with a smoking pistol was being overpowered and wrestled to the ground by a group of men. "That varmint stole my land," he yelled.

"Hang on, Jake." Mason hugged his brother-in-law to his chest, feeling the liquid warmth of blood on the hand that cradled Jake's back. "Someone get a doctor!"

"Too late," Jake wheezed. He pushed slightly till he was away from Mason's chest. Slowly, he reached inside his vest and withdrew a rolled-up piece of paper.

"Yours." Jake fought to lift his arm but lacked the strength. It dropped to his chest. "Take it," Jake whispered. Mason held Jake with one arm and took the paper. "Take care of my kids, Mase. You always were—a better father—than me."

Jake labored to take one more breath; then his eyes and head lulled back as he released the sigh of death.

"No!" Mason roared. "This wasn't how things were supposed to be."

"C'mon, Mason." His mind slowly registered Luther's deep voice speaking to him. A warm hand squeezed his shoulder. "Jake's gone." Mason glanced up to see Luther's concerned face peering down at him. "Nothing you can do here. Ella says you got a train ta catch."

Mason laid Jake on the ground and stood, feeling the deep grief of a wasted life. Moments before his death, Jake seemed to have finally found the one thing that satisfied him—this land. *This stupid land!* Mason wanted to scream. *Was it worth dying for?*

Mason shook his head and unrolled the parchment—the deed to Jake's 160 acres of land. Something wasn't right. Mason closed his eyes tightly, then opened them and stared at the paper again. It was a deed all right, but the name on the deed was Mason Danfield, not Jake Conners.

He glanced at his brother-in-law's silent body. Why had Jake done this? Had he known he wouldn't be any happier tending this patch of land than he had the other places he'd once called home? Jake had seemed so happy. Was his happiness brought on by the fact he'd given the land he'd wanted so badly to Mason?

Mason knew those questions would remain unanswered. He knelt beside Jake's body, wondering what to do. There were things that Jake might have for his children. A watch, a bit of money, but Mason didn't have the heart to rummage through the man's vest. It had to be done, though. He reached out with his fingers twitching in hesitation.

Luther cupped his shoulder. "You go on now, son. I'll tend to Jake. You go get that little lady and bring her back to us. Me and Ella will watch your young'uns till you git back."

Mason nodded woodenly. He took a final look at his brother-in-law and numbly moved toward the train depot. He wanted to be mad at God, but Jake had made his own choices. Jake knew about God—Danielle had made certain of that. In the end, everyone must make up his own mind about God. Jake had made the wrong choice, and now he'd live all eternity with his decision.

Instead of being angry with God, Mason embraced Him even more. If nothing else, Jake's death had reinforced the truth about how short and precious life was.

The train whistle sounded, cutting into his thoughts. He broke into a run. He had to make that train. His whole future depended on it.

❧

Now that her mind was made up to return, Rebekah felt at peace. She'd enjoyed her luxurious bath, thankful for the warm, clear water. Last night's dinner had been scrumptious. Not stew or deer or half-burned biscuits but tender roasted beef and potatoes with dinner rolls. And this morning's breakfast had been a masterpiece. She licked her lips and sighed at the memory.

There was also much to be said about the glory of beds; she'd slept soundly for the first time in weeks. Walking back to the train depot, the town didn't seem quite as intimidating as it had yesterday.

She smiled, wondering what Mason's expression would be when he saw her again. Rebekah nibbled her lip. Would he be angry that she'd run off when his back was turned? She knew he didn't like how she kept running from her problems instead of facing them head-on. Mason had probably never run from a fight in his life. Well, this time she wasn't running. She'd come face-to-face with her problem and see what his response was.

"There she is! I told you I saw her."

Rebekah stopped dead in her tracks and turned her head at the familiar voice.

No, it couldn't be. Not when she was so close to realizing her dream.

"Well, lookee here, Giles. If it ain't my lovely runaway daughter." Curtis Bailey's words dripped with undisguised hatred. "You really put us through the ringer, girl. You're gonna be real sorry."

Rebekah was already sorry. Giles Wilbur and her stepfather stood in her path. Her heart felt like it had lodged itself in her throat. Her gaze darted in every direction, searching for an escape.

"Ain't nowhere to run." Curtis grabbed one arm while Giles latched on to the other. She realized the two men had picked the only spot between the hotel and the train depot where they could have overpowered her without a crowd noticing. She never should have tried to take a shortcut through the alley. They pulled her toward two scraggly horses tied up at the other end of the alley.

"No, I won't go. I can't." Rebekah jerked her arms, hoping to get free. *Please, God, help me. Don't let this happen.*

"Ain't no use fightin' it, pumpkin. Your pa and me had a deal. You're mine now."

Rampant fear like she'd never known before raced up Rebekah's spine. She struggled against their firm grip, her body wrenching and tugging till her arms hurt.

"You can't do this. It isn't right."

"What ain't right is your runnin' off when I had me a business deal with Giles." Curtis slid a look her direction that could curdle milk.

Rebekah's fine breakfast roiled in her stomach. Is that all she was to him? A piece of property to be traded at his whim? She wouldn't go willingly. She kicked him in the ankle. When Curtis's steps faltered, she booted Giles's ankle, too. Both men spat out foul words, but Curtis turned toward her with his hand raised. Ducking her head, Rebekah braced herself for the blow.

"I wouldn't do that if I were you."

Mason!

Still struggling against her captors, Rebekah peered over her shoulder. Mason's smooth Southern voice was like a balm, but it was the look on his handsome face and the pistol in his hand that gave her hope.

"Let her go," he hissed. The muscle in his jaw twitched, and she knew he was angry. She only hoped none of his anger was directed at her.

"Stay out of this, mister. You're not a part of this," Curtis yelled back.

"You're wrong there," Mason said.

Giles and Curtis spun Rebekah around so they could face Mason. With eyes narrowed and that gun in his hand, he looked like a gunfighter.

"How you figure, stranger? This here's my girl, and he's the man she's marrying." Curtis jerked his thumb toward Giles.

"Nope," Mason said, shaking his head. "You're wrong."

Curtis and Giles still maintained their death grips; her wrists throbbed.

"Wrong 'bout what?" Curtis crinkled his brows in a stern glare.

"Well, the way I hear it, you're not Rebekah's pa, and I know for a fact that he's not the man she's marrying." Mason pointed his pistol at Giles, and the man slunk back as if trying to get out of range.

"What makes you say that?" By now, Mason had obviously stirred up Curtis's curiosity. Rebekah was beginning to wonder what he meant herself. Glancing past him, she felt a small amount of relief when she noticed the crowd gathering at the end of the alley. Maybe someone would help them.

"I know she's not marrying that ol' coot because she's marrying me." Mason cast her a glance, almost daring her to disagree.

Hope burgeoned within her, but tinges of doubt soon followed. Was he just saying that to save her, or did he really want to marry her? He pulled his gaze from hers and refocused on her captors.

"Look, I don't want to shoot either one of you. But if you don't let Bekah go right now, I will."

Giles looked at Curtis. "Much as I want your gal to come live with me, I don't want to git killed over her. Look, you can keep that half side of beef I swapped for her, but I want my moonshine back."

Rebekah closed her eyes. Could she be humiliated any further?

"I ain't giving you back that moonshine. Look at all the money I spent helpin' you look for her."

Giles slowly released his grip. "I didn't force you to come. You wanted to. You said no girl was—"

"I know what I said," Curtis hollered back.

Giles gave Curtis a shove. "I want my moonshine back." Curtis stumbled, releasing Rebekah's wrist, and fell to the ground. Lumbering back to his feet, Curtis took a swing at Giles. Rebekah crept back against the alley wall toward Mason just as the sheriff and two deputies rounded the corner.

Instantly the sheriff pulled his gun. He eyed the two men wrestling in the street, then pointed his gun at Mason, who still had his pistol drawn.

"No," Rebekah screamed. She raced toward Mason and threw herself in front of him.

"Now just hold on, missy, and move away. I don't want you to get hurt," the sheriff said.

"You don't understand, sir. He was rescuing me." She pointed at Curtis and Giles, who still tussled in the dirty alley, kicking up dust and yelling a string of expletives. "Those men tried to kidnap me."

"That's right, sir. I was only trying to save her."

Rebekah heard Mason holster his gun then felt his warmth as he wrapped his arm around her waist and pulled her back against his chest. The sheriff cast him a studious gaze as if trying to decide if he was holding her against her will. Rebekah didn't hesitate. She turned and wrapped her arms around his waist.

Thank You, Lord.

"Bekah," he whispered into her hair. "I thought I'd lost you."

"Me, too," she cried into his chest. "Me, too."

Mason held her tight. The noises behind her faded as she realized that being in Mason's arms was the fulfillment of all her dreams. She didn't need to go to Denver. Everything she needed and wanted was right here. If only he really wanted her.

"Shhh, it's okay. You're safe now." Mason kissed her head and tightened his grip on her.

"Uh, miss?" she heard the sheriff say. Rebekah turned her head, staying in Mason's arms, and peered at the tall man. "I'll need you to come to my office and make a statement."

"Yes, sir," Mason answered for her. "Just give her a few moments to calm down."

She heard the sheriff give Mason directions to his office and watched as he and his deputies marched Curtis and Giles away. The crowd seemed to follow, and in a few moments, she and Mason were alone in the alley.

Rebekah buried her face in his chest, afraid now that he'd scold her for running away and getting herself into this mess.

"Bekah?" Mason whispered against her hair. "Are you okay, sugar?"

She nodded against his shirt.

"Look at me."

Rebekah released her hold on Mason's waist and leaned back. He loosened his grip only enough so that she could look up into his face. His expression took her breath away.

"I meant what I said. I want you to be my wife."

A gasp caught in Rebekah's throat. Could she dare hope he was serious? "Why?" she squeaked.

"You know, don't you?" Mason smiled, and a butterfly war was loosed in her belly.

Rebekah shook her head. Mason glared teasingly at her.

"I think you do know." He lowered his face to hers, stopping to gaze deeply into her eyes. His eyelids lowered as his lips touched hers. She wrapped her arms around his neck, hoping this moment would never end. Mason truly wanted to marry her.

"Why do you want to marry me?" she murmured against his warm lips after a few moments.

"I love you, Bekah. Can't you tell?" He deepened his kiss, pulling her tighter against his chest.

He loved her. Rebekah couldn't seem to grasp it. He really loved her. But she still had unanswered questions.

She pulled back and waited for his eyes to open. His onyx gaze burned with love and promise, but she still had to know one thing. "What about Annie?"

Mason closed his eyes for a moment. "Annie's dead. She'll always be a part of me, but she's my past." He opened his eyes and captured her gaze. Leaning forward, he rested his forehead against hers. "You're my future."

Rebekah's heart leaped for joy. He *was* serious. Somehow he'd put his wife's death behind him.

"I've made my peace with God, in case you're wondering." A sweet smile graced his lips; then his eyes twinkled. "Any more questions?"

Rebekah bit the inside of her cheek. Mason raised his hand and ran his knuckles down her jawline. She nodded. "What about Jake? Why did you want me to marry him?"

Mason's gaze darkened. "I'm sorry you overheard that. Very sorry. Guess I just went loco for a while." He flashed her an embarrassed grin. Then his smile faded.

"What is it?" she asked, cupping his stubbly cheek.

Raw hurt glittered in those dark eyes, and he looked away. "Jake's dead."

Rebekah sucked in a stunned breath. "How?"

"Shot. Some ol'-timer thought he'd cheated him out of his claim."

"Did he?" Somehow she could see Jake doing something like that. Instantly she felt guilty for thinking bad of the dead.

"I don't know. It doesn't matter anyway. The old man will probably hang for shooting Jake in the back just for a little piece of land."

"Oh, Mason, I'm so sorry." Rebekah leaned against his chest and hugged him with all her might. "Those poor kids. What will happen to Jimmy and Katie?" Even before she uttered the words, she knew the answer. Mason would take care of them—just as he'd taken care of her.

"Looks like I'm gonna be a daddy after all." His soft chuckle resonated across his chest, tickling her cheek. "You reckon you're ready to be a momma?"

She leaned back, looking into his handsome face. She still needed to hear three little words again before she could answer that.

As if reading her hesitation, he said, "Ah, sugar, can't you tell I'm crazy in love with you?"

Rebekah couldn't hold back her grin. "It's about time," she said.

Smiling, Mason pulled her back into his arms and thoroughly kissed her again. "I'm still waiting for an answer," he said on a breathless whisper. "Will you marry me?"

"Yes! Oh, yes."

"Wahoo!" Mason yelled.

Standing on her tiptoes, Rebekah lassoed his neck with her arms, hugging him until her toes began to hurt. Finally, she dropped back down and looked around, realizing what a spectacle they were making.

She gazed up at the man she loved with all her heart and remembered her mama's words. *"Sooner or later, some handsome man is going to sweep you off your feet and make you his wife."*

Her mother's words rang true. Soon, very soon, she would be a wife and a mother.

Mason smiled down at her, obviously wondering what was going through her mind. She smiled back at him. Taking his cheeks in her hands, she rose up and placed a kiss on his soft, warm lips. "Let's go get our kids—just as soon as we finish with the sheriff. All right?"

"Yes, let's. But first, how about if we visit a minister?"

Rebekah smiled. Mason wasn't one to waste time once a decision was made.

"Don't you want to wait so Jimmy and Katie can be there?"

"No, I'm not taking a chance. It would be my luck to get you back to the tent city only to find out all the ministers have left town."

"Okay."

"Okay?" He eyed her with suspicion. "You never give in this easily."

"You've never made me such a generous offer before." With a coy smile, she batted her eyelashes at him.

Mason's laugh echoed through the alley. "All right, sugar, I'd better be happy winning this battle so easily. Don't expect I'll be so lucky in the future."

"Shall we, Mr. Danfield?" Rebekah held out her hand to him. With a smile that warmed her insides more than a campfire on a cold night, Mason took her hand and headed toward the street.

Rebekah looked up at the bright blue sky and smiled. She'd found a family to love and one that loved her. She knew in her heart that she'd never be on the run again. She was home.

THE BOUNTY
HUNTER AND
THE BRIDE

Dedication

This book is dedicated to my parents, Harold and Margie Robinson. Mom and Dad never failed to allow me to stretch my adventurous wings, even when that meant buying a horse, though we lived in the city, or buying a motorcycle when I was only fourteen. I think the freedom they allowed me as a child gave me the boldness I needed to begin writing and pursue publishing. Dad is now playing his trumpet in heaven and keeping the angels laughing, and Mom is encouraging me with her faithful prayers.

Chapter 1

Y ou oughta be right proud of yourself."

City Marshal Dusty McIntyre's chest swelled at Deputy Tom Barker's comment. Then he heaved a sigh of relief, knowing the crafty swindler he'd been after for months was finally behind bars. He eyed the solemn prisoner in the cell. "I have to admit, there were days I wondered if we'd ever catch this weasel. Feels good to have him locked up."

Ed Sloane's eyes narrowed as he glared through the bars. "Just 'cause you got me locked up today, Marshal, don't mean you will tomorrow." One cheek kicked upward in a cocky sneer.

Dusty wanted to smack that belligerent look off Sloane's face, but he wouldn't. As a law officer, he was bound by a different code than the man in his jail, and as a Christian, he was called by God to walk a straight path and control his temper. He recognized Ed Sloane for what he was—a lost man. A man on the road to hell if he didn't change his ways real fast.

Sloane stuck his hands between two bars. "Think you could take these cuffs off now that you got me safe in your jail?"

Dusty didn't miss the sarcasm that laced his prisoner's voice. The man still didn't seem to realize he'd been caught. Much as he'd like to leave Sloane hand-cuffed, he crossed the room, his boots echoing on the wood floor. He pulled a warm metal key from his shirt pocket, but then stopped and glanced at Tom. "If he tries anything, shoot him."

Tom pressed his lips together and nodded as he pulled his pistol from his holster and pointed it in Sloane's direction. "Be happy to."

Dusty approached the cell with caution. Ed Sloane was more slippery than a greased hog at the county fair. A chill slipped up Dusty's spine when an evil glint flashed in the man's light blue eyes. What could bring a man to be so depraved that he would prey on the elderly and widows, stealing them blind and leaving them penniless and heartbroken?

With a few rattles and clicks, the handcuffs were off, and Dusty moved back. Sloane gave a guttural laugh that sounded like a snarling, wounded animal. Shaking his head, Dusty crossed the room to his desk and tossed down the key. Tom picked it up, stuck it in the desk drawer, and then holstered his weapon.

"Don't you reckon you oughta head home to supper and tell that fine wife of yours all about your exceptional day?" Tom grinned, and his thick mustache twitched. "If she's fixin' that rhubarb pie of hers, you might save me a slice—if you've a mind to. Mmm-mm, it's mighty fine."

"I may do just that." Dusty smiled at his deputy. Tom had been his best friend since school days, and it seemed natural to hire him as his deputy when Dusty's father retired as city marshal of Sanders Creek, in the Oklahoma territory, and Dusty took over. Most of the time he worked days and Tom evenings, but lately they'd both been pulling almost twenty-four-hour shifts as their search for Sloane narrowed. They'd gone from house to house, ranch to ranch, searching for Sloane and his gang. His trail resembled that of a cyclone, leaving in its wake a path of desperation and destruction. Now that Dusty had captured Sloane, it shouldn't be too hard to get the rest of his gang.

Dusty's belly grumbled, and he yawned. All he wanted was to eat one of Emily's fine meals, then hit the hay and sleep a full day and night.

Except for Sloane and the havoc he and his gang had caused lately, this past year had been the best Dusty could remember. First, he'd given his heart to God. Then five months ago, he'd fallen in love and married the new banker's daughter.

He longed to run his fingers through Emily's thick, auburn hair. Soft as a horse's muzzle but as sweet smelling as the rose bushes in front of their porch. He imagined her pine green eyes twinkling with merriment as she played one of her little pranks on him. An only child, Dusty couldn't wait until they had a house full of children. Emily would be a wonderful mother, and he could only hope he'd be a decent father. God would help him in that area.

Ah yes, life was good.

A cowboy on a bay horse rode past at a quick trot, slinging dust on him and yanking him from his thoughts. Frantic shouts at the end of the street chased away his warm feelings, and a snake of apprehension slithered down his spine. Looking around, he noticed men running and women with skirts lifted high hurrying around the corner up ahead. He picked up his pace and jogged to the end of Main Street, then turned onto Haskell Avenue. Two blocks down, he saw the source of everyone's anxiety. His heart thudded to a stop just as his feet did.

One of his neighbors' houses was engulfed in flames, but the billowing smoke was so thick that he couldn't determine which one it was. He narrowed his eyes and studied the scene. Men ran everywhere, using anything from hats to mixing bowls to dip in the nearby horse troughs and get water to throw onto the fire.

Dusty charged forward, fearing for his friends. Was it old man Harper and his sickly wife's home? Or maybe the two-story clapboard building that housed a pair of widowed sisters who had recently been victims of Ed Sloane? They sure didn't need any more trouble.

Dusty's legs propelled him closer. As the roof collapsed on the only blue house in the area, he felt as if he'd been speared by an Indian's lance. Realization dawned like a heavy, dark curtain being lifted on a stage of performers. Only this was no theatrical show. This was his life. His home.

Dusty raced forward, screaming for his wife. "E—Emily! Emily!"

Heads turned his way, and shoulders drooped. Dusty didn't want to read the expressions in those faces covered with black soot. Strong arms pulled him back just as he reached his porch. His face stung from the heat of the flames, and he fought his captors but wasn't strong enough to outmaneuver four big men.

He turned away from the scene, feeling the heat bleed through his shirt onto his back. Across the street from the flaming remains of his house, a group of women stood, each one holding her hand or a handkerchief over her nose. Sympathetic eyes stared back.

No! This couldn't be happening. Everything he owned was in that house. Dusty backed out of his friends' hold and ran to Harmon Styles, a neighbor who lived around the corner. "Have you seen Emily? I need to make sure she's okay."

Harmon's concerned gaze darted toward the man standing next to him. Pastor Phillips reached out his hand to Dusty's shoulder. "I'm sorry, son. We tried hard to save her."

A fog enveloped Dusty's head, making it hard to see and comprehend. "What? Just tell me where she is." He looked right, then left. Nowhere did he see his beloved's face.

"E—Emily!" Choking on the swirling smoke, he dropped to his knees. Where was she? His tired mind struggled to remember if this was the day she'd gone to her sewing circle. No, that was Tuesday. This was Wednesday.

God, no. Please find my wife. Let her be safe. I need her.

Pastor Phillips stooped down beside him, offering a cup of water. Dusty shook his head. He didn't want water. He had to locate Emily. As he started to rise, he caught the minister's pained expression. "I'm so sorry, son, but she's gone. Thelma Sue—she saw Emily in the side windows hurrying toward the front door just before the roof collapsed. We tried to save her. We truly did. It just happened too fast."

Dusty ducked his head, unable to grasp the pastor's words. His legs trembled like never before, forcing him to press his hands against the ground to keep from collapsing. *God, don't do this to me. Emily is my life.*

The top of his head touched the ground as tears blurred his vision and grief pierced his heart. Friends gathered near, patting his shoulder and offering whispers of sympathy.

Dusty lifted his head, peering through several pairs of legs to see the burning mass that had been his home. The flaming remains of the roof rested at an odd angle, like a sinking ship. As he watched, the bricks of the chimney he'd repaired only a month ago crashed down, sending more smoke and fiery embers into the air.

Anger surged through his being as he realized all his dreams had just gone up in smoke. He growled and shoved upward like a wounded bear, sending his friends scattering from the force.

His eyes burned as his hopes and dreams were reduced to ashes. He had to get away from this crowd.

Pressing his hat down low on his forehead, he turned away from the scene. Why hadn't Emily answered his call? *No!* She couldn't be gone. His mind couldn't comprehend the emptiness of life without her. Just this morning, she'd kissed him good-bye and promised to have her delicious fried chicken waiting for him.

He pressed the heel of his hand against his forehead, trying to make sense of it all. *Oh, Emily.*

Somewhere behind him, he heard running footsteps and someone screaming. "No! Please. Emily Sue!"

He recognized his mother-in-law's frantic pleading but had no power to comfort her. The woman's screams tore at his battered heart. How could God let this happen? "Marshal! Where's the marshal?"

A voice from far away pulled him out of the darkness sucking him under. Hank Slaughter, owner of the mercantile across from the jail, plowed through the crowd of gawkers and hurried toward him. "There's been a jailbreak, Marshal. Tom's been shot."

Shoving down his hat, Dusty moved forward as if living a nightmare. His mind refused to believe Emily had perished. She was simply at a friend's house. He had no trouble slipping into work mode. It was just what he needed to drive the frightful thoughts from his mind.

His boots pounded out a cadence on the boardwalk as he jogged toward his office. *Emily is gone. Emily is gone.* Even the wood under his feet screamed the words.

No! He wouldn't believe it. He couldn't. Any minute now he would wake up and find out this was just a nightmare.

He hurried inside the jailhouse, blinking as his eyes adjusted to the dim lighting. The faint odor of gunpowder clung to the air, and the empty jail cell with the door swung open mocked him. Doc Michaels knelt on the floor beside Tom, examining his bloody shoulder wound. He looked up as Dusty skidded to a halt. "He'll live."

Relief coursed through him like a flash flood. Squatting, he stared into Tom's pain-filled eyes. "What happened?"

"Three men." Tom's eyes closed, his mouth contorted as he fought for control. "Got the best of me. Sloane escaped." He heaved a deep breath. "Headed north."

Dusty turned around to start recruiting a posse but then decided he needed to do this alone. Reaching down, he squeezed Tom's good shoulder. "Don't worry about it, pardner. I'll get him back. You just get better."

He started to turn, but Tom grabbed his pant leg. "Wait—"

The glazed look of despair in his friend's eyes nailed him in place.

"Your house. It's okay?"

Dusty crinkled his brow. Tom had no way of knowing what had happened. He stooped to get closer, pushing back an ominous premonition. "Why?"

"As Sloane left, he looked back—said he'd left a present at your house."

Dusty stood and backed up until he hit the wall. A muscle in his jaw twitched.

Sloane couldn't be responsible for the fire, could he? Had the fire simply been a diversion to allow Sloane's escape?

"Glad things are all right. . . ." Tom lost consciousness as Doc Michaels wrapped his shoulder.

"You men, carry the deputy over to my office," the doctor said.

As several men shuffled around him, Dusty mentally listed what supplies he needed. Two rifles and ammunition. Some food. His canteen and horse. He unlocked the rifle case, grabbed two Winchesters, and then locked it back up again. On his way out the door, he yanked his brown duster off a hook and studied the crowd. He couldn't stand seeing the sympathetic looks from the townsfolk. His gaze landed on Steve Foster, a local businessman who had once been a deputy. "You'll watch over things till I get back or Tom's on his feet again?"

Steve pressed his lips together and nodded.

Dusty strode back into his office, yanked open the middle drawer of his desk, and grabbed a deputy's badge. He flipped it to Steve as he tramped outside. As he moved off the boardwalk, the crowd in the street parted like the Red Sea. Dusty turned toward the livery, pulling his hat down low on his forehead so he wouldn't have to meet anyone's gaze.

Tears blurred his vision. Emily was gone. . .and Sloane was to blame. For now, he'd focus on capturing Sloane and seeing him hanged or imprisoned for life. Later he'd think of his beautiful wife and all that he'd lost.

❧

Dusty followed Sloane's trail until dark. He dismounted and tried to grab a few hours' sleep, but every time he closed his eyes, he saw flames and imagined Emily screaming for him. If only he hadn't dawdled at the jail, gloating over Sloane's capture. Maybe he could have stopped the fire before it had gotten out of control. Maybe he could have gotten Emily out of the house before it was too late.

By sunup, he'd eaten a dried-out biscuit and an apple and was on the trail again. Thankfully, last night about dusk, he'd happened upon the unusual, square-shaped hoofprints he recognized as belonging to Sloane's horse. After weeks of trailing Sloane before, Dusty would never forget that unique track.

As the sun reached its zenith, Dusty stared out over a valley that led into Kansas. He had no jurisdiction there. Truth be told, he hadn't had any legal authority to chase Sloane since he left Garfield County. His horse snorted, impatient to move on.

A red-tailed hawk glided across the sky, then dove toward the ground and soared upward again with a squirming rabbit in its grip. Dusty felt like that hare.

His life was over. His home gone. His wife dead. And his God had abandoned him.

Dusty glanced down, and a ray of sunlight flashed off his marshal's badge. Yanking off the metal star, he rubbed his thumb over its smooth surface. He'd dedicated his life to protecting the townsfolk of Sanders Creek in the Oklahoma Territory, but he'd failed to protect the person he loved most. Clenching his jaw, he flipped the badge in the air and watched the sun reflect off it as the silver star spiraled to the ground.

With his heels, he nudged his horse forward. If it was the last thing he did, he'd find Ed Sloane and see justice done.

Chapter 2

Fall 1904, a farm near Claremont, in the Oklahoma Territory

Katie Hoffman jumped at the fervent pounding on her bedroom door. "Yes?"

"Uhh. . .Miz Hoffman, the judge is here, and that feller you're fixin' to marry is gettin' fidgety."

Katie smiled at her shy ranch hand's muffled comment, knowing he must be embarrassed to his boot tips to be talking through her bedroom door. "Thank you, Carter. Tell them I'm almost ready and will be out in a moment." She could imagine Allan King, her fiancé, pacing the parlor, checking his pocket watch over and over, and driving everyone loco. He'd been after her to marry him for two months now, and he wasn't one to be patient.

She turned and studied her reflection in the tall mirror. "Katie King. Mrs. Allan King. Has a pretty nice ring to it, if I do say so myself." She fastened the final button of the blue-gray cotton dress, which draped over her protruding stomach and fell in soft waves to the ground. The ecru Irish-lace collar looked pretty against her tanned neckline. Her spirits soared to be wearing something colorful again instead of widow's black.

She touched her cheek. Did Allan mind that her skin wasn't fair, as was popular with the women in town? Jarrod had said he loved her coloring, but then, even her tanned skin had looked pale against her first husband's bronze complexion. Growing up a tomboy, she'd been outside so often that her skin was always a golden brown and her hair a light blond. After she married, she'd tried harder to stay inside or always wear a bonnet, but since Jarrod's death, the farm demanded so much more of her that she now spent much of her day outside. With the brisk winds that often swept across the Oklahoma plains, she found it easier to work without a hat, which frequently blew off anyway; thus her hair had again lightened and her skin darkened.

Katie pushed in another hairpin to secure her thick bun, then eased down onto the chair beside the window to put on her shoes. As her palm came to rest on her large belly, the child within heaved a mighty kick, making her hand bounce. Not for the first time, she wondered if Jarrod had given her a son or daughter.

Leaning her head against the tall back of the rocker, she studied the bedroom that she had shared with Jarrod. White eyelet curtains fluttered as a cool breeze tickled their hem. The Wedding Ring quilt she'd labored over most of one winter was pieced together from blue and white scraps of fabric and now covered the bed she would soon share with her new husband. It had been Jarrod's suggestion to paint the room a pale blue, and she had to admit she liked it. But would Allan? He seemed a tad particular about things.

Tears stung her eyes, but she batted them away. This wasn't the time for crying. Those days were past. She was getting married for the second time in less than a year and should consider herself fortunate to have found a man willing to wed a woman in her condition.

She thought back to the day she'd met Allan. He'd shown up on her doorstep with a cheery smile on his handsome face and holding a newspaper carrying the ad she'd placed for the sale of her farm. Selling would allow her to pay off the mortgage and give her funds to live on until the baby arrived and she could find some type of work to do.

Before purchasing the farm, Allan had insisted on examining every aspect of the property and equipment. As they'd spent hours together going through the barn, touring the land, and reviewing the books, Katie had grown accustomed to his presence. One afternoon, he'd taken her to nearby Claremont for dinner at the new hotel. She smiled at the memory of the fancy dining room and delicious food. Her mouth watered just thinking about the fresh trout, the abundant vegetables, and the creamy ice cream she'd eaten that night. Maybe he'd take her there again sometime.

Allan's charming personality and constant pampering were a balm to her lonely, grieving spirit. Soon, instead of talking about buying the farm, he was begging her to marry him. And she'd finally given in. It hadn't taken too long for her to see that marrying him was the only way to save her baby's inheritance. By marrying Allan, she could keep the farm and have him, too.

Katie sighed. She would have preferred to grieve over Jarrod longer, but Allan had swooped in and taken her by surprise. In this day and time, a woman did what she had to do to get by. It was very common for women, especially those with children, to remarry quickly, foregoing the customary mourning period. Surely God had sent Allan to her. Katie shook her head. Enough of this debating. She'd made her choice.

Standing, she crossed the room and stared out the window at her large farm. She and Jarrod had made such great plans for this place. What would he think about her marrying again so soon after the accident that had taken his life? Would he understand the farm was simply too much for her to handle without him, especially with a baby on the way?

Crossing the room to the oak chest of drawers, she picked up a photograph taken on her first wedding day. She'd been so hopeful and naive, with no premonition of the disaster soon to come. She studied Jarrod's sturdy face, then placed a kiss against the cool glass covering the picture. Who could have imagined things would turn out like they had? Jarrod died never even knowing he was going to be a father. "You'd have been a wonderful dad. I'll never forget the love and laughter we shared, sweetheart. Good-bye, my love. See you in heaven someday."

Katie opened the top drawer and slid the picture under her unmentionables. Her fingers lingered on the smooth gold of her wedding band. After a final moment of hesitation, she slid it off and placed it on Jarrod's picture.

She smoothed her hand across her stomach. She might not love Allan as she had Jarrod, but he would be good to her, her child would have a father, and she would no longer have to struggle with running the farm alone.

She slipped on a pair of cream-colored gloves to hide her rough hands and chipped fingernails, and inhaling a strengthening breath, she lifted her head and opened the bedroom door. It was time to get married.

Her footsteps echoed down the narrow, dimly lit hallway to the parlor. The smells of old wood and furniture polish battled with the fragrant scent of chicken baking in the oven. Being so much with child, she had decided to get married at home rather than at the church in town, and afterward, they all would enjoy a good meal before the judge departed.

As she glided into the parlor, all heads turned in her direction. Allan looked striking in his new three-piece gray suit, and she was sure that was a glint of victory she'd seen flash in his icy blue eyes. They reminded her of a cold winter's morning when the fog still clung to the earth. He had a right to look satisfied; he'd finally gotten her to consent to marry him.

The smile she gave him turned to a frown when she noticed Judge Simons sitting on the sofa, nursing a glass of whiskey. Allan moved his hand, and the lamplight reflected off the empty glass he also held. Disappointment coursed through her. She lifted an eyebrow at him. He knew she objected to having liquor in the house, so why was it here?

His expression remained cool, and he shrugged. "Surely you can't object to a man toasting his own wedding." He slapped the glass down with a clink on the fireplace mantle as if daring her to oppose him.

She certainly could object but didn't want to start an argument before she was even married. Turning away, her gaze fell on the Hoffman family Bible. In that instant, she realized she'd never asked Allan if he believed in God. Since he'd been so kind and helpful, she'd assumed he was a Christian. Surely, he must be. He'd gone to church with her nearly every Sunday since they'd met. She shook off a shiver of concern.

The rotund Judge Simons smacked his empty glass on the end table next to the settee. "Shall we begin?"

He looked over the top of his spectacles at her, and a flash of regret pierced her heart for not having a minister marry them. Using the arm of the settee for support, the judge heaved his large body upward and ambled toward the fireplace.

As she crossed the room to stand beside Allan, she smiled at Carter and Sam, her two ranch hands. They were the only guests in attendance. Another stab of guilt sliced at her for not letting Uncle Mason and Aunt Rebekah know she was getting married again. She wasn't up to all the hoopla and family members they would have brought with them. Uncle Mason would have drilled Allan on his family history and his spiritual well-being. Aunt Rebekah would never have let her have such a simple wedding. And she'd been too embarrassed to admit to her neighbors that she was marrying so soon after Jarrod's death—not that six months was all that soon. She couldn't help wondering what her friends would say when they found out she had married Allan King.

The judge cleared his throat, and Katie cast aside her reservations and feelings of guilt. She was doing what she had to do to keep her farm and to provide her child with a father.

"Dearly beloved." The judge's huge cheeks puffed up even bigger than normal as a belch escaped.

Katie closed her eyes, blinking back stinging tears. This wedding so paled in comparison with her first one. She didn't even have a flower bouquet or anyone to give her away.

She looked into Allan's eyes to draw support but was met with his smoldering gaze. His slicked-back black hair glistened like a raven's wing, and his full lips twitched, reminding her of the times he'd stolen kisses. She shivered, wondering if she could be the wife he'd surely want. She moistened her dry lips with the tip of her tongue, and his mouth pulled sideways in a one-sided grin.

Her heart pounded a frenzied beat. This was what she wanted, wasn't it? To be Mrs. Allan King?

Turning back to Judge Simons, she realized she hadn't heard a word he'd said.

"If there be anyone here who objects to this union, speak now or forever hold your peace." The judge lowered his spectacles, his bushy eyebrows pulled together into a single line, and he glared at Carter and Sam. The two ranch hands looked at each other, then shrugged. Katie knew Carter didn't approve of Allan, probably because he was still loyal to Jarrod; but Sam was a new employee, and Katie had no clue why he, too, seemed uncomfortable in Allan's presence. Still, she had faith Allan would soon win both men over as he had her.

When nobody responded, the judge continued. "Do you, Edward Allan King, take Katherine Ann Hoffman to be your wedded wife?"

"You bet. She kept me waiting long enough." Allan smiled down at her, his eyes filled with something that made her swallow hard. Her quivering legs barely held her up. He squeezed her hand and turned back toward the judge. Funny, he'd never told her Allan was his middle name.

The judge looked over his glasses at her. "Do you, Katherine Ann Hoffman, take Edward Al—"

The front door burst open and slammed against the wall, rattling the window-panes. Katie jumped and whirled around. Cool October air charged in, followed by a cowboy with a gleaming silver pistol in his hand. Dressed mostly in black except for a stained brown duster, he stood surveying the room, his eyes barely showing under the black hat pulled low onto his forehead. Allan grabbed her upper arms and pulled her in front of him as if she were a shield. His quickened breath warmed her nape even as chills of fear raced down her spine. *Who is this stranger? What does he want?*

Footsteps echoed on the front porch, and Marshal Dodge from Claremont strode in. "I told you to wait for me, McIntyre." His gaze flew past Katie and landed on Allan. "That him?"

The cowboy's lips thinned to a straight white line, and a muscle in his jaw twitched. He shoved his hat back on his forehead. Coal black eyes glared at Allan, and he nodded. "We meet again, Sloane."

Allan's fingertips dug into Katie's arms. Her heart pounded like a black-smith's hammer. *Who is Sloane? Why is the marshal here?*

She glanced at Carter and Sam, who'd backed up against the wall, eyes wide in confusion. Too bad they weren't wearing their holsters. If only she hadn't requested they not wear them during the wedding. But then if the marshal was there, surely they were safe from this stranger.

The judge slithered away, leaving only Allan and Katie in the gunman's path.

The marshal reached for his gun, and Allan muttered a curse that made Katie cringe. Suddenly, he shoved her forward. Her heart jolted; confusion cir-cled her mind. She took two quick steps, then stumbled on the hem of her long dress, falling forward. Fear clutched her being, and her only thoughts were to protect her child. Katie reached for the side of the settee but missed. Her shoul-der collided with the settee's wood trim as she fell under the round-topped end table. She reached out to break her fall, but a stinging sensation shot through her hand and wrist, stampeding up her arm. She landed hard, the table's wooden feet biting into her side. Pain surged like a flash flood throughout her body.

"Get 'im!" the cowboy yelled as he charged toward Allan. A ruckus erupted in the room. Men flew in different directions.

Katie sucked in several slow breaths, trying to maintain control and keep from fainting. Had Allan actually shoved her? The ache in her heart matched the one in her wrist.

With her good hand, she pushed herself onto her back. She lifted her injured arm and laid it across her chest. Wincing, she watched the judge slink out the front door like a fat snake with Sam close on his heels. Marshal Dodge fanned out to the left, the cowboy inched forward toward Allan in the middle, and Carter moved to the cowboy's right side.

Squinting through her pain, Katie saw Allan's gaze, steady and measured, as if trying to figure out how to take on three men. She wanted to yell that this was a mistake. They had the wrong house. The wrong man. But she couldn't find the strength to force the words out.

"So, McIntyre, how's your deputy? He still alive?" Allan hiked his chin and hissed the words in the cowboy's direction. His eyes glinted. "And how's that pretty little wife of yours?"

The stranger stiffened, then yelled and charged Allan. Moving at the same time, Allan rushed toward her. Katie's heart soared. Was he coming to help her?

The next instant, he leaped onto the gold brocade chair that sat beside the end table, stepped up onto the back, and then dove through the window above her head. Glass shattered and rained shards on top of her like a hailstorm. The chair spun around on one leg, then toppled back, landing with a dull thud and sharp stab on her left ankle. She squealed from the intense pain.

The cowboy lunged out the window right behind Allan. Marshal Dodge and Carter charged out the front door. The marshal shoved Carter out of his way, knocking him against the hall tree that sat next to the door. Carter regained his balance and hurried outside, leaving her alone.

The hall tree teetered back and forth, then tumbled away from her, landing with a crash on a small round table. Katie held her breath as the beautiful hurricane lamp Jarrod had given her as a wedding gift toppled to the floor and shattered. A sharp stab of loss lanced her heart. Flames ignited, licking at a zigzag trail of oil across her carpet. The breeze blowing through the door fed the blaze that grew in frantic intensity. Katie's eyes widened, and she covered her stomach as she realized the danger she was in.

"Dear Lord, please help me!" she cried, fighting her overwhelming fear as the room filled with smoke and she watched the home she and Jarrod had built being destroyed.

She had to get out of the house! Was nobody was coming to rescue her? Where had all the men gone? She wanted to cry over Allan's desertion, but she had to stay focused.

"Stay calm. Don't panic." She took a steadying breath, ignored the shooting pain in her hand, and tried to get up. Pressed against the wall with the heavy chair across her legs, she couldn't move her cumbersome body. Her heart pounded. Her breath came in staccato gasps.

Flames fanned out in all directions like a furious lynch mob seeking its victim.

Her long lace curtains *poofed* ablaze, and she watched as the fire raced upward. Fighting her fear, she struggled and squirmed with all her might. One foot broke free, but the chair still held her dress and other leg prisoner. She'd always hated that chair. Why hadn't she gotten rid of it before now?

Hampered by her long skirt, in desperation, she shoved with her foot, trying again and again to move the heavy chair. Each kick only made the chair bite into her leg more. *This can't be happening.*

Tears burned her eyes as thick smoke scorched her throat. She coughed and covered her face with her sleeve. Would this be her last day on earth? Would she die without seeing her baby's face? Without her child taking its first breath of life?

No! She wouldn't give up without a fight. She writhed and wrestled with the chair that held her captive. The child inside her tumbled around as if joining in the effort to get free.

"Help me, Lord. Somebody help me!"

Chapter 3

Dusty tucked in his chin and closed his eyes as he dove out the window right behind Sloane. His hard landing jolted his shoulder and hip. He rolled off the edge of the porch and onto his feet. Sloane was only ten paces ahead, dashing toward the marshal's horse. Dusty burst into a run, hoping his long legs would give him an advantage.

Just as Sloane slowed to mount the bay mare, Dusty lunged through the air and hit him behind the knees. Sloane smacked hard against the horse and bounced off, tumbling backward over Dusty and onto the ground. The mare squealed and pranced sideways. Dusty struggled to his feet and flung himself across Ed Sloane's body.

Weak with relief at finally catching his man, Dusty pressed himself across Sloane's back as the man bucked and struggled to get free. Dusty heard footsteps, then the rattle of handcuffs as the marshal secured Sloane's hands—then Sloane's curse.

"Got him." Heaving from exertion, the marshal waved Dusty off.

He sat back on his heels, breathing hard and staring at the lowly scoundrel who had ruined his life. He wanted to pummel Sloane's face and watch him beg for mercy, but he wouldn't yield to that temptation.

Although dirt and dried grass clung to Sloane's disheveled hair and clothing, he smirked. "I got away once. I can do it again."

Dusty clenched his fist and ground his teeth together as the memory of that awful day resurfaced—the day his wife had died and Sloane had escaped. He stood and took a step toward his nemesis, but then turned away with his fists at his sides, staring out across the acres of barren farmland. Slugging Sloane wouldn't bring Emily back or ease his pain.

"You ain't gettin' out of my jail."

Dusty turned around at the sound of the marshal's voice, grateful for the man's help in capturing Sloane.

The lawman hauled Sloane to his feet. "You there—" He pointed to the other man who'd helped chase Sloane, one who had been at the wedding. "Help me get this crook on that gelding."

Dusty watched as the two men lifted Sloane onto the spare horse the marshal had brought with them. A wave of relief and satisfaction washed over him at finally capturing his man. Dusty sucked in a breath and nearly gagged on a whiff of smoke. Spinning around, heart pounding, he faced his nightmare again.

Flames raced up the curtains inside the two-story farmhouse, sending a cloud of smoke barreling out the broken window and open door. The memory of another house burning singed his thoughts.

A woman's scream rent the cool afternoon. Dusty surged into motion, realizing Sloane's bride was still inside. He wouldn't let another woman die—not if he had the power to save her.

The marshal turned to assist him, but Dusty waved him off. "Stay with Sloane."

Running toward the house, he pulled his bandanna over his mouth and nose and jerked off his duster. He leaped up the steps and stopped just inside the front door. Angry flames had branched out from what looked like the remains of an oil lamp. Thick smoke clung to the ceiling and drifted downward.

Where was the woman? He dropped to his knees and crawled inside, his gaze darting one way and then another, eyes stinging from the thick smoke. Where had he last seen her?

By the broken window! He had reached out to try to break her fall when Sloane had cast her aside, but she'd been too far away. Pivoting to his left, he noticed a chair had tumbled across the lady's skirt. He crawled forward, ignoring the sharp stings in his hands as they landed on shards of glass.

Dusty tossed the chair to the side. Frantic blue eyes softened with relief. The woman coughed and tried to rise, but he could tell that she was in terrible pain. He swooped down and picked her up, even as she struggled.

"I—I can walk."

With her in his arms, he hurried toward the front door. Behind him, a wall crashed down, sending billows of smoke around them. The woman's harsh cough blasted his ear again and again.

Dusty didn't want to think how close he'd come to causing another woman's death. At least this one should survive. He could only hope the fall and the smoke wouldn't somehow affect the child she carried.

When they neared the barn, Dusty set her on the back of a buckboard. Tears streamed down her face, making rivulets in the soot on her cheeks. She gazed past him at her home. The look of total loss on her face made his heart clench.

This was his fault. If he'd waited a few more minutes for the marshal instead of plunging ahead on his own, they might have captured Sloane without this woman losing her home or getting hurt.

As he considered the scene inside the house when he had barged in, he realized a wedding had been in progress. He narrowed his eyes and studied the woman again, not allowing her tears to affect him. Why in the world would she be marrying Ed Sloane? Could the child she bore possibly belong to him?

Katie couldn't stop the tears blurring her vision. She laid her throbbing wrist across her stomach, cradled it with her other arm, and stared at her home. Like an angry monster, the fire roared and popped, devouring everything in its path.

Gone. Everything was gone. Her picture of Jarrod, her wedding ring, the home they'd built out of hard work and sweat. The Hoffman family Bible. Even the chest of baby gowns and blankets she'd hand made. All of it gone.

Except her life and her child's life.

In spite of her gratitude for that, a devastating sense of loss weighed her down. Why had God allowed this to happen?

Katie sniffed. She didn't know whether to punch the stranger standing beside her or hug him. If he hadn't come charging into her house like a mad bull, ruining her wedding, her home wouldn't be a burning mess now, and she'd be Mrs. Allan King. Her foggy mind couldn't comprehend how someone as charming as Allan could be wanted by the law.

The stranger stared at her with an unreadable expression. Though fairly young, he looked rugged and tough. His tanned face sported a day or two of whiskers, but his dark hair and eyes reminded her of Uncle Mason's and her brother, Jimmy's. Somehow he'd lost his black western hat and duster, and his hair hung across his collar, too long and unruly to be civilized. She shuddered at his nearness.

Looking past him, she saw Allan on a horse with his hands cuffed in front of him. A sick feeling threatened to upturn her stomach as she realized her dreams were dying. She glanced at the stranger. Her throat hurt from crying and choking on the smoke, but she had to know. "What did Allan do?" Her voice sounded weak and hoarse.

Something flickered in the man's eyes. A muscle in his jaw twitched. "His name's Ed Sloane, not Allan. He's a thief and a murderer, ma'am. You should be thankful we arrived before you married him. You would have lost all you had to that scoundrel."

Katie shivered. Could what he said possibly be the truth? Was Allan really a murderer? She narrowed her eyes, somehow wanting—needing—to blame this man for all her troubles. "Looks to me like that happened anyway."

The man glared back. "Homes can be rebuilt, but people don't come back from the dead." He turned and stormed off.

Katie hiked up her chin. She had never met anyone so rude and insensitive.

A loud crash pulled her gaze back to the fire. The second story collapsed onto the lower floor. Carter ran back and forth, futilely tossing bucket after bucket of water on the flames.

What would she do now? How could she get by without a house?

If not for her child, she might be able to live in the barn's storeroom for a while, but she had the baby to think of—and Carter lived there. She still had a small pittance in the bank; however, that money would have to go to pay the mortgage, or she'd lose her land.

Katie used her sleeve to wipe off her damp face. How could such a beautiful morning so full of hope turn into such a tragedy?

She knew she should be relieved that she had escaped marrying a criminal, but her whole body felt numb as if she were still trapped in the choking smoke.

The stranger stopped to talk with the marshal. Katie glanced around and realized that Sam and the judge were nowhere to be seen.

The marshal trudged her way while the stranger held Allan's horse. He stopped in front of her and removed his hat. "I'm right sorry about your house, Mrs. Hoffman. I didn't mean for this to happen."

Katie wanted to console him, but the words couldn't quite make it past her throat. She'd never met the marshal, though she'd seen him in town.

"Anyway, just be glad you didn't marry that scoundrel. You'd have been sorry, I'm sure."

As the marshal strode away, Carter dropped the bucket he had been using to douse the fire beside the trough and turned in her direction. With shoulders sagging, he shuffled forward and stopped a few feet in front of her.

"I'm sorry, Miz Hoff—" His brows dipped. "Uh—it is still Miz Hoffman, isn't it?"

Tears burned her eyes, and she nodded.

"I tried to save the house, ma'am. But it was too far gone after we got your. . . uh, that fellow corralled. What do you reckon he did?"

She shrugged and cleared her throat. "That man"—she nudged her head toward the stranger—"said something about Allan being a thief and a murderer."

Her voice cracked, and Carter glanced at her with sympathetic gray eyes. "If you don't mind me saying so, I never liked that feller much. Can't tell you why, but there was something shifty about him."

Katie glanced down at her throbbing, swelling wrist. She didn't dare move it for fear of feeling that stabbing pain again. "I think deep down I felt that way, too. I was just so desperate that I thought Allan was the answer to my problems."

"I reckon he wasn't." Carter swiped his arm across his forehead. "You need to see the doctor about that arm."

She nodded, dreading the long drive to town. "Could you please hitch the horses?"

"Sure thang. And I'm real sorry about your house, ma'am." He ambled toward the barn.

Katie watched the smoke spiraling up, disturbing a perfectly beautiful autumn sky. How she wished she could just drift away like a cloud, feeling only the warmth of the sun surrounding her instead of this hollowness.

With her good arm, she wiped the tears from her face. She'd cried enough. She'd never been an overly weepy female and wasn't going to start today. Staying angry with the stranger would help.

Right now, she had to make some plans. First was get to town and see the doctor. Then maybe she could stay at the boardinghouse or at the pastor's home a day or two. Somehow, she had to keep her land. Her child's inheritance. It was all she had left to give her baby.

She watched the marshal mount his horse and lead the one carrying Allan away. Funny, Allan was the only thing she didn't regret losing. She should have listened closer to that inner voice filling her with apprehension. But hadn't she thought he was God's answer to her prayers? Somehow, she'd missed hearing God's voice.

The stranger walked toward her, carrying the bucket. He ladled water into the dipper and handed it to her. She took it, surprised at his kindness, and drank like a water-starved woman crossing a desert. When she finished, he carried it back to the well, then filled up a canteen he took off his saddle.

Behind her, horses snorted and a harness jingled. She needed to mentally prepare herself for moving onto the wagon bench. It would hurt—and she couldn't imagine enduring that pain all over. Though her wrist still throbbed, if she sat still, it was bearable. At least her leg wasn't broken where the chair had fallen on it.

The stranger strode toward her again, his hat back on and pulled low on his forehead. She wondered what his story was. He looked more like an outlaw than Allan ever had. The man stopped at the end of the wagon and tied up his black gelding. "What are you doing?" Katie glared at him.

"I'm fixin' to drive you into town to see the doctor." He glowered back, his lips pressed tight in a straight line.

"Carter can drive me."

The man shook his head. "He needs to stay here and make sure the fire doesn't jump across the dirt and ignite your barn and fields."

Katie cast a frantic look toward the barn. She hadn't thought of that. Her cattle needed the hay stored there to make it through the winter. Glancing back at the remains of the house, she could see how the dried grass had burned right up to the dirt line, which had been made by cows and horses moving back and forth to the south pasture.

As much as she didn't want to admit it, he was right.

She closed her eyes, took a steadying breath, and scooted off the end of the wagon. Immediately, her whole body seemed ablaze. Instead of supporting her, the injured leg gave way. Letting go of her wounded arm, she threw out her good arm to break her fall, sending jagged pain charging through her wounded hand and wrist. Before she hit the ground, strong arms pulled her back and scooped her up.

Once again, she rested in the stranger's arms. Too tired and hurt to complain, she laid her head on his shoulder. Maybe she could rest for just a moment.

❧

Dusty carried the woman to the wagon bench and helped her get situated. He wished he had some blankets so she could lie down in back or had a pillow that she could rest her broken wrist on.

He nodded his thanks at the farm hand for hitching up the team. "Keep an eye on those sparks. We don't want to lose the barn."

The man nodded. "I'll get a shovel and throw some dirt on it." He strode back into the barn, looking relieved to be able to do something to help.

The wagon tilted and creaked as Dusty climbed on, and the woman grimaced. He had to admire her spunk. Most women would have fainted dead away after enduring the pain she had when she hopped off the wagon, but she wasn't even crying.

He clucked to her horses and heard a soft moan as the wagon jerked forward. An arrow of guilt pushed its way clear to his heart. This was all his fault. Somehow he had to make it right.

"I. . .uh, I'll stay on and rebuild your house for you."

The woman gasped and looked at him with wide blue eyes. Her flaxen, smoke-scented hair, probably fixed perfectly before her wedding, now hung in disheveled waves over her shoulders and down to her waist. Would it feel as soft as Emily's had?

Clenching his jaw, he looked away. What kind of an idiot was he, comparing her to Emily and telling her he'd rebuild her house?

"No."

Her single-word response forced him to look back. "No, what?"

She narrowed her eyes, and the nostrils on her cute little nose flared. "I don't want any more of your help. You've done quite enough already."

Dusty clenched his jaw and stared straight ahead, knowing she spoke the truth. His all-consuming quest to see Ed Sloane behind bars had caused him to lose control. This woman had paid the price. He darted a glance at her. Marshal Dodge had told him that Sloane had been wooing a widow woman, but in the mayhem, he'd forgotten what the marshal had called her. "What's your name?"

She stared straight ahead, cradling her injured arm on the top of her big belly. He sure hoped she didn't have her little one before they reached town, because he had no idea how to birth a baby.

"Katie Hoffman." She heaved a sigh as if giving her name was a big effort.

"Dusty McIntyre." He touched the brim of his hat.

They rode the next half hour in silence, but he kept a close eye on Mrs. Hoffman. She looked done in. "If you need to, I don't mind if you lean against my shoulder."

She peeked sideways at him, her eyes wide. With lips pressed together, she shook her head and looked away.

Dusty sighed. Who could figure out a female? It had taken a lot to offer his shoulder to her, and she just shrugged off his kindness even though she looked exhausted.

He stared ahead, watching the flat, barren landscape of western Oklahoma Territory. He longed for the gently rolling hills of his home in Sanders Creek.

Only he had no home. No job. No family.

He'd spent the last year and a half chasing after Sloane, and now that he'd caught him, Dusty felt empty.

Maybe once Sloane was hanged or in prison, he'd feel satisfied.

Maybe not.

Maybe he should have left vengeance to God. But he hadn't been able to. As long as Sloane was free, good, decent people like Katie Hoffman were in danger of being swindled—or worse. He shuddered to think what would have become of her and her property at the hands of Ed Sloane. He seriously doubted she or her child would have lived very long.

The small town of Claremont came into view on the horizon. As they edged closer, Dusty wondered if such a place would even have a doctor. He glanced at Mrs. Hoffman. Her bobbing head hung down so far it nearly touched her stomach.

Stubborn woman. She could have rested against him if she weren't so thick-headed, but then again, her dignity was about all she had left.

He gently nudged her shoulder, and she glanced up, looking confused. When she moved, pain contorted her pretty face. Her expression cleared as she realized they were in town. "Third house on the right," she spat.

He pulled the team to a stop at the house she'd indicated: a small, wood-frame structure that needed a good paint job. He could only hope the doctor was in better shape than his home.

Dusty lifted Mrs. Hoffman off the wagon and carried her inside, not bothering to knock.

An hour later, the doctor stepped out from behind a white curtain. "Her wrist is broken, and she has a badly bruised leg and hip, not to mention some minor cuts and bruises. Far as I can tell, the baby is fine. You can take her home, but don't let her do anything. For the next few days, she'll feel like she was run down by a herd of cattle. She needs plenty of rest."

Dusty blinked. Didn't the doctor know he wasn't the woman's husband?

The curtain moved, and Mrs. Hoffman hobbled out. He rushed to her side, thinking she shouldn't be walking.

"I don't need your help." She glared at him, daring him to disagree.

He stepped back but stayed close in case she needed him.

"I'll stop back by and pay you, Doc," she said, "after I visit the bank."

The doc waved his hand in the air. "No hurry, ma'am. I'm sure you're good for it."

She took another step, wavered, and then collapsed in the chair Dusty had been sitting in. Her chest rose and fell from her exertion. Holding her arm, now wrapped in stark white plaster of paris, she peeked up at him.

He knew she didn't want his help but suspected she had no choice. Not making a big deal of things, he bent over and scooped her up. "Where to now?"

"The bank."

Half an hour later, after they'd been to the bank and paid off the doctor, Dusty sat beside Mrs. Hoffman again on the wagon seat.

"What now?" He glanced at her out of the corner of his eye.

She pressed her lips together and looked like she was contemplating things. "Were you serious about offering to help me?"

Dusty nodded, knowing it was the right thing to do.

"All right then. Take me to the pastor's house; then tomorrow you can take me home."

Dusty turned on the seat to face her. "You can't go home. There's no place for you to stay."

She looked at him with pain-filled eyes. "I don't mean the farm. You can take me home to my aunt and uncle's place near Guthrie."

Chapter 4

Katie turned sideways on the wagon seat, hoping to ease her aching muscles. Just about the time she'd quit hurting from her fall, she and Mr. McIntyre had left Claremont, and now her body ached for a different reason. Someday, someone had to make a comfortable wagon seat.

She'd wanted to leave town the day after the fire, but her stubborn escort had refused. There was wisdom in his decision, not that she'd ever acknowledge it. They had waited three days for her to rest up and make arrangements to sell her cattle. At least her land was secure until next April, when she'd need to make another mortgage payment.

Peeking out the corner of her eye, she studied Dusty McIntyre. He'd been quiet—even distant—rarely talking since they'd left Claremont. But he was always courteous and gentle with her. Who was he, and where had he come from? And who was Allan—no, Ed Sloane—to him?

Taking a deep breath, she put words to her thoughts. "How did you know Ed Sloane, Mr. McIntyre?" The real name of her almost husband left a bitter taste on her tongue.

He glanced at her with those dark-as-midnight eyes peering out from under the western hat that he kept pulled down over his brows. Was that his way of hiding from the world?

"Call me Dusty." A muscle twitched in his shadowed jaw. In a rugged way, he was rather nice-looking. "He was a prisoner in my jail."

"Your jail?"

He nodded. "I used to be the marshal in Sanders Creek."

She blinked, trying to process this new information. How did a man go from being a marshal to a bounty hunter?

"Sloane liked to take advantage of the elderly." He looked her way, a grim set to his lips. "And widows."

Her sudden breath caught in her throat. *Widows?*

Not for the first time in the past few days, guilt washed over her for almost marrying a man without knowing his true character and spiritual condition. She'd assumed Allan believed in God since he had willingly gone to church with her, but that must have been his cunning way of winning her over.

Katie looked down at her hands. She'd ruined everything. If she hadn't agreed to marry Allan—Ed—she'd still have her home, her belongings, and her self-worth. But now she was returning to her aunt and uncle's with her tail tucked between her legs.

Her aunt and uncle would be terribly hurt to learn that she had planned to remarry and hadn't invited them to the wedding. She'd wanted to prove that she was independent and capable of caring for herself.

Now she'd have to face them, carrying a baby she hadn't told them about. Aunt Rebekah had her hands full caring for her four children and her husband. Katie knew if she'd told her about the baby, Rebekah would have found some way to assist her, and Katie hadn't wanted to add more to her aunt's already heavy load.

Katie swallowed the tight lump in her throat. She should have taken her brother, Jimmy, up on his offer and allowed him to help her with the farm. He'd helped her for a month after Jarrod's death, but she'd turned him loose once he got that wandering look in his eyes. If she had encouraged Jimmy to stay, she never would have put her home up for sale or met Allan.

Her stubborn independence had cost her everything. Tears blurred her vision, and she stared at the dry landscape. The leaves on the few trees in the area had changed to yellow, red, and bright orange. Most of the fields were plowed under, leaving only a few dried stalks exposed. Everything was barren and dying—just like her hopes and dreams.

What would she tell Uncle Mason and Aunt Rebekah? Maybe she could avoid mentioning Allan altogether.

She sighed, and Dusty glanced at her.

"Need another break?"

She shook her head. Could she be any more embarrassed? Having to ask this man to stop nearly every hour so she could relieve herself was so humiliating. She probably shouldn't have even tried traveling, being eight months into her pregnancy, but she didn't have a choice. At least they could make the journey in a day and wouldn't have to camp out overnight.

Katie watched a hawk circle lazily in the sky and wished her life were as carefree. She pressed against the wagon seat, hoping to relieve the ache in her back, and crossed her arms over her stomach. God had deserted her.

First, she'd lost her sweet, loving husband after only four months of marriage.

Now, she'd lost her home and nearly all she owned. She might even have to sell the land she and Jarrod had loved.

Where was God in all this?

She dreaded facing Uncle Mason, who had raised her. He was such a devout Christian man and would be disappointed in her decisions. Still, she longed to be wrapped in his protective arms. He'd comfort her and say that God had a plan—even in this.

Katie hardened her heart and clenched her fists. Well, she wouldn't believe it for a minute. How could losing a husband, a fiancé, and her home possibly be part of God's almighty plan for her?

❧

"Why are you going to your aunt and uncle's instead of your parents' home?"

Katie's surprised blue gaze darted in Dusty's direction. "I lost my parents when I was young, and Uncle Mason and Aunt Rebekah raised my brother, Jimmy, and me."

"Sorry about your parents."

She shrugged. "It's all right. I don't even remember them. I was only three when they died."

What would it be like to lose your parents at such a young age? At least his had lived until he was grown, having died just a year before Emily.

Gripping the reins in his hands, he looked across the heads of the horses pulling the wagon and tried to decide what to do after he dropped off his passenger. The need to compensate her for her loss weighed heavily on him. He'd offered her the hundred-dollar bounty he'd received on Sloane, but she had refused it.

After being a marshal, he hated accepting bounty money, but he'd spent the past year and a half hunting Sloane and capturing several other outlaws in the process. The little money he'd earned had bought food, ammunition, and the other things he'd needed while he was on the trail.

But what should he do now?

A sense of dissatisfaction swirled in his belly. He had imagined he'd be relishing his victory instead of feeling hollow and empty.

"Vengeance is mine; I will repay, saith the Lord." The scripture his mother often quoted came to mind.

But he was after justice, not vengeance. Wasn't he?

The sun reflected off Mrs. Hoffman's cast, making him wince. It was his fault she was injured, and therefore it was his responsibility to care for her until she could support herself again. Maybe he could get a job working for her uncle or in the town closest to their farm.

A fly buzzed in his face, and he swatted it. Looking around, he realized they'd arrived at another town. GUTHRIE, CAPITAL OF THE OKLAHOMA TERRITORY read a banner fluttering in the light breeze over Main Street. People strolled up and down the boardwalk, while wagons and riders on horses filled the streets. Two- and three-story brick buildings stood side by side, lining the dirt road. Fragrant smells of fresh-cooked food mingled with the pungent odors of animals and dust.

Katie cleared her throat. "Uncle Mason says that on the morning of the land run in 1889 there was just the rolling hills of the prairie here, but in less than six hours, Guthrie became one of the largest cities west of the Mississippi."

Dusty glanced sideways at her. He'd learned the same information in school but kept silent. This was the most relaxed her voice had sounded since they'd left Claremont. "That a fact?"

"Yes." Her dark blue eyes twinkled, doing funny things to his insides. He focused on a fat old woman dressed in widow's weeds so he wouldn't dwell on how pretty his passenger looked, now that she wasn't scowling.

"Uncle Mason and my pa rode in that first land run. I wish I could remember more about it. Aunt Rebekah told me that there were thousands of people. She's never seen that many people and horses in one place ever again."

The awe in her voice made him wish he'd experienced the historic event. "So I'm guessing your uncle won some land. You said he lives near Guthrie."

She shook her head and brushed a strand of white gold hair from her eyes. "Actually, my pa won the land, but he signed it over to Uncle Mason."

That seemed odd. Why would a man give away land he'd won fair and square?

"People say my pa was a scoundrel." She pressed her lips together and looked off in the distance as they pulled out of town.

Why would she be attracted to a man like Sloane if her own father had been a rascal? But then, being a scoundrel didn't mean her pa had been a thief or a murderer.

About an hour later, they pulled into a farmyard. A furry brown and white dog barked a greeting and wagged his whole backside. A homey, white, two-story clapboard house with dark green trim stood on a little rise with rolling hills surrounding it. At the bottom of the rise sat a barn with a creek running past.

Beside him, Mrs. Hoffman sighed, probably relieved to have their journey over and to be rid of him. She didn't know it yet, but she wouldn't be rid of him that easily.

A matching pair of dark-haired boys who looked to be five or six years old raced out of the barn and headed straight for the wagon. A man dressed in a plaid shirt and overalls followed them at a slower pace, wiping his hands on a rag. As he drew closer, the man lifted his hat off his forehead and stared at them, a slow smile making him appear younger than Dusty had first thought. Must be her uncle Mason.

The horses snorted and jerked their heads as the boys ran in front of them. Dusty tightened his grip on the reins to keep the animals from bolting. When they settled, he locked the brake in place.

The boys slid to a stop at the same time, scattering dust over their feet. "Who are ya?" the twin on the left asked, wiping his arm across his nose.

"That's Katie." The boy on the right pointed his skinny finger at Dusty's passenger.

"Nuh-uh. You don't know nuthin'." He gave his brother a shove. "Katie's at her farm."

"Is too her." He looked up with big brown eyes that matched his hair. His hand snaked out to pat the wiggling dog at his side. "Ain't you?"

"But she's fat—" The last word echoed on a loud whisper.

Katie sighed and nodded. "These are my twin cousins, Nathan and Nick."

"Ha-ha! Told you so." Nick grinned.

Nathan scowled and crossed his arms over his chest, obviously not happy about being wrong. Dusty bit back a laugh. He imagined the twins could be quite a handful.

"Katie!" The farmer waved and broke into a jog but slowed when his gaze landed on her cast. "What happened?"

She peeked at Dusty, then looked back at her uncle. "It's a long story. This is Dusty McIntyre. He was kind enough to drive me here."

She waved her good hand toward him, though he didn't miss the hint of sarcasm in her voice when she said the word *kind*.

"Dusty, this is my uncle, Mason Danfield."

"Pleasure to meet you, sir." Dusty nodded at Katie's uncle.

"Same here." Mason tipped his hat, and then his gaze landed on his niece's stomach. His surprised gaze darted from her face to her belly and back. His brows dipped. "Why didn't you tell us you were carrying a baby?"

Katie shrugged and eased to her feet. Dusty blinked, stunned that she'd kept her child a secret. Why had she done that?

Mr. Danfield lifted his arms to aid her. She stretched and then pressed her fists into her back. After a moment, she turned to back down the side of the wagon. Dusty held her shoulders and steadied her until Mason had a good hold on her.

"It's so good to have you home again, sweetheart. And just look at you." Mason offered her his arm and shot a curious glance in Dusty's direction. "Rebekah will be so. . .so surprised—and happy."

Feeling a bit left out of the family reunion, Dusty jumped down, dust scattering as his boots hit the ground. He strode to the rear of the wagon to check on his horse.

What would it be like to have a big family? Or any family for that matter? Would he and Emily have children by now if she hadn't died? Shaking off a wave of self-pity, he patted Shadow's muzzle and untied the gelding's reins, then led him to the water trough near the barn. His horse was all the family he needed. Less painful that way.

As he approached the barn, a lean adolescent boy who resembled Katie's uncle walked out carrying a pitchfork. He cast a curious glance at Dusty, nodded a greeting, and then looked toward the wagon. "What's going on, Pa?" Suddenly, the boy's eyes lit up. He leaned the pitchfork against the side of the barn and ran toward the house.

Behind Dusty a door slammed, and all manner of squeals erupted. He turned to see a brown-haired woman and a young girl hugging Mrs. Hoffman on the porch. Smiles were abundant, and the older woman stared at Mrs. Hoffman's stomach and dabbed at her eyes with the corner of her apron.

"I like a man whose first thought is to care for his animals." The farmer held out his hand. "Call me Mason."

Dusty shook hands, noticing the farmer's firm grip and curious stare.

"Thanks for bringing our Katie home. We didn't expect to see her again until maybe Christmas. And to find out that she's carrying her late husband's child"—he rubbed the back of his neck—"well, that's wonderful news. It'll give her something to remember him by."

Dusty knew the man wondered why he'd brought Katie home, but that was for her to tell.

"You can put your horse in the third stall and give him some oats. I'll unhitch the team and water them."

"Thanks." Dusty nodded, grateful that Mr. Danfield didn't pressure him into explaining. After tending to Shadow, he helped Katie's uncle brush down the team. Together they walked out of the barn, the setting sun casting long shadows across the ground.

"Did y'all eat?"

Dusty shook his head. Katie hadn't wanted to stop in Guthrie long enough to eat dinner since they were so close to their destination, even though the food she'd packed that morning was long gone.

"We got room for you to stay the night. You planning to head back to Claremont come morning?"

Dusty nearly stumbled but caught himself. How could he explain to this man that he had no plans for tomorrow—or the next day for that matter—other than trying to repay Mrs. Hoffman for all the trouble he'd caused her? He stopped and studied the ground for a moment, trying to decide how much to say.

Mr. Danfield slowed, halted his steps, and waited.

Finally, Dusty looked up. "I want you to know that I'm responsible for Mrs. Hoffman getting hurt. I never meant for it to happen, but it did—and there's more. I'd explain it to you, but I feel she needs to do that. Maybe we can talk after she tells you what happened."

Katie's uncle looked to be sizing him up. The man stood only an inch or so shorter than Dusty, but the breadth of his shoulders was wider, probably from working his land for years. Mason nodded. Dusty waited for him to say something with that slow Southern drawl, but he turned and jogged up the stairs. Not knowing what else to do, Dusty followed.

For some reason, he liked Mason Danfield. There was a quality to the man.

And the fact that he hadn't needled Dusty about how Katie had gotten hurt helped set him at ease. He half expected the man to grab him and shove him against the barn until Dusty confessed his part in the event.

The screen door slammed shut as they stepped inside the cozy home. Dusty could hear women's voices chattering like a bunch of magpies and dishes clinking in a room down the hall. The twins raced from room to room, whooping like Indians and merely slowed their pace when their father scolded them. Everywhere Dusty looked were signs of a happy family, making him feel his loss even more. He'd gotten over the deep, aching pain of losing Emily and his home, but he doubted he'd ever forget what he'd lost.

He didn't understand this overwhelming need to protect and care for Katie Hoffman. She didn't belong to him—and probably would be happy to never see him again. Maybe guilt was motivating him.

He removed his hat and hung it on a hook near the front door like Mr. Danfield had done. Dusty needed to figure out what to do next. After spending a year and a half on Sloane's trail, he wanted to settle down, and he had to somehow learn to live a normal life again. For now, Katie Hoffman was part of that life, whether she liked it or not.

Chapter 5

Katie yawned and stretched, then opened her eyes. The sun glistened in her window from a high angle, and she realized her family had let her sleep in. She knew she ought to feel guilty, but she was too worn out to worry about it.

The babe in her womb flip-flopped as if it, too, had just awakened. She rubbed her hand across her stomach, wondering how many more days would pass before she would be a mother. Would she handle the birthing as well as Rebekah had? She shuddered, not wanting to think of that scary but exciting event. She knew birthing would be painful, but the joy of seeing her child for the first time would give her the strength she would need.

Lying on her side, she studied her brother's sparse room but failed to notice much change. Excitement tickled her insides as she thought about seeing Jimmy again. The last time she had seen her brother was after Jarrod's funeral, when he stayed on to help her for a while.

Katie lumbered up until she sat on the edge of the bed. How did women bear children when they had a whole passel of young'uns to care for?

Her stomach grumbled, reminding her that she'd skipped breakfast. She slipped off her gown, washed in the water basin, and dressed, grateful for the button-up front of her blue gingham that enabled her to dress herself, even though one hand was in a cast. The sound of deep masculine voices pulled her to the window as she ran the brush through her hair.

Jimmy!

Her eyes drank in the sight of her brother. Though he was four years older than she, they had always been close, and she'd missed him terribly when he'd gone to fight in the Spanish-American War several years ago. Mason had told her last night that Jimmy had gone to Guthrie to pick up supplies and had probably stayed overnight. She'd laughed and wondered if she'd driven straight past him as she and Dusty had ridden through town.

When she saw Dusty, her heart gave a rebellious jump, and she scowled as she watched him shake Jimmy's hand. If a person didn't know better, they might think the two men were brothers, with their matching black hair and eyes and similar build. But her sweet brother was nothing like the man who'd ruined her life, no matter how good-looking that man might be.

With the window closed, she couldn't hear what they were saying. Turning,

155

she bypassed her shoes and plodded barefoot down the stairs.

" 'Bout time you woke up, sleepyhead." Her cousin Deborah's eyes glinted with humor.

Katie reached out and tweaked her nose. "You're getting taller, Deb."

"I am?" The twelve-year-old stretched up on her tiptoes and hugged Katie around the neck. "How's Junior today?"

"Hungry!" Katie laughed with her cousin and took her arm. "But first, I want to see Jimmy."

The front door groaned as Deborah pulled it open. The men stopped talking and turned in their direction.

"Katie!" Jimmy left Dusty and jogged up the porch steps. "Whoa! Look at you."

A nervous giggle escaped her as her brother stared at her huge stomach. She smacked him on the arm. "Give me a hug, you big galoot."

Deborah laughed as she hopped off the end of the porch and disappeared around the side of the house.

Jimmy stepped forward, arms opened, but then stopped. His dark brows furrowed. "Just how am I supposed to do that?"

Katie smiled and shook her head at his teasing. "Just lean over." She grabbed him by the shirt and tugged him down so she could wrap her arms around his neck. Over his shoulder, she caught Dusty coolly watching them. When she met his gaze, one corner of his mouth quirked up in a roguish grin. Her stomach lurched—probably because she hadn't eaten anything yet.

"Good night, sis, you're as big as a—"

She cupped her hand over her brother's mouth. "Don't you say a word, if you know what's good for you."

Jimmy's black eyes glimmered with mischief. Oh, how she'd missed him.

"C'mon in and have some coffee with me."

"Can't. Gotta unload the wagon. Dusty's gonna help." Jimmy adjusted his hat. "We can talk later. Work won't keep."

Jimmy bounded down the stairs and walked past Dusty toward the loaded wagon that sat outside the barn. She was glad he was back home. He'd been restless the past few years. Couldn't seem to find a place to settle. He'd stay home a couple of months, then ride out again as if he were searching for something—or someone.

Instead of following Jimmy, Dusty ambled toward Katie, making her heart skip a beat. She wanted to dart back inside, but a woman her size didn't do much darting. She lifted her chin and held her ground, ignoring her swirling stomach.

"Mornin'." Dusty yanked off his hat and held it in front of him, leaving his black hair in need of straightening. "How you feeling today? I know yesterday's ride couldn't have been easy on you."

Katie blinked, taken off guard by the concern she saw in his onyx eyes. "I'm doing fine. Thank you."

He smiled and donned his hat. "That's good. You look more rested than you did yesterday. Well, I'd better go help your brother."

He turned and sauntered to the wagon, his long-legged gait eating up the ground in quick order. She narrowed her gaze. Why did he have to be nice to her? It made blaming him for her troubles that much harder. Her stomach gurgled, and she went back inside.

As Katie entered the kitchen, Aunt Rebekah glanced up from the worktable where she was sitting, making dinner rolls. Her blue eyes lit up, and she smiled. "Feeling better?"

"Yes, but I desperately need some food—and some coffee." Katie poured herself a cup, then pulled out a chair and sat down.

"I saved you some breakfast." Rebekah wiped her flour-coated hands on her apron, stood, and crossed the room to the stove.

"Why is Mr. McIntyre still here? I figured he'd head out early this morning." Katie closed her eyes and savored the coffee as it slid down her throat and warmed her belly.

"He told Mason he thought he'd stay in the area. Maybe look for work in Guthrie."

Katie froze, her mouth agape, as disappointment surged through her. Of all the places Dusty McIntyre could settle, why did he have to pick Guthrie?

Rebekah set the plate in front of her, and the scent of fresh biscuits, bacon, and eggs wafted up. "Mmm. Smells wonderful. I'm just glad I can eat eggs now. When I was first carrying, I couldn't stand to see or smell them."

"I know just what you mean. About all I could stomach those first months were grits and oatmeal." Smiling, Rebekah sat back down, pinched off a section of dough, and rolled it into a ball. "He seems like a nice man to me."

"Who?" Katie slathered butter and plum jam onto her biscuit, then stuffed a huge bite into her mouth.

"Mr. McIntyre." Rebekah set her hands in her lap and stared off in the distance. "He reminds me of Mason when I first met him. He has that same haunted, hurting look. I wonder if he lost someone he loved."

"I don't know. He doesn't talk all that much." She forked some eggs into her mouth, wishing Rebekah would change the subject.

"So, are you going to tell me why you came to visit so unexpectedly?"

Maybe changing the subject wasn't the greatest idea.

"Is it because of the baby or because you got hurt?" Rebekah glanced at Katie's arm.

"Not exactly. It's a long story."

"I've got all day. Or would you prefer Mason was here when you talk about it? He didn't want to push you last night because you looked so tired."

Katie pushed her eggs around on her plate. Suddenly, they didn't taste so good. She closed her eyes and sighed, knowing she couldn't keep the truth from her aunt.

She told Rebekah how she'd met Allan and how he had swept her off her feet with his charm and persistence, even going to church with her. After taking a swig of coffee to steady her nerves, she told her aunt about the wedding and about Dusty storming in and Allan pushing her down and running away. Rebekah's eyes widened, and her hand lifted to cover her mouth as Katie told her about the house catching on fire and Dusty rescuing her.

Rebekah reached her flour-coated hand across the table and laid it on Katie's arm. "I'm so sorry about your home, sweetheart. So, Mr. McIntyre saved your life? Remind me to give that man a hug."

Eyes moist at the memory of her loss, Katie sputtered and her back stiffened. "Well, yes, he saved me, but he's also responsible for ruining my wedding and burning down my house."

Rebekah's mouth quirked to one side, and her brows lifted in disbelief. "Sounds to me like he kept you from making a terrible mistake, besides saving your life—and your child's."

"Yes, but. . ." Katie considered her aunt's words. Aunt Rebekah had a way of putting everything in its proper perspective.

"No buts. I know you, Katie. You've always needed someone to blame when things go wrong. From what you've told me, Mr. McIntyre wasn't even in the house when the lamp was knocked over, so it couldn't be his fault."

A door banged, and the twins stormed into the kitchen. "We're starved, Mama," they said in unison.

Rebekah smiled. "Are you now? Well, perhaps I could find a cookie to hold you over until dinner."

The twins' eyes gleamed, and they nodded their heads.

Grateful for the reprieve, Katie closed her eyes as her aunt stood. She wasn't ready to let go of her anger, even though she knew that's what God wanted her to do. For some reason, she needed to stay angry at Dusty. Was she afraid if she didn't that she might just discover she liked him?

Even though she dearly loved her aunt and uncle, Katie didn't want to live in their home again. Her independence was too important to her.

Considering her options, she nibbled a piece of bacon and watched her aunt, who'd returned to making her dinner rolls. She could sell her farm and would have the money to get a small house somewhere, maybe in Guthrie. She'd be closer to her family and still be living on her own. But then her child would have no inheritance, and she'd feel as if she had failed Jarrod.

She had to do something. Having lost her mother and father when she was just a tiny girl, she'd always felt something was missing. Oh, Uncle Mason and Aunt Rebekah had loved her as much as real parents, but she'd always wondered what things would have been like if her parents had lived.

She shook that thought away. For now, she'd keep the ranch and find some other means of support, like sewing. Though it would be difficult with the cast, she could manage. Maybe she could get Jimmy to drive her back to town so she could scout out her options.

She stared into her coffee cup and swirled the black liquid. One thing was for sure: She was done with men. She couldn't stand the pain of loving and losing again—or being taken in by another con man. No, she'd find some work and raise her child without a man's help.

❧

Dusty patted Shadow's rump and walked out of the livery. While his horse received a new pair of shoes, he needed to find some work. The livery owner didn't need any help but thought that the man at the mercantile might. Dusty clenched his jaw. Working in a store wasn't exactly his area of expertise, but if it would enable him to fulfill his obligation to Mrs. Hoffman, he could do it for a time.

As he stepped inside the mercantile, he paused to allow his eyes to adjust to the dim lighting. All manner of scents tickled his nose, from leather, to spices, to the pickle barrel at his side. His mouth watered at the thought of eating a juicy pickle, but he was here on business, not for a snack.

A heavyset woman behind the counter smiled. "Good morning. What can I help you with?"

Dusty looked around, hoping to speak with her husband, but no one else was in the store. He removed his hat and plodded toward the counter, his boots echoing on the wooden floor planks. "Morning, ma'am. Your husband around?"

She shook her head, and wisps of curly gray hair danced around her wrinkled face. "No. He had to pick up some orders at the train depot. I can help you with 'bout anything he could."

Dusty cleared his throat. "The truth is, I'm looking for work."

"Oh." Her gaze took him in from top to bottom.

He figured he looked more like an outlaw to her than a store clerk. "I can assure you that I'm honest and trustworthy. Mason Danfield will vouch for me."

"Oh, well, that's good. Mr. Danfield is a fine judge of character. But the truth is, we just hired a man last week. We needed someone to make deliveries. I'm truly sorry."

Her compassionate gaze soothed Dusty's disappointment. He looked around the store, and his eyes landed on a colorful sign advertising soda pop. "I'd like to try one of those." He pointed at the sign.

The woman smiled. "Those new soft drinks are quite the rage now." She moved to the back of the store and returned with a small bottle. Using an opener, she flipped off the top, and a hissing sound erupted.

Dusty took the cold bottle and laid a coin on the counter. He took a sniff of the sweet-smelling drink, then a taste. Fizzy bubbles tickled his tongue, but the drink was cool and refreshing. Much better than the lukewarm, metallic-tasting water in his canteen. He swigged down the drink in three swallows and contemplated getting another. Maybe later. He clunked the bottle onto the counter. "Thank you. I may be back later for some supplies." Dusty tipped his hat at her and licked the remaining sweetness off his lips.

"We'll be here, and we're glad to help." She smiled and waved, making Dusty wish he had a grandmother alive somewhere.

He stepped outside and blinked against the brightness as his boots clunked on the boardwalk. Guthrie was an active town. A number of men and several women moseyed along the sides of the street, stopping at different establishments.

He'd heard that Guthrie was one of the most progressive towns west of the Mississippi. One building even had an underground area for storing buggies and stabling horses for the people who worked there.

Sanders Creek was a far cry from Guthrie. Dusty reckoned the town had a new marshal by now—maybe Tom. Even though he'd never formally quit, he'd been gone more than a year and a half. He scowled, not wanting to think of his hometown and all he'd lost there.

Looking at Guthrie again, he remembered the stories Mason and Jimmy had told him. When they first came here, shortly before the first Oklahoma land rush, thousands of people lived in tents and covered wagons. Dusty tried to imagine the scene.

As he stood in front of the mercantile, leaning against a post, two young women dressed in frilly gowns and carrying parasols crossed the dirt street and walked in his direction. They giggled and talked behind their hands, leaning close to speak in one another's ears. Something told him they were talking about him. He glanced down at his denim pants. A streak of dirt lined one leg where he had leaned Shadow's hoof as he checked the shoe earlier this morning.

The women neared the steps next to him and stopped at the bottom. The cute brunette cleared her throat, making him realize they were waiting for his assistance. He pushed away from the pole and held out his hand. The brunette batted her lashes at him, and a coy smile tugged at her pretty lips. Dusty helped her up the steps, then turned to aid her friend, a shy auburn-haired gal. After he assisted her, the two ambled on their way, giggling and looking back over their shoulders at him.

He jogged down the steps and crossed the street, heading toward the marshal's office. Why hadn't their attention affected him? He ought to consider it a compliment, but his thoughts kept traveling back to Katie Hoffman's dark blue gaze glaring at him. She obviously couldn't be rid of him quick enough, but something inside him wished she felt differently.

Dusty nearly stumbled as the realization hit him—he liked her. For some odd reason, he felt an attraction to the prickly woman. Oh, sure she was pretty enough with that mass of golden hair and those simmering eyes, even though she was with child.

He'd always been drawn to needy people. Maybe that's why he liked his job as marshal, because it allowed him to help those in need. As he looked up, his gaze landed on a sign indicating the marshal's office, and he headed that way.

The door rattled as he entered, and a lean man sitting behind the desk looked up. The small office smelled of cigar smoke and gun oil.

"Howdy, stranger. What can I do for you?" The man leaned back in his chair, surveying Dusty as if he expected trouble.

Hoping to put the man at ease, Dusty crossed the room and held out his hand. "Dusty McIntyre. I drove Katie Hoffman from her farm in Claremont to her uncle's farm."

"I'm Homer White." The marshal stood and shook Dusty's hand. "McIntyre, huh? That name sounds familiar. You're not wanted for something, are you?"

Dusty could tell the man was partly serious with his question. "I was marshal in Sanders Creek a few years back."

Marshal White's eyes narrowed as if he was searching his mind for a memory. Suddenly, his gray eyes widened. "Oh, you're that McIntyre. Sorry to hear about your wife and home. D'you ever catch the man that caused all your troubles?"

Dusty nodded. "Just did." He glanced around the room. "I was hoping to take a look at your WANTED posters. Now that Ed Sloane is locked up, I need to find something else to do."

A drawer squeaked on the desk as the marshal pulled it open. He took out a stack of papers and flopped them on the desk. "Have at it."

Dusty thumbed through the stack, recognizing several faces. He handed one to the marshal. "That man's in jail in Enid. Caught him last month."

Marshal White nodded. "Glad to know that. I'll put his poster in my CAPTURED file." He opened the bottom drawer of his desk and slid the paper inside.

Dusty smiled and studied some more posters. The problem was, if he went after another outlaw, he wouldn't be able to stay around and help Mrs. Hoffman. He sighed. What he needed was a job in town.

"You're welcome to have a seat. I don't get too much company—unless there's trouble."

Dusty nodded his thanks and sat down. "You know of any honest work around here? I'd kind of like to stick around these parts for a while."

The marshal grinned, showing his yellowed teeth. "That Katie Hoffman is a fine-looking woman, isn't she?" His expression sobered. "Heard tell she lost that young husband of hers. Downright shame. They weren't married but a few months."

Dusty stared out the window. Was his attraction to Katie that obvious?

"Tell you what. I could use a deputy. The one I had left town a few weeks ago when he got word his father was dying. You interested?"

Dusty's gaze darted back to the marshal. The man was serious. Dusty studied the dirt on the wood floor. Was he ready to pin on a badge again?

"I know what you're thinking, young man. Wondering if you still have it in you after getting gut shot like you did back in Sanders Creek." The man leaned back in his chair with his hands crossed behind his head. "Best thing to do is get back on the horse once you've been thrown."

Dusty knew it was the truth, but sometimes climbing back on wasn't easy.

"You got a place to stay?"

Dusty shook his head. "Not yet."

"Good. You can stay with me. I live by myself. Got a spare bedroom and a place out back to stable your horse—assuming you've got one. And I'll pay you seventy-five dollars a month, just like I did the other fellow."

Dusty blinked. Rarely in his life had things come so easily. He waited for the *however*—but it never came. He reached out his hand. "Marshal, you've got yourself a deputy."

Chapter 6

Katie brushed her damp hair and paced the length of the porch and back. She desperately needed to find some way to get to town. Uncle Mason was too busy to take her, and Jimmy had gone down to Texas to scout out some cattle. She would ask her cousin Josh but didn't want to get the fourteen-year-old in trouble with his father.

A sharp pain forced her to take a seat in the nearby rocking chair. She rubbed at a spot on her upper leg where the babe tended to sit on a nerve, sending sharp stabs into her hip and down her leg. How in the world had Rebekah managed to do this five times? A picture of two small graves on the hill behind the house reminded her to be thankful for her active child. She remembered the gripping pain when Rebekah's third child had been stillborn and the horrible shock when Mason and Rebekah woke up one morning to discover their youngest daughter dead in her cradle at only five months old.

No matter how much discomfort her babe caused, Katie was determined not to complain. If not for Dusty McIntyre, she could have lost her child.

Katie shook her head, not wanting to think of being beholden to the handsome bounty hunter. A man like that was a loner, destined to travel the countryside, ever in search of his prey. It must be lonely. What would drive a man to want to live such a solitary life?

Besides, he was gone now. He'd ridden out nearly a week ago and hadn't returned. At least her anger had cooled somewhat, not having to be around him daily.

She stood, rubbing her back. There had to be some way she could get to town. Perhaps the dress-shop owner could use some help. Katie had mastered her sewing skills by helping her aunt make clothes for their big family and surely would be an asset to a dressmaker, even though it would take her much longer to sew with the cast on.

The porch thudded as the twins charged up the steps. She loved her young cousins, but they just about wore everyone out with their active natures. They stopped running but still bounced around her.

"Nathan says you swallowed a punkin. That true?" Nick stared up at her, his brown eyes wide. Nathan elbowed Nick in the side, but he didn't look away.

Katie's cheeks warmed as she considered how to respond. The door behind her squealed open, and Rebekah stepped outside.

"There you are. You boys wash up and wait for me in the parlor. It's time for your reading lesson."

"Aw, Ma. Why do we have to learn readin'?" Nathan's shoulders sagged.

"Yeah, we ain't never even been to school yet." Nick glanced at his brother and took a similar posture.

Katie tucked her lips together to keep from laughing.

"I'm determined for you to start school already knowing your alphabet." Rebekah stared down at the boys, her hands on her hips. "Now go inside."

"Aww," the boys whined in unison.

Rebekah grinned and shook her head. "Katie, are you doing all right?"

"Yes, but I'm so bored that I asked Deborah to help me wash my hair—and it's not even Saturday. I want to ride into town and see if that new dressmaker needs some help."

Her aunt's eyes widened. "You'll do no such thing. A woman in your condition has no business traveling. You risk doing injury to your child, not to mention tiring yourself out."

Katie heaved a deep breath. "I did fine on the trip from Claremont. Besides, I need to get work so I can start saving money to rebuild my house and make my next mortgage payment."

Rebekah laid her hand on Katie's arm. "Sweetheart, don't worry about that now. You have a home here for as long as you want. We love having you here."

Inside the house, Katie heard the sound of breaking glass. Rebekah yanked her hand back and spun around, hurrying inside. "Don't stay outside so long that you catch cold," she called over her shoulder as she shut the door.

Katie sighed. Nobody understood how she felt. She loved her family, but after being on her own, she craved her independence. She wanted her cozy home back.

A gentle autumn breeze tickled her cheek and sent leaves from the nearby oak tree spiraling to the ground. Summers might be hot in the Oklahoma Territory, but autumn was wonderful with the cooler yet comfortable temperatures.

She stared off in the distance, wondering how she could get to town. Rebekah didn't understand her driving need for independence. And why all the fuss? Riding to Guthrie didn't take nearly as long as the trip from Claremont had taken, and she'd managed to travel that distance just fine. Well, maybe not fine, but she'd made it.

She'd have to keep thinking on it. Uncle Mason would tell her to pray, but God had let her down. He hadn't saved her home or kept her from breaking her wrist.

Emotions swirled through her. She knew it was wrong to blame God. Bad things happened in life, like Jarrod's accident and the fire. She'd drive herself crazy trying to sort it all out. Uncle Mason believed there was a purpose for everything that happened in life, and she thought she believed that also—until so many bad things occurred.

She looked up at the beautiful sky. She knew in her heart that God was in control and cared for His people, but she needed her mind to align with her heart.

A horse's whinny drew her attention to the road coming from town. She narrowed her eyes and placed her hand on her brow to block the sun as she tried to see if she knew the rider on the dark horse.

Her heart flip-flopped. Dusty McIntyre had returned.

Hope surged through her body, making her limbs tremble. Dusty had said he'd do anything he could to help her. Perhaps she could get him to take her to town.

❧

As Dusty rode up to the Danfield farm, he had a strange sense of coming home. Katie stood on the porch, leaning against the railing, as if waiting for him. Her long, damp hair hung down to her waist, drying in the light breeze like the flaxen mane of a wild mustang. Tingling sparks shot through his body, making him wish he had the right to run his hands through her hair.

Other than when he met Emily, he'd never cared if a woman favored him or not. But for some reason, he wanted Katie to be partial to him. Maybe it would assure him that she'd forgiven him for the trouble he'd caused her.

He nudged Shadow into a trot and quickly ate up the distance separating him and Katie. After hopping off his horse, he tied the gelding to the porch railing and climbed the steps. Katie now sat in a rocking chair with her hair behind her.

Dusty yanked off his hat, feeling a bit shy in her presence. He was never sure whether she'd be pleasant or bite his head off. Marshal White had told him that women were often extra-emotional when they were carrying. At least that had been the marshal's experience with his wife.

"Afternoon. Why don't you have a seat?" Katie waved her hand toward the other rocking chair.

He hesitated a moment, taken off guard by the kindness in her voice. As he passed her, he tried not to notice that her middle looked even bigger than it had last week. He averted his gaze but wondered how a body could stretch so much.

"I didn't expect to see you again." She laced her fingers and rested her hands across her big belly.

Dusty rolled the brim of his hat, not used to making small talk. He'd been alone for so long that he figured he wasn't the best of company.

"Aunt Rebekah said you thought you might settle in Guthrie."

He nodded and glanced her way, trying not to notice how pretty she looked when she wasn't scowling. "I took a job as deputy marshal." He didn't think it proper to tell her he was rooming with Marshal White.

165

"That's good. I'm sure the marshal was delighted to be able to hire someone with your experience and capabilities."

Dusty wanted to allow his chest to swell with pride at her first compliment, but too many years of chasing crooks had taught him that when someone was handing out favors, it was usually because they desired something. Disappointed, he sat back in his chair and faced the barn instead of Katie. Was it too much to hope she might actually like him? What was it she wanted?

"So, did you come out to see Uncle Mason?"

"No, I rode out to check on you."

"Me? Why would you feel that's necessary? Uncle Mason and Aunt Rebekah are quite able to care for me, not that I need them to."

Dusty darted a glance in her direction. Her cute little chin was lifted in the air as if he'd greatly offended her, and her eyes sparked with indignation. She reminded him of a fancy hen strutting around the barnyard.

"I intend to make sure you're all right and to figure out a way to make up for the pain I've caused you."

She peered at him, both curiosity and anger flashing in her eyes. "I don't need you to take care of me." She pushed herself up. "That's the whole problem. I want to care for myself, but everyone seems bent on doing it for me." Turning away, she awkwardly crossed her arms over her stomach.

Dusty stood and walked over to stand behind Katie. Her hair fell in golden waves, teasing him to reach out and run his fingers through it. He jerked his hand back as he came to his senses. This woman wouldn't appreciate his advances.

Suddenly, she spun around. "There is one thing you could do for me, if you're serious about helping me."

Dusty held his breath as he studied her face. Her tanned complexion was much prettier and more natural than that of pale-faced city women who hid from the sun. Up close, her sapphire eyes had flecks of gray and several shades of blue. A smattering of soft freckles dotted her small nose, giving her a spunky, carefree look.

He knew he should be suspicious of her quick turnabout, but his mouth had suddenly gone too dry for him to respond.

She stepped closer, laying her uninjured hand on his arm. Goose bumps erupted at her touch, making him feel like a giddy schoolboy. He glanced at her lips, wishing he had the right to kiss them.

Katie stared up at him, as if she, too, were caught up in the magic of the moment. Was it possible she had some feelings for him? Why did he even care?

Katie cleared her throat, blinked her thick lashes, and took a step back. "I. . . uh. . .need to get to town. Uncle Mason is busy, and Jimmy's gone. Could you possibly take me?"

Dusty stepped back and turned away, disappointed that her attentions had only been a ploy to get him to help her. He remembered Rebekah's comment that Katie shouldn't have traveled to their ranch in her condition. It could be bad for the baby. Well, he wouldn't be part of causing her more pain. If he drove her to town and something happened to the baby, she'd just have another thing to blame him for, and he'd never forgive himself.

He faced her again. "I'm sorry, but I can't do that."

Katie hiked up her chin again. "Can't? Or won't?"

"You've got no business traveling to town in your"—he waved his hand toward her stomach—"condition." Dusty was certain his ears were bright red.

Katie glared at him. "You're just like the rest of them—wanting to keep me tied here to the ranch. All I want is a chance to talk to the dressmaker to see if she needs any help. I want to support myself and my child, not live off my relatives."

He could understand her frustration, but she had a baby to worry about. "All you need to be thinking about right now is your child. The rest you can worry about later."

She crossed her arms over her chest, the cast on her wrist reminding him once again of the pain he'd caused.

Katie dipped her brows, her eyes taking on a stormy glare. "What would you know about it? I lost my husband after only four months of marriage, my home, and everything I owned except my land. There's no way this side of heaven you could know how I feel."

Dusty closed his eyes and waited for the thunderstorm of pain and anger to subside. His stomach ached as if he'd been sucker punched when he wasn't looking. He narrowed his gaze and took hold of Katie's upper arms. Her eyes widened in surprise and apprehension. "Oh, I know how you feel all right. The difference is, you have a child to remember your husband by, but I've got nothing."

He released her, ignoring the curiosity and repentance he saw in her gaze. He ran down the stairs, jumped onto Shadow, and rode off, hoping he'd never see Katie Hoffman again. He was done trying to please that persnickety woman.

Chapter 7

Dusty kicked Shadow into a gallop. Katie had no way of knowing how closely their losses were related. The difference was he bore his alone, while she had a whole houseful of people to help her, even if she didn't want their help.

Even God had deserted him.

No, that wasn't fair. He was the one who'd run off and left God behind when he was aching over Emily's death. If only he knew how to find his way back.

But it was too late for him.

He eased Shadow to a trot, sorry for taking his frustration out on his trusted steed.

Had there ever been a more stubborn woman than Katie Hoffman?

The wind suddenly whipped out of the north, bringing with it colder temperatures and a threat of snow, which chilled his bones after the warm weather of the past week. It never ceased to amaze him how quickly the weather could change here. Though it was a bit early for snow, in Oklahoma anything could happen weatherwise. Dusty reined Shadow to a halt, dismounted, and untied his duster from behind his saddle. He shrugged into the long brown coat, leaving it open and billowing around his legs.

He studied the yellowed rolling hills. Some leaves still stubbornly clung to the trees, but in another month they'd be gone. He had never cared too much for winter and the hardships it brought.

Dusty sighed, wrestling with his feeling of unease. He'd thought after capturing Ed Sloane he would be content and could finally put his past behind him. Instead, he felt like something was missing in his life. Was it that he no longer had a goal? Had he been focused so long on capturing Sloane that he couldn't settle down and live a normal life?

Shadow nickered, and Dusty tugged on the reins, pulling his horse closer. He patted the gelding's soft muzzle.

He didn't want to admit it, but he was jealous of Mason Danfield. Mason had a loving family, a nice home, and his heart was right with God. Maybe this restlessness in him had more to do with his walking away from God than capturing Sloane.

Dusty pressed down his hat, mounted Shadow, and urged the horse into a trot. His parents had been God-fearing people and raised him to be that way.

But when things turned bad, he had ridden away from his friends and from God, preferring to suffer alone.

Was it possible for God to forgive a man who had hardened his heart against Him?

Dusty shook his head. No, he had to face facts. He'd blown his chance with God. There was nothing else left but to endure the rest of his life the best he could.

He thought about Katie. It was obvious she wanted nothing to do with him, unless was willing to do things her way. That shouldn't bother him, but it did.

He had to admire her stubborn desire for independence. Most women in her shoes would be satisfied to sit back and allow their family to take them in. But not Katie.

As he rode toward town, he considered how he might help her regain her independence. He wouldn't bring her to town like she requested, but there had to be something he could do.

A strong gust of wind blew, chilling his belly. Lowering his eyes, he noticed the spot where he'd torn off a button when his shirt had snagged on the chair this morning. He shouldn't have worn it this way, but his only other shirt was dirty. He'd traveled light when he was on the road, taking only one change of clothing. He would find a place and wash his dirty things, trading back and forth, but now that he had a town job and needed the respect of the people, he figured he ought to get some new clothes.

He sighed and thought of the store-bought clothes he'd had in the past. The problem was, being tall with long arms, he had trouble finding shirts with sleeves that fit comfortably. He much preferred custom-made shirts. As he rode into Guthrie, he scanned the signs for a tailor. It would be a good idea to get some made.

As if one of those newfangled electric lights had lit up in his mind, an idea started forming. A plan to help Katie and himself. He turned Shadow around and headed back to the mercantile.

Yep, he had just the idea that would help her take the first step to regain her independence.

※

"Aunt Rebekah, you need to let me help you more." Katie dropped into the kitchen chair and watched her aunt and cousin washing the dishes. She'd cleaned off the table but didn't want to admit the going back and forth had winded her.

"You do plenty around here. You need to take it easy these last weeks and save your strength for the birthing."

Katie wanted to ask Rebekah just what was involved with that, but with Deborah in the room, she held her tongue.

Josh sauntered in, reminding her of her brother when he was fourteen. Tall, lanky, three-fourths man and one-fourth boy. Josh's hair more closely resembled Rebekah's medium brown than Mason's black hair, but his features were more like his father's.

"Pa said for me to get the food scraps for the hogs."

Rebekah nodded her head toward the wooden bucket that held the vegetable scraps. Josh grabbed the pail and hurried out, looking uncomfortable in the women's domain.

"There's something I've been meaning to show you." Rebekah wiped her hands on a towel. "Deb, after you finish rinsing, dump the water and join Katie and me in my room."

"Yes, ma'am." Deborah gave a smile that looked much like her mother's.

It was interesting how Deborah had her father's dark coloring, but her features more resembled her mother's, just the opposite of Josh. Would Katie's baby be a combination of her and Jarrod, or would it favor one side of the family more than the other? Katie stuck her little finger down the end of her cast and rubbed her itching arm as she followed Rebekah to her bedroom. Warm memories flashed through her mind of tiptoeing into her aunt and uncle's bedroom with Jimmy and the other children and waking up Mason and Rebekah early on Christmas morning. As she glanced around, she noticed a new Flying Geese–patterned quilt covered the bed, and curtains from a matching fabric hung from the window.

At the foot of the bed was an old trunk. Her aunt lifted the latch, and Katie peered over Rebekah's shoulder to see what was inside. Her heart leaped when she saw the folded stacks of baby gowns, diapers, and blankets. That was another reason she needed to get to town—to get fabric to make some baby clothes.

Rebekah lifted a pale pink flannel gown and caressed it. "I made this for Susanna right after she was born. The twins pretty much wore out the clothing I had saved from the other children, so I needed new things for Sus—"

"I'm sorry, Aunt Rebekah." Katie laid her hand on her aunt's shoulder. "I never considered how my being here would stir up old memories or make things harder for you."

Rebekah dotted her eyes. "No, I'm sorry. It's just that I haven't looked at these things since I put them away after Susanna's death. It was too painful at first, but it's good for me now. God has healed my pain, though I still miss my baby girl."

"I know. I miss Jarrod, too, but the pain of his loss isn't as sharp as it was at first."

Rebekah hugged Katie. "Yes, God's grace softens the ache of losing those we love because we know we'll see them again in heaven."

Katie wanted to believe that—knew it was true. She needed to forgive God—and Dusty—but she didn't know how.

"Look at this! Oh, I hope you have a girl. My friends gave me so many darling things after I had Susanna." She held up a tiny mint green cotton dress with smocking across the chest and flowers embroidered over it.

"Oh, how precious! That dress almost makes me want a girl, though I have to be honest. I'm hoping for a son to carry on the Hoffman name."

"I don't blame you. Mason was so excited our first child was a boy. Do you remember? You were only five back then."

Katie shook her head, reached in the trunk, and picked up a soft, crocheted blanket. "No, I don't remember his reaction, just that I wanted to hold Josh all the time."

Rebekah dug farther down in the stack of clothes and pulled out a long, white, lacy gown. "All my children were dedicated to God in this. It would make me so happy if you were to have your child dedicated in it."

Katie blinked. She hadn't even thought about that. Could she dedicate their child to the Lord if she was still angry with Him?

"You are planning to have your child dedicated, aren't you?"

Katie looked at her aunt. "I hadn't even thought about it until you mentioned it."

Rebecca glanced down and fingered a pastel blue blanket. "Katie, are you letting your grief build a wall between you and God?"

She heard the concern in her aunt's voice and nodded her head.

Rebekah put her arm around Katie's shoulders. "I can't pretend to know what it feels like to lose a spouse. I lost my mother, younger brother, and two children, but to be a newlywed and to lose my husband. . . Well, I don't know the pain that you've endured because of that. But Mason does. You should talk with him, Katie. He can help you."

Her aunt squeezed Katie's shoulders. "I can only love you and encourage you to talk to God. He knows your pain and can help you through—if you'll let Him."

Katie gave her aunt a weak smile. "I hadn't thought to talk to Uncle Mason. Actually, I've avoided it because I knew he'd tell me I shouldn't be angry at God."

"Having lost his wife when he was young, he knows what you're feeling. He was mad at God, too—ready to turn you and Jimmy over to your unscrupulous father. Then he was heading west, planning to leave behind everyone he ever loved."

Katie nodded, remembering the story of how he had lost his pregnant wife and his sister—Katie and Jimmy's mother—in a wagon accident. Why hadn't she realized before that he would understand what she was feeling?

She folded up the blanket and laid it back in the trunk. Tonight, if he had time, she'd talk with her uncle.

"You've been fussing about wanting something to do." Rebekah glanced at Katie with an ornery twinkle in her eye. "I thought maybe you'd want to get started mending these diapers. Some of them need to be rehemmed. You're welcome to use whatever you want in here."

Katie hugged her aunt, inhaling her faint scent of lavender mixed with the aroma of the cooked food. "Thank you. This is just what I need to keep me busy for a while."

"If you find it difficult to sew with that cast on, I'm sure Deborah wouldn't mind helping you." Rebekah handed Katie a little basket with various colored threads, a couple of needles, and a pair of scissors. "I need to check on that apple pie I have baking."

Katie sorted through the diapers and took out the ones that needed mending; then she took them and the basket into the parlor and sat down in the chair by a large window. She preferred to sit on the porch, but cold weather had blown in several days earlier; now it was simply too chilly.

Half an hour later, she heard steps on the front porch and glanced out the window. Her heart skipped a beat, and she pricked her finger with the needle when she saw Dusty McIntyre. Katie wiped off the dot of blood, wrapped a scrap of cloth around her finger, and went to the door. Just about the time she got Dusty McIntyre out of her system, he showed up again.

He held a large package wrapped in brown paper and tied with twine in one arm and yanked his hat off with his other hand. "Afternoon."

Katie didn't want to think how intriguing he looked with his hair messed up like that and a shy grin on his nicely formed lips. His long duster hung open, and a deputy's badge pinned to his vest gave him an air of authority. Having seen him in action, Katie knew she wouldn't want to be on his bad side.

Realizing she was staring, she moved back. "C'mon in."

He stepped inside, hung his hat on a peg, and shrugged out of his duster and draped it on a hook—just as if he belonged there. He smelled of horse and leather and the faint hint of some kind of aftershave.

"Did you come to see Uncle Mason?"

Dusty shook his head and grinned, sending her heart into spasms.

"Seems we have this conversation every time I show up. I came to see you."

Katie didn't want to consider that she was actually glad he'd come to see her. She motioned him into the parlor and closed the front door.

Rebekah peeked out of the kitchen. "We got company?"

"It's just Dusty. He came to see me."

Her aunt's eyebrows lifted, and an ornery grin tugged at her lips. "Oh, I see. It's chilly out. I'll just fix you two some hot tea."

"I imagine he'd prefer coffee." Katie darted a glance at Dusty, and he nodded his head.

"Coffee it is." Rebekah disappeared back into the kitchen.

Katie ambled into the parlor, wondering how she knew Dusty wanted coffee instead of tea. Perhaps it was just that manly look of his that made her think he was a coffee drinker.

She motioned to Dusty to sit down and took a seat across from him. His long form looked awkward in the small side chair. "So, what brings you here today?"

Dusty glanced at the package in his lap. "I. . .uh. . .got to thinking about what you said about wanting to ask the dressmaker for some work. Trust me, I understand your desire for independence."

Katie watched him, wondering where this was leading. Seeing a tough lawman blushing was rather enchanting.

"Well, the truth is, I need some new shirts, and I can't find store-bought ones that fit since I have long arms. I got some cloth and was hoping I could hire you to make a couple."

Katie stared at him, stunned by the thoughtfulness of his offer. He wouldn't take her to town, but he brought some business to her. "I. . .well, sure! I'd be happy to. Show me what you've got in your package." She couldn't help grinning.

He untied the twine, and the paper crackled as it fell open to reveal a soft blue denim and a stark white cotton fabric. Katie crossed the room and fingered the cloth.

"This should do nicely." On top of the fabric lay a colorful tin box. "What's in that?"

Dusty's bronze cheeks took on a dark rosy shade. "I told Mrs. Whitaker at the mercantile how you lost everything in the fire, and she gathered some sewing tools she thought you would need. Consider it a gift from me for all the trouble I caused you."

She blinked. Who was this man? Why was he treating her so kindly after she'd been so mean to him? Guilt washed over her, making her realize how rude and unmannerly she'd been. She swallowed the lump in her throat and fought the tears in her eyes. Turning away, she stared out the window to gather her composure.

The settee squeaked as Dusty rose. She could feel him standing behind her.

"I'm sorry if I upset you. It wasn't my intent."

Katie closed her eyes. The concern in his voice was for her. Never once did Allan voice apprehension on her part. How could she have been so blind about him?

With her emotions under control, she turned to face Dusty. She owed him the truth. "You didn't upset me. I was just moved by your thoughtfulness."

Relief softened his gaze. Katie eased around him, her insides quivering like warm custard at being so close to him.

"Let's just see what's in that box. I'll need to measure you if I'm going to make those shirts." She pulled off the lid, and excitement coursed through her. The box held a shiny new pair of scissors, threads of all colors, a whole package of needles, a thimble, buttons, and a measuring tape. "Oh my, this is wonderful! But it's too much." She turned around. "You must let me make one shirt to pay you back for all these supplies."

Dusty shook his head. "No, they're a gift. I'll pay for the shirts."

"But—"

He held up his big callused hand. "No buts. Or I'll take my business elsewhere."

Dishes clinked as Rebekah entered the room. "It's a pleasure to see you again, Mr. McIntyre."

"Look what he brought." Katie held out the tin box. "I'm going to make him some shirts."

Rebekah set the tray of coffee and cookies on the round table in front of the window. "How nice. That will keep you busy and out of my hair for a while." She smiled. "Well, I'll let you get back to your business."

"Thank you." Dusty nodded at Rebekah on her way out of the parlor.

"Let me measure you; then we'll take refreshment."

"All right."

Katie stretched the tape along Dusty's arms, noticing that he was correct in his assessment. He did have longer arms than an average man. She stood in front of him, trying to figure out how to best measure around him. "Hold up your arms so I can size your chest."

He did as he was told, but his cheeks looked a tad more flushed than normal. Katie held one end of the tape measure in the hand with the cast and leaned forward, running the tape behind Dusty's back. For a split second her cheek rested against his chest, and she could hear the steady beat of his heart. Her hands shook, and her mouth went dry. She noted the size, quickly moved away, and jotted the numbers on a piece of paper. Stepping behind him, she measured his shoulders across the back and the length the shirt needed to be.

"So, how do you come by the name McIntyre? Isn't that Irish?" she asked, hoping he wouldn't notice her nervousness.

Dusty cleared his throat and lowered his arms. "My father came from Scotland years ago, and his family moved to Kansas. After awhile, Dad got itchy feet and decided to travel south. He didn't get very far. Fell in love with the daughter of a Cherokee chief and married her."

Intrigued, Katie motioned him to sit; then she served the coffee. "So you're half Cherokee. That explains your coloring."

Dusty nodded and sipped his coffee. "I wondered if your uncle might have Indian blood."

Katie sat down and shook her head. "I don't believe so. I've always heard he's part French."

He shrugged. "I just wondered."

Katie picked up the fabric. "So you want a shirt from the denim and the white cotton, but what about this?" She held up a soft, light blue flannel. "A nightshirt, perhaps?"

Dusty eye's widened, and he looked as if he'd choked on his cookie. "No! That's for the baby." If his cheeks hadn't been red before, they sure were now.

Katie bit back a grin at his embarrassment, then realized what he said. "I can't accept another gift from you, no matter how kind it is. It simply wouldn't be proper."

This time Dusty grinned, making cornmeal mush of her emotions. "I didn't say it was for you. It's for the baby. And I can give the baby a gift if I want to."

Katie studied the man before her. She'd been so wrong about him.

Chapter 8

A week later, Dusty rode up to the Danfield barn and reined Shadow to a halt. The front door of the house banged, and the saddle creaked as he twisted toward the noise. Nathan jumped off the porch, ignoring the steps, and Nick followed.

"I'm gonna git you, ya mangy outlaw," Nick yelled at his brother.

"Nuh-uh. I'm Jesse James, and you can't catch me." Nathan dodged around the water trough, then made a wide arc around Shadow's hind end.

Dusty tightened the reins. Shadow was a steady mount but not used to noisy little boys.

Nathan smiled and waved as he ran by. "Howdy, Dusty."

"Ma said to call him Mr. McAtire," Nick countered as he and his brother plowed to a stop beside Shadow.

Dusty bit back a smile at the mispronunciation of his name. He dismounted and held the reins loose while Shadow drank from the trough.

"Well, I cain't say that." Nathan blew out a breath that lifted his straight bangs in the air.

"You boys reckon you could tend to my horse in exchange for a peppermint stick?"

The twins' eyes widened, and they nodded. "Boy, howdy!"

Dusty smiled. How did they always manage to reply in the same way at exactly the same time? "No more water for him, though. At least not for a while."

"We know." Nathan held out his hand.

Dusty laid the reins across the boy's little palm. He pulled the sack of candy from his pocket and handed two red-and-white-striped sticks to Nick. "You be in charge of these since Nathan has Shadow."

Nick nodded and licked his lips as his hand closed around the candy.

Mason moseyed out of the barn and smiled when he saw Dusty. "You boys can put that horse in the third stall. And don't overfeed him." He lifted his hand in greeting. "Howdy."

Dusty closed the distance between them and shook Mason's hand. "Afternoon."

Mason eyed him until Dusty squirmed. What was he looking at?

"I halfway expected to see you two days ago."

Dusty blinked, wondering if he'd missed an appointment. "The marshal had me escort a forger he had in jail up to Tulsa. I just got back last night. Why were you expecting me?"

"You mean you don't know?"

Dusty searched his mind but had no idea what Mason was talking about. He shook his head.

Mason's whole face lit up like a child peeking in his Christmas stocking. "Katie had the baby. I guess Marshal White forgot to tell you."

All manner of emotions swarmed Dusty at the same time. This baby was alive because he had rescued Katie. On the other hand, the child would have been born in its own home if not for the fire caused by Dusty's charging in and capturing Sloane. At least the baby wouldn't be raised by a ruthless outlaw.

"It's an amazing thing when a child is born," Mason said, probably misinterpreting his silence for awe.

"Yes, you're right. I probably should come back another day to give Katie time to rest up. I just wanted to see if she'd had a chance to sew up one of my shirts, but it sounds like she's been busy with other things."

"I believe she managed to get one done." Mason clapped him on the shoulder. "Let's go ask her. Maybe you can see the baby if he's awake."

Dusty walked beside Mason. "He?"

"Yep, she had a son. That's what she wanted—a son to carry on Jarrod's name."

"That's good. How's she doing?" Dusty hoped he wasn't crossing too many rules of propriety with his personal questions, but the Danfield family didn't seem too big on those rules.

"Great." Mason chuckled and glanced at Dusty with a twinkle in his dark eyes. "Nathan was disappointed to discover Katie had swallowed a baby instead of a pumpkin."

Dusty laughed, imaging the boy's confounded expression. He followed Mason into the house, where they shed their hats and coats, then meandered down the hall and into the kitchen. Rebekah and Deborah both looked up and smiled.

Rebekah wiped her hands on her apron and crossed the room. "Welcome, Mr. McIntyre. Come to see the baby?"

Dusty nodded. The fragrant scents and cozy atmosphere of the crowded kitchen made him long for a home of his own. For now, he was satisfied to live with the widower marshal and save money, but down the road, he'd like to get a little place of his own.

"Deborah, would you please tell Katie she has company?"

The young girl nodded, skirted around Dusty with a whimsical grin tilting her lips, and disappeared into the hall. The kitchen door thudded open, and the twins charged in, both talking at once.

Rebekah grinned and looked at Dusty. "Why don't you wait in the parlor?

It's much quieter there."

Dusty stood in the parlor a few minutes later, looking out a large window. South of the barn, he could see Josh chopping wood and could hear the dull thud as he tossed the split sections into a pile. Mason must have put the twins to work, because they were now stacking the chopped wood against the side of the barn.

Behind him, he heard footsteps and turned. A much slimmer version of Katie strolled in, followed by Deborah carrying the baby. Katie smiled, and his heart flip-flopped. She had never looked so beautiful. Her blue dress matched her eyes, but it was the glow emanating from her face that choked off his breath.

"It was so nice of you to come see us." Katie slowly eased down onto the settee, and Deborah handed her the baby, then quietly left the room.

Katie patted the cushion beside her. "Come sit beside me so you can hold Joey."

Dusty knew his eyes must have widened about as far as possible. He shook his head. "Uh. . .no, ma'am. I never held a baby before."

"Then it's time you know what it feels like. Come sit down, Dusty."

When she said his name like that, he could do nothing but obey. He dropped down beside her, trying to maintain a proper distance on the narrow settee. Katie unwound the blanket that enshrouded the baby. The infant squeaked, a tiny fist popped out, and the child stretched.

Dusty's heart pranced in his chest as he watched the little boy. This child's round face slightly resembled Katie's, and his fuzzy blond hair reminded Dusty of a duckling.

She lifted the baby and handed him to Dusty. His hands trembled as he took the light bundle.

"This is Jarrod Joseph Hoffman Jr. But we call him Joey."

Her smile and the warmth in her eyes stirred something in Dusty that he hadn't felt in a long while. Worried that his big, rough hands would scratch the baby, he moved with caution.

"Support his neck with your left hand and his hind end with your right."

Dusty did as she suggested but held the baby away from his shirt. The child jumped and flung his arms out, nearly causing Dusty to drop him. He darted a gaze at Katie.

"Babies prefer to be held closely. Put Joey's head in the crook of your arm and cuddle him against your chest."

As Dusty tucked the baby against his shirt, he wondered again if he'd have been a father by now if Emily had lived. He studied Joey's cute, expressive face, and a deep longing for a family of his own enveloped him. Dusty thought he'd given up wanting a family, but in that second, he knew the truth. He wanted it all—a home, a wife, and children.

Katie held her breath as Dusty hugged Joey to his chest. The longing in his eyes made her heart ache. She knew if she didn't get ahold of herself, she'd be in tears again. Aunt Rebekah said it was the natural way of things for a woman to cry a lot after a birthing.

She dashed to her feet, and Dusty looked up, bewildered. "I'll be right back. I need to get something."

If he hadn't looked so nervous, she might have laughed at his expression.

"You can't leave me here with—him. I wouldn't know what to do if he started crying."

Katie pressed her lips together at seeing this big, capable man floundering at holding a baby.

"Just jiggle him a little if he fusses. I'll be right back."

"No, Katie, wait—"

She rushed out of the parlor and slowly climbed the stairs to her bedroom, savoring her name on his tongue. She liked the sound of it way more than she should. In her room, she found the denim shirt she'd finished and pressed for Dusty and then made her way back downstairs.

As she entered the parlor, she heard Dusty talking and expected to see someone with him, but instead, she found him cooing softly to Joey. The baby stared at him with wide-eyed fascination.

For a fleeting second, a shiver of remorse coursed through her. Jarrod should be holding his child instead of this stranger. Katie closed her eyes and pushed away the angry thought. Nothing could change the past, and like it or not, Dusty had saved her life and Joey's. At the least, she owed him her kindness and gratitude. Putting her anger aside, she had to admit she was starting to like the quiet man. He reminded her of Uncle Mason.

He looked up, and relief flooded his eyes. "Good. You're back."

"Looks to me like you're doing just fine." Katie smiled and checked on her son. He wiggled as if he wanted Dusty's attention again.

"Well, what do you think?" She shook out the denim shirt and looked at Dusty, wondering if he'd be pleased.

His eyes lit up, and she watched his gaze travel down the length of the sleeve. "That looks mighty fine. If you'll just take back your baby, I can get the coins I have in my pocket."

Katie grinned this time. He might enjoy holding the baby in private, but this tough deputy marshal didn't want to seem too soft in public. She folded the shirt and laid it on the coffee table, wishing she could ask Dusty to try it on but knowing that wouldn't be proper. She'd like to make sure the sleeves were long enough before she cut out the other one.

After settling back onto the settee, she reached out, and Dusty laid Joey in her arms. Katie tried to ignore the way her heart pitter-pattered when Dusty brushed against her arm.

He heaved a sigh that she was sure was relief. He stood and pulled two gold dollars from his pocket and set them on the table.

His boots thudded on the rag rug as he paced across the room. With his hands on his hips, he stared out the window. Disappointment surged through Katie. Did he dislike being near her that much?

Dusty stood tall and straight. Wide shoulders angled down to a narrow waist and long legs. His straight, dark hair hung past his collar in an appealing manner. Where Jarrod had been solid and stocky, Dusty was long and lean. She couldn't help being curious about him. And curiosity had gotten her into more trouble as a child than any of her other traits. She was tired of wondering why he was tracking Ed Sloane—or if he had a wife somewhere—or why he kept coming to see her.

"So, Dusty, do you have a family somewhere waiting on your return?"

Dusty's back stiffened, and he remained quiet so long she thought he wasn't going to answer. Finally he shook his head. "No."

She barely heard his soft whisper. Determined to plod through the rock-hard soil of Dusty's past, she considered her next question. "You told me you spent a year and a half hunting down Al—I mean, Ed Sloane. Can I ask why? It just seems to me most lawmen would have given up a long time ago.

Dusty spun around, his mouth puckered and eyes blazing. "Not if that man had burnt down your home and killed your wife." His fists clenched so tight that his knuckles paled. He glanced down at Joey, and his expression quickly relaxed.

Confusion and pain muddled Katie's thoughts. It was true then. Ed Sloane really was a murderer. Dusty had saved her from making the worst mistake of her life. Losing her home was a small price to pay.

As she considered Dusty's words, surprise shot through Katie at the similarity of their experiences. She had been so wrong when she said he didn't know what she was feeling. Her angry statement that day must have hurt Dusty terribly. Compassion swirled through her, knowing he'd lost his spouse just as she had. "I'm so sorry. I didn't know."

He turned away and stared out the window again. "So now you can see that I do understand what you're going through and why I'm sorry for all the trouble I've caused you."

She wanted so much to go to his side, but with her hand still in the cast, she refused to carry Joey while she was walking. "Dusty, please look at me."

❧

Dusty was ready to bolt like a captured mustang that had broken its restraints. He wanted to walk out the door and ride off on Shadow, but he didn't want to be rude. He hated the pain of remembering. But as much as it hurt to talk about

Emily and Sloane, in an odd way, it felt good. He turned to face Katie, and the sympathy in her gaze took his breath away.

"I'm so sorry for all the mean things I said to you." She looked away for a moment, then faced him. "People say things in anger when they are hurting. I blamed you for the fire—"

He winced at her words, knowing he was to blame for all her troubles.

"That was wrong. You weren't the one to knock over the lamp. You weren't even in the house when it happened."

He blinked, considering her words, and searched his mind, realizing she was telling the truth. There had been no lamp near the window that he dove through when he followed Sloane. He didn't start the fire. Sighing, he felt as if an anvil had been lifted off his chest.

"The truth is, I owe my life to you—and Joey's life." Katie stared up at him, sincerity blazing in her gaze. "And you kept me from making the horrible mistake of marrying—Ed Sloane."

She looked as if she could barely voice the words.

The remorse and condemnation he'd felt the past few weeks melted away. As he considered her words, he recognized the truth in them. He studied Katie as she watched her baby.

He admired her spirit and stubborn determination. She was lovely to look at with all that golden hair and her pretty eyes—even more so now that she was no longer tossing angry glares his way. She glanced up at him, making his heart skip.

"So, you see, you've helped me so much. I feel bad for the way I treated you. Will you please forgive me?"

Dusty didn't know how to respond. It was God's business to forgive, not his. But how could he resist those pleading eyes? He nodded, instantly rewarded with her glowing gaze.

Her bright smile broke down the walls of his heart, and he knew then that he cared more for her than he should.

He turned away again and stared out the window. "Thank you for making the shirt. It looks real nice." In truth, he couldn't imagine how she had managed to sew a whole shirt with her hand in a cast. That stubborn independence of hers was a driving force.

"You're quite welcome. After you get a chance to try it on, let me know how it fits. I'll wait to cut out the other one until I'm sure this one fits all right."

"Sure. That sounds sensible."

His heart soared, knowing he had a legitimate excuse to ride out and see Katie again, but he clamped down his emotions. He'd decided a long time ago that he didn't want to experience again the pain of losing someone he loved. He had to distance himself from Katie, yet he felt compelled to care for her.

Dusty hated these tugging emotions pulling him in two different directions.

The cast would surely come off in a few weeks. Until then, he'd maintain his distance and think up some other way to help Katie. But he wouldn't let his heart get any more involved. He'd help her until she was free of her cast. Then he'd ride off and try to forget about her.

Chapter 9

Dusty sat at the marshal's desk and studied the latest WANTED posters. It had been two weeks since he'd ridden out to the Danfield farm and seen Joey and retrieved his denim shirt. Looking down, he fingered the fabric and wondered if Katie had gone ahead and finished his other shirt even though he'd never told her how well the first one fit. He wanted to ride out and see her but knew he had to stay away if he was going to keep his heart intact.

The door creaked open, and a shadow darkened the doorway a moment before Mason walked in. Dusty smiled, happy to see the man again. He stood and held out his hand.

"Good to see you, Mason. What brings you to town?"

Mason solidly gripped his hand and smiled. "Jimmy's still down in Texas, and I needed some supplies."

Dusty waved his hand toward the empty chair in front of the window. He glanced outside, making sure things were quiet, then sat down in his chair.

Mason narrowed his eyes. "Why haven't you been out to the farm lately? Been busy?"

Dusty sighed, not wanting to talk about Katie and his feelings, but he couldn't lie. "No, things have been pretty quiet around here."

"Katie's missed you coming around."

Lifting his eyebrows, he looked at Mason, hoping he'd elaborate.

"She thinks maybe she scared you off because she asked about your past. Is that true?"

Mason's pointed question threw Dusty off guard. Though Mason was an honorable, God-fearing man, he didn't understand the depth of Dusty's pain. He didn't know how it felt to walk away from God and not be able to find your way back.

Mason stuck his feet out, crossed his ankles, and laced his fingers together behind his head, looking like he planned to stay for a while. "Let me tell you a story. I bet you didn't know that Rebekah is my second wife."

Dusty blinked, trying to imagine Mason married to someone else.

"A little over twenty years ago, I had a farm up St. Louis way. My sister and her husband owned the farm next to us. One day my wife and sister rode off in a wagon to help care for a sick neighbor. It started to rain while they were gone, and on the way home, they were crossing a low water bridge—" Mason closed his eyes as if remembering hurt him.

He looked at Dusty again. "They must have been in the middle of the river when a flash flood swept through. We found their bodies downstream near one of the dead horses. The wagon had broken apart, and most of it was gone."

Mason sat up and leaned forward. "Annie—my wife—was seven months pregnant with our first child."

Dusty's mouth went dry as he absorbed Mason's story. The man had experienced losing his wife, too. His pregnant wife. And his sister.

"Danielle, my sister, left behind two children—Jimmy and Katie. Jimmy was seven, and Katie only three. I buried the two women I loved most on this earth, sold my farm, and traveled to the Oklahoma Territory to find my brother-in-law, Jake. He was a low-life scoundrel who'd abandoned Danielle, preferring adventure over family."

Mason sighed and tightened his lips. "I was hurting so bad that I was determined to deliver Jimmy and Katie into his care, even though I'd been more a father to them than Jake ever had. Then I planned to head west and forget all those I'd ever loved."

"Wow, that's some story." Dusty ran his hand through his hair, feeling as if he should say something more comforting, but not knowing what.

"It's not a story. It's the truth. Jake talked me into riding in the Guthrie land rush. He got land, but I didn't. Afterwards, I was ready to leave town, though leaving the kids behind was about to do me in. Jimmy barely knew Jake, and Katie didn't remember him at all."

Dusty leaned forward with his elbows on the desk, engrossed in the tale. "So what happened? Obviously you didn't ride west."

"Jake approached me in the street. Said he wanted to talk to me. At the same time, an old man started hollering about how Jake had swindled him. The next thing I knew, Jake was shot and dying in my arms. Before he died, he pulled out the deed to his land and asked me to take care of the kids. After he died, I looked at the deed. Jake had put the land in my name instead of his."

"Whew! So what did you do?"

Mason settled back in his chair. "By then, I'd met Rebekah and fallen in love with her. But when I got back from the land run, I discovered she'd left town. I went after her. Rescued her from a couple of no-goods in Wichita, married her, and brought her back here. But before that, I had to let go of my anger. I was furious with Jake for abandoning his family. And mad at God for allowing Annie and Danielle to die. The pain was almost unbearable at first."

Dusty sat back, analyzing how similar their stories were. A spark of hope flamed to life. If Mason had found his way back to God, there must be hope for him, too. "How did you get past it all?"

"Falling in love with Rebekah helped. But I came to a point where I had to let go of my anger. Holding on to it was only hurting me—and nearly cost me the woman I was growing to love. I still don't know why God allowed what happened, but I would have never met Rebekah or had the family and life I have now if Annie hadn't died. We only see a speck of what's happening in our lives, but God sees the whole picture. I had to believe that He was watching my back. That's what you need to believe, too."

Dusty knew Mason was right, but how could he turn loose of his anger? It was what drove him to be who he was. And he couldn't get past the nagging question that haunted him: Why would God forgive a man who turned his back on Him just because life bucked him from the saddle?

Mason stood and stretched. "Well, don't be a stranger. We've all taken a liking to you. Come on out for dinner sometime and see how much Joey is growing. Katie would like to see you—oh, and she's got that other shirt ready. I offered to bring it to you, but she said no."

Mason grinned and moseyed out the door, not waiting for a response. The door clicked shut, and the sounds of the street faded. Dusty considered his words. He liked Mason and trusted him. But Mason had never hated anyone as much as Dusty had Ed Sloane.

No, surely God wouldn't welcome him in His house, but maybe Katie would.

⁓

"I can't believe how much Joey has grown since I last saw him."

Katie watched as Dusty held the baby against his chest. Her bright-eyed son made an O with his lips and stared up at him. Dusty put his finger against Joey's fingers, and the babe grasped it tightly.

He glanced wide-eyed at Katie. "Got quite a grip."

His smile tickled her belly. "Yes, but that's natural. All babies do that."

Rebekah walked in and set a tray of coffee and slices of cake on the table in front of the settee. "We're so glad to have you visit again, Mr. McIntyre."

Dusty peeked up at her. "Please call me Dusty."

Rebekah smiled. "All right then, Dusty. But you must call me Rebekah. Mason is finishing up in the barn and should be in soon. He'll be happy to see you again."

"I saw him when I rode in. Offered to help, but he said he and Josh could handle things."

"Well, I need to go help Deborah get the twins in bed. You and Katie go ahead and enjoy your cake and coffee. I'll be back in a little while."

Katie watched Dusty talk to her aunt. She enjoyed watching his lips and the way his mouth moved. When he looked down at Joey, his thick, dark lashes fanned his tanned cheeks, and his straight, coffee-colored hair hung down over his forehead. He'd often brush it back with his hand, but the straight strands seemed to have a mind of their own.

Dusty glanced up and caught her staring. Her heart stampeded, but she couldn't look away. His gaze held hers, and she read the longing that she felt herself. Finally, she turned her head and stared at the sunset. Pinks and oranges wafted across the navy blue sky, silhouetting the barn in a dark shadow.

Now that she'd gotten over being angry with Dusty, she feared she was falling for him. How could she trust her heart after succumbing to the charms of an outlaw?

But Dusty was nothing like Ed Sloane. He was an honorable, law-upholding citizen.

Katie hated the confusion swarming in her mind. Was it possible to fall in love this quickly? Had she stayed angry with him so she wouldn't admit her true feelings?

Katie rose from her chair, pushing aside the unwanted thoughts. "You can lay Joey against the back of the settee so you can eat your cake. He doesn't turn over yet, so he'll be fine."

Dusty looked unsure but did as she suggested, making sure Joey was nestled safely against the back of the settee before he let go. His caution with her son made her value him more. If only she could trust her heart.

❧

Dusty savored the spicy apple cake as his eyes feasted on Katie. Her face had filled out a bit, and she didn't look as tired as she had right after having the baby. She took a small bite of cake and licked her lips, making him wish he had the right to pull her into his arms.

Would she accept his kisses?

She glanced up from her plate, checked on Joey, and then smiled at Dusty. He looked away, not wanting to think about what that smile did to his insides.

Why did he keep coming back here and torturing himself? Even if he carried affections for Katie, nothing could come of it. He quickly finished his cake and swallowed down his coffee. It had been a mistake to come here.

She'd gotten over being angry with him, but the warm look in her eyes made him wonder if she was beginning to care for him. He couldn't continue to lead her on.

Nothing could come of their relationship other than friendship. He wouldn't allow it. To care for Katie meant he had to release his anger over Emily's death—and that wasn't something he was prepared to do.

Dusty stood, then realized he'd left Joey unsupervised and sat back down. Katie stared at him. "I should be heading out. It's nearly dark, and I've got a ways to ride."

Disappointment filled her eyes. "I suppose you're right. If you can sit there with Joey for a minute, I'll run upstairs and get your other shirt."

He nodded, and she flitted out of the room. Joey squeaked, so Dusty lifted up the baby and held him out in front of him. Making sure nobody was looking, he smacked his lips together. Joey turned his head and settled down, gazing intently at Dusty.

"You're some little fellow; you know it? Katie's mighty lucky to have you."

Moisture gathered in his eyes, and he blinked it away. He would have loved to have had a child, but if he had, he never would have tracked down and captured Sloane. And if ever there was a man who needed to be locked up in jail, it was he. Things were the way they were meant to be, and "what ifs" wouldn't change that.

Katie entered the parlor, holding his shirt up in front of her. "What do you think?"

He stood, cradling Joey in one arm, and nodded his approval of the finely constructed garment. Deborah followed Katie into the room and took the baby.

"I'll go change him for you, Katie. Good evening, Mr. McIntyre."

He watched Katie's cousin glide out of the parlor, taking Joey with her and leaving his arms empty. Dusty crossed the room, digging some coins from his pocket. He handed the money to Katie and held the shirt up between them. "Very nice. This will look good with my vest. Do you suppose you could make me another one?"

He lowered the shirt and saw Katie smiling at him. "Yes, I'd be happy to. I get my cast off next week, so it should be a lot easier and quicker."

Glancing at the cast, he wondered if it pained her to work on his shirts. "There's no rush. It can wait until you get the cast off."

"Well, I'll have to wait until you bring the fabric anyway."

He gazed into her eyes and watched the amusement die away as he stared at her. She didn't look away but licked her lips, making him want to yank her into his arms and kiss her until she forgot all about Ed Sloane and her late husband.

Her warm breath tickled his face, and he took a step closer. Kissing her would be a huge mistake, but it would be worth it. Her eyes widened as he leaned forward, but she didn't move away.

Dusty closed his eyes.

A loud thud sounded at the front door, making him jump. Katie moved back as the door banged open.

Josh ran past the parlor entrance, skidded to a halt, and dashed back. "It's Pa. He's hurt!"

Chapter 10

"S tay here," Dusty ordered Katie, as he charged out the door after Josh. He heard Katie sputter, but she didn't argue or follow him.

"What happened?" Dusty asked as he ran beside Josh.

"Loading bales—in the loft. Some fell—on Pa."

The frantic look in Josh's eyes told Dusty the boy was scared. They raced to the barn and through the open doors. Dust and stems of hay still sprinkled down from where Mason and Josh had been stacking bales in the loft.

Close to a dozen bales lay haphazardly in a pile, and somewhere, Mason was buried beneath them. The horses in their stalls nickered and stamped their hooves. Dusty grabbed the first bale and slung it aside, ignoring how the binder twine bit into his hands.

Josh tossed him a pair of gloves. Dusty slipped them on and yanked another bale off the pile. Behind him, he heard someone running in their direction. Josh tugged and heaved a bale to the side, revealing a boot. Dusty heard a gasp behind him and looked over his shoulder. Rebekah watched with one hand over her mouth, her eyes wide with concern.

Dusty flung aside another of the heavy bales. He moved around to where Mason's head should be and jerked off two more bundles. Rebekah set the lantern on a wooden crate and moved to Josh's side to help him.

Dusty heard a groan and pulled off another bale, revealing Mason's head and shoulders. Mason coughed but didn't look up. Quickly, they removed the last few bales covering him.

Rebekah darted to his side and knelt in the hay. "Mason, honey, are you all right?"

Mason lifted his head, coughed, and grimaced.

Rebekah pulled little stems of hay from his dirty hair and brushed off his shoulders. "Tell me where you hurt."

"My side. Broken rib, maybe." Mason tried to push up but collapsed on the ground. "Got the wind knocked out."

"Can you move your legs?" Dusty hoped his friend wasn't seriously hurt, but he suspected Mason had more than one broken rib judging by the pain etched on his face.

Mason wiggled his feet, then moaned.

"We need to get him back to the house." Rebekah glanced up at Dusty. "Do you think you and Josh can carry him?"

"No, I can walk." Mason attempted to push up on his hands.

Dusty stooped and lifted Mason's arm over his shoulder, knowing it must pain him, but the act would allow Mason to keep his dignity in front of his family. Josh hurried to the other side, and they slowly made their way toward the house.

❧

"I can't thank you enough for staying at the farm and helping us while Uncle Mason mends." Katie lifted her head and peered out from beneath her sunbonnet, her sparkling blue eyes revealing her gratitude.

"I'm just glad things were quiet in town and Marshal White said he could do without me for a few days." Dusty clicked his tongue in his cheek and urged the team of horses to pick up their pace. The outline of Guthrie appeared on the horizon as they topped the hill.

For the past week he'd helped around the Danfield farm while Mason recovered. Thankfully, Mason's ribs had only been bruised and not broken, but he did have a concussion. Rebekah's and Katie's hands had been full trying to keep the restless farmer in bed so he could heal properly.

Dusty had been thrilled when Rebekah suggested he take Katie to Guthrie for the big fall festival.

As they followed other wagons into town, excitement coursed through Dusty at spending the day with Katie at the big gathering. He glanced at Joey, sleeping quietly in Katie's lap. The baby sucked his thumb, and his eyelids moved as if he were dreaming.

Contented warmth oozed through Dusty. He had tried to fight his growing attraction to Katie, but being around her daily and eating meals with her made it nearly impossible. Dare he dream that she might one day return his affections? And was it being disloyal to Emily to hope Katie might?

Katie fidgeted on the seat beside him as he pulled the team under one of the last unoccupied trees. "I'm so excited. I've always loved coming to town for big celebrations like this."

Her excitement was infectious, and he couldn't help smiling. It had been a long time—years even—since he felt so lighthearted.

"Don't let me forget to buy flannel before we leave. I need to make some more diapers for Joey. It seems like I'm doing laundry every day."

"You want me to carry Joey for a while?"

Katie nodded and handed the baby to him; then he helped her alight from the wagon. "I'm so glad Doc cut off my cast when he came out to check on Uncle Mason. My wrist is still a bit stiff, so it's a challenge to manage Joey and my long skirt." She twisted her arm in front of him as if to prove her point.

The townsfolk cast curious stares in their direction as they walked down the boardwalk. Dusty could only imagine what they were thinking. Many had known Katie all her life, and most knew him from his job as deputy marshal. He ushered Katie toward the mercantile. "Ever had one of those new soda pops?"

"Oh yes!" Her eyes sparkled with delight. Katie loosened her bonnet and tugged it off. "Jarrod and I tried one in Claremont. It was delicious. And so bubbly."

Dusty peered out the corner of his eye at Katie. Mentioning her deceased husband hadn't seemed to dampen her enthusiasm. He breathed a sigh of relief. He didn't want anything to spoil this day.

After drinking a soda at the mercantile, they meandered around the booths and shops. The morning sped by as they watched the horse races and cheered on their favorite riders.

"Would you look at that!" Katie pointed at a trick roper and stared with her mouth open. "That's amazing."

The cowboy swung an eight-foot circle of lariat over his head. Then he lowered the loop and danced in and out of it, all the time keeping the rope spinning. Dusty nodded, impressed by the man's expertise, too.

Joey squirmed in Dusty's arms and started fussing. Katie studied the ground, a nice blush tinting her face. "I probably should change him and find somewhere to feed him."

Dusty could tell she was uncomfortable discussing the subject with him. "Let's go back to the wagon. It's shady there and probably about as quiet as any place in town."

Katie nodded and took his arm as he led her back to the wagon.

After fixing a blanket for Katie to rest on, Dusty moseyed through town. He'd seen signs of a rifle shoot at the far end of Guthrie and made his way over there, stopping at the marshal's office long enough to pick up his favorite Winchester. He'd always been an expert marksman, and a shooting contest was just the thing to take his mind off Katie for a time.

❧

"I still can't believe you won that beautiful quilt in the rifle shoot. I've always admired Maude Wilson's handiwork. Her quilts are the loveliest ones around these parts." Katie glanced at the colorful coverlet lying in the back of the wagon, then smiled at Dusty. She couldn't believe he'd given her something so nice. She probably shouldn't accept the gift but didn't want to hurt his feelings, and she desperately wanted the lovely Flying Geese quilt. "Are you sure you don't want to keep it?"

"No, I want you to have it. Too fancy for me." Dusty shook the reins and clicked his tongue to keep the team moving.

Katie tried to ignore the way her shoulder bumped against Dusty's whenever the wagon traveled through a rut in the road. She glanced at Joey, who lay in her lap, looking around. He stuck a finger in his mouth and frowned, probably realizing it wasn't his thumb. Love for her son bubbled up inside her.

With the sun behind her, she shed her bonnet and tossed it in the back of the wagon, allowing the light breeze to cool her. Though she hated leaving town before the evening festivities, they needed to get home before dark. She'd had a wonderful time and gotten the flannel she needed. She'd hoped to chat with the dressmaker; however, the woman's shop was closed, and Katie never saw Miss Petit in town. At least Dusty had picked out material for two more shirts.

Katie peeked sideways at him, noticing the pleasing way he filled out the denim shirt she'd made him. A shadow of dark stubble shaded his cheeks, and his hair hung just past his collar, giving him a wild, untamed look. No wonder the single women in town kept casting him shy glances. Dusty was a fine-looking man.

He'd spent the day with her, even though he could have his choice of women. That thought sent a shiver of delight surging through her.

Katie hid a yawn behind her hand. She'd had a nice time, but it was a long day for a woman who'd recently had a baby. She wanted to lay her head on Dusty's shoulder but resisted the temptation. Riding home like this felt almost as if they were a family returning from a pleasant day in town.

Dusty laid the reins across his leg, lifted his hat, and rubbed his brow. He looked sideways and caught her staring. His gaze held hers, and she couldn't look away. She stared into his searing black eyes, her heart stampeding.

Joey let out a squeal, and she broke the connection and glanced at her son.

What had just happened?

She lifted Joey onto her left shoulder, creating a barrier between her and Dusty.

Did Dusty feel what she did? And just exactly what did she feel?

Once she'd gotten over being angry with him, she realized what a kind, considerate man he was. She knew he only kept coming around because of his guilt over the fire and her injury, but she wished that he harbored an attraction to her like she felt for him.

Yet Dusty still loved his first wife. She could tell from the things he'd said to her. He held on to his anger over Emily's tragic death, just as she'd clung to her anger about the fire and her ruined wedding. But she'd been wrong to do so, and he needed to see that it was bad for him. Holding on to anger only hurt the one doing the holding. It had turned her into a grumpy, bitter person. But no more.

That night, after they returned to the farm and Joey had nursed and was asleep, Katie knelt down beside her bed.

"Father God, forgive me for all the anger I've harbored against Dusty. I know now that he was only doing his job and that he saved me from marrying an outlaw and making a horrible mistake. I was angry about the fire and losing my possessions, but You saved my life and my sweet son's. Thank You, Father.

And please help Dusty to turn loose of his anger and make peace with You."

❧

"That Deputy McIntyre is a mighty handsome man." Emmylou Tompkins batted her eyelashes in Dusty's direction. "You're fortunate to be keeping his company."

Katie watched Dusty darting back and forth, trying to corral the twins. They'd brought the children to church so that Mason and Rebekah could enjoy the morning alone. Uncle Mason was finally getting around again, but he couldn't do much yet. Aunt Rebekah feared the jarring of the wagon would set him back, so they'd stayed home from church.

Katie looked at Emmylou. "I'm not keeping company with Mr. McIntyre. He's helping out on the farm because my uncle got injured."

Emmylou flounced beside Katie. "Well, that's just my point. Why him? Why is the deputy marshal doing menial labor on your farm?"

Katie sighed. "It's a long story, and I don't want to get into it now."

Emmylou's lips puckered and twisted to one side. "Well, any of the unmarried women in town would gladly trade places with you."

The nosy woman didn't like being kept in the dark. Katie could only imagine what Emmylou would do if she knew that Katie had nearly married an outlaw. She tightened her lips to keep from giggling at the aghast expression that surely would have been on the woman's face.

Dusty strode toward her with a squirming, giggling twin under each arm. "Got these two hooligans corralled. Did you find Deborah?"

Katie peered across the churchyard to where her cousin stood holding Joey, surrounded by a group of chattering girls. Josh stood off to the side with two friends, feigning lack of interest and at the same time covertly watching the group of females. Katie sighed. Her cousins were growing up.

Dusty deposited the twins in the back of the wagon. "Now stay put until we get underway. I don't want to have to go hunting you down again."

Both wide-eyed boys sat down and stared at him. Katie wondered if they were surprised at this sterner version of Dusty. He'd used his lawman's voice to get the spirited boys under control, and it seemed to be working.

Katie allowed him to help her onto the wagon seat. She tied her bonnet strings under her chin and adjusted her skirts, ready to get home and out of the warmth of the Indian summer that had settled over the land. The wagon tilted and creaked as Dusty climbed up beside her. He let out a shrill whistle that made both her and the horses jump.

She gave him a questioning stare, and he grinned, sending her heart into spasms. He nodded his head toward the girls, and Katie saw that Deborah was walking toward them. "Civilized folk would simply walk over and tell Deborah it was time to leave."

He pushed back his western hat and looked at her, nudging his shoulder into hers. An ornery glint flashed in his eyes. "Who ever told you I was civilized?"

A delicious shiver snaked down Katie's spine. Dusty might like to believe he was as wild as a mustang, but she knew better. The man had a heart of gold, even if he'd never admit it.

Deborah handed Joey up to Dusty, who passed the baby to Katie. She cuddled her son and watched the clusters of church members break up and head for their wagons. Deborah climbed into the back of the wagon with Josh's assistance.

"I want to ride with Josh," Nick shouted.

"Nuh-uh. I want to." Nathan bounced to his feet and started to climb over the side.

Dusty turned around and stared at the boys, and they both sat back down. It amazed Katie how he could command the mischievous boys' obedience without even a word, when they'd barely listen to her and she'd known them all their lives.

"I don't mind if they take turns riding with me." Josh pulled his mare to a stop beside Dusty. "That is, if it's all right with you."

Dusty nodded. "Pick a number between one and twenty."

"Five." Nick jumped to his feet again.

"Ten." Nathan looked hopefully at Dusty.

"Nate wins. The number was twelve."

"Aw, no fair." Nick flopped down and crossed his arms.

"Nicholas David Danfield." Katie shot him a stern glare for his unruly response.

He ducked his head. "Sorry."

Nathan climbed on behind Josh and beamed his victory until Katie also gave him a look. Deborah pulled Nick against her side and started telling him a story as Dusty clucked to the horses.

"What did you think of the sermon?" Katie peered sideways at him.

"Good." He stared ahead, guiding the team around the McPherson and Robinson families, who stood beside the road, visiting. The women smiled and waved as they passed by. Dusty touched the brim of his hat.

Katie waved and smiled back. "Just good. That's all you have to say?"

"It's been a long time since I've been to church, and it felt good."

Katie stared at the dried prairie grass swaying in the warm breeze as the wagon rocked back and forth down the dirt road. Dusty's comment made her realize how little she really knew about him.

She couldn't deny her feelings had taken an unexpected turn. At some point, she'd grown to care for him. He was so kind it was hard not to care.

But she couldn't expect Dusty to hang around forever. One of these days, he would feel that he'd done enough penance and move on.

What would she do then?

She'd miss him, for sure.

She shouldn't be pondering on Dusty, but rather on how she was going to become independent again. She couldn't live with her aunt and uncle forever, no matter how loving and gracious they were. But how could a woman with a young child find work?

And what should she do about her feelings for Dusty?

Chapter 11

Katie crossed the small bedroom, jiggling Joey on her shoulder. The baby cried and cried. Aunt Rebekah thought he was colicky or possibly teething, though he was still a bit young for that. Katie had tried to nurse him, but Joey pushed away and fussed. He wasn't one to refuse a meal, so her concern mounted. She even tried rubbing his stomach, but that didn't work.

She cooed to her son, aching for him. After another ten minutes of walking and humming church hymns to him, Joey finally drifted off into a restless sleep. Her arms and back ached from standing and holding him so long. Did she dare try to lay him down?

When her arms and shoulders burned so much she was afraid she might drop her son, she carefully eased him into his cradle and covered him with a small quilt. Breathing a sigh of relief, she tiptoed out of the room and into the upstairs hallway.

"Yahoo! I'm gonna get ya, you mangy outlaw." Nathan barreled up the stairs, feet pounding on the wooden slats, right behind his brother, whose face was covered with a bandanna.

"You ain't catching me," Nick shouted over his shoulder. He dodged past Katie, and she grabbed his arm, then got ahold of Nathan.

"Hush!" she squealed in a loud whisper. "I just got Joey to sleep. And you know your mom doesn't want you running in the house."

"But I'm an outlaw, and I gotta get away." Nick shrugged out of her grasp and charged for the stairs.

"Let me go, Katie. I gotta catch that mangy varmint." Nathan twisted and squirmed, then pulled free, racing after his brother.

Katie held her breath, hoping and praying their ruckus didn't wake Joey. When he didn't cry, she tiptoed to the stairs. As her foot hit the first step, Joey squeaked. Katie closed her eyes and uttered a quick prayer for strength for herself and peace for her son. How did a new mother ever get anything done?

As Joey's crying intensified, she turned around and went back into the bedroom. Maybe if she took him outside he would quiet down. Carrying her son, Katie reentered the hallway but found Deborah blocking her path.

"Sorry, I was looking for the book I've been reading. Mom doesn't need me for a while, so I thought I'd read a chapter or two."

Katie stepped to her left at the same time Deborah did. She moved to the right side of the hall as her cousin did the same.

Deborah giggled. "Pa keeps saying this house is too small, and I think he's right. It wasn't so bad when you and Jimmy were gone, but it's crowded now that you're both home."

Katie knew Deborah was just stating the obvious, but her cousin's words cut her to the quick. Deb was right. Both Jimmy and Katie were grown adults and should be out on their own. She couldn't fault her brother, though. After getting wounded in the Spanish-American War, he'd come home to recuperate. Now that he was well, he couldn't seem to find a place to settle. He would stay here a few months and then just ride off without anyone knowing where he'd gone.

She hated that he was so restless and missed him terribly when he was gone, but she knew war changed people—and it had changed her brother.

With the flannel blanket secure around Joey, she felt a driving ache to find Jimmy. He'd returned two days ago but had been so busy she hadn't had time to have a good chat with him.

She looked in the kitchen and found it empty, then peeked in Rebekah and Mason's bedroom and found her aunt sitting in her chair in the corner of the room, sound asleep with a book on her chest. Katie hurried away lest Joey fuss and wake her.

Outside, she saw the boys running around the barn. One would think they'd need a nap by the hectic pace they kept, but Rebekah had given up when they turned four. It became such a battle to keep the active boys in their beds for a half-hour rest that she and Rebekah needed an hour-long nap to recover. At least the boys collapsed at night once in bed.

The barn door was open, so Katie wandered in, hoping to find Jimmy. She heard someone moving around in the loft and glanced up. "Who's up there?"

Jimmy peered down and smiled. "Hey, sis. Whatcha doing?"

"Walking Joey. He has been fussing all afternoon. How about you?"

"I'm just rearranging these hay bales so we can get some more up here."

"Can you take a break and talk to me for a few minutes?"

Jimmy swiped his arm across his forehead. "Sure. I could use a short rest." He grabbed a rope hanging from the ceiling and shinnied down. "What's wrong with my nephew? I could hear him crying clear out here."

Katie sighed. "I wish I knew." She looked at Joey and realized he'd fallen back asleep.

"Let's sit on the porch." Jimmy's boots thudded on the hard dirt floor as he walked out of the barn.

"Where are Uncle Mason and Josh?" Katie asked.

Jimmy stopped at the well and took a swig of water from the bucket. "They're out in the field, loading more hay in the wagon."

"Should Uncle Mason be doing such difficult work so soon after his accident?"

Jimmy shrugged. "I offered to do it, but you know how stubborn he is. Rebekah should be glad he rested up a whole week. That's nothing short of a miracle."

"Just goes to show you how badly he was hurt. Plus Dusty was here to help out until you got back."

Jimmy lowered himself into the porch rocker, dusted off his shirt, and reached for Joey. Katie eyed his shirt and dirty hands.

"Aw, c'mon, sis. It's just hay. I promise I haven't shoveled any manure today."

Katie winced, then laid her son in her brother's arms. Jimmy loved kids and would make a great dad someday. If only he could get over his wanderlust.

"Are you planning to stay long?" She sat in the rocker next to him and watched Jimmy's face.

He looked at Joey with a hunger that surprised her. Then he gazed off into the distance. She followed his stare and saw the twins galloping in the field toward their father. She felt a pang of regret that she wasn't watching them better, but then nobody could keep up with those two.

"I'm not sure how long I'll stay. I probably ought to be finding a place of my own before too long."

"You could always come live with me."

Jimmy looked at her, a lopsided grin pulling at one cheek. "I am living with you."

"Oh, you know what I mean." She smacked him on his arm.

"I'm guessing you mean your farm. Last I heard, you didn't have a house to live in."

"Maybe you could rebuild it?"

Jimmy pressed his lips together and stared at Joey. "I don't know, sis. I've heard there's talk of an oil strike up near Tulsa. I've been thinking of heading up there and seeing if I can find work."

"Tulsa! But that's at least two days' ride."

"Not by train."

"Well, no, but who has the money for a train? I sure don't." Katie hiked her chin, hurt that her brother wanted to leave again.

Jimmy laid his head back and closed his eyes.

She had no right to stop him if he wanted to go to Tulsa. And as much as she loved her family, she'd leave, too, if she had a choice. An eighteen-year-old woman had no business mooching off her relatives. And as crowded as her aunt and uncle's home was, she knew it would be a blessing to her family if she weren't there.

But where could she go?

If only Dusty returned her affections. Maybe they could—no. She'd come close once to marrying a man she'd only known a few months, and here she was toying with the idea of marrying a man she'd known only a few weeks. Was she daft?

But wasn't this different? God had brought Dusty into her life. Then again, hadn't she thought the same thing about Allan?

Katie sighed and leaned her head back against the rocker. Life was so complicated at times. How could her feelings for Dusty have grown so quickly? A few weeks ago she despised him, but now he claimed a chunk of her heart. If she moved away, she'd never see him again, and that thought hurt as much as losing her farmhouse to the fire had. But she couldn't live with her aunt and uncle forever.

She looked toward the cloudy gray sky—a sky that mirrored her emotions. *What do I do, Lord? Show me the way You want me to go.*

❧

Katie stood in line to exit the church building, the children behind her nudging her in the back and side in their anxiousness to get out and see their friends. "Hold your horses," she murmured.

Uncle Mason shook the parson's hand. "Mighty fine message today."

Parson Davis smiled. "Thank you, Mason. It's good to have you with us again."

"Good to be here."

After Rebekah and Josh greeted the minister, Katie stuck her fingers out from under Joey's blanket and shook the parson's hand. "Thank you for your message, sir."

He nodded and looked past her to the next person. Katie slipped outside, and the twins and Deborah dashed around her and down the porch steps. She found Rebekah talking with some of her friends. Joey was getting hungry, but there was no place in this crowd where she could feed him. Glancing around, her heart jumped when she saw Mrs. Howard, her teacher for her first few years of school.

The middle-aged woman caught her gaze and waved. "Katie dear, how are you?"

Katie smiled as the woman drew closer. "Fine. Thank you. How about you?"

Mrs. Howard pressed her lips together. "I'm doing well, though I miss Albert something awful."

"I know just what you mean."

"Oh, Katie, I'm sorry. How could I be so insensitive?" She laid her hand on Katie's arm and tilted her head. "I'd forgotten you also lost your husband. At least I had Albert for a good ten years. But let's not talk about sad things. Who's this sweet little fellow?"

Katie beamed a smile. "My son—Jarrod Joseph Hoffman Jr. But we call him Joey."

"My, my, but that name is a mouthful." She leaned over and touched Joey's head. "What a little darling. Albert and I were never blessed with children."

Katie winced. At least God had blessed her with a son. She empathized with Mrs. Howard and thought how lonely she must be.

"I'm teaching again—up in Cushing."

"Oh, that's wonderful. You always were my favorite teacher. I hated it when you left, even though I was happy that you got married."

"I missed all you children, too." Mrs. Howard pushed her wire-framed glasses up on her thin nose. "I thought you'd moved away. Are you living back in Guthrie again?"

"For a time. I have a farm near Claremont, but my house burned down, so I'm staying at Uncle Mason's for now. But I hope to find a place of my own soon."

"Oh, you poor dear. You've been through so much for someone so young." She rested her elbow in her hand and tapped the forefinger of her other hand against her lips. "You know, I've been thinking about taking in a boarder or two. Would you possibly be interested in coming to live with me?"

Katie gasped. Could this be God's answer to her prayer?

Her first thought was that she'd probably never see Dusty again. But then wouldn't that be the best thing since he'd never care for her like she did him?

And he hadn't been at church today. This must be God's confirmation and provision.

"You know, Mrs. Howard, I just might take you up on your offer. That is, if you wouldn't mind a boarder with a child."

A smile broke out on the woman's face. "I'd be delighted!" She pulled a piece of paper from her handbag, fished out the stub of a pencil, and wrote something down. "Here's my address. I'll be in town for several more days, visiting my sister, Ida Johnson. Think about it and let me know before I leave town, if you can. But right now I believe the marshal's deputy would like to speak with you." Her twinkling gaze focused on something past Katie's shoulder. "I'll look forward to hearing from you." She squeezed Katie's hand, then walked off to join her sister.

Katie whirled around, and her heart leaped at the sight of Dusty. He wore the white shirt she'd made him, although it wasn't too white at the moment. His black pants and vest were covered with dust, and Dusty stood twisting his sweat-stained hat in his hands. He looked as if he was trying to live up to his name. He must have just gotten home from a long, hard ride.

"You're moving away?"

The distressed expression on his face took her breath away, making her sorry that he'd overheard her conversation. Maybe he did care for her after all.

❧

Dusty felt as though a horse had kicked him in the chest.

Katie was leaving.

Just when he realized that he cared deeply for her.

Katie blinked. "Well, it's not for sure yet, but yes, I'm thinking about moving in with Mrs. Howard, who lives in Cushing."

Dusty studied the ground and stood with his hands on his hips, knowing it was the only way he could keep them from trembling. How could he let her go? He'd lost the first woman he loved, although he couldn't help that, but this time, maybe he had a chance. He looked up and noted they were surrounded by people. All around him he could hear the chatter of small groups of townsfolk, squealing children at play, and laughter. What he needed to say couldn't be said here. "Will you walk with me for a bit?"

Katie nodded. She glanced around, found Deborah, and then motioned for the girl. "Would you mind watching Joey for a few minutes?"

Deborah's eyes lit up. "Of course not. My friends all love him." She carried off the baby and was quickly surrounded by a throng of adolescent girls.

Katie slipped her arm through Dusty's, and her hand felt warm against his solid arm. He guided her past the church and away from staring eyes.

While he was off chasing some cattle rustlers the past few days, he had considered his options. Now that Katie's cast was off, she no longer needed him to be responsible for her. The problem was he liked caring for her.

He'd thought things through, over and over again. There was only one answer. If Katie were to marry him, she'd have a husband to care and provide for her, and Joey would have a father. She could live in Guthrie and still be close to her family, but not dependent on them. If only she would agree.

He walked her past the parsonage, where the minister's wife had planted a multitude of chrysanthemums in front of her porch. Gold, dark red, and deep purple flowers brightened an otherwise barren landscape. "Pretty, aren't they?"

Katie nodded, but Dusty thought she was prettier than any flower. She looked beautiful in that dark blue dress. Her hair was piled up onto the back of her head, with rebellious wisps that had escaped their binds curling around her face in an appealing manner.

He cleared his throat. "Listen, Katie, we don't have a lot of time before you'll need to go. I want to ask you something." Dusty's heart ricocheted in his chest as it did when he was closing in on a dangerous outlaw.

She stared at him wide-eyed, as if she expected him to say something strange. "What is it?"

"I don't want you to leave."

Katie blinked, and her brows dipped down. "Why not? You know how important my independence is to me."

Dusty crossed his arms, then uncrossed them and wiped his moist palms on his pants. He shoved his hands in his pocket. "Yeah, I know. That's why I've come up with a solution." He took a deep breath, then looked into her eyes. "I want you to marry me."

Katie opened her mouth, then closed it, staring at him as if he'd gone loco. "And just why should I consider such an idea?"

Dusty knew he wasn't much of a catch, but surely he hadn't been wrong in noticing the interest in Katie's eyes. "I. . .uh. . .have some money saved; we could get a little place of our own, and you wouldn't have to stay with your relations. It wouldn't be what you're used to, but you'd have a home again."

Katie's expression softened, and she looked off. "Is that the only reason? So I'd no longer have to mooch off my relatives?"

When she faced him again, anger smoldered in her gaze. "You don't have to take care of me forever. I appreciate your thoughtfulness, but you've done enough."

Dusty stood dumbfounded as she walked away. How had he managed to mess things up so thoroughly? She'd completely misunderstood him.

He jogged past her, blocking the way. His hands rested on her shoulders. Katie stopped and looked up at him. His chest clenched at the tears shimmering in her eyes. One tear escaped, and he wiped it away with his finger.

"Katie, I think you've misunderstood. I want to marry you because I care for you, not because I feel some obligation."

She blinked her eyes as if in disbelief. "You care for me? Truly?"

A slow smile tugged at his lips. "Yes, I do. Truly."

Katie swiped her tears with her hand and gazed up at him. "I've grown to care for you, too. A lot."

A joy unlike any he'd experienced in a long time surged through him. "So is that a yes?"

"Yes!" Her cry bubbled up on a laugh, and joy illuminated her countenance. "Yes, I'll marry you."

Stunned, Dusty stood there, unsure what to do next. He was getting married again. A slow ecstasy flooded through his body. He picked up Katie's hands and pressed a kiss on her knuckles.

She tugged a hand free and reached up, caressing his cheek. "I love you, Dusty."

He closed his eyes and savored the moment, then hauled her into his arms and kissed her. The warmth of her lips on his was the ultimate reward for all he'd been through. Walking away from a job he loved, leaving his hometown, and recklessly searching for Sloane—all had been worth it for Katie's kiss and hearing her say she loved him.

Behind them, someone cleared his throat. They jumped apart, breathless. By the red stain to her cheeks, Dusty could tell Katie was embarrassed; but then she looked past him, and all color drained from her face.

Dusty turned around, still breathing hard and his body trembling. His emotions skidded to a halt when he saw Mason standing there with his arms crossed over his chest, glaring at them.

Chapter 12

Katie had done her best to avoid Uncle Mason's stare ever since arriving home from church. She busied herself in the kitchen, helping her quiet aunt get dinner on the table, then hid out in her room after the meal. Now that Joey had eaten and was sleeping, she sat in her rocker, making a list of things to do for the wedding.

Disappointment surged through her when she realized neither her aunt nor uncle was pleased with her decision to marry Dusty. How could they not approve when they both liked him so much?

Surely she wasn't making another mistake.

No, she couldn't be, not when she saw such affection in Dusty's eyes. He hadn't come right out and said he loved her, but he said he cared for her. And that kiss. . .*oh, my!*

If he cared as much as his kiss indicated, surely love would soon follow.

Katie touched her lips. Jarrod had never been much of a kisser. He hadn't expressed his affections well, though she never doubted his love. And Allan. . . *eww!* Just the thought of his urgent kisses gave her the shivers.

But Dusty's kiss—well, he made her quiver, too, but in a nice way.

She rested her hands in her lap and stared out the window. She had prayed and asked God to show her the way to go, and He'd given her two separate paths to choose from. Had she picked the correct one?

A soft knock sounded on her bedroom door, and it slowly opened. Aunt Rebekah peeked in and gave her a weak smile. "If you're not too tired, Mason and I would like to talk with you in the parlor."

Katie swallowed the lump in her throat. How many times in her life had she endured the "parlor talk"?

There was no sense in avoiding the inevitable, and she nodded. She checked on Joey, wishing with all her heart that he'd wake up and need her, but he slept soundly. For a brief moment she was tempted to give him a little pinch to make him cry, but she shook off that desperate thought.

In the parlor she took a chair near the window. Rebekah sat on the settee, and Mason paced in front of the fireplace. Katie rubbed her finger back and forth on the wooden trim of the chair, took a steadying breath, and waited for her uncle to speak.

Finally, he looked at Rebekah, who nodded her head. He turned toward

Katie. Her pulse kicked up a notch, and she felt like she had when she was eight years old and had nearly set the barn on fire because she'd decided her dolly was cold.

"Katie, you know your aunt and I love you dearly."

She nodded, knowing they couldn't have cared for her any more than if she were their own child.

"Rebekah and I have discussed it, and we both feel you're making a huge mistake. I haven't pushed you to talk about this other man you nearly married, but the fact that you didn't want to tell us about him leads me to think you sensed marrying him was the wrong thing. You tried to hide the news from us until it was too late to stop it. And now here you are, ready to marry another man you've known only a month or so."

Katie winced. Spelled out so clearly, she could understand why he'd be concerned.

Mason rubbed the back of his neck. "I think you know we both like and respect Dusty."

Katie tightened her grip on her skirt. "Then why do you disapprove of us marrying?"

Mason glanced at Rebekah as if he needed backup. She pressed her lips together and nodded. "For one, you seem to be rushing into this marriage."

Rebekah tugged a sofa pillow onto her lap. "Katie, you've always been one to make hasty decisions instead of taking the time to think things out and pray over the situation."

"But I did pray for God's guidance. And then Dusty asked me to marry him. Isn't that confirmation?"

"You're confusing confirmation with coincidence. They aren't the same thing." Rebekah heaved a sigh and looked out the window.

Katie heard the twins race by outside, followed by Josh, who yelled at them to slow down.

"The biggest issue is that Dusty isn't right with God. He's still angry over losing his first wife, and that's no way to start out a new marriage. Trust me, I know." Uncle Mason's gaze begged her to believe him.

"But he said he cares for me." She blinked back the tears stinging her eyes and burning her throat.

"I believe he does. Dusty is a man who takes responsibility very seriously, and he feels somewhat responsible for what happened to you." Mason lowered himself to sit by Rebekah. "But he has no business getting married to you when he's at odds with the Lord."

Suddenly, Katie felt the blood drain from her face. She'd done it again. She had plowed ahead and agreed to marry a man without making sure he was walking with God.

203

How could she be so dumb?

"Are you all right, sweetie?" Aunt Rebekah's concerned tone nearly did her in.

Was she so desperate to not mooch off her relatives that she'd marry the first man who asked her? How could she be so naive?

She closed her eyes and muttered a prayer. She knew it in her heart now—she was wrong to accept Dusty's proposal. As a Christian, it would be a mistake to marry a man whose heart wasn't right with God, no matter how good that man was. The thought of hurting Dusty caused her stomach to clench, but she had to put a halt to their marriage plans.

❧

"What do you mean Katie is gone?" Dusty leaped to his feet. The chair he was sitting in clanked against the wall. He stared at Mason, fighting the confusion and an unwanted numbness that made his whole body feel heavy and sluggish.

Mason twisted the brim of his hat. "She decided to move to Cushing and live with the widow Howard for a time."

Dusty ran his hand through his hair. "I don't understand. When I talked to her Sunday, she agreed to marry me."

Mason studied the floor for a few moments. Dusty knew from the look on his face when Mason had caught them kissing that he'd been upset. His fists tightened. Had Mason influenced Katie in leaving him?

"Mind if I sit down?" Mason motioned to the chair in front of the window.

Dusty nodded and grabbed his own chair, dropping into it, feeling as if he'd lost something precious.

"Katie has been through a lot lately. You know that more than any of us since you experienced some of it. On top of that, after women have a child, their emotions are all aflutter, and they can't seem to think clearly for a time. Trust me, I experienced it enough times with Rebekah."

Mason's ears turned red as he looked at Dusty, then at the floor again.

"I won't lie to you. Rebekah and I discouraged Katie from marrying you."

Dusty lunged to his feet again, feeling as if his friend had stabbed him in the back. "Why would you do that? You know I'd take good care of her and Joey. I care deeply for them both."

Mason grimaced, then nodded. "Yes, I know that, but the problem is, you're still angry at God for what happened to your first wife. You can't be the husband Katie needs until you make peace with Him."

Dusty stared at Mason. He clenched his jaw, biting back his angry retort. Katie was a grown woman who could make her own decisions. What right did Mason have to dissuade her from marrying him?

"Katie needs time to heal and to get her heart right with God. She's been dodging so many arrows sent her way that she hasn't had time to think things out. She's always been one to rush into things, then have to pay the consequences later." A gentle smile of remembrance tilted Mason's lips. "Did I ever tell you about the baby skunks she found?"

Dusty heaved a sigh and fell back into his chair, imagining what must have happened.

"She thought they were kittens." Mason glanced up. "They weren't, though, and Rebekah used nearly her whole store of tomatoes trying to get the stink off that little gal."

Dusty allowed a smile that didn't reach his heart. "Sounds like she had her share of trouble as a child."

"Yep, she did at that." Mason leaned forward, elbows on his knees, and laced his fingers. "Katie will do the right thing in the end. If you and she are meant to be together, this time apart won't affect your relationship. In fact, it will make it stronger."

Dusty failed to understand that reasoning. He'd already lost Emily. He didn't know if his heart could stand losing Katie, too.

But what Mason had said about God made sense, even if he didn't want to admit it out loud. After Emily died, Dusty had plunged forward without thinking. He was afraid if he stopped to sort things out, he might just wither up and die from the pain of loss. Having Sloane to chase after gave him a target for his anger. But Sloane was in jail now, and Dusty needed to step back and turn loose of his hate.

His pride had taken a hit with Katie leaving town without explaining why she couldn't marry him or even saying good-bye.

"Dusty, I know what you're feeling." Mason looked at him with pleading eyes. "I lost my wife—not to a madman but to an act of nature. Something God could have easily prevented. I don't know why it happened, but I nearly let my anger and unforgiving spirit destroy my life."

He stood, crossing the small room to the desk, then placed his hands on the wood and leaned forward. Dusty wanted to back away from the intensity of his stare.

"You've got to put aside your anger, Dusty. Get right with God. Nothing in this world will make sense until you do. And Katie can never be a part of your life if you don't."

Mason blew out a warm sigh that smelled of coffee and stood. He looked spent. For a man of few words, he'd sure spewed a lot today. Probably used up a whole fortnight's worth.

Mason settled his hat on his head. "I like you, Dusty. I consider you a friend, but you need to consider what I've said today. If you ever want to talk, you know where to find me."

The door clicked shut, and Dusty watched Mason stride by as he passed the window. Leaning his elbows on the desk, Dusty rested his head in his hands.

Katie was gone, and with her, his dream of starting over. He should have known better than to allow his emotions to get in the way.

He thought about the little house he'd just found and paid the first month's rent on. Now he wondered if he'd ever live there.

A restless energy zipped through him. He needed to get Shadow and ride out of town, shedding his pain as they soared across the prairie. He pulled open the drawer that held the WANTED posters and thumbed through them. Maybe he'd set out bounty hunting again. If he rode long enough and far enough, maybe he could outride his pain.

Mason's words came back to haunt him. *"You can't be the husband Katie needs until you make peace with Him."*

He rose and walked to the window. Pressing both hands to the glass, he stared outside. People ambled down the street, talking and laughing, oblivious to his struggle.

He'd felt God's gentle tugging, urging him to come back to the fold. He knew he should have sought God's forgiveness a long time ago, but he'd felt so unworthy. God didn't walk away from him; he left God. And what kind of a man runs away just because times get rough?

But Mason had done a similar thing—and he'd made peace with God. Perhaps Dusty could, too. God's arms were wide enough to wrap around a hardened warrior—if only that warrior would yield.

Dusty strode out of the office, slamming the door behind him and rattling the windows. It was past time he had a long talk with Parson Davis.

Chapter 13

Katie pulled a clothespin from her apron and hung another diaper on the line. The flannel squares snapped in the stiff breeze and would be dry in an hour. She picked up her empty basket and stared down the street.

Though she'd been at Alice Howard's home for a week, she still couldn't get used to living in town. Every direction she turned, there were houses or tall buildings blocking the view. Katie longed to jump on a horse and ride out to the open prairie, where the land rolled on until it reached the horizon.

She swiped at a tear tickling her cheek. Even worse was this horrible ache deep within her. She had never considered how much she would miss Dusty. Though soft-spoken, he was all man. Tall, strong, and even kind when she wasn't.

When she first returned to her aunt and uncle's after the fire, Dusty's visits irritated her, but at some point, she had begun to look forward to them. Now she longed to see his face again.

Was he angry with her for leaving without talking to him? Without telling him why she couldn't marry him?

She wondered for the thousandth time if she'd done the right thing in letting her uncle tell him. Katie closed her eyes. It cut her to the soul to think that she'd hurt such a good man.

And why did obeying God have to hurt so badly? If this was the right thing to do, shouldn't God take her pain away?

With a sigh, she hoisted the empty basket onto her hip and headed back to Alice Howard's white clapboard house. The woman maintained a meticulous home. Though her old teacher seemed delighted to have Katie staying with her, Katie wondered how she would react once Joey started getting around and could bother her things.

With Alice gone all day teaching school, Katie had the house to herself. And way too much time to think.

In her heart, she knew she couldn't marry Dusty when he wasn't right with God. But why did it have to hurt so much?

The door clicked shut, and she set the basket in the kitchen. She needed to check on Joey, and then she'd go dump the rinse water on Alice's garden, though the only thing still growing was pumpkins.

She remembered how the twins had thought she had swallowed a pumpkin when she was carrying Joey. A wave of homesickness washed over her.

She moved slowly through the house, allowing her eyes to adjust to the dim light inside. Upstairs, she crossed the hall to her bedroom and peeked at her son. The blanket on his back rose and fell with his soft breathing. His tiny thumb lay just outside his open mouth.

Love for Joey surged through her. How was it possible to care so deeply for someone who'd been part of your life for such a short time?

She'd asked herself the same thing about Dusty—many times.

Her love for Jarrod had grown slower. She'd see him weekly at church services in Guthrie and occasionally at a barn raising or town event.

She'd never loved Allan. For some reason, she still had trouble thinking of him as Ed Sloane. Maybe doing so forced her to admit how wrong she'd been about the man. Why hadn't she yielded to the apprehension and doubt she had felt about marrying him?

It was pure stubbornness. She wanted to keep her land and was willing to do almost anything—and she nearly had.

Katie lay down on her bed, suddenly weary. Joey hadn't slept well since the move and was restless during the daytime. She suspected he missed all the attention he had gotten from her family.

Stuffing the pillow under her head, she longed for Aunt Rebekah's warm embrace. To see Deborah's quick smile or the twins whooping it up. She had wanted her independence, and now she had it. But she missed her family and Dusty something awful.

Tears stung her eyes and clogged her throat. Why did life have to be so difficult?

Her thoughts drifted back to Dusty. Was he still in Guthrie? Or had her desertion caused him to ride off in search of other outlaws?

She thought of the three letters she'd tried to pen him. None of her words seemed appropriate, and none relieved her guilt. She'd told him she loved him and would marry him but had ridden away without even a good-bye. Difficult as it would be, the next time she saw him, she'd need to apologize for running away without telling him why she was leaving.

A picture of Allan dressed in his swanky suit flitted across her mind. Then that miserable scene was obliterated with her first view of Dusty standing like a majestic warrior in her parlor with the wind whipping his long duster around his legs. His raven black eyes focused steadily on his prey. Who would have thought such a man capable of being so gentle and loving?

Overcome with homesickness and longing for Dusty, Katie turned her face into her pillow and wept. As she prayed, peace filled her soul. As hard as it was, she knew leaving her family and Dusty had been the right thing.

Every day as she prayed and drew closer to God, the ache lessened. Her problems were generated from her impulsiveness in plunging forward without seeking God's will first.

"Lord, forgive me for being so headstrong and independent. I need You. I need You to show me the way and to save me from myself and my hasty decisions. I promise to pray over decisions in the future and to never again charge forward like I know the answer to everything.

"And please, Father, if this gripping love I have for Dusty isn't from You—please take it away."

Dusty sang the words to "Amazing Grace," feeling as if the song had been written personally for him. He was the wretch that God had saved—the one who was lost but now found.

And it felt so good to be back home with God.

Two weeks had passed since Katie had left, and he knew without a doubt that he loved her and wanted to marry her. But she had to be sure of that, too, and he was determined to give her all the time she needed to figure things out.

In the meantime, he'd strengthen his faith and become the man of God she needed.

He bowed his head for the closing prayer, then slowly made his way outside. After shaking the pastor's hand, he replaced his hat and nodded a greeting to several clusters of people as he passed them. His stomach growled, reminding him it was time for dinner. A warm meal at the café was just what he needed, and then he'd head over to his little rented house and finish painting the parlor.

If Katie ever decided she'd marry him, he wanted to have a place she'd feel comfortable calling home. If she never wanted to marry, he could always move out of the house. But he didn't like that alternative and prayed that God would speak to Katie and that her love for him was strong enough to endure this time of separation.

"Dusty!"

He looked up to see Mason jogging in his direction. Excitement zinged through him. He hadn't had a chance to tell Mason about his talk with Pastor Davis. Smiling, he held out his hand.

"Good to see you." Mason shook his hand. "I've been praying for you and wondering how you're doing. I was also hoping my talk with you wouldn't affect our friendship."

"Oh, it affected our friendship all right." Dusty struggled to keep a straight face.

Mason's eyebrows furrowed, and his lips tightened. "I'm real sorry to hear that."

"Don't be. I'm grateful you were a good enough friend to be honest with me. You made me realize that it was time I made things right with God. I had a long talk with the parson."

Mason's face beamed with joy. "You don't know how glad I am to hear that." He pulled Dusty into a bear hug and pounded on his shoulders. "That's the best news I've heard in weeks."

When Mason released him, Dusty stepped back and glanced around. He wasn't used to a man hugging him—or anyone, for that matter. He'd been a loner much too long.

"Now I understand."

"Understand what?" Dusty looked at Mason.

"God has been prompting me to ask you over for Thanksgiving dinner, but Rebekah thought I must have gotten into some locoweed." He grinned and peeked over his shoulder at his wife, who stood nearby talking with several women.

"Are you sure? I don't want to cause any trouble."

Mason nodded. "I'm sure. I've prayed about it for days. It wouldn't be a concern normally—you know you're welcome anytime—except that Katie is coming home for a week."

Dusty sucked in a gasp, then smiled. Would she notice a difference in him? Would she even want to see him? His joy deflated like a balloon. "I don't know if that's a good idea. Maybe she'll feel awkward with me there."

"I thought about that, too." Mason rubbed the back of his neck. "But I've prayed and believe this is what God wants. So you'll come?"

Dusty stared across the churchyard for a moment. How could he say no to seeing Katie and Joey again? "Yes, I'll come. Thank you for inviting me."

"There's just one thing. I hope you won't press Katie to marry you—now that you've made things right with God." Mason stared into Dusty's eyes, as if measuring his sincerity.

"I think you know I won't. I'm willing to wait until she knows her heart. It's like you said: If God wants us to be together, He'll work it out, and spending this time apart won't hurt things."

Mason nodded again and clasped Dusty's shoulders. "You make me proud to call you a friend. God always works things out. We'll see you on Thursday around noon."

Dusty watched Mason gather his family. He helped Rebekah onto the wagon seat and then lifted Deborah up beside her. Josh waved at him as he mounted his horse, and Dusty waved back. The twins darted toward him, but a sharp yell from their father made them stop and return to the wagon.

Dusty didn't realize how much he'd missed Katie's family until he saw them again. He'd never been part of a large family, but he'd come to love the Danfields.

Jimmy walked toward him, leading his horse. "You've been a stranger lately."

Dusty shrugged, not sure what to say.

"I just wanted to tell you not to give up on Katie. We've talked, and I know her feelings for you run deep. She just needs some time to sort things out."

"Thanks. I'm trying to be patient, but I miss her more than I could have imagined. And little Joey, too."

"Katie's always been one to rush into things without thinking, but when she does step back and look at the whole picture, most of the time she'll make the right decision—as long as her stubbornness doesn't get in the way."

Jimmy offered a smile resembling Katie's so much that Dusty's insides clenched. He sorely missed her and could only pray she felt the same.

"Thanks for the encouragement. Will you be home for Thanksgiving? Mason invited me to dinner."

Jimmy gazed off into the distance. He had a restlessness about him that Dusty recognized because he'd once felt the same. A bolt of shock zigzagged through him as he realized he no longer had the restless spirit that made him travel from town to town, searching for outlaws for so long. He was ready to settle down again.

"I reckon I'll be there. But I've been thinking about going up to Tulsa. There's been several oil strikes there, and I've heard tell drilling companies are hurting for workers."

"Your family will miss you if you go."

Jimmy nodded. "And I'll miss them, but I can't explain this tugging I feel. It's almost as if I'm compelled to go."

Dusty wondered if it might somehow be God encouraging Jimmy to go, but he didn't see how any good could come of it. Katie had told him how restless Jimmy had been since he fought in the war.

"Have you tried praying about it?"

Jimmy scowled. "I don't pray anymore. It didn't do any good during the war, so I washed my hands of God."

Dusty laid his hand on Jimmy's shoulder. "I felt the same way, but Mason helped me see that I was wrong. God didn't move away from me; I moved away from Him."

Jimmy shrugged off Dusty's hand. "Yeah, well, that's fine for you, but I don't feel the same."

Dusty's heart ached for Jimmy as he watched him ride away. He looked around and realized they were the last two people left in the churchyard. As Dusty made his way toward the diner, he prayed for Jimmy. He knew so much of what Jimmy was feeling, but God had turned Dusty's life around. He could do the same for Katie's brother, too.

Chapter 14

Katie pulled the blue flannel gown over Joey's head and stuck his arms in the sleeves. Her little boy smiled up at her, turning her insides to warm grits. She'd never known such love in her life.

A soft knock sounded on her bedroom door, and Uncle Mason leaned against the door frame. "We all missed you while you were gone but understand your need to be independent."

"Thanks. It's so good to be home again, even if it's only for a visit." Katie smiled at her uncle as she slid the gown over Joey's wiggly legs. "I'm done here and should get downstairs and help with dinner."

"There's something I need to tell you." Her uncle rubbed the back of his neck, and apprehension washed over her at the familiar gesture. "Dusty's downstairs."

"What?" Katie pressed her hand to her chest, startled to the core.

"I invited him."

She sat on the edge of the bed as frustration battled excitement. "Why would you do that after you told me we couldn't marry?"

He straightened and shoved his hands in his pockets. "I never said you couldn't marry—just recommended against it at the time."

"But I still don't understand why you would invite him for dinner, knowing I'd be here."

He pressed his lips together. "I can't say I understand, either, but I felt the Lord wanted me to invite him. Besides, it won't hurt you and him to talk. You did leave without saying good-bye."

Katie studied the dark red-and-blue-floral pattern on the rug. She knew leaving without talking to Dusty had been wrong. She needed to face him and apologize, and it looked like that would happen in the next few minutes.

Uncle Mason walked over to the bed. "Let me haul this critter downstairs for you."

"Why didn't you tell me sooner, so I had time to prepare?" Katie darted a glance in the oval mirror on the dresser, reattached some loose strands to the bun at her nape, and pinched her cheeks.

"You just would have worried and stewed over things like you are now." Joey squirmed and wiggled his arms as Mason tickled the boy's belly. He picked up her son and walked out into the hall, then turned around. "Don't be afraid to talk to Dusty. You might discover things have changed."

Katie wrinkled her brow. What could have changed in such a short time? Her love for him certainly hadn't. If anything, it had grown stronger, even though she'd begged God to take it away. With each step she took downstairs, her anxiety rose. Had the separation proven to Dusty that his feelings for her were false? Was that what Uncle Mason had meant?

The parlor was empty, so she followed her uncle into the kitchen where the family was already seated for dinner. The kitchen buzzed with excitement as the twins hovered around Jimmy and Josh, both talking at the same time. Deborah and Rebekah placed platters of fried chicken and biscuits onto the table. Dusty jumped to his feet and captured her gaze.

Katie's heart nearly stopped. For a time, it seemed as if no one else existed. Her heart pounded a ferocious tempo, and she wiped her slick palms on her skirt. Dusty's ebony eyes bore into hers, but she failed to interpret their message.

"Look who's here." Nate pounded Dusty on the arm, then sat next to him. "We ain't seen ol' Dusty in a coon's age."

"Stop hitting him, Nathan, and don't say ain't." Rebekah waved a spoon at her son.

The connection broken, Katie grabbed a bowl of mashed potatoes and set it on the table, then returned to the stove for green beans and sweet potatoes. When all the food was on the table, she took her seat across from Dusty. She needn't have pinched her cheeks because she was certain they were flaming after blatantly staring at Dusty like she'd done. It was so good to see him again.

Still, she couldn't help glancing up at him as she ate. There was something different about him, but she couldn't pinpoint it. He seemed to have a glow that wasn't there before.

The twins kept chattering, and Mason, Josh, and Jimmy talked about winter coming. Mason struggled to butter his biscuit as he held Joey in one arm. Katie pushed her plate back, having eaten only half her food. She was amazed she ate anything at all with Dusty constantly looking at her. "Pass Joey to me. I'm done."

Mason did as she requested, then picked up his fork in one hand and the knife in the other and dove into eating. Katie couldn't help smiling.

After enjoying her aunt's delicious sweet potato pie, she helped clean up the kitchen while Dusty and the men watched Joey. Katie dried a dish as she peered out the window. She longed to get out of the house to cool off from the hot kitchen and have time to think.

"I suppose you were surprised to see Dusty here." Her aunt glanced out the corner of her eye at her as she washed a mug.

"I can't deny it was quite a shock."

"He likes you." Deborah's youthful smile beamed from ear to ear.

Katie couldn't help giving her cousin a nudge with her hip. "You think so?"

Deborah nodded her head, making her opinion obvious.

"I tried to dissuade Mason from inviting him, thinking it would make things awkward for you." Rebekah set a cup in the rinse pan and gave her a sympathetic smile.

"It's all right. Honestly, I'm glad to see him again, even if we're only friends."

Rebekah's brows lifted, and she gave Katie a who-are-you-kidding smirk.

Katie heard Joey's frantic wail and could tell whoever was holding her son was coming toward her. Her heart nearly stopped when Dusty walked in, jiggling Joey on his shoulder.

"Sorry, but he only wants his mama."

Katie laid down the towel, walked into the hallway, and took the baby from Dusty, trying not to touch the man she loved for fear he'd sense her affection. Joey suddenly quieted and turned his face toward her chest, mouth open. Katie moved him to her shoulder, sure her cheeks were flaming. She followed Dusty down the short hall and stopped near the stairs.

"You want me to carry him up for you? Must be hard to manage stairs, a baby, and that long skirt."

Katie was moved by his concern. She jiggled Joey to keep him from squawking. "I can manage, but thank you." She made the mistake of looking into his black eyes and lost herself there.

"I missed you, Katie." Dusty's lips tightened.

She looked away, then glanced back, knowing he deserved the truth. "I missed you, too, and I'm sorry for leaving without saying good-bye or explaining why I was going."

"It's all right. I understand your need to live somewhere other than here."

His compassion was almost her undoing, and tears blurred her vision.

Joey's patience evaporated, and the boy started crying. Katie jiggled him faster, but he wouldn't be soothed. "I need to feed him."

"Go ahead. We can talk later." Dusty lifted his hand and held it to her cheek. The look in his eyes took her breath away.

Half an hour later, Katie stood at the bedroom window, buttoning her blouse. As she tucked it into her wool skirt, she saw Dusty enter the barn with her uncle. Joey was asleep, and Dusty occupied, so now was her chance to take a walk.

She donned her cloak, thankful that Deborah had agreed to keep an eye on Joey. He'd eaten so well that he should sleep a good two hours or more, so she wasn't worried.

The chilly November breeze teased her cheeks and lifted loose strands of hair. Autumn was a pretty time of year, but she dreaded the upcoming winter. Even though winters were often mild in the Oklahoma Territory, the colder weather made life on a farm more difficult.

Her thoughts turned to Dusty. He'd looked better to her than Aunt Rebekah's pie. Even though her love for him hadn't diminished, there was still nothing to be done about it. She wouldn't marry a man who didn't love God as she did. She had nearly made that mistake twice, and it wouldn't happen again.

The dried grass crunched beneath her feet as she trod across the field toward the dirt road. It felt freeing to be out of the town, where she could see gently rolling hills clear to the horizon. The past few weeks away from home had given her plenty of time to read her Bible and seek God. She didn't understand why God hadn't taken away her love for Dusty, but rather than pine for him, she prayed.

"Father God." Katie stared up at the clear blue sky as she walked. "I ask You to take away Dusty's anger and unforgiving spirit over what Ed Sloane did to him. Bring Dusty back into the fold, so he can know Your love and not have to live alone. He's such a good man; You know how much I love him, but I give that love to You. If we are meant to be together someday, You'll have to make it happen."

A warmth flowed through her. Giving her love for Dusty to God was the right thing to do. She bent down to pick some burrs from her skirt, but when she looked up, she realized she had walked farther than she thought. She turned around and headed back to the house, which was a good mile away.

Behind her, she heard the pounding of horses' hooves and turned to see if a neighbor was coming to visit. She lifted her hand over her eyes and scanned the riders. Her heart nearly plunged to her feet. She sucked in a gasp. *No, it can't be.*

Katie lifted her skirts, turned back toward the farm, and ran for all she was worth. *Father, help me!*

The horses quickly closed the space, and Katie found herself surrounded by a pack of unkempt men whose expressions reminded her of ravenous wolves. The horses snorted and stamped their hooves. Katie stopped to catch her breath while her mind raced for a way to escape.

"Well, well, who would have thought you'd make things so easy?"

Katie cringed at the grating voice she had never expected to hear again. Gathering her courage, she turned to face Ed Sloane.

Though trembling so hard she feared her legs would give way, she hiked up her chin. Showing her fear would only please her ex-fiancé. "How did you get out of jail?"

His mouth, topped with a pencil-thin mustache she had once thought pleasing, turned up in an ugly sneer. "I always get out of jail, darlin'."

Katie dashed toward an opening between Ed's horse and another. Ed charged his mount forward to close the gap. He nodded at two riders behind her. Katie suddenly felt herself being lifted in the air by two of Sloane's henchmen and tossed in front of him on the horse. He'd slid back so that she now sat in his saddle. His arm slinked around her waist, and he tugged her back against his chest.

His warm breath touched her ear as he chuckled. "Well, well, you've lost some weight since I last saw you. Not bad."

Katie pried at his tight grasp with her fingers. "You let me go. I have a baby who needs me." She jabbed him with her elbow and kicked, making the horse prance sideways.

His grasp loosened, but when Katie prepared to lunge off the horse, the cold metal of a pistol to her temple froze her in place.

"You're coming with me, and there's no point fighting."

Katie blinked back her tears. Her throat burned. "Please, my baby is dependent on me. I can't leave him behind."

"Too bad. If you want that sniffling baby to stay alive, you'd better cooperate."

Katie's heart thundered at the thought of Joey in Ed Sloane's evil hands, and she struggled to breathe.

She settled in for the ride, knowing she couldn't fight Sloane. For now, Joey would be safe with her family. They'd care for him. And her life would be in God's hands.

But how could she live without her son—even for a day?

And how could she live without Dusty for the rest of her life?

❧

Dusty knocked on the kitchen door, and Rebekah looked up from her worktable. "Has Katie come back downstairs? I'd like to talk to her."

Rebekah nodded and wiped her hands on a towel. "Yes, she went for a walk close to an hour ago. She headed down the road away from town."

"Thanks." Dusty closed the door, walked to the barn, and saddled Shadow. If Katie had walked a long ways, she'd probably be relieved to have a ride back.

Excitement churned in his belly. He'd talked in the barn with Mason, and Mason agreed that Dusty should tell Katie how he'd made things right with God. She'd be so happy to learn he'd put his anger behind him and was ready to get on with his life. Mason had even told Dusty if Katie still wanted to marry him, he would give them his blessing as long as Dusty gave her the time she needed to decide.

He followed her footprints down the dirt road for close to a mile. His heart clenched. Fresh hoofprints surrounded Katie's prints. Dusty lifted his hat and stared out over the desolate landscape. Far off, he saw what looked to be dust stirred up by riders.

He swallowed hard and dismounted to examine the hoof marks. His eyes landed on familiar square-shaped hoofprints made by Sloane's horse. Chills charged up his spine. The ache in his heart became a fiery gnawing. Sloane had Katie.

His Katie. The woman he loved with all his heart.

Dusty pressed his palms against his temples and cried out. "God, how could You let this happen again?"

He grabbed Shadow's reins, leaped onto the saddle, and kicked his mount forward. Suddenly, he reined the horse to a stop. He had taken off his holster at dinner and couldn't chase after Sloane unarmed. Stopped in the middle of the road, he wrestled between following his beloved and returning to the farm. Good sense won out over desperation, and he turned around, racing for the Danfield home.

Chapter 15

Armed with his pistol and a borrowed rifle, Dusty kicked Shadow into a gallop down the road after Katie. Mason and Jimmy followed right behind him. He'd lost valuable time going back, but at least he wouldn't have to face Sloane and his gang alone and unarmed.

How could Sloane have escaped again? And how did he manage to find Katie? Dusty pondered the questions for the hundredth time.

At a fork in the road, he dismounted and examined the hoofprints. Fortunately, with today being Thanksgiving and most people at home enjoying the holiday with their family, there weren't any other fresh prints on the road.

He glanced at the sky as he remounted. In another hour, it would be dark. Fear for Katie melded with a desperate need to hold her in his arms and make sure she was all right.

A heaviness pressed against his chest, making it hard to breathe. Somehow this had to be his fault. If he hadn't talked in the barn with Mason for so long, maybe he would have caught up with Katie before Sloane had. Or maybe...

No! He shook his head, refusing to give in to the negative thoughts that would steal his peace and try to sever his newly restored relationship with God.

This wasn't his fault, but he sure could change the outcome.

He nudged Shadow to go faster, all the time checking the trail and scouring the countryside for some sign of Katie. The giant orange orb of the soon-setting sun cast long shadows from the few trees on the prairie. When the sun set, so would any hopes of tracking Sloane and Katie.

God, please, help us find Katie before anything bad happens. Protect her.

Just before twilight, they reined their horses to a stop at a crossroads to give the animals a breather and to allow Dusty to check the trail. Several sets of hoof-prints covered the area. Finally he decided to take the path to the right. They walked their horses so Dusty could scour the trail for signs of Sloane's gang.

After a few minutes, Dusty halted and stooped, examining the ground. "What's wrong?" Mason stopped his mount beside him.

Dusty pressed his lips together, hating to admit the truth. "We turned the wrong way. I haven't seen Sloane's trail once since we took this path."

"Then let's go back to the fork and go the other way." Jimmy didn't wait for confirmation but spurred his horse around and into a run.

Dusty and Mason joined him and were soon back at the fork in the road.

Dusty clenched his teeth together, angry with himself for wasting valuable time going the wrong way.

He studied the path as they walked the horses. The tracks angled off the road and onto a faint trail through the tall grass. Up ahead, Dusty could make out the beginnings of a large wooded area. If Sloane wanted to hide, that would be the place.

Mason and Jimmy moved up beside him and examined the ground. "What do you think? Will they ride all night or make camp somewhere?"

Dusty shrugged, wishing he knew for certain. If Sloane did make camp and they continued their search in the dark, they could ride right past him and his cohorts without knowing it.

He stared at the woods. "Sloane's a creature of comfort. My gut instinct says he'll make camp, but I don't know for sure. He's smart, but sometimes he underestimates people."

"You think he'd leave a guard behind?" Jimmy glanced at the woods and back at Dusty, then pulled his rifle from the scabbard. "We could be riding into a trap."

"Could be. What do you want to do?" He studied both men, unwilling to put their lives on the line. Even if they backed down, he knew he'd continue his search. He wouldn't quit until he rescued Katie.

"We've got to find her." Mason pressed his lips tight.

"But you have a family depending on you. Maybe you should ride back and let Jimmy and me continue."

Mason shook his head. "I'm not going back without Katie. Let's quit burning daylight."

Dusty nodded, relieved Mason was still at his side. As he stuck his foot in the stirrup, he heard the faint sound of a man's laughter, far off in the woods. He settled in his saddle and looked at Mason. "Did you hear that?"

"Sure did. What do you make of it?"

He held his finger to his lips. "Listen."

All three men held their horses steady and turned an ear toward the trees. A faint breeze blew in Dusty's face as he listened intently. He caught a few words of a man's curse, and his skin crawled. He'd recognize Ed Sloane's voice any day.

"That's him. I heard Sloane."

They secured their mounts to a lone tree and slowly crept through the tall prairie grass toward the edge of the woods. A hundred feet inside the tree line, the voices grew loud enough that they could make out all the words. Dusty peered around the side of a thick oak tree.

"We ought to keep going. We're too close to her home to stop." One of Sloane's cronies stood with his hands on his hips.

Sloane rubbed a finger over his thin mustache. "It's getting dark, and they probably haven't even missed her yet. I think we're safe here."

Dusty scanned the area, looking for Katie's rose-colored dress. When two men stepped forward to join the discussion, he saw her sitting in front of a tree, her hands tied and her eyes wide. Anger at Sloane for causing her fright roared through him like a wildfire, but at the same time, he ached to march in and comfort Katie. He pressed his hat down, ready to do battle for the woman he loved.

He whispered to Mason and Jimmy to make their way around, one to the right and one to the left. If push came to shove, they just might be able to fool Sloane and his gang into thinking they were surrounded. Dusty was thankful that the family had taken time to hold hands and pray for Katie and their safe return before they had left the house.

Joey's fervent cries for his mother echoed in Dusty's mind. *I'll get your mother home to you, little buddy. Just hang on.*

"Tell you what, I'd like a little time alone with my bride. You men go ahead and make for the hideout. Me and the little woman will get reacquainted."

Even from this distance, Dusty saw the panic that crossed Katie's face. She didn't want to be left alone with Sloane. She closed her eyes, and Dusty hoped she was praying. They'd need all the prayers they could muster to capture Sloane again.

❧

Katie's heart pounded in her chest as she watched Sloane argue with his men. She hoped they'd stay here and make camp to give Dusty a chance to catch up, but she didn't want to be alone with Sloane. She knew Dusty would come looking for her and blessed God that her uncle had invited him for dinner. She hated to think of her sweet uncle and brother going up against Sloane without Dusty's experience and help.

Katie's shoulders ached from tension, and her whole body trembled. She longed to see Joey and wondered again what Rebekah would do when he got hungry. Maybe she'd make him some warm sugar water, but would that satisfy her famished son?

Father God, please watch over Joey and help him. Show Dusty the way to find me. And soon, Lord. Please. I don't want to be alone with this evil man.

Tears stung her eyes. How could she ever have considered marrying Sloane? How could she have been so desperate that she had been swayed by his counterfeit charm?

She no longer thought him appealing, only despicable. And evil.

She longed for a bath to wash his touch off her skin.

Her stomach churned at the thought of riding with him again. His whispered words of romance and what he had planned for her chilled her to the core. Shivering, she watched with dread as Sloane's men mounted their horses and rode off. Soon the last faint rays of the sun, which painted the dusky sky bright pink and orange, would fade, and she'd be left alone in the dark with this dark man.

God, no. Please, Lord.

One horseman reined in his mount and turned around. Katie held her breath. "Are you certain you want us all to leave? What if they catch up with you?"

"They won't catch me in the dark. I don't need a fire for what I have planned, and I don't need an audience."

"All right then. See you at camp, boss."

The man rode off, taking with him Katie's last hope of not being alone with Sloane. She quivered, knowing exactly how a rabbit felt caught in a snare. She searched for some way of escape and wrestled with the rope that held her hands captive until it bit into her skin. The glint in Sloane's eyes as he talked about his plans for her threatened to cut her fragile thread of control.

A chilling silence surrounded them and grew tight with tension. Sloane stared at the woods as if searching for someone, then finally faced her. A knot formed in her stomach as his gaze traveled over her.

Father, give me strength.

"You don't know how long I've dreamed of this moment while I spent those weeks in that rotten jail." He leaned forward, his eyes narrowed. "Thoughts of having my way with you kept me going," he said in a frigid whisper.

Sick to her stomach, Katie swallowed. *Help me, Lord. Help me.*

Though frightened beyond anything she'd ever experienced, Katie felt God's peace surround her like a woolen cloak. Somehow, she'd make it through this night.

Sloane stood and shed his jacket. "You know, I never really wanted to marry you. I just needed your land—to fund my gambling operation up in Kansas. But by marrying you, I got you and your land—or would have if that stupid marshal turned bounty hunter hadn't interfered. He's next on my list—after I take care of you."

Katie shuddered. She didn't want to die but knew in her heart that her family would take care of Joey and raise him up properly. At the thought of never seeing Joey, Dusty, or her family again, tears coursed down her cheeks.

Her aunt had been right in saying that Dusty had saved her from marrying an outlaw. She shivered as Sloane unbuttoned his vest and dropped it on the ground. If only Dusty could save her again.

Chapter 16

Sloane yanked his shirttail from his trousers and began unbuttoning his shirt. Frantic, Katie tore with her teeth at the rope that held her bound. Maybe, just maybe, if she could get loose, she could put up a good fight. She was no longer the slow, cumbersome woman that he had known when she was with child.

Maybe she could stall and give Dusty more time to find her. "Why me? I mean, there are widows all over the Oklahoma Territory. Why did you choose me?"

Sloane's arrogant chuckle resonated in the air and sent goose bumps charging up her arms. The cool breeze blew dust against her cheeks and made her shiver.

"I was in the right place at the right time. Saw you crossing the street in Claremont. You pulled off your hat and made an adjustment to it, and the sun glistened on that yellow hair of yours. At the same time, two women passed by me and muttered something about how it was a shame that you were a widow at such a young age." He rubbed his finger over his thin mustache. "Didn't take long to find out where you lived and learn your farm was for sale."

Sloane turned his back to her, sauntered over to his horse, and took a slow drink from his canteen.

Katie struggled to her feet. If she couldn't get her hands free, at least she could run. She looked to her left and then right as she tried to figure out the best direction to go. If she got far enough away, Sloane might not be able to find her once the sun set. She lunged to her right, away from her captor, but she stepped on the hem of her skirt and nearly fell. She glanced over her shoulder. Panic bolted through her.

Leaves crunched under his feet as Sloane stomped toward her, evil glimmering in his icy blue eyes. He grabbed her by the shoulders, spun her around, and pulled her toward him. She shoved against his chest and felt a small victory when he winced from the abrasive rope scratching his skin.

He held her against him, Katie's left arm crushed against the cold metal of a pistol in his waistband. If only she could get ahold of it, then maybe she'd have a chance.

Sloane grabbed her hair, which had long since come loose of its pins, and he yanked her head back. Katie grimaced from the pain.

"I like a woman who doesn't give in easily."

Katie quivered as his lips angled toward hers. Suddenly, she heard a click, and Sloane froze, his eyes wide open.

"Let that woman go—or you're a dead man."

Katie gasped at the sound of Dusty's voice, low and calculated. She saw the indecision in Sloane's eyes. Then he shoved her away so fast that she fell to the ground, landing on her backside.

Katie's heart leaped at the sight of the man she loved standing there with his hat pulled low, pistol aimed at Sloane, and his duster flapping in the breeze, looking like a warrior.

"Get those hands up where I can see them."

Sloane lifted his left hand, but ever so slowly, his right hand eased toward the weapon in his waistband.

"Look out! He's got a gun!" Katie screamed.

Dusty glanced at her, and in that split second, Sloane grabbed his pistol and pointed it at her. Katie squeezed her eyes shut, certain she'd never see her baby again.

The nearby blast of a gun echoed in her ear, making her jump. She winced, waiting—expecting—to feel pain, but when she didn't, she opened her eyes, taking in the scene before her.

Sloane lay on the ground, grasping his arm and cursing in pain. Mason and Jimmy stood beside him with their rifles pointed at him. Dusty stepped through a cloud of gun smoke and hurried to her side. He scooped her up in his arms and held her tight.

Tears of joy and relief streamed down Katie's cheeks.

"I thought I'd lost you," Dusty whispered in her ear.

He held her so tight Katie could barely breathe. "If you could untie me, I could hug you back properly."

Dusty blinked in confusion then looked at her hands. "Oh, sorry." He gently set her down and pulled a knife from his boot. Ever so carefully, he slit the rope, freeing her hands. Katie rolled her shoulders, then rubbed her wrists while Dusty put away his knife.

"You're bleeding." He took her wrists and examined them, placing tiny kisses close to the scrapes.

Katie stepped into his arms, feeling safer than she ever had. This man she loved would protect her, even at the cost of his own life.

❧

Jimmy started a fire while Uncle Mason tied up Sloane and tended to his wounds. Katie winced as Dusty dabbed a damp handkerchief on the scratches on her wrists. He hated that she'd been hurt but was so grateful to God that they found her before something worse had happened.

He kissed her wrists again; then they walked away from Sloane's menacing gaze. Dusty kept a firm hold on Katie's arm so that she didn't stumble. When they were in the shadows but could still see the light of the campfire, he stopped and turned her to face him.

"I knew you'd come." Katie's breath was warm against his cheeks. "I prayed you would find me."

Dusty ran his hand over her head and down to her soft cheek. "I couldn't stand the thought that Sloane had you. I'd have searched the whole nation to find you."

Dusty gently pulled Katie against his chest and laid his cheek on her hair. "I love you, Katie."

She leaned back and looked up at him. He could barely make out the right side of her face, illuminated by the campfire. She gazed at him for a long while. "I love you, too, Dusty. I've tried not to, but I can't help it. But that doesn't mean there's a future for us. I can't marry a man who doesn't love God and doesn't put the Lord first in his life."

Despite her words, hope soared in his chest, and love for this woman made his knees weak. He cupped her cheek in his hand. "Then I guess it's a good thing I made peace with God, isn't it?"

Katie gasped. "What? You did?"

Dusty nodded. "Yes. I had a long talk with Mason. I realized that he and I were in the same boat: Both of us lost our wives due to tragic circumstances. Mason had been angry with God for a time, just like I was. I didn't think God would forgive me for walking away from Him when things got tough. But Mason had done the same thing, and if God could forgive him, He could forgive me."

Katie fell into his arms. "Oh, Dusty, you don't know how happy that makes me. I longed for you to make peace with God and to lose your anger over Emily's death."

Dusty chuckled. "I guess I owe Sloane a big thank-you."

Katie leaned back but didn't step out of his arms. "Why ever for?"

"If I hadn't found Sloane at your house like I did, I'd probably never have met you."

"Oh!"

He placed his hands on Katie's cheeks. "I'm going to kiss you now—unless you don't want me to."

Proving she had no objections, she leaned forward. His lips touched her velvet-soft lips, and Dusty's pulse leaped as if he'd been plugged into one of those new electric lights. Katie's arms went around his neck and pulled him closer. She kissed him back with a promise of their future together. Too soon, he pulled back, his breath ragged.

Katie touched his cheek. "I love you so much, Dusty."

He wanted to stand there and kiss her all night but was afraid her brother and uncle might shoot him like one of them had Sloane. "I love you, too, Katie. Is it too soon to ask you to marry me again?"

She shook her head no and opened her mouth to respond, but he placed his finger over her lips.

"Before you answer, there's a condition."

Katie's eyebrows dipped. "What condition?"

"That you don't run away this time."

Her lips parted in a wide grin. "I can assure you, that won't happen. In fact, you'll have a difficult time getting away from me. I would love nothing more than to marry you."

He kissed her again and then reluctantly escorted her back to the camp. Mason and Jimmy strode forward and enveloped Katie in a hug. Mason glanced over her head and looked at Dusty with a questioning gaze. Dusty couldn't hold back his grin, and he nodded his head to let Mason know Katie had agreed to marry him.

Chapter 17

Dusty's heart pounded as he rode into Sanders Creek. The last time he'd been in his hometown was the day his life had changed forever. But he knew in order to move on and begin a new life with Katie, he had to close the door on his past life—and the only way to do that was to return to Sanders Creek.

The town had changed in the time he'd been gone. New buildings had sprung up, and older ones had been repainted or spruced up. People ambled along the boardwalk, while a few wagons and riders on horseback dotted the dirt street. He could hear the sounds of an active town—a blacksmith hammering, a train whistling, and some cattle lowing. Fragrant aromas from the café wafted on the morning breeze. Life had continued here as if nothing bad had ever happened.

His gaze was automatically drawn toward the marshal's office. A man sat polishing a rifle in a chair that hadn't been outside the office when he was marshal. The man watched him with interest. He slowed his polishing, then leaned the rifle against the clapboard wall and stood. He sauntered over and rested his shoulder against a pole holding up the overhanging roof.

Dusty's heart pinged as he recognized his old friend Tom. The man now wore the marshal's badge on his vest. A slow smile brightened Tom's craggy features. " 'Bout time you returned. Folks pretty much gave up on ever seeing you again, but I told them you'd be back. Course, if you're planning on gettin' your old job back as marshal, you've got a fight on your hands."

Dusty slid off Shadow, hopped up the steps, and shook Tom's hand. "Your job is safe. I've got my own job back in Guthrie."

"Guthrie! Whatcha doing there?"

"It's a long story, trust me."

Tom leaned back and crossed his arms over his chest. "Did you ever catch that fellow who—well, you know."

Dusty nodded, glad to have good news to share. "Ed Sloane is finally in the state penitentiary, along with the rest of his gang. There's no longer anyone running loose who can rescue him." He'd spent two weeks chasing the men who had helped kidnap Katie, making sure that he caught every last one of them. He never wanted to have another encounter with Ed Sloane again.

He studied his friend. Tom had barely aged since he'd last seen him, making

Dusty wonder if he himself had. Life on the trail hadn't been easy and must have taken a toll on him. "How's the shoulder?"

Tom flexed his arm. "Good as new, though it was slow going at first. Came as close to meeting my Maker back then as I ever have. Took a good two months before I could work again."

"Glad to hear it's better. I'm sorry you got caught in all that mess."

Tom shrugged. "It's just part of the job."

Dusty looked down the street, not really wanting to voice his next question but knowing he must. "Whatever happened to my old house?"

Tom narrowed his eyes. "Guess you knew about the fire, huh?"

Dusty nodded.

"Well, Lawrence Spenser, the man who owned that property, had the mess cleaned up and a new house built there. Then he sold it to a family new to town."

Dusty clenched his jaw. "And what about Emily?"

Tom's lips tightened, and he looked away. "Her pa had her buried in the town graveyard right after the fire. They waited a month for you to return before finally going ahead with the funeral."

"Guess I'd better head over there and say my good-byes."

Tom studied him. "So you don't plan on staying around these parts?"

"No." Dusty shook his head. "I'm a deputy marshal in Guthrie. Figure I'll stay on there." Finally he smiled. "Met a feisty little gal that I'm getting ready to marry."

Tom's cheeks pulled up in a grin. "I'm right glad to hear that. You deserve to find some happiness after all you've been through."

Dusty shook his friend's hand and rode over to the graveyard. Birds chattered and chirped their cheerful songs, which seemed out of place for a cemetery. He tied Shadow to the picket fence. The three-foot-high gate screeched as he entered.

He wandered around, passing mostly the graves of people whose names he didn't recognize. He nearly stumbled when his gaze landed on the recent grave of Jed Harper, the old man who'd been his neighbor. Beside Mr. Harper, Dusty noticed the grave of Mrs. Harper. She had died only a few days after the fire that killed Emily. He wondered if those traumatic events had been too much for the sickly woman.

He meandered toward the back of the graveyard, his eyes scanning for Emily's grave. His gaze landed on a grave with an iron fence surrounding it, and he felt pulled in that direction. Emily's wealthy parents would have wanted something that nice for her.

His heart jolted when his gaze collided with the white marble tombstone. Emily Anderson McIntyre. Beloved wife and daughter. 1883–1903. Here only a brief time, but she touched many lives.

Dusty wished it was the season for flowers so he could lay some on the grave, but instead he twisted his hat in his hands. Emily's parents had picked a nice spot for her grave. Several dogwood trees and a redbud stood behind the headstone. In the spring, they would add the pretty colors Emily had cherished. A shallow creek trickled along about fifty feet from the edge of the cemetery.

Dusty stared at the tombstone. "I miss you, Em. I want you to know I caught that scoundrel who was responsible for our troubles, and he'll never hurt another innocent soul again. I'm so sorry for the pain he caused you and for not being able to rescue you."

Dusty wiped his damp eyes on his sleeve. "I want you to know I'm getting married again. You'd like Katie. She's pretty and spunky and has the cutest little boy who needs a pa.

"I can't pretend to understand why God took you home to be with Him. All I can think of is Katie needed me more. And I need her. You'll be happy to know I've made peace with God."

Dusty pressed his lips together. Sanders Creek had been his home for a while, but his future rested in Guthrie. With his good-byes said, he smacked on his hat and mounted Shadow. Excitement coursed through him as he thought of his future.

"Let's go, boy. Katie's awaiting."

❦

Katie studied the reflection of her new dress in Rebekah's tall oval mirror. The ecru-colored fabric fitted her narrow waist and lay in soft pleats around her hips. Irish lace at the neck and cuffs gave it a bit of fluff, but it was still sensible enough that it could serve as her Sunday dress after the wedding.

A delicious shiver of excitement wound its way through her, making her stomach queasy. She shoved another pin in her hair and patted one side, hoping her curls would stay put throughout the day's activities.

Rebekah strolled in, holding Joey against her shoulder. "You look beautiful, dear."

Katie smiled. She felt beautiful and hoped that Dusty would agree.

"So, no regrets?"

"No, not a one. Well, except I'm still not sure about leaving Joey here with you all overnight. He hasn't yet taken a bottle."

Her aunt patted Joey's padded bottom. "He will when he gets hungry enough."

"I just hate leaving him—after what happened."

Rebekah wrapped her arm around Katie's shoulders. "I know, but that's in the past. We'll take good care of him for you."

Katie moved behind Rebekah and looked at her son's face. His eyes were shut, and his thumb rested in his mouth. How could she bear to leave him overnight?

"I know what you're thinking, but he'll be just fine. He knows us and can get by without you for such a short time. Besides, you and Dusty need time alone on your wedding night."

Katie touched her warm cheeks, making her aunt grin. She had no concerns or fears about her wedding night with Dusty. She was certain that if she loved him any more, she just might explode. No, she had no regrets. Not a one.

Deborah glided into the room in her new rose-colored dress. "Oh, you look so pretty!"

Katie took hold of both her hands and studied her cousin, then gave the girl a hug. "So do you."

Deborah's cheeks turned bright red. "Thank you. Pa says it's time to go."

With hands shaking from excitement, Katie donned her cloak and headed for the wagon that would take them to the Christmas Eve service, followed by her wedding. The month she and Dusty had waited after agreeing to marry had been the longest of her life. But this time she hadn't rushed into things. She had taken the time to pray and make sure that marrying Dusty was God's will for her life. It amazed her how she'd come full circle and was once again starting her life over. She'd sold her land and had put the money in a savings account. They used some of the funds to buy a house in Guthrie so she could stay near her family and Dusty could keep his job, and what was left over would be saved so that Joey could attend college one day or buy his own land.

Uncle Mason's eyes beamed as he lifted her into the fancy buggy he'd borrowed just for the day. Today she and Dusty would marry, and tomorrow they'd celebrate their first Christmas together with the family.

✢

Dusty straightened his new suit for the hundredth time and tugged at the string tie at his neck. Only for Katie would he wear the crazy thing that nearly choked off his breath. He figured he knew what a calf felt like when some cowpoke lassoed it.

"Stand still. You're gonna have folks thinking you're about ready to bolt." Jimmy chuckled in Dusty's ear. Serving as best man, he looked just as uncomfortable as Dusty felt. "It's not too late to salvage your freedom before you're tied to my sister's apron strings for life."

He didn't think he'd mind that one bit, but this waiting up in front of the whole community was getting old. "I thought the women were ready to get this show on the road."

Jimmy shrugged, and the pastor cleared his throat and gave them a stern look.

The pastor's wife began an elegant tune on the pump organ. The whole church was filled with their friends and townsfolk. Josh stood in the back, serving as usher. Deborah, looking pretty and mature in her new pink dress, entered the back of the church. A combination maid of honor and flower girl, she dropped flower petals along the aisle floor and took her place as maid of honor next to where Katie would stand. A faint floral scent wafted in the air as she passed by. Dusty couldn't imagine where the women had found flower petals in December.

The twins, dressed in white shirts and dark pants, began their walk down the aisle. Each boy held one side of a frilly pillow to which Katie's wedding ring was tied. All the men had questioned the females as to the sense of allowing the feisty boys such an important duty, but the women were certain the twins would behave.

Nathan tugged on the pillow. "You're holding too much," he whispered, loud enough that Dusty heard up front.

"Nuh-uh. You are." Nick gave a little yank and regained his hold.

Nathan scowled and pressed his lips together. Dusty watched Rebekah glare at the boys from her perch in the front row. Suddenly, Nathan jerked on the pillow. It went sailing into Homer Johnson's head and then bounced onto the aisle floor. Stunned shock widened Mr. Johnson's eyes; then his lips twitched, and he burst out laughing, many in the audience joining him.

Both boys lunged forward at the same time. Nick fell on top of the pillow, and Nathan fell on Nick.

"I got it! Get off me!" Nick screamed.

Rebekah leaped to her feet, handed Joey to Mrs. Whitaker in the second-row pew, and marched down the aisle. Men chuckled, and women stared wide-eyed at the wrestling boys. Dusty had a feeling this wedding would be talked about for weeks.

Rebekah grabbed both boys by the earlobes and tugged them to the front row. Once seated, the twins nudged each other with their elbows. Dusty couldn't help smiling.

Rebekah retrieved the pillow, handed it to Jimmy, and then sat down between her two sons.

"But we's s'posed to be up there with Jimmy and Dusty," Nick whined.

At his mother's stern glare, the boy crossed his arms and hunkered down, glowering.

"Bet you never forget that." Jimmy chuckled softly beside Dusty as he untied the ring and tossed the lacy pillow aside. "Good thing Katie didn't see it."

Dusty grinned. He heard a ruckus at the back and saw Mason and Katie enter the church. The music became louder, and the organist played another tune.

Dusty held his breath as Katie glided down the church aisle toward him. Her pale-colored dress emphasized her tanned skin. He loved that she wasn't afraid to allow the sun to color her skin. It made her blue eyes stand out that much more. Her glorious golden hair was piled on top of her head in delicate curls. He couldn't wait until he had the right to yank out all those pins and run his hands through her flaxen mane.

Mason walked with Katie on his arm. His eyes beamed with pride, making Dusty glad they'd waited to marry until both Mason and Rebekah could give their blessing.

Katie's eyes gleamed. His insides turned somersaults. Oh, how he loved this woman! Mason handed her off, and Dusty took his beloved's hand and turned to face the minister.

It amazed him how God had taken a man filled with anger and grief and washed him clean, even giving him a future as a husband and father. Only God's forgiving grace could change a man that much.

Dusty glanced at the cross behind the minister's head as he listened to Katie pledge her love.

Thank You, God, for new beginnings.

A WEALTH
BEYOND
RICHES

He that trusteth in his riches shall fall:
but the righteous shall flourish as a branch.
PROVERBS 11:28

Chapter 1

New York City, April 1906

A knock sounded on the door of Sasha Di Carlo's hotel room, and her mother glided inside without even waiting for a "Come in." She eyed Sasha's evening gown, hiked her chin, and sniffed. "There's been a change of plans."

Always one to make a grand entrance, Cybil Di Carlo flipped open her oriental fan and waved it back and forth, fluttering the coal black tendrils of hair around her temples. The lavender silk of her Liberty and Co. evening dress swished back and forth as she moved farther into the room. The scent of expensive perfume overpowered the lemony smell of oil the maid had used earlier to polish the furniture.

"What do you mean? What's changed?" Sasha stared at her mother and sucked in her breath as the maid secured the back of her frilly party dress.

Cybil waved her fan at the maid, which sent the dark-skinned servant scurrying out of the hotel room. Her mother lifted her nose in the air with a hint of disinterest. "I know it's your birthday, dear, but Nigel just surprised me with tickets to *The Earl and the Girl*. You know how I've been dying to see the Casino Theater ever since it was rebuilt after the fire. It's all the rage now. I can't disappoint Nigel. Those tickets cost him a fortune and are almost impossible to acquire."

Disbelief clogged Sasha's throat, and tears burned her eyes. Her mother wouldn't dare disappoint her latest beau—a wealthy Englishman Cybil had known a mere month—but her daughter was another thing. Sasha's frustration bubbled out. "But it's my eighteenth birthday. We've planned this evening for weeks."

"Oh, for heaven's sake, Anastasia, don't be so melodramatic." Cybil clicked her fan shut and eyed Sasha with a narrowed gaze. "You know if Nigel had an extra ticket I would drag you along with us."

Sasha pressed her lips together, doubting Cybil's last statement. Her famous actress mother had never been affectionate, but she had always treated Sasha to a birthday dinner each year. It was a rare, special time that Sasha cherished. One of the few times she was certain to have her popular mother's undivided attention. She closed her eyes and pushed aside her aching disappointment. She wouldn't cry in front of her mother no matter how much her heart hurt. That would only bring a stern reprimand.

"There is more."

With her emotional control tied together by only a thin thread, Sasha composed herself and opened her eyes.

Her mother tugged off her white kid glove, held out her left hand, and smiled. "Nigel asked me to marry him. Don't you just adore the ring he gave me?"

Unable to believe Cybil had finally accepted a man's offer of marriage, Sasha stared at the gaudy diamond ring on her mother's finger. She imagined after wearing the huge stone for a day her mother's wrist would be aching.

"It's—uh. . .large."

Cybil pressed her lips together in a proud gloat. Her gaze caressed the oversized rock. "Yes, it is. Quite. That snooty Thelma Crowley will be green with envy." Her mother's black eyes glinted.

"I suppose congratulations are in order." Sasha couldn't help wondering how this change would affect her. Whenever her mother turned her back when all three were together, Nigel Grantham's leering gaze at Sasha made her shudder. She couldn't stand the man.

Her mother's painted lips tilted up in a sickly sweet smile. "Yes, well, you could be a bit more enthusiastic." While she wrestled her hand back into her glove, Cybil's gaze traveled the room that had been Sasha's home for the past twelve months. "I simply can't fathom why you're happy staying in such quaint quarters."

"I don't need all the space you require, Mother, and it's affordable. Besides, it has the same view of the city as your suite." Sasha stifled a sigh, wondering how her mother could consider any room at the fashionable Castleworth as quaint.

Cybil sashayed over to the chest of drawers and fingered a small statue of the Eiffel Tower. Sasha had picked it up as a souvenir of their two-year stint in Europe, where her mother had acted in several plays while Sasha had worked as a makeup artist. Now they made their home in the Castleworth Hotel where her mother's luxurious suite took up one-fourth of the top floor, while Sasha's more conservative single room was on the third floor.

Though physically she was almost an exact replica of her beautiful mother, on the inside, they were very different. Cybil craved attention and fawning from anyone who was willing, but Sasha only yearned for her mother's love. Now it looked as if she might never achieve that dream.

"I am quitting the theater, darling. Nigel is wealthy enough that I no longer have to work. Instead, I will content myself with sitting in his private theater box seats and being part of the adoring audience. I suppose your salary with Geoffrey's troupe will keep you living in the style you are accustomed to."

Sasha blinked, confusion fogging her brain. "What do you mean?"

Her mother snapped open the fan again. "Anastasia, you are eighteen now.

It is past time you were on your own. I will no longer be supporting you."

All manner of emotions assaulted Sasha. Her mother hadn't truly supported her since she was sixteen when Sasha had been hired as the head makeup artist and had also begun serving as her mother's understudy. A measure of fear snaked up her spine. Even though she was already providing for herself, her mother had been there to fall back on if things hadn't gone as planned. Not that it had ever happened.

Still, she couldn't help feeling she was losing something precious—even if it was only her dream.

"Anyway, Nigel is downstairs waiting. I must be off. You and I will catch dinner together another time." Cybil stared at her as if she wanted to say more, then snapped shut her fan and stuffed it in her beaded handbag.

The door clicked shut as Cybil left, and Sasha felt more alone than she ever had. Tears blurred her eyes, but she forced them away. She'd learned long ago how hard-hearted and selfish her mother could be. But her birthday had been the one day she could count on having her mother to herself.

Ignoring the hunger pangs rumbling in her stomach, she wandered over to the window and stared out at the busy traffic on 32nd Avenue. People on their way to dinner, others heading home from work, and still more on their way to theater shows continued on their merry ways, oblivious that her heart had just shattered.

It had taken a lot of effort to persuade her boss, Geoffrey, to allow her and Cybil to have the evening off. Up-and-comer Lorinda Swanson had been only too happy to play the lead role, and fortunately, she was up on all the lines. But all Sasha's efforts had been for naught.

She continued watching the people below. How could someone feel so utterly alone in such a mass of humanity?

Sasha clenched her fist as she remembered her mother's coldhearted glare. The woman didn't care one whit that she'd chosen her new fiancé over her own daughter.

Sasha's satin dress rustled as she crossed the room and flopped onto the bed. All she ever wanted was to belong. To someone. To some place.

Her mother had always considered her a nuisance. Sasha shuddered as she thought of the times as a child when she'd sat quietly alone in the dark of a hotel's wardrobe while her mother entertained her male friends. Sasha had learned to hide in the silky long dresses and pretend she was a fairy princess.

She picked up the Bible on the night table beside the bed. She'd meant to return it to the desk clerk but had forgotten. Some nice organization had donated it to the hotel. She didn't understand everything within the thick book's pages, but certain passages warmed her heart and gave her hope.

At eighteen, she was already tired of the theater, but it was the only life she knew—the only way she could support herself. Unshed tears burned her eyes and made her throat ache. If only she had some clue who her father was—maybe she could go to him. But her mother had always refused to talk about him. Sasha didn't even know his name.

A yawn forced its way out. She'd looked forward to her birthday dinner for weeks, and disappointment weighed heavily upon her. Though it was only 8:00 p.m., Sasha closed her eyes and hugged the Bible to her chest. Maybe tomorrow would be better.

❧

An incessant pounding pulled Sasha from her sleep. She yawned and glanced at the window, noting the sun must have been up several hours. The Ansonia Chamberlain on the fireplace mantel read nine o'clock.

"I'm coming. Just a minute."

She slipped off the bed, padded across the room in her bare feet, and unlocked the door, hoping to see her mother. The theater had been closed on Sunday and Monday, so the last time she'd seen Cybil was that disappointing Saturday evening.

The maid's dark eyes widened. "Mercy me, Miz Di Carlo! For such an early riser, you sho' have been sleeping late these past few days." The young colored woman hurried behind Sasha and flung open the drapes. Sasha squinted, for the bright light hurt her dry, gritty eyes. She'd slept late because it had taken until after 2:00 a.m. to fall asleep the past few nights. Sasha yawned and stretched, wondering if she'd see her mother today.

Prissy opened the wardrobe, revealing the wrinkled pale green evening dress Sasha had purchased especially for her birthday dinner. She had hoped her appearance in the fancy new gown would please her critical mother, but Cybil hadn't even noticed.

Disappointed again, Sasha removed her nightgown and flopped onto the Victorian sofa, dressed only in her undergarments. Today would be better than yesterday. She'd spent enough time upset, and she needed to put the past behind her.

Prissy rummaged through the wardrobe. "What would you like to wear? Your pale blue day dress? Or perhaps the yellow one?"

Sasha waved her hand in the air. "It doesn't matter. You pick." Her stomach grumbled, reminding her she hadn't eaten much lately. She'd had little appetite. Breakfast was usually a lonely affair as her mother rarely rose before noon.

Prissy fluffed the yellow gown. "You need something cheery today." She laid the dress on the bed, then pivoted. "Oh, I almost forgot. Your mama gave me a package to give to you. And I have one from the hotel manager, too."

Hope sparked within Sasha. Had her mother perhaps sent her a birthday gift to make up for missing dinner?

Prissy pulled two envelopes from her apron pocket and handed them to her, one bearing the hotel insignia. "I'll just go get some fresh water whilst you read your letters."

The door clicked shut as the maid slipped out. Sasha turned over the thicker, plain white envelope. It didn't look like a present.

Business first, then hopefully pleasure. She loosened the flap on the hotel envelope and pulled out a heavy linen sheet.

Dear Miss Di Carlo,
> *We here at the Castleworth Hotel are very sorry to see your mother leave.*

As she read the short missive, her heart stumbled. Sasha crinkled her forehead. What was he talking about? Her mother wasn't going anywhere. She still had ten months left on her contract.

> *We have enjoyed having you both as our guests this past year. However, I regret that I must inform you that the rate for your room must be increased. We have graciously charged you only half price, due to the fact that your mother was also staying in one of our top-floor suites. Now that that is no longer the case, we must charge you full price for your room. The rate increase goes into effect beginning Monday.*

She lowered the letter to her lap, trying to make sense of it. If she had to pay full price, she would be forced to find a room in a less expensive hotel. But what was all this chatter about her mother leaving?

With shaking hands, she picked up her mother's thick envelope, loosened the flap, and peered inside. There was a folded sheet of what looked like hotel stationery and a yellowed envelope. She pulled out the paper, and a pile of money fell into her lap. Curious, she read the note.

Sasha darling,
> *By the time you read this letter, Nigel and I will have departed for England. He persuaded Geoffrey to release me from my contract, and we are getting married at Grantham Manor, his family's two-hundred-year-old castle. This will come as a shock, but you are a capable girl and will be fine without me.*
>
> *I know you have been curious about your heritage. You certainly needled me enough with endless questions about it. I must confess that my past is a grievance to me. I couldn't bear to voice the horrible truth out loud. You will understand when you read the enclosed letter. I will see you on our return in a year or two.*

> *Thinking of you,*
> *Cybil Angelina Di Carlo*

Stunned, Sasha stared at the letter. Her mother was gone? To England?

Cybil must have planned this for weeks. She couldn't simply secure passage on a ship so quickly. Her mother hadn't even had the nerve to tell her good-bye in person. Sasha pressed her hand against her aching heart. She thought nothing could feel worse than the pain she'd encountered on her birthday, but she'd been mistaken.

She wadded up the letter and tossed it across the room, then grabbed the dollars, slinging them aside, and watched as they spiraled down to the carpet. Penance money—that's what it was. Money to ease her mother's guilty conscience.

Pressing her lips tightly together, she locked her hands in her lap to keep them from trembling.

"Am I so worthless my own mother doesn't want me?"

Cybil hadn't even had faith that her daughter could take care of herself and had to shame her by giving her money. She hadn't even signed the letter with "Mother," but instead used her full name.

Well, she was truly on her own now. Sighing, Sasha took hold of the aged envelope and turned it in her hands. The letter was from a Dewey Hummingbird in Indian Territory. She closed her eyes and searched her memory to see if that name held some meaning.

No, she'd never heard it before.

The yellowed envelope crackled as she withdrew the paper from inside. An unfamiliar scribbling covered several pages. Sasha rubbed her eyes and began reading.

Dearest Myrtle,

Myrtle? She glanced at the envelope again. *Who is Myrtle?*
Only one way to find out, so she continued reading.

> *Or should I call you by your theater name—Cybil? How I long to see you again. I hope you and Anastasia are well. Your aunt Kizzie married Raymond Arbuckle and is living on the land next to mine. They are very happy and would love to have a whole tribe of children, but Kizzie has been unable to become with child. My Jenny is gone now. Buried her last August under the big oak on the hill behind my cabin.*
>
> *I wish you and Sasha could come visit. How old is she now? Three? Four?*

Sasha laid the letter in her lap. Confusion swirled with excitement. She had family! An aunt and this man who wrote the letter. But how could her mother have kept this correspondence for nearly fifteen years and never have mentioned it?

I feel I should have done more to make you happy, but you were never the same after your parents were killed. I know living on a farm in Indian Territory was hard for you. You always had such big dreams. Forgive me for my shortcomings. And please, if you find the time, come and bring your daughter for a visit. She deserves the chance to meet her Creek relatives and to learn about her rich ancestry.

Always yours,
Your uncle, Dewey Hummingbird
Creek Nation, Indian Territory

P.S. Things have greatly changed around here, so I've included directions to my home, in case you decide to visit.

Numb, Sasha stared out the window across the room. She'd always dreamed of and longed for a heritage, but to be an Indian! People in New York referred to Indians as savages.

Was it true?

The man in the letter sure didn't sound like a savage. He could even read and write.

Did her mother never tell her about their Indian heritage because she was ashamed? Or because she thought people would treat her unkindly? She must have been ashamed since she'd changed her name and had kept the information a secret all these years.

Sasha closed her eyes, trying to take it all in. All her life she'd thought she was Italian because of their last name. Was Di Carlo her father's surname—or just another name her mother had made up?

Being Indian also explained her mother's high cheek bones and black hair and eyes. Sasha crossed the room and stared in the mirror. Her facial features were similar to her mother's, but her complexion and hair color were quite a bit lighter.

What would her friends say if they knew she was Indian?

What about Geoffrey, her employer?

Now she understood the secret burden her mother had borne all these years. Myrtle Hummingbird must have left home, changed her name, and become an actress.

All her life Sasha had wanted to belong to a family and to settle down and live in a real house. For as long as she could remember, she wanted to quit living in hotels and have a place to put down roots. To be accepted for who she was on the inside, not because she was pretty or had a famous mother.

But to be an Indian—a half-breed, most likely—was more than she could comprehend. Would the theater troupe members despise her if they learned the truth?

She looked down at the letter in her fist. It was the only link to her family. Pressing the paper against her lap, she smoothed it. Somewhere, far away in Indian Territory, she had a relative—an uncle who wanted to meet her.

Sasha glanced at the money strewn across her floor. Was there enough to get her to Indian Territory and back? Would Geoffrey allow her to take a leave of absence from the theater, especially since her mother had just left?

Or maybe she should quit. There were plenty who could take her place.

Then again, if they learned she was part Indian, they might boot her out of the troupe without even a second glance. She and her mother would most likely become pariahs.

But she had family—family who longed to see her.

She paced the room, wrestling with her discovery. Should she go to Indian Territory and meet her uncle and learn of her heritage? Or should she stay in New York and live a lie, doing a job that didn't hold her heart?

She had toured the richest cities of eastern America and Europe with her mother and other members of the acting troupe, but did she dare travel west—to primitive Indian Territory?

With a quick knock, Prissy slipped back into the room and eyed the money on the floor. Having worked several years at the hotel, she ignored the scene and set her bucket of water beside the basin. "You ready to wash up, ma'am?"

Sasha nodded. "Did you know my mother was leaving, Prissy?"

The maid ducked her head and fiddled with her apron. "Yes'm, but Miz Cybil threatened to have me fired if I said a word. I'm so sorry, Miz Sasha."

"It's all right. I understand."

"Pardon me for saying, but your mama is jealous of you."

Sasha's head jerked up. "Jealous? Of me? Why ever for?"

"You're prettier than her. She's afraid you'd soon steal the lead from her, and she couldn't handle that thought, so she done run off."

Sasha blinked in disbelief. Was that truly what her mother thought? That she'd try to take her place? The thought had never even entered Sasha's mind and only emphasized how little Sasha knew her own mother.

Pushing aside her disappointment, Sasha allowed an excitement that she hadn't felt in a long time to surge through her. She had family. Family who wanted to meet her.

She spun around. "Yes, I want to wash up, and then I need you to help me pack."

Prissy blinked in confusion. "But your mama's already gone. It's too late to join her."

A grin tugged at Sasha's lips. "I'm not going with Mother. I'm going to visit my uncle."

Chapter 2

Creek Nation, Indian Territory, May 1906

S asha stared out the window of the gently swaying train, wondering how much longer it would be before she arrived in Tulsa. They had already crossed into Indian Territory, but she'd yet to see a tepee or an Indian out the window. Though many of the passengers looked as if they might carry Native American blood, their clothing seemed nearly as modern as her own.

Still, she couldn't stop the chills that charged up her spine. Did Indians still go on the warpath?

She'd heard stories of pioneers meeting up with bands of renegade Indians who shot zinging arrows and whooped eerie cries. Some adventurers had even lost their scalps and lives. She shuddered and reached up, tugging her hat forward, hoping and praying those days were past.

But then, she was of Indian blood. A half-breed most likely. Would that make any difference if the train were attacked?

A man across from her cleared his throat, and Sasha jumped.

"I was wondering, ma'am, would you do me the honor of accompanying me to dinner at our next stop? I'm rather tired of the dining car's food and fancy something different."

She stifled a sigh and stared at the gentleman dressed stylishly in his gray three-piece suit. Hope sparked in his pale blue eyes. He ran a neatly manicured finger over his thin moustache.

She'd lost count of the number of men who had offered to buy her meals and pushed their unwanted attentions her way since she'd left New York. A few men had even asked her to marry them. She now understood why most women traveled with an escort. But for her, that hadn't been an option.

It had been a mistake to dress in her tailored Edwardian suit. The short bolero jacket only helped to emphasize her narrow waist, but the dark blue color was perfect for traveling because it didn't show dirt or coal dust.

She glanced at the man, patiently awaiting her response. "I sincerely appreciate your kindness, sir, but I do not intend to disembark the train for dinner at our next stop." No, but she would locate her trunk and fetch a change of clothing.

"But surely you must eat." He leaned forward, resting his elbows on his knees.

Oh, how she wished these train seats didn't face one another. She shook her head. "Thank you, but I have something leftover from my last stop."

He pressed his lips together and sat back. "As you wish."

Relieved that he acquiesced, Sasha focused her attention on the passing landscape again. Growing up the daughter of a famous and beautiful actress, she'd had her share of men's attentions. Though her mother craved the limelight and being fawned over by adoring men, Sasha had never liked it. Somehow she felt there had to be more to a relationship between a man and a woman than physical attraction. She longed for friendship and even love. But she'd seen few examples in the theater world of happily married couples.

Sasha could feel the man across from her staring, and she sighed, wishing she'd worn her old woman's costume. When things in New York became more than she could bear, she'd skillfully apply some theater makeup and dress as an old woman. Incognito, she was free to ramble the streets of New York without an escort or sit in a park without disturbance. Her old woman's costume had served her well and had given her the freedom to wander where she wanted without drawing the attention of half the men on the street.

A half hour later, the train stopped in a small town that resembled ten others they'd passed through. In the washroom of the depot, Sasha changed out of her travel clothes and put on her costume that a kind freight conductor had helped her retrieve from her trunk. Now she shuffled down the aisle, dressed as an elderly woman. Her cane tapped out a slow rhythm as she made her way to the final seat, which faced the wall of the train. Her makeup was good at a distance but most likely wouldn't hold up to close scrutiny.

As she settled herself on the wooden seat, she set her cane on the bench beside her to discourage anyone from sitting there. She readjusted her fringed scarf and stared out the window with a smile tugging at her lips. Several men, including the one who'd asked her to dinner, had looked her way and tipped their hats, but not a one had pressed his attentions. Perhaps she'd have solitude for the final leg of her long trip.

From her satchel, she dug out a hard biscuit left over from breakfast, as she eagerly anticipated her arrival. What would her uncle think when he finally saw her?

She'd left New York so quickly that she hadn't taken time to write a letter or send him a telegraph message. Would he be happy to see her?

Mile after mile of low hills and wild acres of tall prairie grass sped by. The gently rolling landscape was refreshing after the flat, treeless plains of Kansas.

Her thoughts drifted back to the big buildings of New York. Would she ever return? She wasn't sure that she wanted to. Deep in her heart, she hoped that she'd find the family she'd always longed for. But she hadn't yet reconciled herself to the fact that she was part Indian—Creek Indian.

What would her theater troupe say if they learned the truth? What would life be like in an Indian village? Was it possible that her uncle live in a tepee?

She had so many questions and nobody to answer them.

The train slowed as it made a sluggish turn to the south. Gradually it began to pick up speed again, and the gentle swaying lulled Sasha into a relaxed state. She closed her eyes and saw a picture of her mother. Had Cybil missed her yet?

A more poignant question was, did she miss her mother?

An ache coursed through her as she realized she did. If she stayed in Indian Territory, she'd probably never see Cybil again, and that thought made her sad, in spite of the way her mother had treated her. They'd never been close, and Cybil had made it clear on many occasions how inconvenient it was to be a famous celebrity and have to deal with the responsibility of a child. Sasha had grown up quickly and learned to depend on herself. Still, as long as her mother was around, she had never been totally alone. Until now. Unshed tears burned her eyes, and her throat tightened.

Please, Uncle Dewey. . .please want me.

❧

Two hours later, Sasha retied her scarf and picked up her satchel and handbag. There was definitely a negative side to dressing like an old woman. She'd already stopped at five of the nicer Tulsa hotels and several of the lower-class ones that people here referred to as "cowboy hotels." Each clerk had refused to rent her a room, saying, "We don't rent to Gypsies."

She'd never even seen a Gypsy before and had no idea that her costume resembled one until now.

Sasha looked ahead and to her left to make sure no one was watching, then darted down a dark alley. Her heart pounded, and she prayed she wouldn't run into any Indians, not that the ones she'd seen so far looked all that fierce. In fact, much to her surprise, most resembled white men with just darker skin and hair. Very few had been dressed in what she assumed was native garb. Most of the hotel clerks had even looked like they were of Indian blood.

She found an unlocked shed behind the Whitaker Hotel and scurried into it. Leaning against the closed door, she willed her heart to slow its frantic pace. Things were so different here in Tulsa. The handful of buildings were only a few stories high, and everything seemed so rustic. The town was so small compared to New York City. She could only hope she was doing the right thing by coming here.

Changing clothes quickly, she considered what the clerk at the train depot had told her. After she had made arrangements to store her trunk until she could return for it, the clerk confirmed that Dewey Hummingbird used to live in Keaton, near where oil was first found at the Glenn Pool strike. The man knew her uncle because Dewey had occasionally picked up freight at the Tulsa depot, but the clerk hadn't seen him in a long time. Disappointment surged through her. Traveling across the country and buying frequent meals had cost more than she'd expected. With her funds dwindling, what would she do if her uncle no longer lived in the area?

As she entered the Whitaker Hotel, again dressed in her stylish travel clothes and with her makeup removed, she noticed the clerk's gaze rivet on her. His eyes sparked, and he straightened his black vest and string tie. A man on her side of the counter also turned to stare, a leering grin tilting his cheek.

"Howdy, ma'am. What can I help you with?" The clerk's interested gaze darted sideways toward his buddy, and he lifted his eyebrows up and down.

Sasha never ceased to be amazed at how men could be so easily swayed by a pretty woman. No one had shown kindness to her when she was dressed as an old woman. Was there not a single man in the world who had character?

Lifting her chin, she pinned the clerk with a stern glare. "I'd like a room for the night, please."

He adjusted his string tie again and cleared his throat. "I'd be happy to rent you a room, but mostly cowpokes and oil workers bunk here. Wouldn't you be more comfortable in a fancier hotel?"

Sasha shook her head. "I've already been told there are no rooms available at those establishments."

"Well. . ." The man leaned on the counter and narrowed his eyes, "I have a room, but I can't guarantee your safety. We don't often get women traveling alone here—at least not of your caliber. If you know what I mean."

Sasha surmised what he meant but didn't want to think about the ladies of the night. "I assure you I'm quite able to take care of myself. So, if you don't mind, I've traveled a long ways and am rather tired."

"Suit yourself." He shrugged one shoulder, pushed the registration book toward her, and collected her coins.

She followed him up the stairs of the bare, wooden structure and down a dimly lit hallway toward two rugged cowboys. Their low rumbling voices halted as she drew near. One man leaned against the doorjamb, and the other stood in the narrow walkway. Whiskers shaded their jaws, and they smelled strongly of cigars and cattle.

"Whoowee! Would you look at that, Sam. A real lady, right here at Whitaker's."

Sasha hugged the wall and hurried closer to the clerk as she passed the men.

"Mmm-mmm. Sure does make your mouth water." The taller of the two men sidestepped and blocked her path. "H'lo there, missy."

Sasha halted and shivered as the second man sidled up behind her. She'd had her share of run-ins with dandies in New York. These men might dress and smell differently, but they were all the same. Stroke their egos, and you could usually get what you wanted—that was one thing she'd learned from her mother. As she formulated her words, she heard footsteps stomping toward her.

"You two leave that woman be. She's a customer just like you. If you cause trouble, you'll be out on the streets." The clerk glared at the two men.

One cowboy smirked, his gray eyes burning holes into her. "I think you're wrong, Dwight. She ain't nothing like me." He tipped his hat, and the floor squeaked as he stepped aside. "Be seeing you later, ma'am."

The clerk opened a door several rooms past the cowboys and handed her a key. "I try to run a clean place, but with all the rough cowpokes and roustabouts who stay here, it's difficult. I'll bring up some fresh water. And I don't have to tell you to stay in your room and keep the door locked, do I?"

Sasha shook her head and hurried inside, closing and securing the door. She looked around the sparse room, so different from the nice one she'd had in New York. The bare, unpainted walls reeked of cigar smoke. The bed was simply a plain, wooden frame with a sagging mattress and worn quilt. No carpet decorated the bare, dusty floor. She dragged the ladder-back chair across the tiny room and wedged the top slat under the door handle.

As she dropped her satchel on the narrow bed, her throat tightened. Had she made a horrible mistake coming here?

Tulsa was so rugged, even though the effects of the recent oil boom were evident. Many of the buildings still smelled of fresh wood, and there were several new brick structures. As she'd strolled down the boardwalk, she could hear the sound of hammering in all directions. But everything was so unlike New York. Even the town's odor was different—more like animals and dirt.

Sasha lifted up the lone window and peered out, watching the people wandering along the boardwalk. Though it was still chilly in New York, a stiff, warm breeze blew in her window, lessening the cigar odor.

Having used nearly all of her money to get here, going back would prove difficult. Her training as a makeup artist and intern actress wasn't likely to do her any good in Indian Territory. Besides, she wasn't even sure she wanted to work in theater anymore.

A tear slipped down her cheek. Her throat burned. In New York she never cried, but this was a world away. And her mother wasn't here to chastise her.

Maybe just this once she'd give in to her tears.

❧

Jim Conners kicked open the door of his hotel room, removed his hat, and tossed it onto the bed. He crossed the tiny room, pushed aside the dingy curtain, and stared down onto Second Street, watching the people.

He hadn't wanted to overnight in town, but when the load of freight he was supposed to pick up hadn't arrived, he'd had no choice. It was too late to drive back to Keaton today and too dangerous to camp out with all the rough oil workers in the area looking for some nighttime fun. Jim heaved a sigh. He hoped his employer wouldn't worry about him.

A raucous laugh across the hall pulled him from his musing.

"She's a looker, that one. I say we see if she wants some company."

Jim tossed his hat on the bed and looked through his open door across the hall where two men in Room Four were talking. One man rubbed the back of his neck.

"Yeah, she's a fine lady, but you heard Whitaker—he said he don't want no trouble."

Sensing something was amiss, Jim slipped behind his open door and peered at the men through the crack between the door and the frame.

"Whitaker's downstairs." The shorter man leaned forward toward his friend and spoke softly. "What he don't know, he cain't object to."

A sickening grin tugged the man's lips, and he cackled a raspy laugh. "You're right, Shorty." He nudged his buddy in the shoulder with his elbow. "I say let's have us some fun. Shhh, here comes Whitaker."

Jim's skin crawled. These two were up to no good, and he suspected an innocent woman would pay the price. Though he had a hankering to head over to the café and get some supper before the place closed, he needed to find out what these two rabble-rousers were up to. If his sister, Katie, ever encountered trouble, he'd like to think someone would help her. How could he do any less?

Jim heard footsteps treading down the wooden hall in his direction. They passed by, and a knock sounded several rooms away.

"I've brung your water, ma'am. I've got customers waiting downstairs, so I'll just leave it here outside your door."

Footsteps rushed in his direction, passed by again, then faded away.

For a few seconds, nothing could be heard except the muffled sounds of outside noises—the whinny of a horse, a faint hint of laughter.

"Dwight's gone, and no one else is around. Now's as good a time as any," the tall man across the hall whispered. "Let's just wait outside her door until she opens it for the water."

"Yeah. Sounds good to me."

The men's spurs jingled as they shuffled into the hall toward the back of the hotel. Jim slipped around the door and peeked out, watching the shorter man's back move away from him. He checked his gun, making sure it was fully loaded, and waited.

In a few seconds, Jim heard the click of a lock and the squeak of a door opening. A woman's brief squeal erupted, followed by a ruckus and the thunk of a bucket being kicked.

Jim sprang into action. He wouldn't stand by and let an innocent woman get hurt, not when he could prevent it.

Chapter 3

Sasha wrestled her two attackers, smacking one across the nose with her hair brush. He howled and grabbed her right arm. The shorter man struggled to keep his grasp tight on her other arm as she tried hard to claw him with her fingernails. Her heart pounded like a frantic animal's fighting to escape a snare. Bile burned her throat as her fear surged. Never had she been so afraid.

She jerked and struggled, but they were too strong for her. Her worst fears were becoming a reality, and there was no one to help her. Oh, why had she come to this wretched place?

Not yet ready to give up the fight, she kicked one man in the shin, making him curse. Her heart plummeted when another man rushed into the room.

For a brief second, their gazes collided, and she knew instantly when she looked into those brilliant black eyes that help had arrived. He was taller than her captors and broader across the shoulders. The handsome cowboy raised his gun as the two men shoved her up against the wall, oblivious to the third man's presence. Their rank breath and evil glares made her feel faint, but she maintained her focus on her rescuer.

"Now we'll have some fun—"

The cowboy pointed his pistol at them. "Get away from that woman."

Her attackers froze. They glanced at each other, then looked over their shoulders.

"Get him!" the tall man yelled.

They tossed Sasha aside like a rag doll and charged the man, all three falling back into the hallway with a loud clamor of men knocking against walls and the scuffle of boots.

The blast of gunfire resounded in the hallway, leaving in its wake the pungent scent of gunpowder and smoke. A man cried out. Sasha could only hope it wasn't her champion.

Heart throbbing, she grabbed her handbag, snatched up her satchel, and darted into the hallway, barely missing getting kicked. She glanced at the pile of thrashing bodies, unable to see who had the advantage because of the dimly lit hall and the lingering cloud of smoke. Hurrying toward the rear exit, she fled the frightening commotion.

Behind her someone yelled, "Get the sheriff—and the doc. Looks like one of 'em is shot."

At least her rescuer had help now. She dearly hoped he hadn't gotten shot or injured.

Sasha's stampeding heart outpaced her feet as she rushed down the stairs and out into the growing dusk. She hated abandoning her rescuer, but she had to get away. If the cowboy wasn't successful in fighting her two attackers, then surely they'd come after her again.

She dreaded being outside at night, not knowing what she would face. At least in New York City, she knew her way around and knew which places were safe and which weren't. But Indian Territory was as new to her as a script she was reading for the first time.

Ducking behind a toolshed, she took a moment to catch her breath. She pressed her hand to her chest and willed her heart to slow its frantic pace as she peered around the corner. A man ran out the back of Whitaker's Hotel. Sasha held her breath. The faint light of the open door illuminated his back, but his face remained in the shadows.

"Miss? Are you out there?" He leaned his hands on the porch railings and stared into the darkness. "It's safe to come back. Those two fellows are tied up, and Mr. Whitaker's gone to fetch the sheriff. They won't bother you anymore."

She recognized the blue plaid shirt as belonging to the man who had helped her, and for a brief second, Sasha considered returning to her room. It wasn't much, but it was paid for and better than sleeping outside with the unfamiliar. But if she could be accosted after being at the hotel only a few minutes, how would she manage staying safe overnight? No, she wasn't going back. Hesitating, she wondered if she should thank him. But she wasn't sure whether to trust him or not. When he stepped back inside, she inhaled a deep breath, feeling both guilty and relieved.

She needed to don her costume to feel safe. Nobody would bother an old woman.

❧

Jim clucked to the horses pulling the heavy wagon. This area was his favorite part of the drive from Tulsa to Keaton. The sandy Arkansas River meandered along on his right, and on his left, farm and ranch land rolled on as far as he could see. He was glad that Tulsa didn't allow drilling within the city limits. Oil might make a few folks wealthy beyond their imaginations, but drilling destroyed the beauty of the land.

He sighed and allowed his mind to drift back to last night's events. The vision of the lovely woman he'd glimpsed invaded his thoughts again. Before his scuffle with the two men at the hotel, he'd made split-second eye contact with the frightened lady. He didn't think he'd ever encountered such a lovely woman. She reminded him of a cross between his sister's porcelain doll and a corralled mustang, with her saddle brown mane that hung in soft waves to her waist and brown eyes that had glistened with fear and anger. She'd wielded that hairbrush like a warrior.

By the time he'd knocked both men out cold, the woman had skedaddled. He'd tried to find her last night but had no luck, and he had hoped to see her this morning at breakfast but was disappointed. He watched for her as he loaded his wagon and drove out of town but had failed to find her.

Who was she? And why was she staying at a seedy place like Whitaker's?

Jim swatted a fly and pulled down his brim to shade his eyes. He'd be happy when the railroad was opened up to Keaton so he wouldn't have to drive the slow-moving wagon clear to Tulsa. The track had been laid, but service wasn't due to start for another week.

Up ahead, he saw someone shuffling down the road. A woman. From her slumped back and grandma-style dress, he suspected she must be quite old. She lugged a satchel in one hand and leaned heavily on a knobby stick, which she used as a cane.

Where in the world was she going? It was at least twelve miles to the Glenn Pool and even further to Keaton.

As the horses pulled even with her, Jim tugged them to a stop and stood. The animals pawed the ground and snorted, as if they knew it wasn't quitting time yet.

"Mornin', ma'am. Can I offer you a ride?"

The woman glanced his way, shook her head, and kept walking.

He didn't blame her for being apprehensive, but he was the last person she needed to fear. Clucking the horses forward, he sat down, drove twenty feet, and then stopped again.

"I don't mean to bother you, ma'am, but it's a good twelve miles to the next town. And with all the oil riffraff in these parts. . . Well, a woman shouldn't travel without an escort."

At those words, she stopped and turned toward him but kept her eyes on the ground.

"Would you mind telling me where you're going?" Jim slid his hat back on his head and watched as she wrestled her carpetbag.

"Keaton," she muttered.

"Keaton! Well, that's a good fifteen miles or more. You won't make it before dark if you walk, and you definitely don't want to be out alone after the sun sets. Not on this road."

She glanced up. Something sparked in her dark eyes, and she looked away again. After a few moments, she turned toward the wagon but kept her face to the ground. "All right, if you're sure you don't mind, I'll ride with you."

"No, ma'am. I don't mind at all." His boots thumped the ground as he jumped down, stirring up a cloud of dust. He set her satchel in the back and helped her up onto the seat, noticing she seemed rather spry for an old woman as she shinnied up the wheel. She was as thin as a sapling, though.

The wagon creaked as he sat on the seat beside her. Leaving a decent gap in between them, he picked up the reins and nudged his canteen with his boot. "There's water if you're thirsty."

She glanced down, then at him, and leaned forward, picking up the canteen. "Thank you." She drank deeply, then laid the container back on the floor.

He clucked the horses forward, wondering where the woman had come from. She looked a bit like a Gypsy, but her accent was different and her speech sounded as if she might even be an educated woman. In fact, her voice didn't sound half as old as she looked.

"My name's Jim Conners." He glanced sideways, hoping for a peek at her face. "Nice day, isn't it?"

"Mmm."

"Where do you hail from?"

"Back East."

He wasn't much of a talker himself and could take a hint. This woman was in no mood for conversation. Well, he knew what it was like not to want someone to poke a nose into his business.

He glanced down, and his gaze landed on the woman's hand, which held her scarf tight under her chin. Surprise surged through him. This hand wasn't the wrinkled, withered limb he'd expected to see. It looked as if it belonged to a young woman—a woman with medium brown skin.

Curiosity just about did him in, but he held his tongue. What did he know of old women's hands? He focused his attention on the road. Soon he'd be back at the ranch and would need to get the wagon unloaded.

He glanced at the woman again, but now her hands rested in her lap, hidden under the folds of her skirt. Jim peeked at her face but could see only the side of her scarf and wisps of brown hair, not the gray he'd expected.

She didn't want to talk or let him see her face. Yep, she definitely had something to hide, but it was none of his business.

❧

The driver looked to his left, and Sasha peeked out the corner of her eye. It was him, she was certain—the man who'd come to her rescue last night. And now he was helping her again. She turned her head to the right, just as he faced forward again.

Used to long walks in New York, she hadn't expected the journey to her uncle's home to take so long and was grateful for the ride. It would probably have taken her two full days to walk it, and she hadn't looked forward to spending another night outside.

But would this man see through her makeup? Would he recognize her?

Right after sunup, she'd applied her makeup, using her reflection in a window in lieu of a mirror. She'd tried her best to avoid letting the man look at her face. Though she was an expert in applying stage makeup, it was meant to be viewed at a distance, not close quarters.

She considered the man's kindness to her—once when she was dressed as herself and now as an old woman. She owed him her gratitude and wished that she could thank him. Perhaps there were kind people in Indian Territory after all.

He was a nice-looking man, with his black hair and eyes. She couldn't help wondering if he, too, was part Indian. His skin didn't have the reddish tint that some of the men in Tulsa had but rather was a healthy tanned shade and far more appealing than the pale skin of city men.

They rode along in companionable silence. Sasha studied the countryside, which ranged from gently rolling hills to flatlands where she could see clear to the horizon. Instead of being afraid of the open spaces, she loved the feeling of freedom that came from not being surrounded by New York's lofty buildings and hordes of people.

A gentle breeze teased her face, making her hold on to her scarf so it wouldn't blow off. She'd love nothing more than to allow her hair to blow free like her spirit, but she couldn't. Not yet, anyway.

She fought back a yawn. The warm sun, gentle plodding of hooves, and lack of sleep the night before lulled her into a relaxed state.

Several hours past noon, Mr. Conners gently nudged her arm with his elbow. He nodded his chin forward, and she pushed aside her sleepiness to stare at the changed landscape. She had to physically keep her jaw from dropping.

Tall wooden oil derricks stood out like sentinels everywhere she looked, blotching the landscape. Not a single tree was left standing, but numerous stumps testified that they once had. Ahead and to her right, the sun shimmered on a lake of some kind of greasy, greenish-black substance.

"This whole area is the Glenn Pool. The Ida Glenn Number One was the first oil strike in these parts. Early last year this was just a cornfield and prairie grass, but now. . .well, you can see for yourself."

Sasha lifted her hand to her nose. "What's that smell?"

"Crude oil. Rather pungent, isn't it?" His smile brightened his whole face, making him look far too handsome for his own good. "Takes awhile to get used to."

Holding her scarf over her nose, Sasha stared with amazement at the lake of glimmering substance. "So, is that where the oil comes from? A lake like that?"

Mr. Conners chuckled. "The oilmen wish it was that easy. These lakes of oil are actually overflows. Drillers are bringing in the oil faster than storage tanks can be built, so they resorted to building these earthen dams to hold the excess runoff."

As they drove through the oil field, Sasha watched grimy men scurrying around the tall derricks and working on pumps. The earth here was blackened from the oil, and nothing grew except a few sprigs of grass and obstinate wild-flowers. She'd heard that the oil boom had made many people wealthy, but it saddened her to see the landscape ruined.

"That's Rag Town, where many of the oil workers live." He pointed at what looked like a city of tents.

Barefoot children ran around whooping and chasing one another while a tired-looking woman hung ragged clothing on a line. Even the cheap hotel room she'd been in yesterday was far better than this. She couldn't imagine living in such squalor.

"Politicians call the oil boom the next great land rush—a run for riches, a run for power, and a run for national security, but as you can see, very few people here are prospering from it."

She considered his words for a time as they continued their journey. Soon the small town of Keaton came into view. Her heart thudded. She'd hoped that the town her uncle lived near would have some amenities, but its mud streets and rough wooden buildings were a far cry from even Tulsa.

Mr. Conners pulled to a stop. "You sure I can't take you all the way to your destination?"

Sasha shook her head. "No, thank you." She'd used this man enough and could easily get dependent on someone as nice as Jim Conners. She'd learned at a young age that depending on others only brought disappointment. She was a grown woman now, and as her mother said, she needed to take care of herself.

A shiver of apprehension wafted through her as he helped her to the ground. With a trembling hand, she took her satchel from him, thanked him, and said good-bye. He shook the reins, and the wagon pulled away with a soft creak. She breathed a sigh of relief. He was curious about her but hadn't pressed her for information. She thought too late that she should have asked if he knew her uncle.

She studied the people walking up and down the boardwalk. Could one of these men be Dewey Hummingbird? He had to be fairly old now, since he was her mother's uncle.

Her gaze landed on a mortician's shop where a casket leaned up against the wall. Several men were laughing and taking turns standing inside its wooden frame. A horrible thought darted through her mind, and she stumbled on a rut in the road. She took three quick steps to right herself.

What if her uncle were no longer alive? Could she have come all this way for nothing?

Chapter 4

Jim tightened the cinch and mounted his horse. He'd unloaded the wagon and worked all afternoon but still couldn't get the old woman off his mind. Things just didn't add up. Her voice and hands didn't match her age and face, not that he'd gotten a good peek at her features. And when he had glanced at her, it was her brown eyes that stood out—glimmering with curiosity, but also guarded.

He'd never been acquainted with an elderly woman beyond polite greetings. His mother died when he was six, and he'd never known his grandparents. An overwhelming urge to make sure the old woman was all right had him heading back to Keaton instead of spending an hour reading before bed like he normally did. He nudged his horse forward into a gallop.

An hour later, Jim sighed as he marveled at the pink and orange sunset. The woman was nowhere to be found. He rubbed his hand across his bristly cheek and turned his horse back toward the ranch where he worked, praying the lady found shelter for the night. In May, nights in Indian Territory were usually mild, but no woman should be on the streets alone with all the riffraff around, especially an elderly one. He asked God to watch over her and keep her safe. Maybe he'd have better luck finding her tomorrow, not that he knew what he'd do if he did.

❧

Sasha attempted to smooth the wrinkles from her dress, but it was useless. Too long scrunched up in her satchel, the poor garment needed a good ironing. A half hour ago, she'd slipped off the dirt road and stopped at a stream to refresh herself and change out of her costume. Now, excitement at seeing her uncle battled anxiety as she stared through the growing darkness at the silhouette of his cabin. A lone light in the window beckoned her.

Nearby, a night creature screeched, and Sasha jumped. Darting forward, she raced toward the cabin and onto the porch, pressing her palm to her chest. She'd never been easily spooked, but all these strange noises of nature were new to her and vastly different than those of a big city. Her recent experience at the Whitaker Hotel and Mr. Conners' warnings about not being out at night still lingered in her mind.

Just walking along the dirt road in the daylight had made her legs tremble, but now that the sun had set and who-knew-what was out prowling in the woods. . . Well, she could only hope her uncle would be happy to see her. She didn't want to think what she'd do if he turned her out. At least she'd learned in town that he was still living when she'd asked for directions to his place. With all the new growth because of the oil strike, she'd found her uncle's map almost useless.

The porch's wooden floor creaked, and she lifted her hand to knock.

"Who's out there?"

She jumped at the sound of a man's voice coming from behind the door and licked her lips. "I'm, uh. . .looking for Dewey Hummingbird. Is this his cabin?"

The door opened a crack, and the barrel of a rifle slipped through the opening, pointing straight at Sasha's chest. Her heart skipped a beat.

"Who are you and what do you want at this hour?"

Oh, if only she hadn't been so hasty to leave New York, but it was too late to succumb to her doubts. She took a deep, straightening breath. "My name is Anastasia Di Carlo, and I'm looking for my uncle, Dewey Hummingbird. Is this the right place?"

She was certain she heard a gasp on the other side of the door. The rifle quickly disappeared, and the door opened, revealing a thin, elderly man. He studied her for a moment, then his mouth broke into a smile, revealing several missing teeth.

"I can't believe it!" He slapped his leg several times, looked past her, and then back. "How did you get here? Where's your mother?"

"I came by train. Alone." She swallowed the lump in her throat.

The small oil lantern on the table by the window illuminated the side of his rugged face in dancing light. Deep lines were etched into dark skin. Though he must have been in his late fifties or sixties, his hair was still raven black. He smelled of wood smoke and stared at her as she examined his features. He shook his head and stepped back.

"Forgive me. Please come in. I just can't believe you're here."

Sasha ducked away from a moth seeking the light, and he swatted it outside. "You are Dewey Hummingbird. . .my uncle?"

Lips that didn't look as if they'd smiled much tilted upward. "I sure am. Come on in, or we'll have half the bugs in the Creek Nation in here. Not that they'd bother me, but you. . ."

Sasha tugged her satchel inside and held it in front of her. On the seat of an old chair, she noticed a copy of *Treasure Island*, and a spark of surprise flickered through her. She had trouble imagining her uncle as an educated man. In New York, Indians were always classified by words like *savage* or *primitive*. But he had written the letter to her mother. And she'd overheard a man on the train who'd said that Creek Indians were considered one of the five civilized tribes, though she wasn't sure what he meant by that.

She glanced around the small, rustic log cabin. Much of it remained hidden in the shadows, but what she saw made her shiver. What had she gotten herself into?

"I know this place isn't much. I'm actually building a bigger house, but it's not quite done yet." He stared at her. "I can't believe you're here. It's so good to finally see you. I'd almost given up hope of you ever coming here."

She smiled at the delight twinkling in his dark eyes. "It's wonderful to meet you, too."

"Here, let me have that." He took her satchel, disappeared into a dark room off to the side, and returned. "You're an answer to prayer."

Sasha blinked. "I am?" She'd never been someone's answer to prayer before—at least not that she knew of.

Her uncle smiled. "Yes'm, you sure are. I've been praying for years that Myrtle would come for a visit and bring you." His expression sobered. "Where is your mother? Is she all right?"

Sasha nodded. "Yes, she's fine—as far as I know. She's gone to England to get married."

"Married! Well, that's a good thing, I suppose. I hope she's happy."

"I'm sure she is." Sasha pressed her lips together. She didn't want to be reminded of her mother's desertion.

He hurried over to the chair and picked up his book. "Have a seat. You must be tired. How did you get here from town?"

"I walked." She dropped down in the chair, realizing just how exhausted she truly was.

"That's a fair distance on foot." He disappeared into the dim shadows across the room and returned carrying a glass. "Want a drink? The water here is good and cold."

She nodded. He handed her a glass with a chipped top, and she gulped down the refreshing liquid.

Her uncle pulled a wooden chair away from the small table and sat across from her. His face burst into a smile again. "Thank the good Lord. I just can't believe you're really here. You look much like your mother did when she was young, Anastasia."

"Please call me Sasha. Anastasia is so formal."

He nodded. "And you may call me Dewey—or Uncle—or whatever you'd like."

Never having met anyone who'd known Cybil when she was young before, Sasha considered his comment about her looking like her mother when she was younger. There was something special about it.

"How long can you stay?"

Sasha tightened her grasp on the wooden arms of the chair, unsure how to respond. The trip to Tulsa had cost much more than she'd anticipated, and unless she found some work she could do, she was stranded.

"I. . .uh, I don't know. How long would you like me to stay?"

His gaze darted around the cabin. "This ain't what you're used to, what with your having lived in those fancy places in New York and all, but you're welcome to stay as long as you like. Or at least as long as you think you can stand it." He chuckled as if he'd made a joke.

"I would like to stay awhile and get to know you, if you're sure you don't mind."

"You're welcome to stay forever if you want." He smiled. "I'm just happy to finally get to meet you and have family here again. But you look all tuckered out. How about you get some rest, and we can talk more in the morning? Unless you'd rather have something to eat first."

"I am a bit hungry, but I don't want you to go to any trouble."

"No trouble." He stood. "You like peaches?"

Sasha nodded. "Yes, that sounds good. Thank you."

He shuffled toward her with a twig in his hand and stuck it in the lantern. It flamed to life, and he used it to light another lamp on the other side of the room. The insides of the primitive cabin shocked her. How could anyone live with so little? Two small pots hung below a wooden rack that held several plates and cups. A tiny table rested against the far wall. The mate to the chair her uncle had used looked lonely sitting there by itself.

"I don't have company too often. Just my workman. He and I take most meals together. Hey, can you cook?"

She shook her head. "Not really. I always wanted to learn, but I never got the opportunity, living in hotels most of my life."

"That's too bad. I'm not much of a cook myself."

He opened a jar of peaches, spooned out several, then handed her a bowl and sat back down in the chair. Though elderly, he seemed to get around well and was able to take care of himself.

The sweet, yet tart, juice of the peach teased her tongue, and she stuffed the slice the rest of the way in her mouth. "Mmm. . .these are delicious. New York's peaches don't taste anything like this."

"Your grandma planted our peach trees when she was young. I share the harvest with a neighbor lady, and she cans them for me."

Sasha looked up. Surprise zinged through her insides at the mention of her grandmother. "Tell me about my grandmother."

He grinned. "I can do that. Her name was Adele Hummingbird, and she was my brother's wife."

"Your brother? My grandfather?"

"James was his name. He was my older brother by four years, but he passed away several years ago. We had a much younger sister named Kizzie." He rubbed his chin and looked away for a moment. "She died last year."

A deep sense of losing something precious left Sasha weak. If she'd only known about her family sooner, she could have met her aunt. "I'm sorry."

He waved aside her concern. "Kizzie lived a good life. It's because of a promise I made her that I'm building a new house."

Sasha finished the peaches and handed the bowl to her uncle.

"I reckon we ought to get you settled for the night." He pushed up from his chair, set the bowl on the table, and returned for the lantern.

Sasha yawned, not wanting to move. She'd barely slept any the night before for fear the two men would find her. When she had fallen asleep, she'd dreamed about the handsome cowboy saving her. Finally, she forced her exhausted body up and followed her uncle into the tiny bedroom. She longed to hear more about her family, but it could wait until morning.

Her uncle set the lantern on a small table next to a single bed. On the far wall were several pegs that she imagined held all of her uncle's clothes. He grabbed a plaid shirt off one peg and a blanket that was lying over the back of the only chair in the room.

"Make yourself at home. There's an outhouse back of the cabin. . .if'n you've need of it."

Sasha was sure her uncle's cheeks had darkened a shade. Suddenly, she realized he was offering her his room. "Oh no, I can't take your bed. I don't mind sleeping on the floor. Truly."

She reached for the blanket, but he tugged it away.

"No, I'll bed down in my workman's tent with him. He won't mind at all."

"But—"

"No buts. You're my guest, and I'm happy you're here. Have a good rest. I'll see you in the morning after the cock crows."

He turned and left before she could argue. Exhausted, she untied her shoes and tossed them under the chair. She blew out the lamp and flopped on the bed, thinking about her ancestors. Her grandparents had names now—James and Adele Hummingbird.

Smiling in the dim lighting, she thought about her talkative uncle. She liked him, but she couldn't help feeling thankful that she hadn't been raised in such rugged circumstances.

But what about now? Could she handle living like he did?

The truth suddenly hit her—she truly was of Indian blood. She might never know about her father's side of the family, unless maybe Uncle Dewey knew something, but at least she now had a heritage. If only she could embrace it.

Chapter 5

Sasha held her uncle's arm as they left the family grave plot where her grandparents and aunt and uncle Arbuckle were buried. It saddened her to think she had family she could have gotten to know if only her mother had brought her for a visit.

"Yes'm, Kizzie led a good life. Her only regret was not having children." He patted Sasha's hand. "She'd have loved you and mothered you half to death."

She smiled. "I would have liked that. May I ask how she died?"

"The doctor said her heart just gave out. Folks around here loved Kizzie. She was always doing something nice for someone."

Dewey led her past the cabin and up a hill. Off to her right she heard a whack, followed by a pause, and then another whack. Her uncle glanced past her as the pattern of sounds continued.

"That's my workman chopping wood. He's a fine boy. You'll like him."

Sasha wasn't so sure of that. Any boys she'd been around had always been ornery troublemakers.

"Kizzie struck oil on her land. She died a wealthy woman." Dewey shook his head. "I didn't want her money, but she left it and her land to me. Made me promise to build a nice house for myself. Said to make it big enough just on the chance you and your mother might come back some day."

Sasha turned her head and stared at him. "She actually said that?"

"Yes'm, she sure did."

With an uncommon lightheartedness warming her chest, she lifted her skirts with her free hand and allowed her uncle to propel her up the hill. As they reached the top, she gasped out loud. The rising sun, hidden directly behind the large house, made it look as if the structure had a shiny golden halo. The two-story brick home, in the final stages of completion, would rival anything in New York, but it looked so out of place here in the wilds of Indian Territory.

"It's too fancy for my blood, but I promised Kizzie—and now that you're here, I'm glad I did as she requested." Dewey glanced at her, and for the first time, he looked shy—hesitant. "You like it?"

"Oh, yes! It's lovely. Can we go in?"

"I don't see why not. The workers should be here anytime, but we'll stay out of their way.

The double doors opened into a tall foyer, which included a beautiful curved staircase. Sasha's mouth hung open, but she couldn't help it. She felt as if she'd walked into Cinderella's castle.

The scent of fresh wood tickled her nose, and her footsteps echoed in the empty structure. Elegant dark wood rose three feet from the wide baseboards and was topped by a delicate wainscoting. Above that, all the walls were plain. Her mind raced with ideas. She envisioned a lovely floral wallpaper in the foyer....

Some time later, they stood in the room she'd picked for her own at her uncle's request. They opened the double doors and walked out on the wide balcony overlooking a small lake. Ducks quacked to one another as they splashed in the pristine water. Far off to her right, she could see the tips of several derricks, but no other oil equipment obliterated the view.

"It's so lovely here."

Dewey moved to her side. "Yes'm, it is. I've had plenty of those oilmen out here wanting me to lease them my land for drilling, but I want to keep it the way God made it. I don't need the money, but I need for the land to stay the way it was when our people first came here."

"I'm glad you feel that way. I know oil has made many people wealthy and the country needs it, but I saw how it ruins the land."

He nodded, and they stood together in silence, enjoying the view and the cool breeze. In spite of the rustic setting, Sasha felt as if she'd finally come home. Was it possible to find her roots in this place?

"I used to farm mostly, but now I run a couple hundred head of cattle. Those oilmen like their beef." Dewey turned to face her. In the daylight his wrinkles were magnified, but his eyes reflected the kindness she heard in his voice. He was no savage, just a man with Indian heritage.

As much as she ached to belong to someone or some place, she still couldn't reconcile with the fact that she was a half-breed. She may not have ever met her father, but it was evident by her lighter skin tone that she wasn't full-blooded Creek. Would she be welcomed into the Creek Nation or considered a despised outcast?

"Did you know my father?"

Dewey shook his head. "No. You're mother must have met him after she left here." He stretched and turned to face her. "So, what do you think? Could you stay and furnish this house for me? I might know building materials, but I know nothing about home furnishings and all the fripperies a fancy house like this needs."

She shook off her disappointment that Dewey didn't know her father and allowed excitement to soar through her at all the possibilities for the house.

"I've more money than I could spend in a lifetime, so you can do whatever suits your fancy."

A wave of apprehension washed over her. Would it be taking advantage of her uncle in some way to spend his money?

He flapped his hand in the air. "I see your mind working, missy. This is your home, too. I want you to feel you can stay as long as you like, and if you need to leave, you'll always have a place to return to. And when I'm gone, this will be yours. You and your mom are the only kin I've got left."

Unshed tears stung Sasha's eyes at her uncle's surprising kindness, and she looked at the lake so she wouldn't embarrass him. Even her own mother had never treated her as lovingly as this man she'd only met twelve hours ago.

A loud whistle broke the natural quiet, and Sasha searched for the source. She could see someone walking toward the house in the shadows of the trees, but he was too far away to tell much about him. It must be her uncle's worker.

Dewey tapped his watch. "Yep, right on time. C'mon, I want you to meet my boy. He's like a son to me."

They reached the bottom of the curved stairs just as the front door opened. Sasha sucked in a breath. The man who'd come to her rescue twice walked into the room. A good six feet tall, he wore a blue chambray shirt and dusty jeans. This was certainly no boy but a handsome, well-built man. Jim Conners, her champion.

Her mouth went dry as she stood on the bottom step and watched him set down his crate of tools. He removed his hat, and his thick thatch of ebony hair flopped back down, giving him a roguish air. Her heart skittered as his dark, surprised gaze landed on her. His eyes were nearly as black as her uncle's, but his skin was a healthy sun-kissed tan, lacking the red tones that Dewey's had.

"Lookee here, Jimmy boy. We've got us a guest."

⚬⌒

Jim's mouth felt dry as a desert as shock rippled through him. The last thing he expected to see in his boss's new house was a beautiful woman. As he continued to stare, her cheeks turned a dark rose, and she finally glanced away.

"Jimmy, this is my niece, Anastasia Di Carlo. She's from New York City."

Unaccustomed to being taken off guard, Jimmy struggled to gather his composure and stepped forward, hat in hand. He crinkled the brim and licked his lips, hoping to find his voice. He held out his hand. "Jim Conners. Nice to meet you, ma'am."

Her eyes sparkled, and she reached out, shaking his hand. "It's my pleasure, Mr. Conners."

Jim's gaze collided with hers. There was something familiar about her saddle brown eyes. His mouth opened, then he slammed it shut. This was the woman from the hotel! He was certain.

She cleared her throat, and Dewey chuckled. Jim realized he was staring and still held her hand. He released it as if it were a rattler and stepped back.

"She's a sight to behold, ain't she?" Dewey waggled his eyebrows.

Jim nodded, searching his mind for any conversation he'd had with Dewey about a niece. He drew a blank. All times they'd worked together and ridden to church or town, Dewey had never mentioned having family outside of Indian Territory. In fact, as far as he knew, all of Dewey's family had already passed on. But now Dewey's niece had arrived, and Jim had a feeling his life would never be the same.

His heart stampeded as he looked at Miss Di Carlo again. She had to be one of the most beautiful women he'd ever seen. She studied him, as he did her. She'd tied her long brown hair back with a ribbon, but rebellious waves that refused to be tamed wafted around her face. His eyes followed her narrow nose down to lips that looked soft and kissable.

He lowered his gaze to the floor. Where in the world had that thought come from?

Maybe he had romance on the brain since his sister, Katie, had recently found love and marriage.

"Sasha is gonna be in charge of decorating the house."

"Sasha?" Jim glanced at Dewey.

The older man waved his hand. "Sasha's what folks call her. You can, too."

Jim glanced at Miss Di Carlo to see if she agreed. She gave him a soft smile and gentle nod of her head, which sent his pulse racing.

Oh brother. This wasn't good. He enjoyed looking at a beautiful woman like any man, but he'd never reacted so strongly to one before. He couldn't afford to have an attraction to his boss's niece. He needed this job so he could save his money and buy land in the Oklahoma Territory near his aunt and uncle's farm.

"It's fine if you want to call me Sasha, Mr. Conners. I imagine we'll be seeing lots of each other since you work for my uncle."

"Then you must call me Jim." He swallowed, grateful that he'd finally found his voice again.

Her pretty smile sent pleasant shivers skittering through him, but he tried to ignore them. Sasha Di Carlo had a sweet, innocent look about her, but the hair on the back of his neck had stood up at the mention of her spending Dewey's money. It made sense to have a woman furnish the house, but he had heard many stories of long-lost relatives showing up when one of the families in the area struck oil. Dewey had only been granted control of Kizzie Arbuckle's money in the last six months. He hoped this woman really was Dewey's niece and not just another fortune hunter. Just maybe he should keep his eye on her.

"You gonna have breakfast with us?" Dewey hooked his thumbs through the straps of his overalls.

Jim shook his head. "I just had some jerky and bread. I wanted to see what else needs to be finished up before we let the workers go. But I think we've just about got it licked." His gaze traveled around the room. Pride for doing a job well swelled his chest. This home would be a legacy to his skills as a carpenter long after he was gone.

"Sounds good. Well, Sasha and me went for a walk before eating, and now my belly button's rubbing against my backbone. We're heading back to the cabin. Maybe at dinner tonight you and Sasha could talk about furnishing this place." He scratched his head. "I don't know what Kizzie was thinking, wanting me to build a house this big, but it's done. Guess we'll just have to let the good Lord fill it."

Jim stood at the door and watched Dewey and Sasha walk back to the cabin. Sasha glided along, her skirts skimming the tops of the wildflowers. She was a sight to behold, for sure. No woman had stirred his blood like she had in a very long time.

He thought about the aunt and uncle who'd raised him. He missed Mason, Rebekah, and their children a lot, but he missed his sister, Katie, and his nephew, Joey, the most. He was glad that Katie had found love again with the bounty hunter who'd saved her life. Dusty McIntyre was a good man and would treat her well. Much better than their own father ever had.

Jimmy remembered the last time he ever saw his father, at the site of the first Oklahoma land rush near Guthrie. Even as a seven-year-old, he knew his pa wasn't the fatherly type. In fact, he was a gambler and a liar and had left his wife and two children alone while he sought adventure.

Thanks to Uncle Mason's patient guidance and Dewey's influence, his heart was right with God again. Jim lifted his gaze toward heaven, praising God for the beauty of the new day.

He liked to think he was honorable and kind, but he had no patience for a liar or a deceiver. He'd seen at a young age the trouble a swindler could cause. "Please, God, let Dewey's niece be the real thing and not just some treasure seeker out to get his money."

It would break his heart if Sasha hurt Dewey. He loved the old man like a father. Maybe he'd just keep an eye on Sasha Di Carlo until he was certain about her.

What could it hurt?

Chapter 6

Dewey's wet shirt snapped in the air as Sasha gave it a quick shake. She pulled two clothespins from her apron pocket and secured the chambray top to the line. As she pulled a pair of socks from the wicker basket, she listened to the sounds of nature all around her. It saddened her to think of all the years that she had rarely heard birds and crickets chirping, except for when she'd ventured out to a park. The clamor of the big city had overpowered the gentle sounds of nature.

She fastened the socks to the line with wooden pins, then shook out a pair of overalls. Dewey had been both shy about her doing his laundry and delighted, telling her that all the bending aggravated the catch in his back. As she straightened a denim strap, she overheard upraised voices coming from the front of the cabin. Just as she'd come outside, she'd heard the hoofbeats of several horses coming down the dirt road, but she had continued with her task, knowing that whoever it was had not come to see her.

She pinned the overalls onto the line, picked up her basket, and walked around the side of the house.

"I've told you before, I won't have my land destroyed by oil drilling. My answer is no."

Hearing the anger in her uncle's voice, Sasha set down the basket and peered through a crape myrtle bush to see three men dressed in suits all but surrounding Dewey. She didn't want to eavesdrop but also didn't want to leave her uncle alone. Glancing over her shoulder, she considered running up the hill to find Jim but decided it would take too long.

"Surely, Mr. Hummingbird, you understand how wealthy you could be if you leased your land to Chamber Oil for drilling. All your neighbors—even your own sister—struck oil." The shortest man of the trio pushed his hat back on his head and set his hands on his hips.

"It's as close to a sure thing as you can get." A heavyset man with a handlebar moustache held out both of his chubby hands.

Dewey shook his head. "I don't need any more money. I'm satisfied with what I have. Preserving the land and raising my cattle is what's important to me."

A tall man who looked part Irish stepped forward. He ran his hand over his slicked-down red hair, and his eyes gleamed as he studied her uncle. "We don't normally do this, but I have permission from the boss to make you a special offer. If you'll lease your land to Chamber Oil, we'll give you a higher royalty rate than normal, like we did with your sister. That's more than fair."

Dewey shook his fist in the air. "Fair! You call it fair when you leased Elmer Red Hawk's land for two hundred dollars an acre and yet you took out millions of dollars in oil?"

The tall man's gaze narrowed, and he stepped forward. "Mr. Red Hawk was more than pleased with the deal in the beginning, but he got greedy."

"And now he's dead." Dewey crossed his arms over his chest. The finality in his voice made Sasha shudder.

The three men closed ranks and stepped forward. "You accusing us of something, old man?" the tall man hissed.

"You'd be wise to lease us your land and stop spreading rumors."

Sasha didn't like the man's tone of voice or his threat. She grabbed Dewey's rifle, which leaned against the side of the house where he'd been cutting brush, and stepped around the bush, out into the open. Cocking a bullet into the chamber as Dewey had taught her the day before, she braced the rifle against her shoulder and glared at the trio. She might not know how to shoot yet, but with a background in theater, she sure could pretend that she did. "Is there a problem here?"

Their eyes widened at the sound of her voice, and at least one mouth dropped open. Tall Man responded first, as his face altered from surprised to sickly sweet. "Well, how do, ma'am. We didn't realize ol' Dewey had gone and gotten himself a woman." He let out a low whistle through his teeth. "Whoowee, Dewey, you ol' coot, you like 'em young."

Surprise rocked Sasha, but she quickly recovered. "I am not his woman; I'm his niece."

"That a fact? Didn't know Dewey had any kin left." The fat man smoothed his forefinger over his moustache and glanced at Tall Man.

Sasha hiked up her chin and the barrel of the heavy weapon. "Well, he does. And it's time you got off his land."

Dewey chuckled and relieved her of the rifle. "I guess you all had better listen to the lady. You've heard all I've got to say, so get out." He waved the rifle toward them, and all but the tallest man stepped back.

"I reckon we'll give you some more time to think things over, but we'll be back."

He turned and stomped toward his horse. The poor animal squealed when the man jerked hard on the reins and turned it toward town.

Sasha sighed as they rode off. It seemed to her as if the white men were the troublemakers in this part of the country rather than the Indians.

Dewey turned to face her. "Sorry you had to see that. Them fellows have been after me for nearly a year to allow them to drill on my land. I keep telling them it's not going to happen, but they don't take the hint."

"Well, maybe now that I'm here they'll leave you alone. They're less likely to bully you if there's a witness around."

Dewey smiled and hugged her shoulders. "I imagine it was the rifle what scared them off, and not you. Though I do appreciate the assistance."

Sasha sagged against him, fearing her shaky legs would give out. Those men would be back—she was almost certain of it. They had to be ready if and when that happened. But how could a woman and an old man fight off three grown men if push came to shove? Her mind started whirling. Somehow she had to help her uncle keep his land and not let those oilmen bully him into doing something he would regret. But how?

❧

"I don't reckon Keaton looks like much of a town to you after living in New York." Dewey jiggled the reins to encourage the horses pulling his wagon to move faster. "It wasn't even here back when your mother lived with us."

"It is a lot different, that's for sure." Keaton was typical of the small towns Sasha had passed through on her way here except, like Tulsa, it sported many new buildings made from fresh wood that hadn't grayed yet. A few brick or stone buildings were scattered among them.

Unlike the day she arrived last week when things were somewhat quiet, now scores of people milled around. Local oilmen had invited the townsfolk to a huge pig roast to celebrate the railroad coming to Keaton. Instead of the long wagon ride to Tulsa, now folks could get there in less than a half hour. Sasha knew trains were good news for the town, but she'd had her fill of them for a while. One good thing was that it would make retrieving her trunk easier and less time consuming. She hoped to make arrangements today to have it delivered to the Keaton depot.

Dewey pulled the wagon alongside several others and set the brake, then climbed down and lifted his hand to assist her. Once on the ground, Sasha shook out her skirts, grateful for the breeze that cooled her legs. She desperately needed her trunk and something different to wear, although she worried that her dresses would be too fancy for this small town.

She took Dewey's proffered arm and allowed him to guide her through the crowd. Poor oil workers dressed in grimy overalls, leading their barefoot children and wives, mingled with businessmen sweating in their fancy three-piece suits. Somewhere above the noise of the crowd she heard some lively music. At booths decorated with red, white, and blue sashes, craftsmen hawked their wares. The fragrant scent of pork being roasted over a fire mixed with the aromas of fresh baked bread and pastries. Sasha's mouth watered, and excitement rippled through her at the chance to sample life in Smalltown, America.

A man stared at her as she and her uncle walked toward him. He nudged another man in the side, and both raised their eyebrows and gawked at her. She averted her gaze and watched some Indian children playing stickball.

"You want to go listen to the music or look through the commodities for sale first?" Dewey glanced down at her.

Sasha shrugged. "It doesn't matter to me."

"Then let's check out the merchandise. I could use a new hat."

As they meandered through the area where various items were displayed in the backs of wagons or on blankets on the ground, Sasha's frustration grew. Everywhere she went men stared at her—young and old. She hated being the focus of their attention and had often longed for plainer features. She wished that she'd been able to wear her costume, but then Uncle Dewey didn't know about it, and she wasn't sure he'd understand why she needed it.

A nice-looking man dressed in a clean white shirt and black denim pants walked toward her, cap in hand. A shy grin twittered on his lips as he cleared his throat. "Hullo, Mr. Hummingbird." Though he acknowledged her uncle, his gaze never left Sasha's face.

"Howdy, Spencer. Nice day for a celebration."

The man nodded and fiddled with his cap. "Yes, it is."

Dewey's mouth tilted up in an ornery grin. "Have you met my niece? Sasha Di Carlo."

The man shook his head. "A pleasure, ma'am. I was. . .uh. . .wondering if you'd do me the honor of eating with me."

Oh no, not again. Sasha stifled a sigh. The man seemed nice, and she didn't want to hurt his feelings. She offered him a smile. "Thank you, Mr., uh. . ."

"Jones. Spencer Jones."

"Mr. Jones, I truly appreciate your kind invitation, but I've just arrived in town and want to spend some time with my uncle today."

Disappointment tugged at his pleasant features. "Maybe another time then."

Not wanting to encourage him, she refrained from smiling. He tipped his hat, bid them good day, and wandered off. She heaved a sigh that made Dewey chuckle.

"You might as well get used to invitations like that. There's two dozen men to every woman in these parts. And few women are as lovely as you."

"Thank you, uncle, but I'm not interested in getting a husband. I just want to spend time with you right now."

"Then I don't reckon you'll want to eat with him, either." Dewey nudged his chin toward the street.

Sasha squinted and lifted her hand over her eyes. Another tall man strode toward her. Her cheeks puffed up as she exhaled a sigh again, but suddenly she recognized the man coming her direction. Jim Conners.

Her heart jolted, and a butterfly war was loosed in her stomach as she watched his easy, long-legged gait. He was a man confident with his body but not arrogant. He lifted his hat in greeting, and Sasha smiled. His damp black hair had melded to his head, and a ring marked where his Western hat had rested.

"You all been to dinner yet?" Jim's hopeful gaze darted from Dewey to Sasha.

"Nope, not yet." Dewey's lips turned up in a wry grin, and he glanced at her, eyebrows raised.

Jim's warm smile melted her remaining defenses, and she gave a little nod. "You want to join us, Jimmy?"

For some reason she welcomed Jim's attentions where she shunned others—maybe because he'd twice come to her aid. He held out his elbow, and she looped her arm through his, ignoring the sparks from his touch and her uncle's soft chuckles. She'd had plenty of handsome men escort her to events in New York, but somehow this simple carpenter intrigued her more than any man she'd ever known.

She peered up at him, wondering again if he maybe had Indian blood. A trickle of sweat slipped down his temple, and he glanced at her, locking eyes. Something sparked in his gaze, and Sasha knew without a doubt that she wanted to get to know this man better.

Chapter 7

What little Sasha had eaten of the roasted pork and the fresh green beans and potatoes seasoned with ham had been delicious. But with Jim Conners sitting directly across from her, making eye contact every few minutes as he and Dewey chatted, her appetite had fled.

She tried to pinpoint what it was about Jim that interested her. He was very easy on the eyes, especially when she glimpsed his quick smile. Where her uncle's teeth more resembled a picket fence, Jim's were straight and white.

Maybe she liked him because he was kind to her uncle and actually seemed interested in what he had to say. Or maybe it was the compassion he'd shown her when he gave an old woman a ride.

Sasha pressed her lips together and watched as a group of Indians in colorful native costumes danced on the vaudeville stage. She especially enjoyed the little children as they pounded out the drum's rhythm with their tiny feet. If she had been raised here, would she have learned to dance like them?

Dewey cleared his throat, and she looked at him. "I'd like to go look at them new-fangled automobiles on display."

Sasha stood and picked up her tin plate. "I'll go with you. I saw plenty of automobiles in New York—even rode in a couple—but I don't mind seeing what they have here."

Dewey glanced at Jim, who'd stood up at the same time as Sasha. "I thought Jimmy might escort you over to watch the show for a while."

Her gaze darted to Jim's and back to her uncle. Did Dewey have some business to attend to and not want her around, or was he perhaps trying to pair her off with Jim?

"You might enjoy the show. You probably haven't seen real Indian dancers before." Jim glanced at her, his hopeful gaze making her waver.

Maybe spending time with Jim was a good thing. If he escorted her, surely other men would leave her alone so she could enjoy herself. She glanced at Dewey. "Are you sure you don't mind?"

"Nah." Dewey waved his hand in the air. "You young'uns go enjoy the show."

Sasha and Jim carried their tin plates to the wash table, then he offered his arm. She looped hers around his, marveling again at the tingles tickling her insides. He found her a seat on a rough bench and sat beside her, keeping a decent distance.

Her gaze riveted to the low stage where children were stomping around in a wide circle, while sometimes spinning around in a smaller one. Off to the side a group of older men chanted a monotone tune and pounded on drums of various sizes.

Jim leaned toward her. "That's called the stomp dance. Can't imagine where they came up with such an original name."

She glanced at him, and his black eyes twinkled with mirth. Smiling at his joke, she watched as the children finished and left the stage. A man with trained dogs followed. The lively animals did some amazing tricks. Next came an opera singer, whose shrill voice made Sasha cringe.

In spite of the woman's less-than-stellar performance, Sasha relished sitting back and being part of the audience and enjoying the show instead of having to race around applying makeup or preparing to go onstage herself.

The singer attempted a high note and missed. Beside Sasha, Jim squirmed on the bench. He leaned forward, fiddling with his hat, but she was certain he held his hands over his ears on purpose.

She pressed her lips together but couldn't help laughing. He glanced back at her, his neck reddening when he caught her watching him. Sasha leaned over, wanting to put him out of his misery. "Would you mind if we go look at some of the wares that are for sale?"

Relief brightened his countenance, and he jumped up, offering her his hand. She took it and allowed him to guide her out of the quickly dwindling crowd. She felt sorry for the performer, but not enough to endure any more of her strained singing.

Jim tucked Sasha's hand around his muscled arm again. She glanced up at him, proud to be escorted by such a nice-looking man. That she felt so comfortable with him surprised her. Still, she didn't want to get her hopes up that he might have feelings for her. They'd barely just met. He might be willing to escort her around town, but what white man would want a relationship with a half-breed?

Her uncle had told her about the Upper Creeks, who were full-blooded like him, and the Lower Creeks, who were of mixed race. Sasha felt stuck between two worlds—that of the whites and that of the Upper Creeks, which was her heritage—neither of which would completely accept a woman of mixed race.

"So, what do you want to look at?"

Jim's question pulled her from her troubled musing. She glanced around, and her gaze landed on a colorful display of handmade quilts. She pointed toward them. "There. Uncle Dewey might like a locally made quilt for his new room, rather than something fancier from a store."

Jim nodded and guided her toward a clothesline tied between two trees. Three beautiful quilts hung there, brightening the stark landscape. Sasha loosened her grip on Jim and lifted the edge of a multi-colored coverlet. Though the fabric in the design looked to be from previously worn clothing, nobody could deny the quality of the tiny stitches.

Jim leaned over her shoulder. "These are made by the oil widows."

She peered up at him, nearly gasping at his nearness. He stared at her a moment before stepping back. "Oil widows?" she finally rasped.

He nodded. "Most often when an oil worker dies, his family has so little money that they continue to live in Rag Town. Some of the widows collect used clothing and make these quilts. Nice, aren't they? I took a couple home last time I went."

Sasha longed to ask him about his home but thought it would be improper since they barely knew each other. She refocused on the quilt. "What colors do you think Uncle Dewey would like best?"

Jim moved to the quilt beside her. "Seems like most of his shirts are some shade of blue. I guess he might like this one."

Sasha studied the design that was mostly blue and white with a little red and green. A woman who'd been helping a customer sidled up beside Jim. "That's a flying geese pattern. See, it loosely resembles a flock of geese in flight."

Sasha nodded but turned her eyes toward the woman. She couldn't be too much older than Sasha, but she had a haggard look about her. The worn dress hung on her thin frame as if she'd lost weight since making it. A towheaded boy about four years old ran toward her and hid behind the woman's skirt.

"I see you, Philip." A darling urchin with wispy blond locks skipped in their direction. She reached behind the woman and touched the boy. "Tag, you're it." The girl smiled at Sasha and darted away with the barefoot boy close on her heels.

"I'm sorry for the interruption, but children are good at that." A red blush stained the woman's pale cheeks as she studied the ground.

"It's all right. I grew up with kids all around." Jim's kind words were meant to soothe the woman, but a spear of shame pierced Sasha's heart. She'd never been wealthy, but she'd always worn pretty clothes and shoes. Never once had she been required to go barefoot or wear frayed rags like those poor children. Though she'd only planned to buy her uncle a quilt, she changed her mind and bought a second one to help out the poor widow.

Jim held her purchase while Sasha dug around in her handbag for the money Dewey had given her. She felt a bit odd spending money that wasn't hers, but she was furnishing his home as he had requested. Sasha handed the woman ten dollars, but a frantic looked passed across her face.

"I'm sorry, ma'am, but I have no change." Her gaze darted between Sasha's and the ground, as if she were afraid Sasha might change her mind about the purchase.

"I have some money." Jim stuck his hand in his pocket.

Sasha touched his arm. "That's all right. I don't need any change."

Jim's eyes sparked with surprise, but the woman took a step backward as if she'd been slapped. "Oh, no. I couldn't possibly accept more than the quoted price."

"But—" Jim's light touch on her back halted Sasha's objection. She didn't mind the woman keeping the whole ten dollars. It was obvious she needed the money.

Jim pulled out eight dollars and handed it to the lady and gave Sasha's money back. "I'll square things with Dewey later."

As they walked away, she glanced up at Jim. "Why wouldn't she accept more than the price?"

"Stubborn pride." He pressed his lips together. "As much as she needed the money, she still wouldn't accept more than what she thought was fair. That would be charity. And she'd never accept charity."

Sasha pondered his words as she purchased a soft pair of beautifully beaded moccasins from another vendor. They would be nice to wear around the house instead of her uncomfortable shoes. She followed Jim to the wagon, where they deposited their purchases. He checked on the horses, then came around to stand next to her, leaning his elbows against the side of the wagon. She nibbled her lip, knowing she still owed him a thank you.

"I want you to know how much I appreciated your help at Whitaker's Hotel."

A charming smile tugged at his lips. "I thought that was you. I didn't get too good of a look, what with things happening so fast and all."

"Yes, well, I did scurry out of there rather quickly." Sasha returned his smile as she studied his handsome face. His hair and eyes were black as midnight. His skin, darkly tanned. He was tall like a towering pine tree, and his powerful, well-muscled body moved with an easy grace. She'd never admit to watching him work, but she enjoyed doing so. He glanced away, staring off at the crowd, and Sasha realized she'd spent too long observing him. Heat warmed her cheeks, and she searched for a safe topic.

"So, you had a bunch of siblings?"

"What?" Jim glanced at her, his brows puckered. "No, only one—a sister."

Sasha blinked. "But I thought you said you grew up around a lot of kids."

Jim chuckled. "I did. But they were my cousins, not siblings. My aunt and uncle raised me after my parents died."

A wave of guilt washed over Sasha for bringing up the subject. "I'm sorry about your parents."

"It was a long time ago." He flipped his hand in the air and pushed away from the wagon. "I guess we ought to track Dewey down and make sure he hasn't gotten into any trouble."

Sasha peeked up at Jim, unsure if he was serious or teasing. She remembered seeing the three men who'd accosted Dewey and wished now that they'd all stayed together. She'd just found her uncle and didn't want anything to happen to him.

"My family lives in the Oklahoma Territory," Jim said, as he guided her back toward the throng of people. "Uncle Mason has a farm there. Ever been on a farm?"

She shook her head, wondering what it would be like to live away from a big city most of your life. Allowing Jim to lead her, she marveled at how comfortable he was to be with and to talk to. It was almost as if they were friends.

Suddenly, Jim stopped, and she stumbled to a halt. "Not again." A muscle ticked in his jaw and his gaze narrowed.

Sasha looked around, trying to figure out what had raised his ire, and she saw her uncle surrounded by the same three men who had visited the ranch the day before. Jim tugged her out of the main flow of people and tucked her up against the millinery store. "Stay here."

Because of the noise of the crowd, she couldn't make out Dewey's conversation, but she did hear "cheat Indians" and "can't read" when he lifted his voice. She edged around some old men sitting in front of the barbershop, hoping to get close enough to hear.

Jim marched up to the trio and shoved his hands to his hips. Dewey glanced at him, looking a bit relieved. "You men are slow learners. Mr. Hummingbird is not interested in leasing his land."

"He's a slow learner." Tall Man waved his hands in the air as he argued with Jim. "He could make hundreds of thousands of dollars from oil rights."

"You're just going to have to take no for an answer." Jim leaned toward the man. "Dewey's answer is no."

Tall Man's nostrils flared, and he clenched his fists. He was a good two inches taller than Jim but not nearly as well built. "You need to learn when to butt out, kid. This isn't your concern." He shoved Jim.

Taken off guard, Jim stumbled back into a picket fence. It leaned sideways from his weight but didn't break. He regained his footing and tightened his fist.

"There's no call to get rough." Dewey stepped forward, holding out his hand, palms up. "We can handle this peacefully."

A man hurried past Sasha, then stopped and turn around, staring at her. A slow smile lifted his lips. "Well, hello there." He tipped his hat, and his dark eyes glimmered. "Pardon me, miss."

The well-dressed, darkly handsome man was obviously Indian. He stepped in front of Jim, virtually ignoring him. With a wave of his hand, the three men backed off and stood to the side, glowering at Jim, who glared back.

The man held out his hand to her uncle. "I'm Roman Loftus. Sorry if these men have been harassing you, Mr. Hummingbird. They tend to get a little over-excited when they smell a sure thing."

Jim relaxed his stance a bit, as did Dewey. Mr. Loftus kept his back to her, but he turned his head, displaying his perfect profile, and waved away the three men. They scowled and grumbled but walked off.

A group of men behind her laughed, and she missed hearing what Mr. Loftus said. He turned, along with Dewey and Jim, looking her way. The man's wide smile didn't warm her as Jim's did, but there was no denying his handsome looks.

She walked over to the group, and the man tipped his hat again. "Roman Loftus. It's a pleasure to make your acquaintance, Miss Di Carlo."

Sasha noticed that he already knew her name. Confidence practically oozed from him. She smiled, accepting his outstretched hand, and he grasped her fingertips, then leaned over and kissed her knuckles.

Surprised, she darted a glance at Jim. He didn't appear too happy.

Dewey nudged his head toward the man. "His father is Gerald Loftus, a prominent Creek oilman."

Surprise surged through her. She hadn't realized that some of the oil companies were actually owned by Indians rather than white men.

"Miss, it would be my great pleasure to escort you and your uncle to supper this evening."

Sasha stifled her desire to roll her eyes at his flowery actions, but the fact that he omitted inviting Jim irritated her. She glanced at her uncle, and he shrugged. She couldn't help looking at Jim, who stood frowning with his hands on his hips.

"Thank you for your kind offer, Mr. Loftus, but we ate not too long ago, and I do believe we are heading home soon, so as to make it before dark."

Mr. Loftus pressed his lips together and narrowed his eyes for such a brief moment that she wasn't sure of his intentions. He didn't look like a man who took rejection well.

"Perhaps another time then." He smiled, tipped his hat, and strode off without a comment to Dewey or Jim.

"Arrogant—" Jim glanced at Sasha and closed his mouth.

There was very little conversation as Sasha, Dewey, and Jim gathered their purchases and readied to leave. The confrontation had broken the wonderful mood of the day.

As they headed home, Sasha peeked at Jim riding his horse beside the wagon. He looked so comfortable in the saddle. He turned his head and caught her staring. A slow smile tilted his finely shaped lips.

She looked away, hoping her time in Indian Territory would be a long one. Just maybe there was hope for a half-breed and a carpenter.

Chapter 8

Sasha studied the two carpets at the Tulsa store. One would go well with the quilt she'd purchase for her uncle, but he told her not to do anything fancy for his new bedroom. Finally, she pointed to the one with the rose design, which would go in her room. "I'll take this one. And I'd like to order some curtains out of that sheer fabric with the rose pattern we looked at earlier.

"Do you have the window measurements?" The store clerk peered up at Sasha over the top of her wire-frame glasses.

Sasha looked at Jim. He pushed away from the window he'd been staring out and reached into his pocket, withdrawing a piece of paper. He handed it to the woman, his eyes glazed with boredom. Sasha pressed her lips together to keep from smiling. Shopping obviously wasn't his favorite chore.

"I imagine you'll be needing some blinds for the windows also." The clerk glanced up from the paper expectantly. No doubt she'd make a hefty commission off Sasha's purchases.

"Yes, I will. For all the bedrooms."

A spark glimmered in the clerk's eyes, but Jim scowled. Apprehension knotted her stomach. Was he tired of waiting on her? Or did he think she was spending too much of her uncle's money?

Dewey had been adamant that money was no object. She was to furnish his home in any manner she saw fit. Still, as much fun as it was to buy furnishings, she couldn't shake feeling guilty for spending so much.

Having to pay her own way at such a young age had forced her to save her money. Spending so freely now went against every fiber of her being.

Jim stood in front of the window, again staring out. He rolled his head to the side and back as if working out the kinks. She'd tried to get him to leave her to shop when they'd first entered Mayo's Carpet store, but he'd refused. Maybe she should try again, because he was making her anxious.

"Jim."

He spun around, hope brightening his onyx eyes. "Ready to go?"

She shook her head, and his expression dimmed. "No, and it may take awhile. The house has a number of windows."

"You don't have to buy everything in one day, you know." A shadow of annoyance crossed his face.

"No, but then we'd have to come to Tulsa another time. I don't want to keep taking you away from your work."

He nodded and turned toward the window again.

"I don't suppose you could go to the hardware store and see about ordering the items we need for the bathroom? That would save us some time."

Jim glanced over his shoulder, looking pleased. "I can do that. Just tell me what you want."

She explained what she and Dewey had decided, and Jim eagerly strode for the door. He stopped with his hand on the knob. "Stay here until I come back."

Sasha nodded, not sure whether to be thrilled about his protectiveness or perturbed by his bossiness.

"That husband of yours doesn't want to let you out of his sight." The clerk pushed her glasses up her nose. "He must love you an awful lot."

Sasha blinked, completely taken off guard. She wanted to explain Jim wasn't her husband but didn't want to embarrass the kind clerk. Still, she couldn't help feeling a measure of delight being paired with such a thoughtful, pleasant-looking man.

That afternoon, Jim escorted her to her seat on the train, then went to see about getting their purchases and her trunk loaded. She thumbed through one of the store catalogs, wondering what type of furniture her uncle would like for the downstairs area.

She'd been able to order some bedroom furniture and a dining set at Harper's Furniture Store but held off buying for the parlor area, hoping to get Dewey to help her. It was his home, after all.

Sasha gazed around the train. This car had seats that all faced the same direction. She let out a sigh, thankful she didn't have to sit across from any gentlemen seeking her attention. Jim slid in beside her, and her heart skipped a beat. A manly scent of sweat and dust drifted her way.

"All set." He shot a sideways glance at her. "The depot clerk said he can ship the furniture as soon as Harper's has it ready. Then we'll just have to pick it up at the Keaton depot."

"That sure makes things easier on you, doesn't it?"

He nodded and glanced at the open catalog on her lap. "More shopping?"

"Well, there's still the rest of the downstairs to furnish."

Jim pressed his lips together and turned to look out the window across the aisle. She couldn't help feeling again as if he were displeased with her for some reason. Maybe he just didn't like spending time in town.

At least she'd had a wonderful time. She thought about her afternoon with Jim. Other than showing a little impatience, he'd been a perfect gentleman all day. She loved that he was relaxed around her and not trying to win her favor. But then, he probably had no interest in a half-breed like her.

Tired, she laid her head against the window and looked out at the people scurrying around the depot. A fancy touring car pulled up and parked near the gate, and a man wearing goggles and a long travel coat hopped out and helped a woman exit the vehicle. Sasha wondered how they could stand to wear a coat in this heat.

The view triggered her memory, and she remembered the few times she had been privileged to ride in an automobile. Other than riding on a train, it had been the fastest she'd ever traveled and had nearly taken her breath away.

"Did you go to church back in New York?" Jim surprised her with his sudden question.

She shook her head. "Not too often. Mother rarely woke up before noon, and I didn't like to go alone."

Jim's eyes widened. "Noon! I never heard of people sleeping that late unless they were sick."

She couldn't help smiling at his bewildered expression. He was a man used to a full day's hard work. Seeing how antsy he was today during his idleness proved that.

"I don't know if Uncle Dewey told you or not, but Mother and I worked in the theater. She is—was—an actress, and I was a makeup artist. Mother often went out with her fans and other members of the crew after performances."

"I never knew anyone in the theater before." He grinned. "I still don't see how your ma could sleep till noon, though." He shook his head. "Anyway, I don't know if Dewey told you yet, but we generally ride together to church on Sundays, though he didn't go last week since you'd just arrived and were tired from your travels. We could take the buggy this week so you can go. That is if you want to." He stared at her as if measuring her worth.

She hadn't considered attending church but thought she might like it and nodded. Jim smiled and leaned back, then tilted his hat so that it covered the top half of his face. His pose looked so manly it made her insides quiver.

During their evening devotions together, she had listened as Jim and Dewey talked about the different Bible verses they'd read. She'd never heard anyone talk about God as if He were a friend, and she longed to know if such a thing were possible. Though she was happier here in Indian Territory than she could ever remember, she still felt a void in her life.

Was that emptiness something a husband could fill? Or would it take Someone bigger—like God?

❧

Jim allowed the gentle rocking of the train to lull him into a relaxed stupor. Though tired from standing around shopping all day, he wasn't sleepy. Other than being half bored, he'd enjoyed his time with Sasha and felt proud walking around town with such a beauty on his arm.

Plenty of other men had noticed, and he'd stared them down, almost daring them to approach Sasha. His jaws puffed out as he sighed, knowing his behavior wasn't very Christlike. Gazing at the inside of his hat, which covered his face, he asked God's forgiveness for being boastful in his actions.

He thought of the excitement twinkling in Sasha's brown eyes and remembered her smiles and how she'd flitted from one item to the next, reminding him of a hummingbird. She had a good time today, he could tell.

But she'd spent a whole lot of Dewey's money. And enjoyed it. As much as he liked her and was attracted to her, he still wasn't sure whether to trust her.

Her timing was almost impeccable, arriving a few months after Dewey was awarded control of Kizzie Arbuckle's property and finances.

Still, he'd watched what she bought, though he doubted she realized that. She never once purchased the most expensive item. Instead, she'd leaned toward midlevel, yet quality items. He had to admit, she'd made wise purchases—practical versus showy—all except for that flowery rug she bought for her own room. Not that it was all that expensive, just too feminine for his taste.

Unable to sleep with Sasha on his mind, he pushed up and set his hat back on his head. She glanced at him, and he took a moment to study her lovely face. Delicate features highlighted an oval face. Her medium brown complexion looked as soft as a horse's muzzle. And those lips—perfect for kissing.

Her cheeks grew rosy, and she looked away. He shouldn't be staring. It might give her the wrong idea, but she was so beautiful that he was compelled to gaze on her face whenever he had opportunity. God sure did put some fine creatures on this earth.

He shook his head. What he needed to do was share the gospel with her. Obviously she'd never had any Bible training. Though she seemed to listen intently when he and Dewey talked scriptures in the evenings, she rarely asked any questions.

Maybe it was just too soon. She'd only been here a week.

Jim leaned back and looked out the window across the aisle. The landscape sped by.

Lord, I pray You give me the opportunity to tell Sasha about You. Perhaps that's the whole reason our paths crossed. You know I haven't always walked Your path, but I am now. Help me to guide this lost lamb into the fold.

Chapter 9

Dressed in her old woman's costume, Sasha peeked out the door of the cabin, hoping Jim and Dewey were up at the new house as they'd told her they would be. Relieved not to see them, she scurried out the door and over to the buggy her uncle had hitched for her. He hadn't liked the idea of her going to town alone but thought she'd be all right as long as she was home well before dark and stayed in the good part of town.

She made a kissing smack and jiggled the reins, guiding the horse down the dirt road. Her hands trembled, and she tried to remember everything Dewey had taught her about driving a buggy. Knowing she had a mission she wanted to complete, she'd paid close attention to his instruction and now felt semiconfident of her skills.

As the horse clip-clopped down the dirt road beneath a shadowy canopy of oak, pine, and elm trees, she thought about the things Jim had told her about God the day they went to Tulsa. He'd said that the Lord was a loving God. He was alive and wanted to come into her heart. That He sent His Son Jesus to die on the cross to pay her debt of sin. It had made her heart ache to think of an innocent man dying for something she'd done.

Some of the things she'd read in the Bible made better sense now that Jim had explained them to her. She wanted the closeness with God that her uncle and Jim had, but she wasn't sure how to get it. Just asking for God's forgiveness as Jim told her to do seemed too simple. There had to be more.

As she steered the horse to the right at a fork in the road, her thoughts turned to the oil widows again. They kept invading her mind, and she remembered that cute barefoot girl dressed in rags. Jim had said the widows continued living in Rag Town because they couldn't afford to go anywhere else and that they sometimes cooked or did laundry for the oil field workers, not that it brought in much income.

The beautiful quilts and braided rag rugs the women had made would bring high prices back East. Just the fact that they were made in Indian Territory would intrigue city folk. There had to be something she could do. As the niece of a wealthy man, she doubted the widows would let her help them—but as an old Gypsy woman. . .well, perhaps.

As she neared Keaton, she drove the buggy around to the far side of town, so if people saw her, they wouldn't know she'd come from Dewey's land. On the edge of town, she parked the buggy and tied the horse to a tree. The bay gelding would be fine since her mission wouldn't take long.

Using a knobby branch for a cane, she shuffled toward the alley behind a row of fancy homes, wishing she hadn't left behind her nice cane in the scuffle at Whitaker's Hotel. Dewey had mentioned one night that some of the woman who'd gotten rich from oil threw away perfectly good clothing. They wore an item once or twice, then bought something new. He said he couldn't tolerate such waste and was perfectly happy with his worn overalls.

Sasha smiled at the memory. She doubted her uncle's overalls could take many more scrubbings on the washboard. They were nearly as ragged as the urchins' clothing.

Holding her scarf with her free hand, she worked her way down the alley. When she noticed the shimmer of bright blue fabric near a trash barrel, excitement whizzed through her. Seeing nobody around, she quickened her steps. The blue dress had been stuffed into a wooden crate. Sasha tugged it out, and a flash of lavender caught her eyes. She shook out the colonial blue skirt, trying to imagine anyone wearing something so bright. Below it lay a nearly new lavender plaid dress with leg-o'-mutton sleeves. Near the bottom of the crate lay a white eyelet blouse with a tiny stain.

She lifted out the final item and gasped out loud at the pristine white Edwardian lawn and lace tea dress. Why would anyone throw away such a beautiful garment?

After carefully folding the items, she looked around to make sure she was alone, then hoisted up the crate and hurried back to the buggy.

An hour later, in a different alley, she found several more items, but caught up in the fun of the search, she wasn't ready to quit. She glanced at the sun, knowing she still had plenty of time before she needed to start home.

Up ahead, she spotted what looked like a dark green sleeve flapping in the warm afternoon breeze behind a solid brick home. She ambled over and discovered a tea gown with a pigeon bust and lavish skirt. The dark green color would look beautiful in a quilt.

She reached for a bluish-gray item, which turned out to be a girl's pleated dress. It reminded her of the school uniform she'd worn as a child. Allowing a smile, she caressed the slightly worn garment. Maybe the little blond urchin could wear this with some minor adjustments.

Sasha couldn't believe her good fortune. She hadn't truly believed Dewey when he told her about the clothing, but she wouldn't doubt him again. She gathered up the two dresses and looked across the street. So far, she hadn't run into anyone, but she didn't want to push her luck. Could she perhaps get arrested for taking people's throw-away items? She hadn't considered that before.

She heard a door slam and some men's laughter coming from the house in front of her. She was only about twenty feet away and noticed that a window near the back porch was open. Something sounded like the squeal of a chair being pulled out, and the soft rumble of men's voices grew louder.

She ducked behind a huge oak that shaded the small backyard as the voices grew clearer. Obviously the men had come into the room where the open window was. Peeking around the tree, she saw a man sitting sideways on the window sill.

"I told you it was easy, didn't I?"

She could make out several voices but couldn't see anybody except the one man.

"Yes, you did, but I have to say I didn't believe it would be so easy to cheat those Indians."

Sasha gasped. Cheat Indians? She glanced around for some place else to hide but saw nothing big enough. She pressed down the dresses so that they didn't show around the wide trunk.

A man's boisterous laugh pierced the air. "If those dumb Creeks had bothered to learn to read English, they'd know before they signed that Chamber Oil leases are written so that landowners only get a fraction in royalties of the income from the oil."

A mumble of agreements flittered around the room, and she heard what sounded like someone tapping a fork against a glass.

"Here's to getting rich."

Sasha gritted her teeth in anger as glasses clinked together. These men were deliberately cheating the Indians. She had to find out who they were so she could report them.

A narrow street passed along the right side of the home, but it would be too dangerous to attempt to go that way. The men might see her and know she'd overheard them. No, it would be far better to go down the alley and circle around. She could cross the street and wait until the men came out the front of the house, and they'd never be the wiser.

Excited that her plan was a good one, she carefully folded the two dresses and turned to hurry back to the buggy. Her heart pounded a ferocious rhythm as she stepped away from the tree. *Please don't notice me.*

She took a step. Her foot snagged on something, and she fell forward. Her right hand darted out as she tried to grab the trash barrel to keep from falling. The rickety metal container tilted her way and clanged to the ground as the pile of dresses broke her fall, making her landing painless. Holding her breath, she glanced at the window as the barrel clattered against some rocks. A man poked his head out the window.

"Hey! Someone's out back."

Sasha had heard enough. She had to get away. Pushing herself off the ground, she reluctantly left the dresses behind and hurried down the street. Everything in her wanted to break into a run, but she tried to remain calm. If she could get past the next house, she could duck between them and cross to Main Street.

Behind her she heard what sounded like a door being thrown open and slamming against the house.

"There!" someone shouted.

"Get her."

Sasha lifted up her skirts and rushed forward, but her legs weren't fast enough.

"You, there. Stop!"

Running for her life, she cut across the corner of a yard, hoping to get away. Suddenly, a large hand latched onto her shoulder, and she felt herself being hauled backward. She twisted and kicked as visions of her previous assault swarmed her memory. A second man charged forward and grabbed her arm.

Panting and with her heart racing, she gazed up at the sky.

Please, God, if You're really up there, help me.

❧

Jim reined his horse away from crowded Main Street and down an alley. He patted his pocket, making sure he still had his package. His goal today had been to finish painting the parlor with Dewey's help, but the handle on his paintbrush had broken, thus he'd made an unscheduled trip to town.

His mind drifted to Sasha, and he smiled. She was so lovely and innocent, and as they were getting to know each other better, she was opening up and sharing more of herself. Her intelligent questions about the Bible had challenged him and Dewey. If she kept seeking God, she'd soon find Him. And that would be a happy day.

The horse jerked his head and sidestepped, making Jim look up. Several houses ahead, three people scuffled in the alley. He started to rein his horse down a different street, but his heart jolted when he realized two men were accosting a woman—the Gypsy woman!

She pushed and shoved but couldn't get free of her captors. Jim kicked his horse and charged ahead, knowing he had to help.

One man looked up. His eyes widened at Jim's approach. He released the woman and ran toward Jim. Hunkering down over his horse's neck, Jim charged his mount into the man, sending the attacker flying. The other man let go of the Gypsy and lunged at Jim. The second man climbed to his feet and ran to his friend's aid.

The old woman hurried down the alley and disappeared around the corner. Jim heard a shout and saw another man running his way. One man jerked his foot from the stirrup as the other yanked on his sleeve. The horse whinnied and jumped, as rough hands pulled Jim out of the saddle.

Chapter 10

Hidden in the shadows of Uncle Dewey's small barn, Sasha quickly removed her costume and slipped on the cotton dress she'd hidden earlier. Even with it being the button-up-the-front style like most of the women in the area wore, she could barely get it fastened because of her trembling hands.

What a close call that had been!

If not for some man riding to her aid, who knows what would have happened. She folded up her costume and put it in the hiding place, washed off her makeup, then unhitched the horse from the buggy. Standing by the pasture fence, she watched the gelding trot over to the pond and lower its big head to the water. She felt proud that she'd learned to handle a horse and buggy, thus gaining some independence.

But that independence had caused her to get hurt. Sasha leaned against the fence post and rubbed her bruised arm where one of the men had grabbed her. Both legs still felt as limp as spaghetti, but her mission had been a success, if only she hadn't lost those two dresses. At last count she'd collected six dresses, three skirts, four blouses, and a nightgown. Surely they would be a big help to the widows.

Glancing up at the lowering sun, she realized Dewey and Jim would be home soon. She needed to check on the stew her uncle had left simmering on the back of the stove and slice up some bread and tomatoes.

Turning toward the cabin, she wondered what to do with the information she'd overheard. She hated to get her uncle involved any more than he already was. Maybe Jim would know what to do. Or maybe that nice man who'd come to her uncle's aid and asked her to dinner could help. He seemed kind and treated her uncle with respect. What was his name? Ro–Roman something.

She grabbed the bucket inside the cabin door and headed to the creek for some fresh water.

"I can do that."

Sasha jumped. She'd been so deep in thought she hadn't heard her uncle's approach.

Dewey grinned. "You'd think you were expecting an Indian attack."

She handed the bucket to her uncle but couldn't resist giving him a hug. "No, not an attack, but it wouldn't surprise me if one asked me to dinner."

Dewey chuckled. "Guess that happens to you a lot, huh?"

"Too much."

"It's to be expected. You're a beautiful woman, and there are many more males around these parts than females."

"I understand that, but I don't have to like it."

Dewey headed toward the creek, chuckling. Sasha sliced a half dozen pieces of bread and cut up two large tomatoes, enjoying the simple domestic activities. After stirring the stew, she set the table, wondering why Jim hadn't returned. He and Dewey usually came back from the big house together.

Her mind drifted to thoughts of the house. Furniture should be arriving any day, and they could start decorating. Excitement made her hands tingle. It would be so much fun furnishing a whole house.

A scuffle outside pulled her from her thoughts.

"Sasha! Come quick."

Dewey's frantic voice set her feet in motion. At first all she noticed was Jim's saddled horse, but as the animal trotted toward the barn, she saw her uncle kneeling in the dirt. Her heart jumped as she saw Jim's battered body lying on the ground.

She rushed to his side, wondering what had happened. One eye was blackened, and his bloody lips were swollen twice their normal size. A goose egg with an inch-long gash had risen on his forehead.

"Oh! What do we do?" She looked to her uncle for guidance.

"Let's get him inside."

Dewey took Jim's shoulders, and she lifted his ankles. His dead weight was much greater than she'd expected. Finally, with both of them heaving and straining, they got Jim onto her bed.

"I'll get some more water. There are some rags in a box near the stove."

Sasha smoothed back Jim's dark hair. She hated seeing him so battered and hurting. Her emotions overcame her normal reserve, and she leaned over, placing a soft kiss on his cheek. Her feelings for him had grown and blossomed more than she realized. Everything in her wanted to pound whoever had done this to him.

He was such a nice man. He'd never once treated her with disrespect or acted like her being a half-breed mattered in any way.

She admired his fine dark looks and the lithe way he moved, like a man confident with his body and skills. He was always patient with her many questions about the Bible and answered her intelligently, not patronizingly, as one would answer a child. Seeing him each day made her heart soar. And when their gazes collided—oh my!

Could this be love?

Jim moved one of his legs and emitted a low groan. He murmured something unintelligible, and then the words "Gypsy woman."

Sasha stepped back with her hands on her cheeks, taking in his bloodied blue shirt. It was the same shirt her rescuer had been wearing.

This was her fault! Once again Jim had come to her aid, but this time, he'd paid a terrible price.

She ran into the kitchen and grabbed the rags, then hurried back to his side. Jim's eyes were open as she stepped back into the bedroom. He grabbed hold of her hand.

"The woman. Did she. . .get away?"

Sasha leaned closer, hoping her assumption was wrong. "What woman?"

Jim licked his puffy lips and winced. "The old Gypsy."

Sasha laid her hand on his chest. "Why would you help an old Gypsy woman?"

"God loves everyone. . .even poor. . .old women. How could I not help?"

Tears stung Sasha's eyes. She couldn't stand the thought that this kind man had been injured because of her.

Dewey hobbled in with another bucket of water. Sasha dipped a tin mug in it and helped Jim drink. He guzzled down the whole cupful, then collapsed against the bed. As she dabbed at his cuts, Sasha hoped that facial wounds were the only injuries he'd received.

"Why would someone do this to him? Jimmy never hurt a soul." Dewey glanced across the bed, his dark eyes looking pained.

"He was helping an old Gypsy that some men were accosting."

Dewey harrumphed. "Sound likes something he'd do. I just hate to see him hurting."

"Me, too." Sasha applied some salve Dewey gave her and bandaged Jim's head. He'd remained silent as she tended him, only grimacing a time or two.

Guilt flooded her. Should she confess she was the one he aided to put his mind at ease? But how would she explain wearing her costume so he would understand?

She desperately wanted to tell him but feared the disgust she'd see in his eyes. No, she couldn't tell him. Soon, but not until he was better.

⁓

Sasha's pounding heart matched the quick hoofbeats of the gelding pulling the buggy.

It had taken Jim three days to recover before he was able to work at the big house again. And even then, he only worked a few hours before coming back to his tent to rest awhile. He'd suffered no broken bones, but his ribs were bruised and his muscles sore.

It pained her to see his handsome face darkened with purple bruises and to watch him being careful with his movements.

If he knew what she planned to do today, he would have insisted on escorting her—and she couldn't have that.

To make things easier, she'd donned her Gypsy outfit, then shrugged her dress over it. A few miles from the cabin, she'd slipped off the dress and applied her makeup. Now, as she guided the buggy into Rag Town, she began to have second thoughts.

The massive tent city sprawled out in all directions. Children sat playing in the dirt or running around. Tired-looking women stood talking in small groups, hanging laundry or cooking at campfires. As far as she could see, not a man was in sight. Most likely the ones who lived here were at work in the oil fields.

Like oil spewing from a gusher, guilt washed over her. She'd never seen such poverty before. New York had its underprivileged areas, but her mother had never allowed her to travel in that part of the city or see where the impoverished lived. How did people survive in such squalor?

Here she'd been gallivanting to Tulsa and back, buying furniture and spending her uncle's money supplying his new house, while these people struggled to put food on their plates. Why did life have to be so lopsided?

Curious stares surveyed her as she drove through the shantytown. She tried to decipher what else she read in the tenants' eyes and decided it must be hopelessness. She knew a bit about that. Hadn't she felt hopeless of ever earning her mother's love? And in the end, she'd failed.

A swath of color grabbed her attention, and Sasha recognized the quilt hanging on the line to be of the same pattern as the one she'd bought Uncle Dewey. A woman in a baggy gray cotton dress stepped out from behind the quilt, and Sasha knew she'd found the woman she was searching for.

Sasha clambered out of the wagon and used her stick to shuffle over to the woman. The lady approached, curiosity dancing in her blue eyes. Sasha hoped and prayed her makeup would hold up to close scrutiny, but she'd do her best not to get too near the woman.

She took a deep breath, then plodded forward, hoping her plan worked. "That fancy bed cover of yours caught my eye at the festival last week."

The woman offered a shy smile. "I didn't see you there, but it was very crowded. My name's Mary McMurphey."

Ack! Sasha hadn't considered having to give her name. She didn't want to lie, but she needed to protect her true identity. "Monique," she said, thinking her middle name sounded a bit like a Gypsy.

"Pleased to meet you." Apprehension battled curiosity in Mary's eyes.

Sasha ambled toward the crate full of dresses in the back of the buggy. "I. . .uh. . .sometimes pick through people's trash before they burn it. Found a few jewels I thought you might could use." She hoped her accent resembled a Gypsy's.

"Me? Why would you bring me anything? We've never met before."

Sasha picked up the dark blue dress and fingered the fine fabric. Mary's gaze darted from the fabric to Sasha and back. Her interest was obvious.

"I can't sew—other than to do some mending. I saw your fine quilts the other day and thought you could use these clothes to make some more."

"Oh. . .I don't know." Mary's suspicious gaze traveled past Sasha, and her eyes widened.

Sasha turned back to the buggy, lifted a dark rose-colored dress out of the back, and shook it open.

"Oh, that's so lovely. I rarely get fabric that color."

Sasha smiled to herself. "It would be a shame to just return it to a trash barrel so somebody could burn it up, but I have no use for it."

Mary licked her lips. "Well. . .if you're sure."

Sasha nodded and laid the dress in the crate. She started to lift it before Mary changed her mind.

"Here, let me get that." Mary hoisted the crate and carried it into her tent.

Sasha prepared to mount the buggy, but Mary halted her with a hand on her shoulder. "Please, you must stay and have tea with me. I have to tell you, I prayed for more fabric, and God sent you. You're an answer to prayer."

Chapter 11

Sasha drove the buggy back home, thinking about her time with Mary. That was the second time someone had said she was an answer to prayer. Was that possible? Could God use someone and that person not even be aware of it?

She shook the reins, urging the horse up the hill. The buggy creaked as it dipped into one rut in the road after another. These country roads were just as rugged as the landscape. She passed field after field littered with oil wells and tanks. Where the derricks stood like angry sentinels, rarely was there a tree or bush. Even the ground was blackened from oil spills. Now she understood why Dewey was so determined to keep his land undefiled.

Sasha breathed a sigh of relief as she entered Dewey's property. Here, knee-high grass and wildflowers wafted in the wind and birds chirped lively tunes. Cattle grazed peacefully on the green hills. The countryside was alive and made her feel cheerful. She'd done a good thing today.

But it hardly seemed enough. Still, she had to be careful not to steal Mary's dignity by helping her too much or too often. An occasional trip now and then should suffice. If only there were more she could do.

The wagon hit a big rut, and Sasha braced herself with her foot. She clucked to the horse as she'd seen Jim do, and the animal heaved forward, pulling her back onto level ground.

The tea Mary had offered her had been weak and sugarless, but the company was cordial, and in the muted lighting of the tent, Sasha's makeup had passed the test. It was evident that Mary held beliefs of faith similar to those of Jim and Dewey. Sasha was beginning to feel left out.

But her mother and their New York friends had rarely gone to church, except on Christmas and sometimes Easter, and they had done all right. Hadn't they?

The theater troupe had worked hard to put on superb productions. They performed in the evenings, then ate dinner afterward and spent time on the town. Sasha had usually preferred to retire to her room after dining to read before going to bed. But what had been the purpose of that life? To entertain others?

Was that a noble cause?

Never once in her life had she done anything that had given her the satisfaction she had received from taking clothes to Mary. She could still see Mary caressing the fabric, looking as if she could hardly wait until Sasha left so she could get to work.

She smiled. Yes, she'd done something good today. Her uncle would be proud, but her mother would have said Sasha had wasted her time and the fine clothing, having given it to someone who couldn't appreciate its quality.

Sighing, she thought again about her uncle's faith and Jim's. Both men were the real deal. They weren't living their lives trying to impress the wealthy people of the world. They cared for others, but more important, they cared about God.

A deep longing coursed through her. She wanted to believe like they did. Believe in a God who loved her no matter if she sometimes messed up. She glanced at the sky, wondering how one went about approaching God. Jim had said you just had to believe in Jesus and confess your sins to Him, but that still seemed too easy. Surely you had to do penance—or something.

Up ahead she saw a corner of the cabin come into view and heard the rhythmic whacking of someone chopping wood. Perhaps it was Jim, though he shouldn't be exerting himself yet. Excitement at the thought of seeing him again made her limbs weak. Suddenly, she remembered her costume, and her heart nearly jumped clear out of her chest.

Using all the muscles she had, she forced the horse to stop on the road. The stubborn animal that longed to be back home where it would be freed from its binding and fed was less than cooperative. Sasha set the brake. She grabbed her dress from under the seat, climbed down from the wagon, and darted into the woods before someone could see her.

Hiking her skirts, she hurried through the thick brush toward the creek. How could she have been so carelessly caught up in her thoughts?

Behind her she could hear the horse whinnying and pawing the dirt. Surely Jim or her uncle would come to investigate.

At the creek, she flopped down on the ground and scrubbed her face with the small jar of cold cream she kept in her pocket. She scooped up some water and splashed it on her face again and again, all the while her hands shook and heart pounded.

Jim was supposed to be working up at the house. Perhaps her uncle was the one chopping wood. She would have to be more careful in the future if she donned her costume. Using her scarf for a towel, she wiped her face. Quickly, she removed her skirt and blouse and pulled the wrinkled calico over her head. She stuffed her costume under a bush and noted the surroundings so she could find it later.

Making her way back to the wagon, she gathered a handful of wildflowers for the table. As she stepped out of the trees, she saw Jim holding on to the horse and looking around. Relief filled his eyes as his gaze landed on her.

"What are you doing?"

Her mind raced. Not wanting to lie to him, she held up her hand and showed him the bouquet. "I thought some flowers would look nice on the table."

Jim's brows dipped, and a muscle in his jaw ticked. "In these parts, we tend to our animals first, then do things like. . .uh. . .pick flowers."

Sasha ducked her head, knowing he was right. But she couldn't very well explain her frantic rush into the woods. "Sorry. I'll do better next time."

"That's all right. You're new to the area." He released the brake, and the horse started of its own accord. The wheels on the buggy squealed as it rolled forward, and Jim followed it into the barn.

With her heart still throbbing, she walked toward the cabin, disappointed at Jim's reprimand. In her heart, she wanted to please him because she liked him and was grateful for all he'd done for her.

Soon, his shadow darkened the open cabin door. Droplets of water still clung to his dark stubble from his washing off. Sasha busied herself, peeling potatoes for supper.

"Got any coffee left?"

She looked up, and their gazes collided. His black eyes glimmered, and his damp, messed-up hair gave him a cute, boyish look.

"Pretty," he said, never breaking eye contact.

Sasha's heart, which had just slowed to normal, skittered out of control again. Was he talking about the flowers in the cup on the table? Or about her?

❧

"So, what do you think? Light blue or floral wallpaper?" Sasha looked at Jim, hoping he'd help her decide which paper looked best for the foyer.

Jim glanced at the paper, then at the walls. "I don't know. I'm not good with decorating."

"Well. . .you built the house. Surely you must have had some picture in your mind how it would look when completed."

He shrugged. "Actually, I never thought about it that way. I was just focused on finishing it."

Sasha turned back to the wall and held up the wallpaper samples she'd gotten in Tulsa. "All right then, let's go with the floral. It seems more natural than blue for the entryway." She held up the blue again. Maybe she'd use it upstairs in one of the bedrooms.

She peeked at Jim, who stood casually with his hands in his back pockets. "Have you always been a carpenter? You do wonderful work."

His neck and ears took on a reddish tint, and he looked out the tall window next to the front door. "No, actually I've been a farmer most of my life. I learned carpentry on the farm, having to repair and build things, but refined my skills during the Spanish-American War."

Sasha frowned. "How did you learn to be a carpenter during the war?"

Jim's brow dipped, and his lips thinned as he pressed them together. "I was on funeral duty for a while. Built a lot of caskets."

She laid a hand on his arm. "Oh, Jim, I'm so sorry. That must have been difficult."

He nodded and heaved a long sigh. "After that, I didn't want to fight anymore." He glanced at her as if she'd scold him for losing heart.

"I don't blame you. I wouldn't have, either."

"I just kept thinking of the families of those men who were hoping and praying their fathers, sons, and husbands would come home."

She squeezed his arm. "It must have been horrible for you."

He studied the ground and nodded. "I was threatened with a dishonorable discharge if I didn't fight, but a captain I was friends with stepped in. He got me put on repair detail—fixing wagons, making a structure safe for temporary headquarters. . .stuff like that."

"God was watching over you."

His stunned gaze matched her own surprise at the comment that had spilled from her mouth.

Slowly, his lips turned up in a roguish smile. "I guess He was at that, though I wasn't walking with Him back then. In fact, I was quite a mess for a while after returning home."

"Why didn't you go back to farming after the war?"

He looked out the window again. "I tried, but I was too restless. As much as I wanted to be with my family, it was hard realizing that I'd changed so much while they'd remained the same. I wanted to buy my own land and heard about all the money to be made around here, so I left home and came to Indian Territory."

"Do you plan to buy land around here so you can drill for oil?"

Jim shook his head. "No, I hope to get land closer to my uncle's farm. He lives near Guthrie in the Oklahoma Territory."

Disappointment washed over Sasha. Jim wasn't staying in these parts. When had she started hoping that he might care for her? That they might have a future together?

She licked her lips, knowing she must be a glutton for punishment, but she wanted to prolong her time with him. "So you're not of Indian blood? I thought maybe because of your coloring. . ."

He smiled, lifting her mood. "No, the way I understand it, we're French and Scottish. I have a grandfather I've never met who owns a big plantation in Georgia."

Sasha fiddled with the samples in her hand. Being French would explain his dark good looks. Still, disappointment raced through her. Jim was the first male friend she'd ever had. Actually, her first true friend. And he didn't seem to mind that she was half Indian, but she couldn't help believing that if he was of native blood, too, he might be more open to a deeper relationship with her. But knowing he was a white man, she doubted he would.

She still felt guilty that he took a beating to help her. His dark bruises had faded to a greenish yellow, and he was getting around well again, but it was her fault he'd been injured.

"You all right?" Jim looked down at her with warm eyes.

She nodded, knowing she had to pull herself out of her mood. Having grown up in a loving family, he wouldn't understand her vital need to hold close those she loved.

Sasha blinked. Did she love Jim?

She gazed up at him. Never having been in love before, how could she know? Turning, she started up the stairs. She needed to get away before he figured out what was wrong. "I'm. . .uh. . .going upstairs to decide what paint and wallpaper I need up there."

"You want help?"

She had to smile at that and looked backed over her shoulder. "I thought you didn't know anything about decorating."

"Aw, you're right. Guess I'll go see what Dewey's up to."

She watched him go out the door and past the window in the entryway. Her heart went with him. How was she supposed to work and eat with him every day without revealing her growing attraction?

Chapter 12

The wagon dipped into a deep rut in the road, knocking Sasha's shoulder against her uncle's. He slapped the reins on the horses' backs, and the animals plodded forward, bringing the wagon back on level ground.

Sasha tightened her grasp on the edge of the seat and thought back to the day she'd been in town, dressed in her costume. If she didn't do something, those men she'd overheard would just keep on swindling the landowners. But who could she trust with the information?

Dewey glanced at her. "Something wrong?"

She nibbled on her lip, wondering how much to tell him. He wouldn't approve of her traipsing around dressed as an old woman and sorting through people's garbage.

"A two-day-old stew is mighty good, but stewing over your problems just makes them seem bigger than they are. Why don't you tell me what's bothering you?"

Sasha heaved a sigh and plunged forward. "When I was in town the other day, I overheard some men talking about how Chamber Oil was cheating Indians."

Dewey exhaled a sigh and looked away. After a few moments, he turned back to face her. "I'm aware of their trickery. I know how they dealt with Kizzie. I offered to help her, but the woman had an independent streak as wide as the Arkansas River. She earned a wagonload of money with her oil leases, but it was only a fraction of what she should have made." His eyes darkened with anger. "I have proof she was cheated."

"Really? Can't you do anything about it?"

He shook his head. "Not now. Too late."

"It's never too late to right a wrong."

Dewey's kind eyes looked small against his leathery face. "I don't need the money—you know that. I wouldn't mind helping my people to keep them from being cheated, though, but I don't know who to trust. The oilmen all seem to be eating from the same bean pot."

"Surely they aren't all bad."

"No, you're right." Dewey shook his head. "But I don't know who I can trust, so I just keep the information to myself. Some landowners have been killed because they refused to sign a lease or wanted more money. I don't need that kind of trouble."

They pulled into Keaton a short while later, and Dewey stopped the wagon under a tree near the train depot. He clambered to the ground, then helped her down.

"I reckon you've got more shopping to do." Dewey smiled. "I know you haven't bought everything we need for that big house yet."

"No, I have a long way to go before I'm done." She studied her uncle for a moment. "Are you sure I'm not spending too much money?"

Smiling, he shook his head. "No, Jim told me how thrifty you're being. I'm proud of you, Sasha. From what he's said, you're buying quality goods but also being frugal."

"Thank you. I'm trying not to spend any more than we need to." Her chest warmed with pride. She'd rarely received such a heartwarming compliment.

"You're doing fine, and I don't want you to worry about it." He patted her shoulder, looking a tad embarrassed.

"Now, I need to see if any of that stuff you ordered has arrived." He pulled out his pocket watch and looked at it. "How about if we meet up around half past noon for dinner at the diner?"

"That sounds fine." As they parted, Sasha walked down the boardwalk toward the dressmaker's shop. She hoped the lightweight, front-buttoned dresses she'd ordered were ready. Her New York gowns were too hot and impractical for daily living here.

She rounded the corner and plowed straight into a solid chest. If the man hadn't grabbed her upper arms, she would have fallen onto her backside. She peeked up to apologize and came face-to-face with—seeing him in person brought the name she hadn't been able to recall a couple of days earlier to mind—Roman Loftus.

"Well, it's a pleasure running into you, Miss Di Carlo." His pearly white smile looked bright against his reddish brown skin. He lifted a derby hat and bowed.

Though embarrassed, she couldn't help smiling at the way he worded his greeting. "Nice running into you, too, although I suppose I should apologize for not paying attention to where I was going."

"No need, I assure you." He waved his hand in the air. "Might I ask where you're headed in such a hurry?"

Sasha's cheeks warmed. "I. . .uh. . .was on my way to do some errands."

"Would you mind if I accompany you? Normally women are perfectly safe in town, but if I were to escort you, then nobody would even consider bothering you."

She preferred being alone, but if his company kept other men away, then maybe she should accept his offer. "Why, yes, Mr. Loftus, I would be happy for you to walk with me."

He offered his arm. "Where to first?"

She slipped her arm through his, giving him a charming smile. "Why, the dressmaker's shop, of course."

Mr. Loftus lifted his gaze to the sky and shook his head. "Why doesn't that surprise me?"

"You are free to withdraw your offer."

He patted her arm. "No, no. To the dressmaker's it is."

They strolled along, and she considered how kind he seemed. Could she possibly ask his advice about what she'd overheard? He was an oilman, after all, and might be able to help her. He'd come to Uncle Dewey's aid the other day. But was he trustworthy?

She ducked into the dressmaker's shop, leaving him gladly waiting outside. She paid for the two dresses that were finished and made plans to return the next week for the final garment. As she exited the store, Mr. Loftus tugged at the package in her hand.

"Do allow me to carry this for you." His amiable smile dissolved her objections, and she handed over the parcel.

"Where to now, Miss Di Carlo?"

"Surely you must have some place you need to be."

"No, I have the next few hours free. There's always paperwork to be done, but it can wait for a bit."

They crossed the street, and Sasha pondered whether to confide in him or not. Two women stared at them as they passed in the road. Sasha glanced up at her escort, realizing again how handsome he was. His features, though clearly Indian, were finer than most, giving him a regal air, and he didn't seem the least bit uncomfortable in her company, even though he must be full-blooded Creek.

In the mercantile, she placed an order for some linens from the Montgomery Ward catalog and purchased two sun bonnets like many of the women in town wore. All the while, she wrestled with whether to tell him about the dishonest oilmen or not.

Jim was the one she ought to be confiding in, and she could just imagine his scowl at seeing her on the arm of Roman Loftus. She pushed that thought aside. She needed someone familiar with oil companies and how they worked to help her.

As they exited the store, Mr. Loftus glanced down at her. His dark eyes shimmered with some emotion she couldn't decipher. Could he tell she was a half-breed? Would it matter to him?

"It's well past the noon hour, Miss Di Carlo. Might you consider having lunch with me?"

"Oh my. I'm supposed to meet my uncle at the diner soon. Perhaps you could join us."

He nodded, though she thought he would rather have her to himself. As they approached the diner, she saw Dewey waiting for her near the entrance. He smiled, then studied her escort.

"Afternoon, Mr. Hummingbird." Roman Loftus tipped his hat.

"Mr. Loftus." Dewey pressed his lips together and nodded, then turned to her. "I'm sorry, Sasha, but some of our order just arrived on the noon train. I need to stay at the depot to make sure everything gets unloaded off the train and into our wagon."

She laid her hand on his arm. "It's all right. Mr. Loftus asked me to dine with him. But you won't get to eat."

Dewey waved his hand in the air. "Just have Sue Ann make me a roast beef sandwich and bring it to the depot when you two are done. I should be ready to go by then."

She nodded, and Dewey gave Roman a stern look before leaving. Did her uncle not approve of her escort?

They took their seats, placed an order, and then sat staring at each other. Maybe being with him would help her better understand her feelings for Jim. If she truly cared for Jim, then Mr. Loftus wouldn't hold her interest. But here she was, and as hard as it was to admit, she was curious about the man across from her.

They made small talk for a time. All the while she was getting up her nerve to confide in him. Surely he could help. Soon their food would arrive, and then it would be too late. She leaned forward, and he copied her action.

"Mr. Loftus, I wonder if you might help me with a. . .uh. . .situation."

His dark brows lifted. "Of course, I'd be happy to assist you any way I can."

She looked around to make sure no one was paying them any attention, took a deep breath, and then plunged forward. "I know someone who overheard some men talking about Chamber Oil cheating Indians."

He blinked and looked stunned at her abrupt confession. "This person actually heard this? I mean an actual confession that the oil company is swindling Indians?"

Sasha nodded. "Yes."

"Would this person recognize these men if he saw them again?"

"I don't think so. I don't believe my friend got a good look at them."

He leaned his elbows on the table and steepled his fingers. "Then, unfortunately, there's not much to be done, but I'll ask around and see if I can find out anything. Sadly, many oilmen are unscrupulous, unlike my father and I, who strive to be upright and fair."

"I see." Disappointment flooded Sasha.

"I'm full-blooded Creek and don't like seeing my people getting cheated."

Sasha studied Mr. Loftus as she fiddled with the edge of the tablecloth.

297

There was no doubting his heritage with his straight black hair, dark complexion, and high cheek bones. She no longer remembered why she hadn't wanted to dine with him the other day. Could it be possible that Creeks, besides her uncle, wouldn't be put off by her heritage?

He reached across the table and laid his hand on her forearm.

"Miss Di Carlo, I promise I'll do my best to get to the bottom of this and see that the people involved are punished."

❧

"Move it a little to the right." Sasha watched Jim and a worker push the heavy dresser two inches closer to the bedroom window.

Jim brushed his forehead with his sleeve. "How's that?"

She eyeballed the chest of drawers, deciding it looked perfectly centered between the window and the wall. "That's fine. Thank you."

"All right, we'll bring up the bed frame next." The men trudged into the hall and down the stairs.

Sasha wiped her hand over the walnut highboy dresser, then untied the sash that had held the attached swivel mirror steady during transport. She doubted her uncle had enough clothes to fill it, but at least he wouldn't have to hang things on pegs anymore. The scent of fresh paint still lingered in the room, making her hope her uncle liked the soft blue color. She'd made him stay away until the room was completed, and now excitement and anxiety both swirled in her stomach.

She crossed the room and wiped off the top of the washstand. What she loved most about this small piece of furniture was that the enamel basin could be pulled out for use and pushed in and hidden under the wooden top when not needed. She tugged the basin out and pushed it in.

Jim backed into the room carrying the bed's headboard. "You're not playing with that washstand again, are you?"

Spinning around, she tried to wipe the guilty look off her face. "Just center that along the south wall."

He flashed her a knowing smile, then focused on his job. Her insides tingled at his teasing look.

Several hours later, Sasha's calves ached from climbing the stairs so many times. Her bedroom and her uncle's were complete, and this would be their first night to sleep in the new house.

"I just don't know if I'll be able to sleep in such a big place." Holding an armload of clothes, Dewey looked around his new bedroom. "It's too nice for the likes of me."

Sasha sidled up beside him as Jim came in carrying a wooden chair. "No, it's not. There's nothing fancy in here. Just basic walnut furniture, a quilt, and curtains."

She pointed to the corner where the chair belonged, and Jim set it down. He wiped the back of his hand across his forehead. She could just imagine how tired he must be after lugging furniture upstairs most of the day. Flashing him a smile of gratitude, she turned back to her uncle.

Dewey shook his head. "Looks mighty fancy to me. But you did a fine job, and I'm proud of you."

She was having the time of her life supplying the house and making it livable, and Dewey's comment gave her a sense of satisfaction that she'd rarely felt before. Deep in her heart, she hoped she never had to return to New York.

✎

A warm sense of admiration surged through Jim as he watched Sasha light up at Dewey's comment. Her uncle was right—she had done a wonderful job so far of outfitting the house. Dewey's bedroom was simple but nice. Sasha's room was a bit more elegant, but still usable and practical. The rose carpeting matched the design on her bedding and the sheer curtains that covered the window.

He loved seeing Sasha's eyes light up. They reminded him of coffee with just a drip of cream. Wisps of rebellious hairs had pulled free from her long braid and danced about her face whenever the wind whipped in the open window.

Blowing out a sigh, he knew he needed to walk down the hill and head to bed, but he was so tired from hauling furniture upstairs all day, he didn't want to move.

"Well, Jimmy, I reckon you can sleep in the cabin tonight."

Jim's heart skipped a beat. "Are you sure? You haven't gotten all your belongings out yet." He wouldn't admit that sleeping on the cabin's bed sounded much more inviting than spending the night on the stiff cot in his tent.

Dewey nodded. "Yep, I'm sure. It's time we called it a night. We're all tuckered out from working so hard, though I don't know how I'll sleep in this fancy bed."

Sasha gave Dewey a kiss on the cheek, waved good night to Jim, then walked down the hall to her room. Jim longed for her to kiss him, too, but he bid them good night and shuffled down the stairs, wishing for once that the cabin wasn't so far away. Parts of his body were still tender from the beating he'd taken, and after today's workout, he longed for a soak in a hot tub. The creek would have to do, though.

As he stepped out into the warm evening, he couldn't get Sasha's lovely face out of his mind. She was beautiful inside and out. She already loved Dewey, and Jim felt sure that she cared for him, too. He longed to get to know her better and deepen their friendship.

But could there be any future for him and a woman of Indian heritage?

It wouldn't be the first time for an Indian and white man to court and maybe marry. In fact, there were many such marriages in the Twin Territories, but what would his family say to such a union?

What would Sasha say?

Chapter 13

Sasha wiped down the buffet cabinet with beeswax. As she moved her flannel rag back and forth, her gaze darted over to where Jim was attaching the legs to the oak dining table that he had just brought inside. With the sleeves of his chambray shirt rolled up, she could see the muscles in his forearm contract as he attached the leg to the table. Sighing, she refocused on her job.

She loved to watch Jim work. He was so meticulous in all that he did. She was sure he'd never done a job halfway in all his life. He was nice-looking, honest, and had a faith in God she admired.

She peeked at him again, and his eyes locked onto hers. A warm blush heated her cheeks at being caught staring. Jim's eyes sparkled. He smiled, then winked at her.

Stifling a gasp at his forwardness, she concentrated again on her polishing. Butterflies danced in her stomach, and she marveled that she'd never met a man who stirred her like he did. She sighed again, wishing, hoping there could be a future for them. But Jim said he planned to move back to the Oklahoma Territory, and now that she had a home and an uncle who loved her, she wasn't about to leave—even if Jim was willing to marry an Indian. She loved her uncle—even though he wasn't refined and sophisticated like her mother's friends—and they were family.

Jim chuckled, making her turn around again. "You're doing some mighty heavy sighing over there. Must be thinking awful hard."

She opened her mouth to correct him but knew he spoke the truth.

"I'm always willing to listen if you need someone to talk to."

Wasn't that just like him? Considerate to the core. But there was no way she could tell Jim that she'd been thinking about him.

"That's done." He stood and stretched, nearly popping the buttons off his shirt.

Her mouth went dry. She longed to lean against his solid chest and have his arms wrap around her.

She shook her head. What was wrong with her? She was acting like an enamored school girl. Everett, Jim's helper, walked in carrying two of the chairs that matched the table. Sasha was grateful for the distraction. "Just put those along the wall for now."

He did as she asked, then helped Jim turn the table onto its legs.

Jim looked at her. "Where do you want it?"

She waved her hand in the air. "Put it in front of the double windows, but leave about three feet so we can put the chairs in. We'll enjoy a nice view of the field when we eat in here."

The men did as told, and she marveled at how lovely the room looked with the furniture in it. The floral wallpaper that Jim and Everett had put up several days ago brightened the room and added a rainbow of color. She picked up a chair and slid it under the table, wondering if life could get any better.

"I'll get the other chairs." Everett disappeared into the hallway.

Sasha glanced at Jim as he retrieved the matching chair. She imagined him sitting at the head of the table with her beside him, eating together every day. Yes, it was possible that life could get better. If only. . .

A knock sounded on the front door, pulling Sasha from her work. She hurried to the front of the house, eager to see who their first official visitor was. She pushed open the screen door and saw Roman Loftus dressed in a dark brown three-piece suit standing off to the side, staring down at the pond. His horse grazed nearby. Mr. Loftus turned and smiled.

"Good day, Miss Di Carlo." He tipped his hat and looked past her. "Mighty fine place your uncle has here."

Sasha smiled, delighted to have someone to show the house to. "Would you like to see the inside?"

"Yes, I would. Thank you."

She stepped back, and he entered, closing the screen without letting it bang. That small feat impressed her, because Jim had been going in and out for days, banging the door each time. She relieved him of his hat and laid it on the entryway table. When she looked back, she noticed him admiring the curved staircase.

"Very nice indeed."

"Yes, Jim Conners and his workers have done a beautiful job."

Mr. Loftus's brows dipped down for a moment. "Ah, so that's what he does around here. I'd wondered."

Sasha ignored his comment about Jim and held out her hand, indicating for him to enter the parlor. "The furniture for this room hasn't arrived yet, so I can't offer you a place to sit—unless you'd care to move to the dining room."

"No, thank you. I actually came out to talk to you about something."

Her heart skittered as she placed her hand against her chest. "Did you find out who those men were?"

He pressed his lips into a straight line. "No, sorry. I haven't had any luck on that account."

Disappointment sagged her shoulders. "Oh, I'd hoped you had. It's a very serious thing."

"I haven't given up, I assure you." He studied her face, and his countenance seemed to brighten. "I was wondering. . .Natalie Carmichael is coming to Tulsa next weekend. Have you heard of her?"

"Oh, yes. She has a reputation as a wonderful opera singer, though I've never heard her perform."

Mr. Loftus looped his thumbs in his lapels and hung on. "Then you must accompany me to hear her."

Sasha blinked, stunned that he'd asked her to go with him to Tulsa. Her thoughts flew to Jim, and she found herself wishing he was the one asking her out. But he wasn't, and probably never would. She needed Mr. Loftus's help in tracking down the dishonest oilmen, and it would be wise to stay in his good graces.

"Miss Carmichael is doing a two o'clock matinee, so we could have dinner, attend the program, and still get back home before dark—thanks to the train."

As she wrestled with what to do, Jim walked in, carrying an armload of window blinds that he had picked up at the Keaton depot. The screen door banged shut, making Sasha wince. Jim stopped quickly and scowled when Roman Loftus stepped out of the parlor. The two men stared each other down like a couple of rams about to butt heads.

Finally, Jim nodded. "Afternoon. If you're looking for Mr. Hummingbird, he's down at the cabin getting some of his belongings."

Mr. Loftus smiled like he was the only rooster in the henhouse. "I found who I was looking for."

Jim's dark brows dipped as he looked from Sasha to Mr. Loftus and back. "I reckon I'll get back to work if you don't need me."

His comment was directed at Sasha, and she shook her head, giving him a gentle smile. She could read his curiosity but knew his good manners would keep him from lingering. He nodded and started up the stairs, looking back over his shoulder.

"So, what do you think? Would you have dinner and go to the show with me?"

Sasha heard Jim stumble at the top of the stairs. Her heart jumped to her throat, and she looked up to be sure he was all right. He stood on the landing, glaring down. He looked fine, but not too happy.

Maybe he was jealous of Mr. Loftus's attention. She turned back to face her visitor, certain that he'd just wiped a smirk off his face. If she didn't need his help, she never would have considered his offer. But she did.

"Yes, I do believe I'd like that, Mr. Loftus."

His brilliant smile could have lit up the whole room. "Wonderful. But since we'll be seeing more of each other, you must call me Roman."

"We'll see," she said, smiling wryly. She wasn't sure that she wanted to take that step so soon.

"I'll pick you up at ten o'clock on Saturday. That should give us plenty of time to get to Tulsa and have dinner before the show." He headed for the front door, picked up his hat, and then cast a victorious glance upstairs.

She escorted him outside and waved as he rode off. Was she doing the right thing? If she'd said no to his offer, would he still have been willing to help her?

Well. . .she'd never know the answer to that question now. As she went back inside, she looked upstairs, but Jim wasn't in sight. Somehow she felt sure he'd be displeased with her.

And she didn't like that feeling one bit.

≫

Jim wanted to slam the blinds onto the floor, but he resisted. It made his heart ache to know that Sasha was going out on the town with Roman Loftus. The thought of her alone with the slimy oilman made his stomach churn.

Couldn't she tell that he had feelings for her? But then he hadn't exactly made his intentions known—partly because he wasn't sure what they were. All he knew was that Sasha was special, and when he was near her, his whole being felt as if he'd grabbed onto an electric light fixture the wrong way.

Jim picked up a blind and unwrapped the paper covering it. He was certain that Roman was just another oilman looking for a way to make more money. It didn't matter that he was Creek; he was still an oilman watching out for his own interests first.

He crossed the room, checked his measurements and the number on the blind to make sure he had the correct one, and then unwound the string that was wrapped around it. He clenched his jaw, concerned about Sasha's safety.

Seeing movement outside, he felt his ire rise as he watched Roman Loftus ride off. The man had put down a silent challenge with the looks he'd cast Jim when Sasha wasn't watching. He had a sneaky suspicion the man was using Sasha to get to Dewey.

Jim leaned the shade against the wall and paced the guest bedroom. He had to face the truth that he cared for Sasha—maybe even loved her—but he had nothing to offer besides a little money in the bank.

He sighed and rubbed the back of his neck. He could never compete with the lifestyle Sasha had lived her whole life. If they ever married, how could he ask her to leave her uncle when she'd just gotten to know and love him? And what about this house that she'd put so much time and effort into? Would she leave all this to live in a soddy with him?

Frustrated, he stomped down the stairs and out the front door, relishing the loud slam the screen made. With Sasha being Dewey's only living relative other than her mother, whenever he died, she would most likely inherit his wealth.

He'd gotten his hopes up about a relationship with her, and now he was paying the price.

There was no way to bridge the differences in their lives.

He didn't even have a home or land of his own, and here Sasha was living in a brand-new house—a fancy one, at that.

The painful truth drove him, and he had to get away. He jogged down the hill to his horse, tossed on the saddle, and rode off at top speed. The wind whipped his face, along with an occasional insect. His horse's hooves pounded out a rhythm he couldn't get out of his head.

You can't have her. You can't have her.

Chapter 14

On Saturday afternoon, Jim reined his horse to a stop. Three hours of riding fence lines, checking for breaks, hadn't erased the picture of Sasha leaving in the wagon with Roman Loftus. The man had resembled a gloating rooster who'd swallowed the biggest insect in the pen as he escorted Sasha to his buggy. And Sasha—she looked like a princess all dressed up in her shimmering blue gown. All satin and lace.

Jim's jaw ached from being clenched so much the past few hours. He was angry at Loftus for asking Sasha to Tulsa. Angry at her for accepting. And angry for not being honest with Sasha and himself.

Swatting at a mosquito, he considered why he'd been hesitant to approach her about his feelings. Besides their differences, there was her Indian blood.

He smacked his leg, angry at himself that he had been prejudiced—even a little bit. Why did it matter? He was of mixed blood himself—part French, part Scot, and who knew what else.

He was a Christian, and bloodlines shouldn't matter. People were created in God's image—equal and valuable—and should be judged on their character and what they did with their lives, not on who their ancestors were.

Of all people, he shouldn't care about bloodlines. Dewey Hummingbird was one of the finest men he'd known. He'd helped Jim become a stronger Christian and helped him overcome his anger and frustrations from fighting in the war.

Maybe what really bothered him was that he had so little to offer Sasha—and he'd used her heritage as an excuse to keep him from facing that fact.

He came to a creek and checked the water for oil seepage before letting his horse drink. Many cattle in the area had died from drinking water that oil had seeped into, but Dewey had been blessed not to lose any of his.

He spent the next hour praying and seeking God as he headed back to the cabin. Finally, his heart found peace. He would confess his feelings to Sasha and let the Lord work things out. A smile tugged at his cheeks for the first time since he'd learned about Sasha's dinner outing with Loftus.

As he rode over the hill, past the new house, his heart stopped. A cloud of black smoke boiled into the sky near where the cabin was.

Fire!

He dug his heels into his mount and galloped down the hill. His heart melted as he saw the cabin in flames, and ten feet away, Dewey lay on the ground, badly beaten. Both eyes were swollen shut, his lip was split, and his arm looked broken.

Jim leaped off his horse while it was still moving and skidded to a stop beside Dewey. Kneeling, his gaze roamed over his friend's battered body. Anger battled pain. Who would do such a thing to a kind, old man?

He carefully lifted Dewey by the shoulders and dragged him away from the fire, wincing when his mentor moaned.

"Jim. . ." Dewey lifted a bloody hand. "Oilmen. . .attacked me. . . . I wouldn't sign their lease."

"Shhh. . .rest now. We'll talk later." Jim patted Dewey's shoulder, hoping there'd be a later.

Dewey clutched Jim's sleeve. "Have evidence. . .Chamber Oil cheating Creeks. . .in box in cabin."

Jim glanced at the blazing cabin. It shuddered, and the roof collapsed with a loud roar, sending fiery debris and ash sprinkling down around them. Whatever evidence had been inside no longer existed, but he couldn't tell Dewey that.

Tears—probably from the smoke and ash—stung his eyes. He brushed the back of his hand across them.

"Jim, I love you. . .like a son. Take care of Sasha." Life seeped out of Dewey, and he went limp.

Jim heaved a sob and brushed his hand over his friend's dark hair. He loved this old man and would dearly miss him. Tears streamed down his cheeks as he gently lifted Dewey, carried him into the barn, and laid him in the wagon bed.

How would he ever break the news to Sasha that her beloved uncle was dead?

❧

"So, did you have an enjoyable time?" Roman put his arm along the back of the train seat and turned sideways to face her.

She looked up at him and smiled. "I had a delightful time. Thank you for asking me. The singer was wonderful, as well as the meal." Even though she had been nervous, she'd had a magnificent time. Perhaps there were some things she missed about New York.

"Good, I'm glad. Maybe we can do it again sometime."

"Perhaps." Sasha gave him a shy smile. Roman had been polite and charming all day.

"I have to admit, I still don't understand why your uncle doesn't want to lease his land. People would kill for such an opportunity."

A shudder charged through her at his sudden change in conversation. Sasha stared out the window at the landscape whizzing by. "My uncle has enough money to satisfy him and wants to preserve his land."

Roman chuckled and shook his head. "How can anyone ever have enough money?"

"It's more than the money—his land is his home, and he doesn't want it defiled."

"Land is land. He could lease his and buy a huge ranch somewhere else with all the money he'd make. He could have the best of both worlds and be unbelievably rich, too."

Sasha sighed, truly uncomfortable for the first time all day. In spite of being full-blooded Creek, Roman couldn't understand that sometimes owning land that family has lived on for years was more important than becoming wealthy.

He waved his hand in the air. "Never mind. I'm sorry for throwing a wet blanket on our lovely day. Let's not talk any more business."

She leaned back in her seat, relieved. Still, she couldn't help being disappointed with his attitude. But he was an oilman—so what else should she expect but that he'd talk oil?

In the back of her mind, she couldn't help wondering if he'd asked her to dinner just to try to persuade her to his way of thinking.

Well, it wouldn't work, if that was his plan.

Her thoughts drifted to Jim. What was he doing right now? He'd looked both hurt and angry when she left with Roman. She dipped her brow. Well, so what. He didn't return her affections, so he had no say in what she did. His opinion didn't matter one whit.

As much as she wanted to believe that, her heart told her it wasn't true.

❧

Sasha paced the depot, her footsteps echoing on the wooden planks of the floor. Roman had gone to retrieve the buggy from the livery and would be returning any minute. He'd asked her to dinner next Saturday, and she needed to give him an answer. Part of her wanted to say yes, but another part didn't.

"Sasha."

She whirled around, surprised to hear Jim's voice. His filthy face looked as if it were covered in coal dust, and he reeked of smoke. He stood there with his hat in his hand, gazing on her with a miserable expression on his face.

"What are you doing here?" She couldn't help wondering if he was spying on her and Roman.

Before he could answer, Roman approached, his brows tucked down. "You couldn't wait until I got her home to talk to her?" His haughty gaze took in Jim's disheveled appearance, and he smirked.

Jim pinned Roman with a pointed glare, then his gaze softened to apologetic as he looked at her. "Sasha. . ." He glanced away, but when he turned back, his eyes glimmered with unshed tears, sending a shaft of fear straight to her heart. "There's been an accident. Dewey. . .is dead."

Sasha gasped as a pang of grief threatened to knock her off her feet. "No, it can't be. What happened?"

Her knees turned to butter, and her head buzzed. She reached out and grabbed hold of Jim's forearm. He looked as if he wanted to hold her, but then he glanced at her clothes and then his.

"The cabin was set on fire, and somebody beat up your uncle."

She sagged, and both men reached for her, but Jim grabbed her first.

"C'mon over here and sit down. Loftus, get her some water."

Roman scowled, obviously not used to being bossed around, but left anyway.

"Dewey told me it was oilmen, trying to force him into signing."

Tears coursed down Sasha's face as she thought of her dear uncle hurting and now dead while she was off having a good time.

Jim handed her a dingy handkerchief. "Sorry, it's clean but smells like smoke."

She shrugged but accepted it and wiped her face and nose. "I can't believe it came to this."

"Me, neither. I talked with the sheriff, but since there were no witnesses except Dewey, there's not much he can do. I told him about the three men who'd been pressuring Dewey, and he said he'd check them out."

Sasha jumped up, her dress swishing. "There has to be something he can do. People can't commit murder and get away with it."

Roman returned with her water, and she downed the whole cupful.

"Let me take you home," Roman said. "You've had quite a shock."

Jim shook his head. "I'll take her."

Roman looked ready for a battle, but Sasha laid her hand on his arm. "There's no sense in you driving clear to the ranch when Jim's already here. I had a wonderful time and thank you for it." She pinned on a no-argument stare.

"But—" Roman opened his mouth to protest, then slammed it shut. He glared at Jim, then bowed to her. "Thank you for accompanying me today. It would be my pleasure to escort you again once you're feeling better." Spinning around, he stalked toward the buggy.

Sasha hated refusing him after he'd been so nice all day and had spent so much money on her, but at the moment, the only person she wanted to be with was Jim. He loved her uncle as much or even more than she, and he understood her agony and grief in a way Roman never could.

Chapter 15

On the way home, Jim pulled the wagon to a stop where the road diverged, one way leading to the new house and the other to the cabin.

"Are you sure about this?"

Sasha nodded, then dabbed her nose again with Jim's handkerchief. "I need to see it."

"It's just a burned down cabin."

She waved her hand to the left. "Just go. Please."

The overwhelming sense of loss she felt as the cabin came into view a few minutes later threatened to knock her off the buggy seat.

Her uncle was gone.

And now she was alone. Again.

Smoke still drifted up, and embers glowed in the debris that once was her uncle's cabin. Ashes drifted like black snow on the light afternoon breeze. Her hopes and dreams floated away with them.

"Seen enough?" Jim asked, his voice laced with compassion.

She nodded, and he clucked to the horses, which moved away at a quick pace, obviously happy to be away from the heat of the debris.

Numb, she watched a waddling mother duck lead her ducklings into the pond as they passed. As they rode up the hill, the house came into view. She sniffed and held back a sob. Such a big, beautiful house, and she alone would live there now.

She looked down at her ruined dress. Soot from Jim's clothing had turned the pale blue gown gray. It was just as well, because she knew she would never wear it again. She'd been off having a gay time while her uncle had suffered and died. The dress would only remind her that she should have been here. Maybe she could have made a difference.

Jim pulled the wagon to a stop in front of the house and came around to help her down. As he set her on the ground, all her pain and fears came gushing out, and she burst into tears. "What will I do without him?"

❧

Sharing Sasha's blinding pain, Jim pulled her into his arms. Her dress was already ruined, so he no longer worried about that. He ran his hand over her soft hair and held her head against his chest. She sobbed and moaned with grief, her tears bleeding through his shirt.

Against his will, Jim's own tears streamed forth. He'd miss his old friend more than anyone he'd ever lost.

Finally, Sasha stepped back a half step, but Jim kept her in the circle of his arms. He loved this woman and wanted to protect her. She glanced up, looking so pitiful with her red, splotchy face and moist eyelashes. "What am I going to do?"

He wiped away her tears with his thumbs and tried to smile. "You'll go on living—here in Dewey's house. He built it for you, you know."

Sasha blinked, looking confused.

"He told me just last week that he'd promised his sister to build a fine house so that when you and your mother came to visit, y'all would have a nice place to stay. He said he'd never given up hope and knew you'd come one day."

Sasha's chin and lower lip quivered. A fresh set of tears escaped.

Jim knew he shouldn't take advantage of her grief, but he couldn't have stopped if a hundred horses held him back. He lowered his face and kissed her, hoping to comfort her. Needing her comfort.

For a brief moment, she just stood there, then she wrapped her arms around his neck and returned his kiss.

Oh, how he loved this woman and wanted to protect her and see her happy. Finally, needing air, he pulled away. A smile tugged at his lips. "I'm afraid I got your face dirty."

A fiery rose blush glowed through the soot and tears. "It's all right. I'm a mess anyway."

He tugged at her hands. "C'mon. Let's get you inside." He escorted her upstairs and stopped in the hall outside her room. "Will you be all right while I get some fresh water so you can clean up?"

She nodded, but the look she gave him was like a puppy that had lost its master. He took her face in his hands and stared deeply in her eyes. "We'll get through this—together."

※

The next morning, Jim paced the entryway to the back of the house, willing Sasha to come down. He hadn't wanted to leave her alone but knew he couldn't sleep under the same roof, so he'd pitched his tent in the backyard. But sleep had eluded him. He couldn't get Dewey's battered body or Sasha's distraught expression out of his mind.

A creak on the stairs alerted him to Sasha's presence. She glided down, dressed in a gray cotton work dress. She flashed him an embarrassed smile and looked at her skirt. "I don't have anything black to wear."

Jim's heart ached for her. "Dewey wouldn't want you to wear mourning clothes."

She shrugged and walked past him into the kitchen. "Thanks for making coffee. I sure need it today."

311

She poured a cup and sat at the kitchen table. Jim pulled a plate of scrambled eggs and bacon off the back burner and set it on the table in front of her.

"I don't think I can eat a thing."

The chair squeaked as Jim pulled it away from the table and sat. "You need to keep up your strength. We. . .uh. . .have to go to town and take care of the funeral arrangements."

Sasha's lower lip quivered.

"I can do it alone if you don't want to."

Her gaze darted up. "No, I need to have a part. It's the least I can do for Uncle Dewey."

Jim picked up the fork and stabbed a piece of egg. "Here, eat this."

She looked at it and shook her head. Jim ignored her resistance and held the bite against her mouth. She peeked up at him, a red blush staining her cheeks, and then she opened her mouth and took the bite.

"I've been thinking. You shouldn't stay here alone." Jim tapped the table while she ate. "I moved my tent to the backyard in case you need me, but you really should have a woman here with you."

Sasha shook her head. "I'll be fine by myself."

"I know it's none of my business, but I was thinking maybe you could help out an oil widow or two and yourself at the same time."

Her eyes sparkled at his comment. "You know, that might not be a bad idea."

Sasha stood in front of Mary McMurphey, trying hard not to wring her hands. The widow had seemed defensive when Sasha asked her if she'd like to come work for her.

"I don't know, ma'am. It's a far piece to travel, and I'd hate to leave my children all day."

"My foreman, Jim Conners"—Sasha waved a hand toward the buggy—"can build a room on the back of the house where you can live with your children."

Something flickered in Mary's eyes. Hope maybe? Then they dulled. "But I would still have to leave them alone all day, ma'am. Here, everyone watches out for the children."

Sasha felt herself losing ground. "Well, the fact is, I could use two people. Someone to tend the house and another person to cook. Would you happen to know someone who is a good cook who might have an older child that could keep the children during the day? I wouldn't mind paying her a little something for the chore."

Sasha could tell the wheels in Mary's mind were churning. She was certain she'd made headway.

Mary looked across the ragged tent city, and Sasha followed her gaze. A thin woman stood holding a toddler while a teenage girl brushed her hair.

"Rita is a mighty fine cook, and she lost her husband a few months back."

"Do you think she'd be interested in employment?"

Mary nodded. "I reckon she would. She's got three young'uns to feed."

The blond urchin Sasha remembered from the festival skipped over and wrapped her arms around Mary's skirt. "Who's she, Mama? Her dress is purdy."

"Miss Di Carlo, ma'am, this here's my daughter, Leah. She's my oldest. My son, Philip, is around somewhere."

Sasha stooped down and held out her hand to the little girl. "A pleasure to meet you, Leah."

The child giggled, then glanced at her mother. When Mary nodded, Leah shook Sasha's hand. Straightening, Sasha looked at Mary again. "So do we have a deal? I can pay you ten dollars a week and provide you with a room of your own and all the food your family can eat."

Mary's eyes widened. "It's far too much, ma'am."

"I disagree. I desperately need the help and wouldn't mind the companionship. My offer is the same for Rita. You'll talk to her?"

Mary finally smiled. "Yes, ma'am, I surely will. And I'd be honored to accept the position. When should I start?"

Sasha figured it would take Jim several weeks to finish the room but hated to think of Mary and her children living in such squalor till then. "What if you pack up your things, and I'll send Jim to fetch you in two days. You can set up your tent in my backyard and live there until he finishes your room."

"That sounds just fine and dandy, ma'am. I'll work hard. You won't be sorry for giving me this chance."

"I have no doubts that you will, and I look forward to getting to know you and your family better."

Jim hopped off the wagon as Sasha approached. Her heart lurched at the smile on his face.

"Was she interested?"

"Yes, after I convinced her how much I needed her assistance. And she's going to ask her friend if she'd like to be the cook."

"You did a good thing today, Sasha. I'm proud of you."

She beamed at him as she thought of the two rooms he would have to build, which meant he'd have to stay awhile longer. "Yes, I think I did. Thank you for suggesting it."

He helped her up, then took his seat again. He slapped the reins on the mare's back, and the buggy lurched forward. "You might need to buy another buggy and a horse so the women can get to work. It would be too far to walk twice a day, and I won't have time to pick them up and bring them back every day."

"I. . .uh. . .told Mary that you'd build her and the cook rooms of their own behind the house."

Jim glanced at her, looking serious. "Did you, now?"

Sasha nodded, hoping he wouldn't mind. "I didn't think they'd feel comfortable living upstairs with me."

"Guess I'll just have to hang around for a while then." The smile he gave her set her heart stampeding.

"I guess you will."

As they drove home, Sasha savored her success. She'd have help with the house and would be assisting two of the oil widows and their children. Not to mention Jim would have to stay longer since he now had two more bedrooms to build.

Jim had been there for her since Dewey's death and seemed comfortable around her—at least until he'd kissed her. Now he seemed to avoid her unless she needed him for something. Was it because he never could think of her as more than a friend? Did he regret kissing her?

She had compared Roman and Jim again and again, and every time, Jim won hands down. But did it really matter? She might have to return to New York soon. Uncle Dewey had said his property would be hers when he was gone, but no one expected him to be gone this quickly. Maybe she should reconsider building those extra rooms.

Jim guided the buggy down the road toward home, but at the fork, he turned the horse toward town. Sasha peeked sideways at him.

"We have to go in to Keaton and make funeral arrangements." He pressed his lips together in a sympathetic smile.

The joys of the day leaked away like milk in a cracked jar.

Chapter 16

The day after her visit to Rag Town, Sasha allowed Jim to escort her away from the small church. It had touched her heart that so many people had turned out for her uncle's funeral. Mary and Rita, along with several other oil widows, offered their condolences, and Mary had handed her a fresh-baked loaf of pan bread.

She clung to Jim's arm as they walked down the hill. Sweat trickled down her back from the warm sun. Sparrows chirped and flittered happily in the nearby trees, oblivious to her pain.

She'd only known her uncle a short time but had loved him dearly. Her heart ached to think she'd never see his twinkling eyes or receive another hug from him again. Using her lace handkerchief, she dabbed at her eyes, knowing they must be red and puffy. Jim patted her arm and gave her a reassuring smile.

A shadow darkened their path. Sasha tore her gaze away from Jim and saw Roman standing in their way, his hat in his hands.

"I'm terribly sorry about your uncle. I've talked with the sheriff, and he's using all his resources to find out who attacked him."

Jim tucked her a bit closer to him. She didn't fuss about his protectiveness but rather appreciated it.

Roman's dark brows dipped. "If there's anything I can do to help you, please don't hesitate to call on me."

"Thank you. That's kind of you." She smiled and stepped around Roman, only wanting to return to the quiet of Dewey's house. But they still had to take her uncle's body back to the ranch and bury him in the family plot. She didn't have the strength within her today to deal with Jim and Roman fussing like two dogs over one bone.

She spotted the wagon parked in the shade of an elm tree and made a beeline for it. Soon they'd be back home, and she needed to decide what to do. Here she'd gone and gotten up Mary and Rita's hopes for a better life and asked Jim to stay and build their rooms, yet she had no idea if she even had a right to stay and live on Dewey's property. Jim had suggested looking for a will before, but she'd been too disheartened to consider it.

Almost to the wagon, Jim stopped suddenly, pulling on her arm. She looked up to see the three men who'd accosted her uncle on several occasions standing near the buggy. She shook her head and heaved a sigh. They were the last people she wanted to see today. In fact, she believed in her heart that these men were responsible for her uncle's death.

The trio lined up, blocking the path to their buggy. The short, heavyset man tipped his hat to her, looking like a fat cat who'd captured a mouse. "We were right sorry to hear about your uncle, ma'am." The sickeningly sweet smile he flashed made Sasha's stomach churn.

Tall Man stepped forward, looking pleased with himself. A wary premonition charged down her spine, raising tiny bumps on her arms. "I'm sorry to be the one to inform you of this on the day of your uncle's funeral, but Dewey Hummingbird willed all his property to the town of Keaton in the event of his death."

Numb with shock, she clutched Jim's arm like a lifeline. She peeked up and saw the same astonishment on his face that she felt.

Jim stepped forward, setting her behind him. "I don't believe that for one second."

Tall Man opened his hands and held them out, palms up. "I'm afraid it's the truth. Dewey had no relatives except you and your mother, and since he hadn't heard from you in years, he decided to leave his property to the town."

Jim's hands rested on his hips, his back rigid. "I still don't believe that. What proof do you have?"

"It's common knowledge. There was big talk all over Keaton after he'd filed his will with the town attorney." Tall Man hiked his chin, rocked back on his heels, and gloated.

"We'll just see about that." Jim's fist clenched, and then he swiveled toward her, taking her hand and pulling her with him. "Let's go talk with the attorney."

"You have two weeks to pack up and clear out." Tall Man's victorious shout made Sasha shudder. How could this be happening?

She took two steps to each of Jim's, trying to keep up. "Do you think that's true? That Uncle Dewey left his land to the town?"

Jim glanced at her. "No, I don't, but without his will, we can't prove it. I can't see the town knowing Dewey's business anyway. He wouldn't have mentioned what was in his will, nor would the attorney."

"Do you have any idea where he might have put it?"

"I don't know. Maybe his new room?" Jim rubbed his hand along his nape and peered at her. "I just hope it wasn't in the cabin."

Two weeks to clear out. What would she do? Since her uncle had put her name on the bank account, she had plenty of money, but she didn't particularly want to return to New York. She wasn't even sure if she'd still have a job with the theater troupe. Geoffrey hadn't been happy when she'd left, right on her mother's tail. He'd wanted her to take Cybil's place.

She probably wouldn't have to work, at least not for a long while, but she needed something to occupy her time. Maybe she could start over somewhere else.

But where?

She dreaded the thought of leaving her new home. She'd finally found a place to put down roots, but it was being stolen away from her.

Jim's steps slowed in front of the attorney's office, and he reached for the door knob. When he lowered his hand, Sasha noticed the cardboard sign affixed to the window. Gone on holiday. Will return on July 16.

She glanced at Jim. "But that's three weeks from now! What are we going to do?"

A muscle in his jaw ticked. "We go home and find that will."

❧

"It's not here." Sasha flopped onto her uncle's bed, looking dejected. "Where could Uncle Dewey have hidden his will?"

Jim wanted to wrap his arms around her and comfort her, but he kept his distance. They had too many other things to worry about right now and didn't need to complicate the situation with romance. He pulled out the lone chair in Dewey's new bedroom, spun it around, and sat on it backwards. Leaning his arms on the top, he surveyed the messy room. Drawers hung open where they'd searched through Dewey's meager supply of clothing. Even the bedding was askew from their quest.

"I don't know where else to look." Sasha stopped crushing the bedcovers in her fist and looked at him. "Do you know of any secret hiding places he had?"

Jim shook his head, wishing he did. "No. If he had such a place, it was most likely in the cabin."

"Maybe we should search through the ashes. Something might have survived."

"Good idea." He offered her a weak smile. He didn't want to get her hopes up, but at the same time, he didn't want to discourage her. She'd already lost her uncle, and now she could well lose the home she'd put so much effort into.

Sasha slid to her feet and walked toward the door. "I'll go make us some dinner, and then we can go check the cabin—and maybe the barn, too."

Jim sighed as she exited the room, wishing he could help her more. What would happen to her if they couldn't find the will? Would Sasha return to New York?

He stood and swung the chair back into the corner, knowing his heart would break if that happened. He shoved his hands into his back pockets, and his fingers rattled some paper.

The letter.

In all the commotion of the funeral, the confrontation with the three men, and burying Dewey, he'd forgotten about the letter from his uncle that he'd picked up at the post office earlier. Jim pulled the envelope from his pocket and tore it open with his finger.

Dear Jimmy,

    I can't tell you how happy it made me to hear that you are satisfied with your job. Dewey Hummingbird sounds like a fine man, and I'm glad that he's been an encouragement in your walk with the Lord. I had my doubts when you left the farm last, but God was directing you to where you needed to be.

    I have some news. My father died. He left me his plantation in Georgia, but I don't yet know what I'll do with it. I have no desire to ever live there again. Only bad memories surface when I think of that place.

    I know I should grieve over my father's death, but the truth is, he was a cruel man, and my only grief comes from knowing he didn't walk with God.

    Father sent me a letter last year when he learned he was dying. I've wrestled with whether to share his deathbed confession with you or not. But given your circumstances and surroundings, I thought you'd want to know.

    All my life, I was told that my grandmother, my father's mother, had come from France. She had fine, dark features and looked like a porcelain doll. I never questioned that, but it seems our family sheltered a secret— grandmother was in truth a full-blooded Creek Indian. Back in those days you were a pariah if you married an Indian. It's amazing the secret was kept for so long.

    I hope this information doesn't dishearten you. I admit it was a shock at first, but there are many fine people who are of mixed blood. And to God, we are all the same anyhow.

    Come back home when you can. We all miss you. Dusty and Katie are doing fine, and Joey is getting big. Bet you miss playing with him. Being an uncle is a fun job, isn't it?

                Yours always,
                 Uncle Mason

Jim's arms fell to his lap as if they bore lead weights. He blinked as he tried to absorb his uncle's letter. Here he'd wrestled with being attracted to a half-breed woman, and he was himself at least one-eighth Creek Indian.

He let out a laugh at the irony of it all.

❧

Sasha watched Jim pace off the outline of the rooms he was going to build for Mary and Rita. Long, lean legs ate up the distance in short measure. Jim glanced her way. She'd struggled with what to do, but Jim had encouraged her to move ahead and not let their problems change things. He believed with all his heart they'd find the will and that God would work everything out. And she wanted to believe that, too.

"Are you sure you want two rooms for each worker?"

She nodded. "Originally, I just thought to build one room, but both women have children. They need a place to call home, and one room just isn't enough."

He pushed his hat off his forehead. "Honestly, I think it might work better if we build some cabins out in those trees, rather than adding on to the house." He pointed to a cluster of pine trees.

Sasha pushed away from the house and followed him. "That's not a bad idea. It would give them some privacy. Although, in bad weather, they'd have to brave the elements to get to the big house."

"True." He walked around, studying the area. "Well, what if we put them here?" He stood in a spot halfway between the pine trees and the house.

Sasha considered it, glancing at the house and then the trees. "No, I think it would work better if you build the cabins near the pines. It's really not all that far—"

She spun around at the sound of hoofbeats. Roman rode along the east side of the house on a pretty roan. Sasha wasn't sure if she was happy to see him or not. The time alone with Jim was special, and Roman seemed like an intruder. As long as she and Jim stayed busy, she didn't grieve as deeply as when she just sat around thinking.

Roman scowled when he saw Jim but reined his horse to a stop and vaulted off. When his gaze landed on her, his smile turned charming. He approached her with bold, confident steps. "How are you doing, my dear?"

She glanced at Jim and could tell he wasn't happy to see Roman or to hear his casual address. "I'm all right," she said, turning her attention back to her guest.

"I'm glad to hear that. I know your uncle's death was a terrible shock."

In spite of her resolve not to cry anymore, tears pooled in her eyes. She studied Roman's fancy alligator-skin boots for a moment until she regained her composure. He reached out, using his index finger to lift her chin.

"I came to see if you still want to have dinner with me this weekend."

Sasha felt as if she'd been slapped. Her uncle was barely buried, and Roman was concerned about their dinner engagement?

"I'm sorry, but I'm still mourning my uncle. I'm afraid I must decline."

Roman glanced at Jim, his brows dipping down, lips pursed. "Is it because of him that you won't dine with me?"

"What?" Sasha blinked.

"Every time I see you you're with him. Is there something going on between the two of you?" He glared at her with black, beady eyes.

Sasha felt suddenly weak. How could Roman turn on her so quickly? Was he truly jealous?

Jim stepped forward, his arms crossed. "I think you'd better leave."

"I don't take orders from hired hands." Though Roman huffed, he backed up a step when Jim moved closer.

Jim clenched his fist, and Sasha knew she needed to intervene. "Please, Roman, this isn't the time. I've just buried my uncle. I can't think about having dinner with you now."

He hiked up his chin when Jim sidled up beside her. "Maybe you just prefer white men to being with your own kind."

Sasha gasped. Jim rushed forward and shoved Roman against his horse.

"It's time you left."

The spooked horse jerked its head and sidestepped, causing Roman to fumble for his footing. Roman glared at Jim as he regained his balance. Then anger twisted his handsome features. He mounted his horse and yanked on the reins, making the mare squeal. After a final glare, he kicked the poor beast in the side, urging it into a run.

Chapter 17

Sasha rinsed the last plate from breakfast and dried it with a towel, then set it in the cabinet. She shut the door and ran her hand over the smooth wood. Such a lovely home. . .but how much longer would she live here?

If they didn't find her uncle's will, she might be on her way back to New York in another week.

Even if she wanted to continue living here, could she do so without her uncle? She'd decorated the home for him, and not having him here to enjoy it stole her pleasure in the house. Tears stung her eyes, and she swiped the back of her hand across them.

The sound of voices outside lured her to the back door. She pushed open the screen and stepped out into the warm sunshine, the air nearly stealing her breath. With New York being so much cooler, she'd not yet gotten used to the heat here. Using her hand, she fanned her face and looked to see who had arrived. Her heart jolted when she saw Mary and Rita. This was the day they were to begin working, and she'd completely forgotten. Should she tell the women they no longer had employment?

Mary glanced up from talking with Jim, her eyes dancing with excitement. "This is a fine house you have here. I'm delighted to be able to take care of it."

Sasha winced and glanced at Jim, who gave a slight shrug. She couldn't disappoint these women. Even if they only worked for a week, they'd probably make more money than they normally would in a month. She looked past Mary and Rita to see an adolescent boy leading a pitiful donkey pulling a cart. Behind him, an older girl held a toddler boy, and Mary's two children squirmed around the girl's skirt.

"That's Rita's boy, Timmy. He borrowed a neighbor's cart and brung our tents. You said we could set them up here until our room is done. It's a far piece to walk every day."

Sasha smiled, hoping to relieve Mary's concern. "Oh, yes, that would be fine. Why don't you have Timmy set your tents up over there?" She pointed to a bare area behind the house that was sheltered by a large oak tree.

The thin woman stepped forward and curtsied. "I'm Rita Lancaster, ma'am. I'll be doing the cooking for ya. I thank ya for the job." Her pale cheeks turned a rosy shade.

Sasha smiled, thinking Rita could stand to eat a few solid meals. "It's a pleasure to meet you, Mrs. Lancaster. This is Jim Conners." She waved her hand at him. "He's the one who built this lovely house, and he helps with other things, too. I'm sure if you ever need his assistance he'd be happy to help out."

The women turned toward Jim, and he tipped his hat. "Nice to make your acquaintance."

Both women smiled and nodded, then turned back to Sasha.

Mary pointed to the children behind the cart. "That there's my two children, Leah and Phillip, and Rita's girl, Angie, and little Christopher. Angie's gonna watch over the young'uns while we work."

Sasha nodded a greeting at the children, feeling a tingle of apprehension snake down her spine. She'd never been around children much.

"What would you like for us to do first, ma'am?" Mary asked.

"Why don't you go ahead and take today to get settled?"

A worried look passed between Mary and Rita. "We'd just as soon get to work, if that's all right with you. Timmy can set up the tents, and Angie and the children can unpack our belongings."

Timmy guided the donkey over to the spot Sasha had indicated and started unloading. Jim crossed the yard and helped him lift the tents from the cart.

"The children are welcome to play, but it might be a good idea if they stay out of the barn. Oh, and there's a pond that the little ones will need to steer clear of." Sasha hoped she wasn't being too bossy, but she didn't want the youngsters to get hurt.

Mary and Rita nodded and glanced at Angie, who also tipped her head in agreement.

"All right then"—Sasha clapped her hands—"I guess we should all get busy."

The women followed her into the house, and she gave them a tour, appreciating their oohs and aahs at her decorating talents. Sasha enjoyed sharing the house with the women and hoped deep within that they all could become friends.

"I should probably get started in the kitchen, iffen we're to have dinner by noon." At Sasha's nod, Rita busied herself in the kitchen.

Sasha left Mary upstairs to straighten Dewey's room and to pack up his clothing so Timmy could take it back to Rag Town and distribute the items when he returned the cart and donkey.

Sasha hurried down the steps. They had to locate Dewey's will. It was no longer just her well-being that depended on finding it, but Mary's, Rita's, and the children's, as well.

❧

Sasha slammed shut the tack room door, sending a cloud of dust and hay particles dancing on the dappled light of the barn. Her pretty mouth sagged with disappointment, and Jim wanted nothing more than to kiss away all her problems. But that would be no solution at all, because after kissing her, the problems would still be there.

"I don't know where else to look." Leaning against the barn, she crossed her arms over her chest. "What are we going to do?"

Jim shook his head. "I don't know. There's still the cabin. The remains should be cool enough by now that I can sift through them."

Sasha pushed away from the wall. "I can help."

He took a stance, knowing she'd object, but he didn't want her long skirts anywhere near those ashes, just in case some were still smoldering. "You'd better go back to the house and check on your workers."

"I trust them to work without me watching over them."

Jim moved closer. "That's not the point. Rita is probably fine in the kitchen, but Mary may not know what you want her to do."

"Oh. I hadn't thought of that. I guess I could have her wash Uncle Dewey's bedding." Her shoulders sagged, like she bore an ox yoke all by herself.

He brushed his hand over her cheek, wishing he could take away her troubles just like the streak of dirt he wiped off her face. "We'll get through this. I can't believe God would bring you here only to see you lose your uncle and your home."

Her lower lip trembled, and her eyes shimmered with unshed tears. "Oh, Jim, I miss him so much. I barely had a chance to get to know him before he was taken away."

"I know, I know." He cupped her face in his hands. "You're not in this alone. I'm here, and God's still here, even if it doesn't always seem that way."

"Why would God allow hoodlums to kill a sweet man like my uncle?"

Jim shook his head. He'd asked the same thing, but there was no answer for such a question. "I don't know, but I do know that God is still in control—and we have to believe that. All right?"

Sasha's lips quivered again, but she nodded.

"That's my girl."

Her mouth turned up in a shy smile. "Well. . .I guess I need to get back to the house. I probably should make a trip into town and stock up on some more food and supplies since we have so many mouths to feed now."

"Want me to hitch up the wagon?"

"That would be very nice of you." She beamed a pleased smile, and it took every ounce of self-control not to pull her into his arms and kiss her. But this wasn't the time. He needed to guard his heart, because if Sasha returned to New York, he feared it might just crack in two.

Down at the cabin, Jim used a rake and sifted through the dirt and ashes for an hour. Having moved his belongings into the cabin the day before the fire, he'd lost everything except his tent, which he had stowed in the barn. Thankfully, his money was safe in the Keaton bank.

He sighed in frustration. Nothing remained from the fire except a tin cup and the cast iron skillet. He threw the rake to the ground, stirring up a cloud of ash, and shoved his hands in his back pockets. This was just a waste of time.

Glancing heavenward, he watched some clouds, gray with moisture, drift along, threatening to drop their precious cargo any minute. He needed to finish sorting through this mess before that happened, or he'd look like he'd been tarred and feathered with ash.

He glanced heavenward again. "Father God, I need some help here. I'm at a loss as to what to do. If we don't find that will, Sasha will lose everything. I can't believe Dewey would build that big house, even though he never knew if Sasha and her mother would ever visit, only to leave it to the town. I know he'd want Sasha to have his property, even if she'd never come here. Dewey would have wanted to keep his land in the family. Help us find that will, Lord. And help me be the encouragement Sasha needs.

"Lord, help me also to come to grips with being part Indian. I don't like to think I'm prejudiced, but I must be. You formed me before I was born. As Your Word says, help me to be the man You want me to be and accept my heritage. It doesn't change who I am."

He heaved a sigh, feeling a weight lift off his shoulders. Stepping forward to retrieve the rake, his foot collided with something hard. The dull thunk indicated a container of some sort. With renewed fervor, he dropped to the ground and dug through the ashes. A blackened box began to take shape, and his hopes soared like an eagle taking flight.

Grabbing the box, he shook it free of the ashes, then he stood and carried it over to the chopping block. Sitting down, Jim held his breath. This had to be it. He used his knife to pry open the latch, misshapen from the heat of the fire. It clinked off and flipped to the ground.

Jim's heart felt like a bronc trying to bust out of a chute. "Please, Lord."

With a shaking hand, he lifted the lid and saw a leather pouch that smelled strongly of smoke. He loosened the tie and pulled out a roll of papers. His heart quickened even more as he unrolled the thick sheaf.

The will!

His gaze swiftly scanned the papers, which left everything Dewey owned to Sasha, except for his saddle horse and five thousand dollars, which he left to Jim.

He gasped. That much money was far more than he needed to buy his land. He could even build a nice house and furnish it—not fancy like Dewey's—but simple, like a farmer needed. He glanced at the date and the attorney's signature.

This will was dated just a week before Dewey's death, and Jim knew in his heart that it was the most current version.

He jumped up, running for the house. He had to tell Sasha that her home was safe.

Chapter 18

Anxious to get to town and back, Sasha gave Mary a list of things to do, then headed for the barn. She'd told Rita not to worry about her being back in time for dinner, but that she'd be looking forward to their first supper together. She hoped it didn't hurt Rita's feelings that she wasn't there for the first meal that the woman was making, but the sky was clouding up. Sasha wanted to get the food supplies home before it rained, or she might have to wait days for the road to dry out. Besides, she needed something to keep her mind occupied other than her troubles. She'd seen Jim digging through the ashes, but he'd been so deep in thought, she didn't think he even saw her leave.

As she walked into the mercantile an hour later, all manner of scents assailed her, from pungent spices to pickles to leather goods. The store owner glanced past the customer she was helping and flashed a smile.

"Be with you in a few minutes."

Sasha nodded and checked her list. Rita would need lots more sugar to cook up goodies for the children. She couldn't help smiling, knowing how much Jim would also enjoy the treats. That man had an appetite bigger than the whole state of New York, not that anyone would notice with his lean, muscular form.

Shaking her head, she pulled her thoughts away from Jim and studied her list. She'd need more flour, canned goods, and fresh vegetables, but she also needed to be frugal. If they didn't find the will, then her little family would be scattered in three different directions. But then again, she could send any left-over food back with Mary and Rita if things turned out for the worst. Making a mental note to up the quantities, she turned back to the counter.

Wilma Plunkett wiped her plump hands on her apron. "Now, how can I help you?"

Sasha borrowed a stubby pencil, changed the amounts, added several items, and then handed the long list back to Mrs. Plunkett. The woman's eyes widened.

"I sure hope you aren't in a hurry. It might take awhile to gather up all of this. Plus, my Henry will have to load it, and he's down at the livery just now."

"My wagon is right outside, so he can load it whenever he's ready." Sasha's stomach suddenly rumbled, and she glanced at the storekeeper, hoping the woman didn't hear. "Perhaps I'll go eat something at the diner while I wait."

Mrs. Plunkett flashed a knowing smile. "Sounds like that might be a good idea."

They shared a laugh, and Sasha walked back outside, peeking up at the sky. The clouds were dispersing and looked less threatening than before. Just maybe she'd get home without getting wet.

As she entered the diner, it took a moment for her eyes to adjust to the dimmer lighting. Fragrant scents tickled her nose, and the hum of conversation mixed with the clinking of silverware. She noticed an empty table in the corner and headed for it, but just before she reached her destination, a man stood up, blocking her path.

Roman Loftus.

Sasha scowled, remembering their last encounter.

He met her glare with one of complete humbleness. "I owe you an apology, Miss Di Carlo."

She wanted to skirt around him or run back out the door but couldn't in the face of his surprising meekness.

"I acted dreadfully the other day. I make no excuses for my ridiculous behavior." His hands drifted open in a stance of surrender. "Please accept my humble apology by joining me for dinner."

She glanced at his table and saw that he hadn't yet received his meal. Never one to hold a grudge—even on an occasion when she sometimes wanted to—she smiled at him. "All right, Mr. Loftus, I'll dine with you—and apology accepted."

In spite of her initial reservations, she enjoyed the meal, although Roman monopolized the conversation talking about his father's oil business. Much to her disappointment, no mention was made of the men whom she'd overheard talking about cheating Indians. Taking Roman's proffered arm, she allowed him to escort her back to the store once they'd finished eating.

Just outside the door, he tugged her to a stop. "I wonder if you'd consider having dinner with me this Friday evening."

Sasha shook her head. In her heart, she knew there was no future for the two of them, and it irked her that he was so persistent, considering she'd just lost her uncle and was still mourning him. And for all she knew, she might well be packing to leave by Friday. "I don't think that's a good idea in light of all that's going on right now."

Roman pursed his lips and stepped sideways to allow two older women to pass. He looked around, then back at her. "Come with me, please. There's something I want to talk to you about."

In spite of her reservations, she followed him into the alley. Her heart picked up its pace, but she felt perfectly safe with so many people walking past on the nearby boardwalks. Roman had never threatened her. His frustration had always been directed at Jim. Roman shoved his hands into the pockets of his fine trousers and paced a few feet away and back.

"This isn't at all how I'd planned this." He glanced at Sasha, with a look of apology.

"Whatever it is, please just say it. I need to be getting back home."

He sighed and stopped in front of her. She took a half step backward to put some space between them.

"All right. I know your uncle's death was a shock—and then finding out that he left his property to the town. . .well, it must have felt like a kick in the teeth. I guess you're planning to go back to New York soon."

She saw the question in his dark eyes but didn't understand where he was going with his little speech. "I've not yet given up hope of finding my uncle's will. I believe it will prove differently than what you've said."

He pursed his lips and shook his head. "If the will was around, you'd have found it by now. In another week, you'll be evicted. I don't want you to go back to New York, Sasha."

She opened her mouth to comment, but when he reached for her hand, she slammed her lips together. Her mind raced, trying to imagine what he wanted.

"What I'm trying to say is. . .I want to marry you." Looking a bit embarrassed, he lifted his derby hat and ran his fingers through his straight black hair. "You'll need a place to live and someone to take care of you. I want to be that person."

Sasha blinked, numb from his surprising proposal. She noticed he didn't ask her to marry him, but simply told her he wanted to. Her mind swarmed with excuses, but she didn't want to seem coldhearted.

"I thank you for your kind offer, but I'm afraid I'm not in a position to marry right now. There are too many loose ends that need to be tied up."

Roman's congenial look shifted to one of displeasure. It was obvious he hadn't expected her to turn him down. Most of Keaton's single women would have considered him the catch of the town, but she saw past his fine looks and into his murky heart. She suspected that by marrying her, he hoped to somehow gain control of Dewey's property, but with it going to the town, she failed to see how that was possible.

"I could help you, if you'd let me." His eyes pleaded with her to accept his offer.

"Thank you, but no. I can't marry you." She pivoted and rushed out of the alley back into the mercantile, praying he wouldn't follow. She'd had her fill of Roman Loftus and only wanted to get her supplies and leave town.

Mr. Plunkett was almost done loading the wagon. The man was shorter than his wife but muscled from years of hauling supplies. As she waited for Mrs. Plunkett to finish with her customer, she watched Roman stalk off. Sasha longed to be married and settled, but Roman wasn't the man she envisioned herself with.

It was Jim. He was the one who made her heart flutter. He was a man to look up to—a kind, caring man.

Why couldn't he show an interest in her like Roman had? Was a simple kiss all he wanted from her?

⁓

Jim tightened the cinch and stepped up into the saddle. His horse snorted and fidgeted, anxious to be off. Jim hadn't wanted to stop and eat dinner, because he was in a hurry to tell Sasha the good news, but he'd gone to the house looking for her and found dinner ready. Not wanting to disappoint Rita, he'd wolfed down her delicious stew and fresh biscuits. He adored Sasha, but his belly sure was glad she'd hired Rita to do the cooking. He swatted his horse with the ends of the reins and clicked out the side of his mouth. His mount took off at a fast clip.

As he rounded the third bend in the road, he saw Sasha and the wagon coming over the hill.

"He'yah!" Jim nudged his horse into a gallop, eating up the distance between him and the wagon. His stomach churned with eager anticipation at the prospect of Sasha's surprised expression.

At the bottom of the hill, Sasha stopped the wagon and stood up with her hand blocking the sun from her eyes. He could tell she was worried. As he pulled alongside the wagon, he yanked his horse to a quick stop and jumped off.

"What's wrong? Has someone been hurt?" Sasha started to climb down, but he lifted up his arms and hoisted her to the ground.

He couldn't quit grinning. "I found it! I found the will!" His hands on her upper arms tightened.

Sasha's concern instantly changed to joy, and she leaned forward, hugging him. "Oh, that's wonderful! Where did you find it?"

He wrapped his arms around her and held her close. "At the cabin. I found a box that must have been under the floorboards. It was charred but still intact." Leaning back, he looked her in the eye. "Your uncle left almost everything to you and nothing to the town."

Astonishment widened her eyes. "Truly?"

"Yes. There was a new amendment to the will dated a week before Dewey died."

"Oh, I'm so relieved. I wanted so badly to stay here and not go back to New York. Everything I love is here."

Jim studied her face until her cheeks turned a dark red. More than ever, he wanted Sasha to marry him, but now, they were even further apart. She was a wealthy woman. And yes, he had the money Dewey had left him—or would soon—and the money in the bank, but it didn't come close to Sasha's wealth. If he confessed his love now, she'd just think he was after her property, like Roman

Loftus. His joy gone, he stepped back.

"What's wrong?"

He shrugged. "Nothing. I'm just relieved we found the will."

"Where is it?"

"Safe. I hid it in the place I used to hide my money before I started putting it in the bank."

"Good." Sasha glanced over her shoulder at the wagon. "I guess we'd better get this food home. Then what should we do about the will since the attorney is gone?"

"I'll go talk to the sheriff and see what he thinks." He lifted her back into the wagon, amazed at her trust in him. She didn't pressure him about where the will was but simply trusted him to take care of it. His chest swelled a bit.

Jim picked up his horse's reins. "You were gone quite awhile. What took so long?"

Sasha glanced down at him, her lips pressed together as if she didn't want to tell him. "Mrs. Plunkett said it would take some time to gather up all my supplies, so since I missed dinner, I ate at the diner."

Jim nodded and mounted his horse.

"I. . .uh. . .ate with Roman Loftus."

Feeling as if he'd been shot with a renegade arrow, he spun his mount around to face her.

"Sasha! How could you—after the way he treated us the other day!" He clenched his jaw, just thinking about Sasha being in that scoundrel's company. Couldn't she see Loftus was a wolf in sheep's clothing?

Jiggling the reins, she made a kissing smack, which set the horses in motion. The wagon groaned as if in pain and creaked forward. "I didn't *plan* to eat with him. He was just there—and so remorseful that it seemed cruel not to accept his apology."

"I don't understand why you can't see him for who he is."

Sasha glared at him. "I realize he's rather shallow, but that doesn't mean we shouldn't treat him as nice as the next person."

"You're far too sweet and naive." Jim reached over and pulled on the reins, stopping the wagon. The two horses snorted and pawed the ground. "Loftus only wants to get control of your uncle's property—and he's not above using you to do so."

"You're just jealous." She sat back and crossed her arms, not mentioning that she'd thought the very same thing about Roman just a short while ago. Why did they have to argue about him? She'd never planned to accept his dinner invitation again.

Jim's stormy black eyes looked as if they would spit forth lightning bolts any second. "Along with your uncle's will was Kizzie Arbuckle's land deed and her oil lease." He looked at her long and hard. "The lease papers were signed by Roman Loftus—*president* of Chamber Oil."

Sasha blinked, confusion numbing her mind. "But how could that be? Roman never even mentioned Chamber Oil."

Jim's gaze softened. "Maybe that's because he *owns* it. He's been stringing you along all this time."

She gasped. Wave after wave of shock slapped at her. "He tricked me."

Jim's horse danced around, and he turned his mount back to face her. "Loftus only wanted the land so Chamber Oil could drill and make him richer. It wasn't about you, Sasha; it was always about the land."

Chapter 19

Sasha unloaded a couple of canned food items from the crate and handed one to Leah and the other to Philip. The children were having a grand time running the cans over to the pantry, handing them to Rita, and skipping back. Their sweet smiles softened her aching heart.

She'd always been so careful to guard her heart. Now Jim was upset with her, and her heart hurt because of it.

She had also thought Roman had become a friend, even though his temper got the best of him at times, but she'd seen his signature with her own eyes. Roman Loftus was president of Chamber Oil—a company he'd never even mentioned to her. He lied and tried to woo her to get at her uncle's property. Those three men who'd pestered her uncle probably worked for him.

But how could he, being full-blooded Creek, be callous enough to cheat his own people—and maybe even his own family?

She should have known by the way Roman always talked about his father's company whenever she tried to talk about Chamber Oil. He was deftly deflecting her to a different subject. How could she have been so stupid?

She slammed the can onto the counter, making Leah jump. The girl stared at her with wide blue eyes.

"Sorry, sweetie. I was just thinking about something that upset me."

Leah smiled and reached for the can before her brother could get it, then she darted back toward the pantry. Philip stared up at her with sparkling eyes, holding his palm out. Sasha handed him the final two cans, and his eyes widened along with his smile.

"She gave me two of dem," he said, trotting back to the pantry, carefully carrying his bounty.

Sasha lugged the empty crate outside, passing Jim as he carried in a twenty-five pound sack of flour. His warm smile made her insides tingle. Perhaps he wasn't so upset, after all.

At least she'd done the right thing upping her food quantities and wouldn't have to return to the mercantile for more supplies for a while and chance running into Roman again. She set the crate next to the others and wandered down the hill toward the pond.

At the water's edge, she tossed in a pebble and watched the ripples it made. A mother duck swam on the far side of the pond with her ducklings, snapping up an unsuspecting insect every so often. Sasha swatted at a mosquito that hummed past her ear.

What was her mother doing now? Did she miss her?

Roman Loftus's character was so similar to her mother's that it surprised her that she hadn't noticed before now. Her mother only cared about fame and fortune, even walking away from her only child when given the choice between Sasha and a wealthy man.

Sasha had tried all her life to be good enough to earn her mother's love, but she'd never succeeded. Until she met Dewey, she'd never known what unconditional love was. In the short time she'd known him, Dewey had loved her that way, but he'd said that God was the only One who could truly give her the security she longed for.

Tears pooled in her eyes and burned her throat. She'd had such high hopes for a new life here in Indian Territory, but the one person who'd truly loved her was dead. Could she live in the big house alone? Did she even want to?

For so long, she'd thought having family, a home, and setting down roots would fill the empty spot inside her. Now she had a home and plenty of money, but that emptiness was still there.

From a distance, she heard the children's laughter, and hope flickered anew. At least she was helping a couple of the widows and their families. Maybe she could somehow figure out a way to help the others. She lifted her gaze toward the heavens. *God, if You're truly up there and care about people, show me what to do with all that I've been given.*

❧

Jim hated to disturb Sasha, but he needed to apologize. She looked so lonely there standing by the pond. His boot snapped a twig, and Sasha spun around, staring at him with damp eyes. He walked toward her, noticing she looked as melancholy as he felt. He came to a stop several feet away and studied the ground. Finally, he looked at her. "I'm sorry for getting upset about you eating with Loftus."

She waved her hand in the air. "No, you were right, but I didn't know everything you knew at the time. I won't ever have anything to do with Roman Loftus again if I can help it."

"Well. . .for what it's worth, I'm sorry. I know you cared about him."

Sasha shook her head, but her tears told Jim that she cared more for Loftus than he'd thought. He felt his own dreams die a little more. She leaned forward, crying into her hands, and he couldn't help pulling her to his chest. He'd hold her one last time, build her cabins, then ride out as soon as things were settled and she had control of her land.

Maybe if he worked hard enough on the land he wanted to buy in the Oklahoma Territory, he could forget her. Forget how her eyes twinkled before she teased him. Forget her long lashes clustered together from the tears she'd shed. He was a simple farmer and carpenter. How could he compete with the likes of wealthy oilmen?

Sasha finally had the home she'd craved for so long. He couldn't ask her to give that up.

He rested his head on her silky, rose-scented hair and held her tightly, wanting to remember this moment with her in his arms and the sun glistening on the pond. A light breeze lifted the rebellious strands of Sasha's hair that had escaped her long braid, and he smoothed them down. All too soon, she sniffed and pulled back.

"I didn't care for Roman like you think. He was a friend—of sorts. A while back, I overhead some oilmen talking about cheating Indians. I needed his help to try to find the men responsible." Her thin brows dipped down, and she uttered an unlady-like snort. "I was asking help of the very man responsible. How could I have been so naive?"

She stared up at him as if she expected a response, but all he could focus on was that she didn't care for Loftus. "You really didn't care about him?"

"What?" She blinked, then her confused expression softened. "Well, yes, as a friend. He could be quite charming, but I never thought of him as anything more. Why?"

A mallard near the pond flapped its wings and took flight, just like Jim's heart. He couldn't help smiling as he stared down at Sasha. He loved her sweet innocence. Her kindheartedness, and her truthfulness. There wasn't a deceitful bone in her body.

"Sasha, do you think you could ever care for *me*?" The question was tough to voice, but he had to know.

She opened her mouth to respond, but he laid his fingers across her velvety lips. "Don't answer that yet. There's something I need to tell you first. All my life, I thought my family was part French. But I recently got a letter from my uncle. He told me about a long-held family secret—my great-grandmother, it turns out, was a full-blooded Creek Indian."

Sasha's eyes widened as surprise engulfed her face. She blinked several times. Then her lips curved up in a smile that sent a vibrant chord of hope strumming through his being. She laid her hand against his cheek, and he leaned into it.

"I already care about you, Jim. It doesn't matter a whit to me if you're Indian or white. I care about the kind, sensitive man you are."

He kissed her then—taking his time, raining gentle kisses on her mouth, then trailing up to her eyes and ears. Holding her tight, he knew she was the woman for him. If only—

Suddenly, he stopped and pulled back, his breath coming fast. As much as he loved Sasha, even if she cared for him, he couldn't have her—unless she gave her heart to God.

In spite of his feelings for her, he couldn't—no, wouldn't—make that compromise, even if it meant riding away and never seeing her again.

Sasha gave him a shy but confused smile and stepped back. "I suppose I should go help Mary and Rita finish putting the food away."

She darted around him, and he let her go.

This time.

He had a lot of praying to do. Surely God wouldn't allow him to love Sasha so deeply if He hadn't meant for them to be together. Sasha had been very open to Dewey's Bible teaching, and she'd asked them both plenty of questions. He'd pray and nurture her, and soon—he felt it in his heart—she would give her life over to God.

And then maybe they could have a future together.

But if not, Sasha would be safe in the arms of his heavenly Father.

Chapter 20

Sasha drove the buggy the final half mile to the barn. One day they'd have a nice, new one, but for now, Dewey's old barn near the burned-out cabin sufficed. Today had been a good day.

She smiled, knowing Jim had shown the will to the sheriff yesterday, and he had said that nothing would be done until the town attorney returned. The sheriff also said he would lean on the three men who'd been pestering Dewey to see if they had anything to do with his death or were connected to Chamber Oil. If only they could discover who had killed her uncle and make them pay the price, then everything would be wonderful.

The light breeze lifted the scarf of her Gypsy costume and threatened to steal it away. Holding the reins with one hand, she grabbed her scarf with her free hand. She tucked it back around her face and pulled on the reins so the horse would slow. The anxious animal resisted, knowing the barn was just around the corner. But she had to be cautious. Jim and Timmy were supposed to be out checking the cattle today, but they could always return early.

With nobody in sight, she urged the buggy into the clearing beside the barn, stopped, and set the brake. As she climbed down, she heard Jim's voice in the stable. Her heart jumped almost up to her throat, and she darted behind the building, thankful to find the back doors closed.

Picking up her skirts, she hurried down to the creek and followed it back to the main house. By staying off the road, maybe she wouldn't be seen. Her change of clothes was hidden in the barn, but if she could get into the house without being noticed, then she could dress in her room.

But that was a big "if" with so many people around the house now.

She hated this deception, but it was for a good reason. Wasn't it?

If she hadn't wanted to help the other widows by taking some clothing to them, she didn't think she would have used her costume again. Here, in Indian Territory, she could be herself and no longer needed a costume to hide behind. Still, the poor but proud widows seemed more willing to accept an old beggar woman's help than a wealthy landowner's, even if she was the same person on the inside.

She jolted to a stop at the sound of children's voices as Rita and all the kids headed her way. Sasha's heart felt as if it would beat clear out of her chest. She ducked down, hiding behind a thick cluster of bushes. Thankfully the dark colors of her clothing blended with the landscape.

"Can we really swim?" Leah asked, her high-pitched voice carrying a bit of awe.

"Yes, but you must stay in the shallow water." Dried leaves left over from last winter crunched as Rita passed her carrying several thin, frayed towels.

Sasha made a mental note to purchase new ones for the cabins. The younger children skipped past, followed by Timmy and Angie.

Timmy snorted and leaned close to the adolescent girl. "Swim—yeah. They don't know this is just Mom's attempt at getting them clean before supper."

Angie giggled and nodded her head. "I don't mind, though. As hot as it's been, the water. . ." Her voice faded as she moved out of hearing distance.

A bead of sweat trickled down Sasha's back, making her wish she could join them in the cool water. She took a final look around and darted to the back of the house, then stopped to listen. Jim had been in the barn, probably talking to his horse. All the children were with Rita, so that left only Mary.

Taking a deep breath, she dashed in the back door and past the kitchen. Mary was most likely upstairs. As she passed the parlor, she heard a bang and jumped.

"Hey there, what are you doing in here? Stop! Now!"

Sasha darted for the stairs, not sure what to do, but Mary snagged hold of her skirt. "I don't want to hurt you, but you don't belong in here. If it's food you want, you only have to ask."

Sasha fought to get away, but Mary yanked on her scarf, and Sasha's mass of hair tumbled down around her shoulders.

Mary gasped and turned Sasha around. "Ma'am?" Her brows dipped.

Sasha heaved a sigh. "Yes, Mary, it's me."

With her hands on her cheeks, Mary stepped back. "I'm sorry for scolding you. . .but why are you dressed like that?" Utter shock replaced her normally pleasant features. "Were you the old woman who brought me that fabric?"

Sasha saw confusion in Mary's eyes and stared at the floor. She nodded.

"But why?"

She looked at her friend. "I didn't think you'd accept help from a wealthy woman, and I wanted so badly to help you. Uncle Dewey told me that sometimes the rich women in town simply wore a dress once or twice and tossed it in the refuse pile afterwards. In New York the wealthy often gave their clothing to their employees or shelters for the poor. I couldn't stand perfectly good clothing going to waste when you had such a need." She was rambling, she knew, but the pain in Mary's eyes cut her to the quick.

"I suppose I owe you an apology." Mary gave her a weak smile. "We have so little in Rag Town that our pride is something we cling to. Pride in poverty, maybe. I'm sorry that I was so proud that you felt you had to use a disguise to help me. Please forgive me."

Stunned, Sasha stared at Mary. The mantel clock in the parlor ticked a steady beat that matched the rhythm of her heart. Mary was asking Sasha's forgiveness when she'd done nothing wrong. "I'm the one who needs forgiveness. I didn't mean to trick you—only to help."

"We all need God's forgiveness—and other people's help at times."

Sasha blurted out, "But how do I get God's forgiveness?" She had never wanted anything so badly in her life.

Mary smiled. "Do you believe Jesus is God's only Son? And that He died for your sins?"

"Yes, I do." Sasha nodded.

Mary took her hand. "Then tell that to God and ask Him to forgive your sins. It's that simple."

She closed her eyes and did as Mary said, then Mary prayed for her and they hugged. Sasha stepped back, feeling whole for the first time in her life. Jim would be so happy to hear she gave her heart to God.

The back door banged shut. "Mary, have you seen Sasha? The buggy's at the barn, but I can't find—"

Sasha sensed the moment Jim noticed her. He tugged off his hat and stepped closer. His smile suddenly dropped and his brow crinkled as he took her in from head to toe.

"Sasha?"

❧

"Yes, it's me." Sasha's voice sounded hollow.

"*You're* the Gypsy woman? It was you all the time?"

She nodded and stood perfectly still. Mary patted her arm, then slipped away, leaving them alone.

"Why?" Jim couldn't voice everything he felt. Betrayed, deceived, lied to—just like his father had done all his life.

"It's complicated, but in New York, dressing like this was the only way I could go out on the streets alone. There were times I had to get away from the theater, and this is how I did it. Nobody bothers an old woman." Sasha's gaze begged him to understand.

"I took a beating for you. Why didn't you tell me?"

Her shoulders lifted in a pitiful shrug. "I wanted to, but after you got beat up, I was. . .afraid to tell you."

Jim had never known such deep emotional pain. "I trusted you. Loved you. But you're a liar, just like my ol' man." He slammed on his hat, turned, and strode outside, savoring the loud bang the screen door made.

"You should forgive Miss Sasha. Her intentions were good."

He halted at Mary's soft voice, his boots slinging pebbles spiraling across the yard. "She deceived me."

"She had a good reason to dress as she did. Sasha didn't mean to hurt you, Mr. Conners." Mary glanced down at her folded hands, then peeked at him. "You'll be happy to know she just gave her heart to God."

Jim closed his eyes. He'd prayed for this. Ought to be joyous about it. But there was nothing on God's earth that he despised worse than a deceiver. He shook his head and stalked away.

Half an hour later, Jim felt only marginally better. He'd ridden out to the fields and checked on the cattle, but he had ended up at the remains of Dewey's cabin, wishing his old friend were there to offer advice. He'd been ready to pack up his meager belongings and head home, but something had stopped him.

One thing he'd learned from Sasha was the value of family. At one time, he'd had to get away from his, but now he ached to see them. His sister, Katie, and her young son. His aunt and uncle. Even their rowdy kids. A smile tugged at his lips. Yeah, he actually missed his family. That was something.

Finally, weak from all the emotions that had roiled through him, Jim look at the endless blue sky. "What do I do, Lord? You know how hard I've prayed for Sasha to give her heart to You, and now she has. But You also know how much I hate a fraud—a deceiver. I fought twice for Sasha and didn't even know it was her.

"Was that why You brought us together? So I could guide her toward You?

"I never wanted a woman in my life until I met her. But now everything's changed."

His horse pawed the ground, restless to move. Jim dismounted and dropped to his knees. "Show me what to do, Lord. Help me to forgive Sasha and trust again. And help me to forgive my father."

❧

With her clothes changed and makeup removed, Sasha still felt awful. She couldn't get Jim's stricken expression out of her mind. He'd been her one true friend, and she'd shattered his view of her.

How could she make amends?

She had to find him.

Grabbing her wadded-up costume, she hurried downstairs. Rita had banked the fire in the stove until she needed it for dinner. Sasha tossed her disguise into the ashes, poked the garments with a stick, and watched them ignite.

As she stepped outside, Mary was pacing back and forth with her hands folded under her chin. She glanced up, an apologetic look on her thin face. "I tried to stop him, but he was just so angry."

"I'll find him. I have to make him understand."

Mary nodded. "I'll keep praying. God will work things out."

"I sure hope so." Sasha lifted her skirts and jogged down the hill past the pond. She didn't know why, but she felt a pull to Dewey's cabin. It was the first place where she'd found true happiness. Where she was valued for what she was on the inside and not what she looked like or who her mother was.

The memory of the pain in Jim's eyes threatened to knock her to her knees. Besides Dewey, he'd been the only person ever to stand by her. To protect her. To be her friend. Somehow, she *had* to salvage their friendship. She didn't think she could live without it.

She loved him, deep in her heart, like she'd never loved anyone else before. This love was different from what she'd felt for her uncle, and it amazed her.

As she neared the rubble that had been her uncle's home, she skidded to a halt. Jim knelt in the ashes of the cabin with his hands over his face, his horse grazing nearby. Her whole body quivered with the need to make things right. To see him smile again.

Help me, Lord.

⤚

Jim felt as if he were two men wrestling. The one man despised Sasha for her deception while the other loved her and wanted to make a life with her. He hated feeling weak and at odds with himself. The conflict was tearing him apart.

He wanted to stay mad. He wanted to forgive her.

The scripture verse where Peter asked how many times he should forgive his brother came to mind.

"Seven?" Peter had asked.

But Jesus had responded, "Seven times seventy."

A smile tugged at his lips. As a boy he'd told his uncle that if he forgave Katie four hundred ninety times, then he wouldn't ever have to forgive her again. He'd followed his ornery sister around saying, "I forgive you," so many times he'd made her fume. In spite of her small size, she'd shoved him down, making him lose count. Too tired to start over, he finally gave up.

Jim heaved a sigh. That wasn't the point Jesus had been trying to make. He needed to forgive Sasha. But how did he do that when she'd shaken him to the very core?

He heard a noise and lowered his hands. Sasha stood there in her pretty dress, looking sad and alone.

She was a gift God was offering to him if he'd only reach out and accept it. But to do so, he had to forgive her—and his father, who, by his behavior, had ingrained Jim's hate of deceit into him.

He stood and dusted off his knees and hands. The scent of smoke lingered, mixing with the odor of leather and a faint whiff of Sasha's floral scent.

Forgiveness was a choice. And now he had to make one that could change his life.

Sasha moved closer. "Jim, I'm *so* sorry for not telling you the truth. I only wore my costume for protection and to help the widows. I didn't do it to be sneaky."

Sasha's eyes pleaded with him to believe her. "I never meant to deceive you."

He took a step toward her, and she hesitated, then did the same.

One step toward forgiveness.

"It's all right. I understand."

Sasha blinked, looking stunned. Tears flooded her eyes, then spilled onto her cheeks. "You do?"

He nodded. "I'm sorry for getting so angry. I understand now why you felt you needed the costume. Will you forgive me for getting upset?"

She wheezed a laugh. "Forgive *you*? I'm the one who should be asking that."

Jim closed the distance between them and took her hands. "Then let's just mutually agree to forgive. All right?"

Sasha nodded, smiling in spite of her tears. "Yes, that sounds wonderful."

Jim grinned and dashed his own tears away with the back of his hand. In one quick swoop, he tugged her into his arms and kissed her firmly on the lips. She returned his affection with a fervor that surprised him. Finally, they came up for air.

She reached out and wiped his face. "You've got ashes all across your eyes. You look like a raccoon."

A smile lifted his cheeks. "Then we're a matched pair, because you do, too."

Sasha's giggle blended with the birds chirping and the locusts singing. Oh how he loved her!

And to think, moments ago he'd been willing to give her up because of his hurt and anger. What a loss that would have been.

He tightened his grip and gazed into her eyes, thrilling to the affection he saw there.

"Sasha, will you marry me?"

Stunned, she opened her mouth, then closed it. Slowly, a smile tugged at her cheeks and joy filled her countenance. "Why, yes, Mr. Conners, I believe I'd like that very much."

They laughed and resumed kissing.

As they walked back to the house arm in arm, Jim marveled at the difference an hour could make.

Chapter 21

Three weeks later

Sasha jumped aside as Jim's twin cousins darted past her, yelling like banshees. She giggled and shook her head. With his family there, the house buzzed with activity like a beehive. Jim, along with his brother-in-law, Dusty McIntyre, his uncle Mason, and Mason's oldest son, were busy raising the cabins. Jim's aunt Rebekah and his sister, Katie, had jumped in to help Rita make the wedding cake and food for after the ceremony.

Sasha moved Joey, Dusty and Katie's toddler son, to her left arm. He patted her chest and kicked his chubby legs, begging for another piece of biscuit to gnaw on to ease his sore gums. The cute little boy had stolen Sasha's heart from the start. Deborah, Rebekah's only daughter, wiped her hands on her apron and ambled toward Sasha. "Would you like me to hold him for a while?"

Before Sasha could answer, Joey squealed and dove at Deborah. At fourteen and lovely, she would have young men lining up to court her in a few years. Mason would have to keep his shotgun handy, or some fellow might soon steal Deb's heart.

Sasha walked to the back porch door and looked out. As if he could feel her gaze, Jim glanced up and grinned at her. They stared at one another, making Sasha's heart sing. Oh, how she loved him. And tomorrow they'd be married. Mason said something, and Jim turned to answer, breaking their connection.

Sasha loved Jim's whole family. They were noisy, the twins especially rambunctious, and could they ever put away the food! But she loved them all. Mason was a kind father figure to Jim. The only loving father he'd ever known. She suspected it wouldn't be too long before Mason held that same position in her heart.

And Rebekah treated her like a daughter and sister both. The kind woman had swooped in and stolen her heart from the beginning. Sasha never knew before how much she'd missed by not having a loving family.

But thank the good Lord, she had one now.

She strolled upstairs to look over her wedding garments to be sure everything was ready for tomorrow. Holding up the lovely gown that Rebekah and Katie had made, she turned to her left and right, surveying herself in the mirror. Would Jim like the dress?

"You'll be a lovely bride." Katie stood in the doorway, leaning against the jamb.

Sasha started. She had been so engrossed in her activities that she hadn't even heard her approach.

"Are you nervous?" Katie asked.

Sasha nodded. "Yes, I suppose all brides are. Weren't you?"

Katie giggled and tucked a strand of her honey blond hair behind her ear. "Truth be told, I couldn't wait to get married. I loved Dusty so much, and we'd gone through some rough times. I'll tell you about them someday." She stepped forward and adjusted a sleeve on Sasha's gown.

"Are you happy with the dress?" Her blue eyes held a trace of apprehension.

"Oh, yes, I love it! You and Rebekah are so talented. I could never have sewn anything like this. In fact, I can barely sew at all. My mother never had time for such domestic things."

Katie laid her hand on Sasha's shoulder. "Aunt Rebekah would be happy to teach you. I would, but Dusty and I live too far away to visit frequently, but we usually get back every couple of months. You'll enjoy living next door to Uncle Mason and Aunt Rebekah. Farming can be lonely."

"I won't mind as long as Jim is there."

Katie chuckled. "I still can't get used to calling him Jim. He's always been Jimmy to me."

Sasha smiled. "I'm sure he would answer to either, especially if you're carrying a tray of sweets."

They shared a laugh, then Katie sobered as she looked around the room. "Are you sure you won't mind leaving this beautiful house? You've done so much work decorating it."

She looked around the room, enjoying the pretty rose theme. "I've learned that a house doesn't make a home. It's the people who live in it. Wherever Jim is, that's my home."

Katie smiled. "You don't know how happy that makes me. We all worried about Jimmy for so long—ever since he fought in the Spanish-American War. He returned home a different man. And he's been troubled for so long."

Katie crossed the room and stood in front of the window, staring out. "None of us wanted him to come here—to Indian Territory. He'd wandered so much that we wanted him home, even if he wasn't the same." She spun around, her long skirt swirling around her legs. "But the old Jimmy has returned, and I have you to thank for that."

Sasha bit back her surprise when Jim's sister hurried over and hugged her. Katie pulled back, looking a tad embarrassed. "So, Aunt Rebekah says you're making this house into a widows' colony."

"Yes. We'll start small and add more cabins if it's successful. Mary has agreed to serve as the overseer, with Rita cooking and assisting her. The first women will move in next week. This room will remain empty so Jim and I can use it when we come back for visits to see how things are going."

"It's a wonderful plan, and I'm sure God will bless it."

They heard a loud cry downstairs, and Katie scurried out the door. "Sounds like Joey's ready to nurse again," she said over her shoulder.

Sasha stepped out onto the balcony and stared at the pond. A tremor of excitement zigzagged through her as she thought about tomorrow. Her wedding day. Tomorrow she'd officially be Jim's wife and part of his family.

❦

"I like Sasha—a lot." Mason cupped his hands, dipped them into the creek, and dumped the water over his head.

Jim flashed him a smile. "I rather like her, too."

Mason looked at him, water beading on his eyelashes. "Yeah, I imagine you do. I'm sure glad to see you happy again."

Jim sipped the cool water he'd scooped from the creek, then wiped his nape with his wet hand, finally feeling some relief from the heat. He stood. "Feels good to be happy again. To have my troubles behind me."

Mason slapped him on the shoulder. "I doubt if all your problems are behind you, but whatever the future holds, God will help you."

Jim nodded. "You know, it's odd. When I was seventeen, all I could think of was joining the army and getting away from the farm. I was sick of farming." He ran his hands through his damp hair and stuck his hat back on. "Now I can hardly wait to get back to the Oklahoma Territory, set up a home with Sasha, and start plowing."

Mason chuckled, pulling Jim's gaze to him. "Now you get to *plant* oats instead of sowing wild ones."

Jim smiled, then sobered. "I'm sorry for all the trouble I caused you, Uncle Mason. There were times I resented you raising me instead of my own pa, but I can tell you now, I'm grateful for all you did for Katie and me. You made a huge sacrifice, taking us in after you'd lost your first wife and child."

"We're family." Mason shrugged. "Family cares for family."

"Yeah, that's right."

They stood shoulder to shoulder staring out past the creek, like father and son. Jim knew in his heart Mason had done a far better job as a parent than his own father ever could have. He'd given him a foundation to build on and a faith in God.

"Did you tell Sasha your news yet?" Mason glanced out the corner of his eye at him.

"No. I haven't had a chance. We'll take a walk after supper, and I'll tell her then. She'll be happy to know they caught the men who killed her uncle but disappointed when she learns Roman Loftus was responsible. She liked him for a time." Jim plucked a leaf from a nearby bush and tore it in half, feeling guilty for how jealous he'd been over Sasha's friendship with Loftus. He hoped his news wouldn't affect their wedding. For a fleeting moment, he wondered if he should wait and tell her after the ceremony.

"That Loftus fellow—he's in jail now?"

Jim nodded. "Yep. Guess all that money he accumulated by cheating folks won't be much help to him there."

"Nope."

"Sasha will be happy to learn that the mayor's put together a commission to explore how the Indians were cheated and to see if anything can be done about it now. Most of the oil companies are fair and legitimate, but Chamber Oil sure caused lots of problems. It's nice to know it's out of business."

The dinner bell clanged, and they turned in unison, walking toward the house. Jim whispered a prayer of thanks for all that God had done. A shiver of excitement surged through him, knowing that at this time tomorrow he'd be a married man.

He couldn't wait until he and Sasha had children—a houseful of dark-headed youngsters running around. The thought made him smile, and he thanked God for his heritage and his bride.

※

Sasha glided down the stairs, knowing her future husband waited. Her heart was so full of joy, she felt sure it would burst. Never in her life had she been so happy. The one shadow on her bright day was that her mother wasn't there. But she and Jim hadn't wanted to wait for her to return from England—even if Cybil would have come. Maybe one day Sasha would see her mother again, but she would be a different woman than the daughter her mother had known.

As she stepped outside, her gaze slid past the small crowd of family and friends and found her beloved. His black eyes beamed his love, and she could tell by his expression that he thought her beautiful. For once, she didn't mind that she was pretty, because it pleased the man she loved.

As she eagerly approached Jim, she thought about the frightened, determined girl who'd left New York nearly four months earlier. That girl no longer existed. God had come into her life and blessed her beyond measure. He had answered her prayers, giving her a wonderful man to marry, the family she'd always longed for, and a place to call home. He'd given her wealth beyond what most people could imagine. But most of all, He'd given her a wealth beyond riches—something for free—His unfailing love.

A Letter to Our Readers

Dear Readers:

In order that we might better contribute to your reading enjoyment, we would appreciate your taking a few minutes to respond to the following questions. When completed, please return to the following: Fiction Editor, Barbour Publishing, Inc., P.O. Box 719, Uhrichsville, OH 44683.

1. Did you enjoy reading *Oklahoma Brides* by Vickie McDonough?
    ❏ Very much—I would like to see more books like this.
    ❏ Moderately—I would have enjoyed it more if _____
    _____
    _____

2. What influenced your decision to purchase this book?
    (Check those that apply.)
    ❏ Cover   ❏ Back cover copy   ❏ Title   ❏ Price
    ❏ Friends   ❏ Publicity   ❏ Other

3. Which story was your favorite?
    ❏ *Sooner or Later*   ❏ *A Wealth Beyond Riches*
    ❏ *The Bounty Hunter and the Bride*

4. Please check your age range:
    ❏ Under 18   ❏ 18–24   ❏ 25–34
    ❏ 35–45   ❏ 46–55   ❏ Over 55

5. How many hours per week do you read? _____

Name _____

Occupation _____

Address _____

City _____ State _____ Zip _____

E-mail _____

If you enjoyed

OKLAHOMA
Brides

then read

ALASKA
BRIDES

THREE WOMEN DON'T NEED MARRIAGE TO SURVIVE THE ALASKAN WILDS

Golden Dawn by Cathy Marie Hake
Golden Days by Mary Connealy
Golden Twilight by Kathleen Y'Barbo
